FULL SURRENDER

The Midwest Stalker Series

Reigna X

GO Publishing House

CONTENTS

DEDICATION

TO THE STAR IN MY LIFE. I LOVE YOU BEYOND MEASURE.

THANK YOU FOR READING

"Love and Hate are not opposites; they are siblings birthed by obsession."

Steve Mariboli

Chapter 1

Palm Tower's Conductor

Tonight, Cinderella's clock was winding down. Love stories are like great fairy tales; pain and suffering must be felt before a princess is rescued by her true prince.

Occasionally, someone must die.

"Finally," he said aloud with a heavy sigh. One last event. The MPowerU Gala. All the waiting, all the blood spilled in the name of love and honor, would at last come full circle.

"Almost, my sweet rose." His hand grazed one of the 24 white O'Hara roses, a gift for his beloved at the end of her night. A scent as original as she was filled the air. Turning away from the desk, he looked around him. Smiling, pleased with himself. No one would ever suspect that a humble cabbie turned executive driver could have created a high-tech masterpiece. All for her.

From the moment he saved her from the mugger, he had foreseen the need — his first genius realization. She was born to be famous, and as a star, needed expert security. Unlike other cabbies, he had used the *sit and wait* to his advantage. While other drivers would play on their phones, texting random women, he had sacrificed for her.

In the last eight years, he had dedicated every day off to online classes. Devoting his time, he pursued degrees in IT and cybersecurity. In secret for her. All for her.

Her goal was to be seen by the world; his goal, to be seen only by her.

He stood in the center of the room, legs spread apart, arms dancing in the air as if conducting an invisible orchestra. The combination of a haunting cello melody with the low whir of computers filled the stagnant room with an electronic symphony.

Almost a decade, he spent grooming her for himself. Teaching her to trust only him. Her trust so full now, she had given him unlimited access to all the plans for her towers. Publicly making him an envoy delegated with updating her on build details. Without realizing it, she gave him the power to watch her every move.

He was the Palm Tower's private conductor and this was his music. He was the executive director and producer of all things her. He was the eyes everywhere around her. Some would view the glow of neon blue coming from the monitors as unsettling or creepy. Not Tim.

He was a visionary with imagination, seeing far beyond the basics. Domination was the holy grail, the feeling he had felt as a young boy being bullied by his drunken father and rich brats from school. The tables were turning, no longer was he the frail one, beaten down. He had the power now and as a man; he found total control at this level erotic. Knowing he was the only one watching XAna in this intimate way turned him on. Watching her with her guard down, not prepped for media, so every movement, touch, and sound she made from any room in the building would activate a monitor.

He loved this room with its false door. He found a thrill in making the machines sing of every detail of his beloved XAna. His heart beating fast, his hands twitchy as he concentrated on fighting the impulse to rush the moment he would see his queen.

Without her understanding, the access she granted allowed him to whisper *good morning* each day and bid her *sweet dreams* every evening. Every interaction with her was planned from this room. Had she not slept well? Then he made a special trip to *Starbies* to buy her fave dirty chai. Was she feeling melancholy about her dad? A perfect remedy — a reminder of a happy memory. Was she rethinking her diet? Then it was gourmet salads. It was in these details that he had made his role in her life irreplaceable—though it was in secret, for now.

Blood rushed, his manhood swelling, tightening the slacks of the slim-fit tux; erections were natural, though they were more frequent now. Delaying gratification was becoming difficult knowing their special uniting was mere days away.

All his plans, his hard-fought impatience and some-times ignored efforts would soon be clear to her. Her full surrender to everything he dreamed of for the two of them was finally coming true.

Four years ago, she had made him her full-time executive driver, and since then—whether it was her personal choices or outside forces — he was in charge. He had lovingly manipulated, eliminated and removed any threats to their unity.

The technology installed was an elegant gentleman's touch. Every optic lens specialized and highly rated was built by a security company out of DC. A company whose reputation wasn't always clean.

The giant screen covering a third of the wall was his artwork; tonight it would be very active. Installed within this special 8x12-foot plasma screen was a signature set to show the scan from her oversized vanity mirror in her glam station, all movements or sounds of his beautiful, adored treasure, XAna.

A cough, a giggle, her hair color, her eyes, even the click of her heels on marble tiles in the halls outside her penthouse had been measured and recorded to produce a visual or audible detection. For optimal secrecy when he was away, the screens were silent until he pressed the neon green button, each of the smaller monitors would be lit with random persons in the Towers, but all of them together would search her out and the precise second she was detected the massive wall unit would alight with her every feature.

The app on his phone found her, sending a notification that linked to his watch, another gift from XAna.

The original install by a local firm he found insulting, sloppy, and highly inadequate. Too few cameras and too many gaps of time lost because they were set on timers rather than biometric feeds.

Clever manipulation on his part, slipping a note on XAna's personal stationery to the decorator with the name of his contact at a preferred D.C. security firm; not only expedited the matter but also allowed him to lend his expertise with suggestions of camera placement.

It was brilliant, but not challenging. His princess was surrounded by fools. Sycophants who obeyed her without question. They didn't care about the cost. They wanted only to share in her fame. No one cares as selflessly for her as I always have. No one was willing to get their hands dirty for her every wish. He was, and not just dirt.

When he couldn't be in the room with her or his sound room, he could monitor everything from his phone. A simplified version of his system through an app remote that angled, zoomed, and adjusted for clearer viewing without the slightest noise or tremor.

His real masterpiece was the mirror. The technology of this mirror was foolproof; clean viewing, a powerful 20dB, and unmatched by any of its kind. SNR, or signal-to-noise ratio, was an important feature that he added himself. He couldn't have background noise vying with his treasure's angelic voice. Every word he wanted to hang the moon and stars on.

Of course, he didn't design this mirror for perversion. This unique reflecting glass was like the mirror in Snow White, but instead of vainglory, Tim could discern XAna's mood of the day. Her worries, her happiness, her anxieties, and her sadness or loneliness. With expert biometric scans.

The vanity was only one of such covert placements; lens and audio equipment were everywhere — sconces, floor lamps, the side table knobs, even the remote control on her TV, her daily compact in her purse as well. He would never leave her unattended. He would always be watching.

He had scoured the dark web for quality-controlled, impeccable mechanics that promised to be undetectable by the latest TSCM countermeasures that sweep for any surveillance equipment by outside professionals. No security detail, private or governmental, would think to scan for a secondary system. Each delicate toe touch on her elegantly planned bamboo flooring, each flip of golden locks, or even a blink within a 20-foot radius of every camera — only his. Redundancy in secrecy was necessary.

The plans delivered to the building's security department were the original blueprints that included only the cameras installed by the commercial security company. They didn't include his personal touches.

After careful planning of every detail, the disappointment he felt when he heard that Arthur and Garrett had convinced her to employ hired guns for the gala threw him off balance. The first weeks when they arrived, he overheard the five men in the garage talking about XAna's body; their words of slanderous lust brought out the killer in him. Nothing but a group of thugs, brawn without brains. They couldn't comprehend how honored they were to even know her. His plans shifted. More blood would be shed.

The arrogant troopers immediately performed a *thorough* sweep for cameras and bugs. Tim sneered, knowing they missed his installs. Background checks on everyone who ever had contact with her, including building maintenance, restaurant staff in the Towers, or her personal staff, came back without a single red flag. After doctoring his background, a name change years prior, his entire digital footprint a lie had cloaked his real identity, but soon his true self, his destiny would be revealed. He hated XAna had fallen for their false sense of safety.

They believed they were the only ones capable of protecting her thanks to their FBI or military training. Educated adrenaline junkies missed every detail he had tailored just for his precious. He loved that ignorance can be found in any field of security. As if greatness can only come from a government-backed program like a university or Quantico. His lips curled back into a sneer. The so-called experts would have no idea what he's capable of or who he was until it was too late.

He hated XAna had fallen for their false sense of safety. Arthur, XAna's friend and attorney with his years of practicing law and defending criminals, had an old-school mentality when it came to security. Big men with big guns. Part of Tim couldn't fault him since they shared a similar goal. Keep XAna safe. But the glorified bodyguards were in his way, their constant mockery of his position, their dismissal of his importance strengthening his resolve to end their cockiness in a very messy way.

XAna's innocence, a reliance on expert advice from anyone, was her downfall, but the sweet part of her that Tim cherished. It made her too trusting. Like the room he stood in, she would never have imagined this level of intrusion into her privacy, and while he hated betraying her in this way, she needed him to do this for her. Until he claimed his rightful place by her side, he would be her eyes, ears, her everything.

Protecting XAna is my job. I am her only need, her secret guardian, her confidante, and someday, though she doesn't realize it yet — her everything; she is mine. Tim had let nothing get in his way of watching over what was his, and tonight was XAna's main event. Her last event before she was to be forever his. Tonight, nothing was getting in his way. Their way.

Loud giggling, the screen lit with cackling mice, that's how Tim saw them. Like the story of Cinderella, rats gathered around her, distractions that only show up to feed off XAna's generosity, come to prep their vain, smug selves for the Gala. A passionate friend, a brilliant businesswoman, and a famous supermodel, she was flawless in his eyes, but she could be naïve. She couldn't see how those around her were using her. Oh sure, there were one or two trusted friends in the room, but those could be a nuisance too. He truly disliked anyone or any-thing that stood between him and what he desired.

Tapping buttons, focusing on the finer details, he could never call himself her authentic hero if he didn't. The mega-screen lit up the blackened room. He angled the lens; the plastic clicking sounded loudly in the stark space; his shoes swished across the cold, bare concrete as he glided closer to the screen; his fingers reached out, the pads slowly tracing the details of her face.

The flare of her nostrils, the prominent forehead, laugh lines perfectly framing her smile, so regal, yet her blue eyes held innocence within their depths. She was his angel of the night. Not yet dressed, make-up not finished; her vanity was nonexistent. While her physical beauty made any man with a pulse buzz with thrill, her true beauty came from within.

Her smile — she had two, each distinctively different from the other. The first practiced for the camera (the model always on cue), the second bright enough it could warm the soul, so sincere this smile, you couldn't take your eyes off her face. This smile was the rarest and had to be earned. This smile came from the heart. She reserved this for special people in her life: her father before he died, her best friend Janice, and me, though it had been weeks since he had the privilege. He often joked with her, calling it her lethal weapon. Her determination to see other's in a good light reflected the simplicity of her heart. Too pure to understand his meaning wasn't a compliment; he had meant it as a warning, how its use put others in danger. No one deserved this smile beyond him. No one lasted long in her world after he spotted the use of that honest emotional response to kindness or humor.

Lately, even he had to work for her special smile. After the guards arrived, he was edged out of conversations. She tried to win him over with arguments laced with gentle reminders that Arthur paid for the team out of generosity and kindness. His retorts made him feel like a petulant teen, a familiar, unwelcome feeling.

Years of watching her beauty bloom into a voluptuous woman fueled his desire. The business atmosphere suited her, amplifying her sensuality far more than her time as a top model. She was always above those shallow magazines. The mega corporations only wanted to profit from her beauty. The eye candy of every man and many women in the world. *But they'll never love her the way I love her.*

Tim leaned closer to the screen. A flicker in her eyes, was it worry or doubt? The shining excitement in her eyes replaced with a sudden fear tinged with disappointment, lips in a firm flat line, she was holding her breath. What was causing his angel to panic? Something in the room had changed.

Engaging other cameras, shifting around the room, the mirror across from the picture window, he spotted them. His eyes narrowed, his grip on the mouse tightened, the plastic crunched. The favored O'Hara Roses, but these weren't from him.

Who dared send her his signature arrangement? Sacred they were, a message only between the two of them. "*Who the f-… How dare they!*" Someone would pay for this overstep.

CHAPTER 2

XANA

Oh please... not tonight.

XAna's breath caught, her heart hammering against her ribs. The heady fragrance of O'Hara white roses was unmistakable. In a room thick with perfume and hair spray, nothing could overpower the scent of an O'Hara.

Her head swayed slowly left, then right in the massive wall mirror, trying to see past the six glamorous women preparing for the gala—searching for a glimpse of the newest floral delivery arriving behind them.

No one else seemed to notice.

Though technically classified as a rose, the large white blooms carried a uniquely soft yet potent lavender fragrance. The scent tightened something deep in her chest.

They had been an obsession of her grandmother's during the final years when she rarely left home. Grandma Melva had planted rows of them behind her father's house after XAna's mother moved out. Her mother had hated the "overly feminine" fragrance, always preferring darker notes—musk, patchouli, anything seductive and heavy.

A small part of XAna had always suspected the garden wasn't planted out of love for flowers at all.

It had been revenge for her ex-daughter-in-law's betrayal of her only son.

In the past, the scent had stirred sweet memories of working beside her grandmother in the garden, learning how to coax the delicate blooms into thriving.

But with both her grandmother and her father gone, those memories—and the flowers' traditional meaning of elegance and romance—had become something darker. The fragrance was no longer comforting.

Now the aroma twisting through the room made her stomach knot, as if danger hid beneath petals meant to resemble love notes.

XAna watched Bryn guide the delivery man through the promenade of furniture and elegantly dressed women, carrying an extravagant crystal vase filled with thirty-six long stems of O'Hara roses.

Bryn caught the apprehension in XAna's eyes.

Few people understood the fear those flowers stirred in her. But Bryn—her publicist—was one of the rare few who could read the anxiety in XAna's expression from a hundred yards away.

She crossed her fingers—and even her toes—silently praying for tonight's success. More than anything, she hoped the gift didn't hold another love note from the "gardener," meant to terrorize her and ruin the event.

XAna held her breath as Bryn accepted the bouquet from the deliveryman. He left quickly after receiving what was probably a very conservative twenty-percent tip. Bryn set the extravagant arrangement on the vanity beneath the bright mirror lights.

Her eyes locked with XAna's as she leaned down and whispered, "Honey... breathe. They're from Ms. Wintaur of *Vogue*."

The breath XAna had been holding escaped a little too loudly. She snapped back into composure just as Bryn stepped away from the vanity, lifting the elegant card for a dramatic reading.

"Ladies, listen to this—from Ms. Wintaur of *Vogue*. Of *VOGUE*, ladies," Bryn added with theatrical flair.

The women gathered closer, offering the appropriate oohs and ahhs.

And despite herself, XAna smiled.

Let these White OHara's wrapped in Emerald ribbon — the color of Success — remind you that no one can take tonight from you.

It's your night now. Take a Bow! L&H's, Gena."

"You heard her, X." Bryn's nickname always steadied her. "Stand up and take a bow."

Smiling, XAna obeyed. Theatrics like this were one of the many reasons Bryn Hudson was the best publicity agent in all of Miami.

Standing among these women—these brilliant, beautiful women who believed tonight would be perfect—XAna dipped into a humble bow and accepted their cheers and applause.

She exhaled again, louder than she meant to.

No note.

Relief loosened the tight knot in her chest.

Her gaze swept the room until it found Janice. Her assistant gave a small nod of understanding before returning to the tablet in her hands. Janice knew exactly what that moment meant. She had been the one to discover the last message—a single white rose with a love note left on XAna's desk at the hotel where tonight's gala was being held.

The words were always sickeningly sweet.

But the knowledge that someone watched her closely enough to know her every movement twisted them into something sinister.

The sender never signed a name. Instead, each message ended the same way: a stamped phrase declaring that soon she would understand her moment of *Full Surrender*.

The implication of intimacy made her shiver—and not in a sexy way.

The police had explained the stamp was deliberate. It concealed handwriting. Worse, it was the same popular stamp brand XAna used when autographing her books.

The notes had left her constantly looking over her shoulder, questioning whether she should even host the gala tonight.

Detective Garrett—Janice's friend—had urged her to cancel the event entirely. When she refused, he agreed to attend undercover as a favor.

XAna inhaled slowly, forcing calm into her lungs.

Everything was fine.

The roses were from *Vogue*.

There was no creepy note.

But the gala wasn't just about her philanthropic showcase. Tonight belonged to all the women gathered with her now—and those waiting for them at the Coral Club.

She had hired an entirely new security team, men with résumés that could make the event look as though Fort Knox itself were being guarded. Their presence ensured everyone could relax and truly enjoy the evening.

As XAna looked around the room at the women surrounding her—new friends, old friends, and trusted colleagues—hope and gratitude swelled in her chest.

She lifted her champagne and took a small sip, releasing another steady breath.

Perhaps tonight her stalker was truly gone. Perhaps tonight these women would finally take their long-awaited bow.

Still...

As the laughter around her grew louder, the faint scent of O'Hara roses drifted through the room again.

And for one brief moment, XAna had the unsettling feeling that someone in the building knew exactly where she was.

So, it wasn't another man.

Just some pitiful excuse of an editor for a trash magazine from who cares Illinois.

I suppose for now she can be left alone, let her career kill her slowly, dying out to the fake social media influencers stealing every bit of their advertising dollars.
A cruel chuckle filled the dark room. Dying breed indeed. Tim snickered. His sense of humor may be dry, but he was funny in a sick, perverse way. His anger was amping up, impatience driving his every thought. If he wasn't careful, his XAna could get hurt in the crossfire of his love.

In the weeks leading up to the gala, XAna had spent a great deal of time getting to know her. Chloe was a single mother to a beautiful daughter she'd named Chleo—a subtle shift of letters that reflected their unbreakable bond.

Even after winning the $75,000 award for Best Entrepreneurial Essay and Business Plan, Chloe still worked two jobs. She had put herself through online college with almost no government assistance.

Her dream was to open her own bakery, with a mission of setting aside fresh baked goods each day for women's shelters across Miami. The idea was not only smart—it was deeply kind.

As an independent businesswoman, XAna understood that kind of determination. She, too, had once chosen not to lean on the security of her upbringing, instead venturing out to prove what she could build on her own.

In that way, she and Chloe had formed a deep bond in the quiet power of kindness.

The foundation's board had voted unanimously to award Chloe the scholarship.

And XAna couldn't have been happier with their choice.

Chloe was a vision in gold lame fabric; the dress fit her perfect curves, and the low heel crystal sandals were the understated perfection of a veritable goddess. She glowed with happiness, making XAna's Gala even more special.

"Bryn, are you certain about this shade of pink? Isn't it a little bright? I mean, my dress is all white, so even a light shade of pink is gonna stand out."

XAna sat on the golden chaise longue in her beloved feather-cuffed robe, studying her reflection. Her full lips —bold and siren-like—stood in striking contrast to the faint iridescent shadow around her eyes. Not an inch of her skin escaped the shimmer of body glitter.

It wasn't her usual style to lean this far into costuming for an event. But tonight she had indulged Bryn's hand-selected, publicity-stunt wardrobe and makeup out of sheer happiness—and the welcome distraction from the ugliness threatening the gala.

"Of course it is," Bryn declared. "Aphrodite is a goddess and a bad bitch. She never does anything without making a statement. And that fuchsia from your Goddess line? To. Die. For."

She squeezed XAna's shoulders from behind and air-kissed her cheek in the mirror.

"You agreed to let me make visionary decisions. So yes—fuchsia, baby. Besides, it's the only color you're wearing tonight that might draw your fans' eyes upward from that magnificent plunging neckline in the perfect dress I chose."

Bryn flashed a triumphant grin at her reflection. "Now stop overthinking my brilliance. I know what I'm doing—and so does Michel."

She winked at the makeup artist and gave his backside a playful pat.

Her publicist could be haughty—sometimes downright vain—when it came to her creative vision. Which was exactly why the black-and-gold gown Bryn had chosen for herself, embodying Bellona, the Goddess of War, suited her perfectly. She looked the part... and sometimes acted like it in her day job.

XAna gave her reflection one last approving glance. She did love the fuchsia lip color—its sunset undertones catching the light whenever a camera flashed. It was one of the standout shades in her Goddess line, fittingly named *Venus* for the Love Goddess.

She smiled and blew a playful kiss at her reflection.

Perhaps it really was her favorite.

"Michel', no complaints." She gave him a flirtatious wink, "You have magic in your fingertips; it just seemed bold for all the white chiffon. Truly, you know I love your work."

"Listen here Ms. X, I have magic in every delicious part of me and tonight you are gonna have men fanning themselves and some ladies with that deep v, so you gotta give them a teensy little chance to breathe, and this brilliant hot pink shouting desire is just the trick needed to give respite before they look back down at your perfect boobies, Trust Michel', he would never steer you wrong. Color is Life." Michel ended every statement with his motto and a snap. He was a true treat every day. She had known Bryn for six years and Michel even longer; they were more than people she employed. They were family and friends to her.

Giggling, she blew Michel' a kiss. "You are too much, but you make a woman feel confident."

"Is the car downstairs, Janice?"

XAna glanced over her shoulder at her assistant, who was scanning her planner and checking items off one by one. If not for the black horn-rimmed glasses, XAna might not have recognized her as the same executive assistant who normally dressed in conservative but feminine suits with sensible office heels.

Tonight, however, Janice wore a stunning silvery-green silk gown. The front rose in a graceful high neck, while the back fell into a deep plunging cowl that revealed the elegant line of her shoulders. It was beautifully refined. For the evening she had chosen Luna—the Goddess of the Moon—and the effect made the concept come alive.

She truly looked like a moonbeam.

"Yes," Janice said without looking up from the planner, her pen still moving. "Mitch's team is waiting in the hall to escort us to the cars. Tim already went down to bring yours to the front of the tower. I saw him earlier—wearing the tux you bought him and carrying his book—but he seemed a little on edge."

Her eyes never left the page. She never stopped working.

Janice's mention of Tim reminded XAna that she would need to soothe his lingering resentment about the new security team.

"Okay then," XAna said, rising slightly from the chaise. "Michel, if you could help me slip into my dress, I'll be ready. Let's not make them wait any longer."

Her eyes rolled as she shot Bryn a pointed look.

"I think the twenty-minute delayed arrival Bryn planned for dramatic effect should be enough."

She giggled softly.

If only tonight were as lighthearted as she felt in this moment.

A flicker of memory pricked her thoughts. The tension of bodyguards and threats still hung over the evening, but the show—and the donations—had to go on.

Tonight would determine the future of her foundation... and the women who would depend on it.

CHAPTER 3

WATCHING

Tim's eyes narrowed as XAna walked toward the dressing room.

Michel followed, clattering beside her about how she'd be the bi-atch of the ball tonight.

Normally, Michel's taste in overly masculine men like Mitch gave Tim a sense of peace.

At least he could trust Michel not to sully his innocent angel.

Motion detection activated a separate camera as they made their way to the hall that led to where her gossamer gown hung. He had visited the room many times this week just to touch the garment, her scent lingered from the many try-ons. He closed his eyes, recalling the silk's whisper against his fingertips, a barely-there brush of cool, smooth fabric. The phantom essence of her per-fume, a delicate floral, filled his mind as he pictured her. A warmth bloomed in his chest as he envisioned her eyes, bright with their moment's promise. He took a deep breath, the air thick with unspoken desires, and thought to himself, *Soon.*

The tinkling sound, like shattered glass, of sweet laughter ripped him from his imaginary world.

Gay wonder had obviously tickled her with his flam-boyant sense of humor.

His skin feverish knowing his princess was prepar-ing to slip on her dress with the assistance of another man, homo or not, the thought of another someone touching her in such intimate ways caused a level of fury that sickened him. His blood boiled; watching Michel fol-lower her around the corner.

"Wait", he said aloud, what's happening, why can't I see them?" Panicking he grabbed the remote stepping closer to the smaller screen, he pushed buttons trying to manipulate the camera lens to the corner, it reached only so far, he could see Michel's tacky purple heels and then only a snippet of XAna's bare feet standing in front of him. Shadows of movement crossed the screen, but not his jewel.

"Damn it, FUCK!" The remote went smashing against the screen, now Michel had his hands on her and he couldn't watch to make sure he was being appropriately mannered. He heard more giggling and muffled whispers.

"Fuck! Fuck! Fuck!" His fingers, his hands numb with rage from squeezing his fist, luckily the room was

soundproof and three stories below anything or anyone to hear his screams.

As Michel zipped up the dress and she finished slipping on the crystal encrusted heels, she gathered her white heart clutch designed by Chanel, she glimpsed her image in the looking glass, the gown was truly a masterpiece designed by the talented Vera Wang, it was a donation to the charity in honor of all that XAna was trying to do for women who needed a chance.

Thanks to Bryn's hard work as the foundation's publicity guru, there was more promised celebrity attendance at her gala than any other charity for the year. She was thrilled with the pledges that had already started to pour in, the monies would lead to an amazing first year of entrepreneurial hopes.

The women already chosen to receive initial funding from MPowerU had been vetted hard, each lady's story was heartbreaking and amazing in some detail. The vetting had been handled by her long-time friend, main benefactor, and attorney for the foundation, Arthur, they were so lucky to have his wisdom and guidance, and she was honored to have him escort her into the Great Hall this evening.

She cherished Arthur's friendship. With her grandmother gone nearly six years, his loyalty had quietly filled a space in her life—especially after her father passed away last year.

Stepping closer to the full-length mirror, the woman staring back at her projected confidence, determination —and yes, a little luck.

XAna smiled, allowing herself a quiet moment of pride.

She winked at Michel in the mirror, the silent signal that she was ready to be the goddess tonight. He lifted the long train of her gown as she moved toward the entrance of the room she named, the *Hall of Mirrors*.

Her place of transformation. The room where glamour began and she could become anything she dreamed.

She paused at the threshold and drew in a steady breath, looking out at the seven stunning women waiting for her.

It struck her then how funny life could be. She stood surrounded by beautiful, confident single women. Only weeks ago she never imagined she would be one of them again.

But perhaps it wasn't so terrible.

If you couldn't be with the one you truly wanted, living fully—side by side with extraordinary women like these—might be the next best thing.

As she came out of her dressing room, Michel made like a horn and tooted her arrival. Chatting hushed, replace with lots of ooh's and ahh's. Their adoration, once again making her realize how lucky she truly was to have such a tribe of support.

"Thank you ladies, we all look like the Queens we are, so Bryn, we will let you lead us out. Let's get this party started!" The ladies cheered and a marching of heels became a thunderously sweet sound of triumph.

At last—what felt like hours but had been barely two minutes—his rose appeared.

The sight of her in that dress snapped his focus into place.

She stole the breath straight from his lungs.

A timer behind him shrieked, shattering the moment with its ugly reminder that it was time to resume his humble role for the evening.

"Fuck it all to hell."

The words tore from him, meant for no one and everyone at once.

He dragged in a breath, killed the lights, and headed for the door. On the way out, he scooped up the shattered pieces of the remote and slipped them into his pocket—a reminder to replace it tomorrow... and repair the camera in the corner.

A mistake like that would not happen again.

She is my destiny.

The white of her dress... the promise of the moment when they would finally be united as one, never to part.

She simply didn't see it yet.

But she would.

Over the next few hours he would help her understand that he was never meant to stand outside her life. He was meant to guide it. To stand beside her through every triumph, every venture—personal and business alike.

No one else deserved her.

No one else would sacrifice for her the way he already had... or would.

No one.

His hand rested on the door handle as a slow, ugly smile stretched across his thin lips.

Perhaps Michel would have to meet with an untimely end after all.

Complications were a pet peeve of his.

And anyone who touched his angel without permission had a troubling tendency to suffer very unfortunate accidents.

Time would tell.

CHAPTER 4
LIGHTS CAMERA BULLSHIT!

Tim eased the limo forward, matching the snail's pace of black sedans and stretch cars creeping along the one-way street outside the Coral Club. They had been placed at the back of the line, just as Bryn had ordered. Her instructions were clear—XAna's entrance from car to hall was meant to be the flashiest, the most anticipated of the night.

Another one of Bryn's hollow productions.

XAna didn't need spectacle to command a room. She never had. Perfection required no staging. She was already far above the shallow theatrics meant to feed other people's egos.

From the driver's seat Tim watched the frenzy unfold. Flashbulbs exploded along the long staircase leading up to the club entrance. Searchlights swept lazily through the dusk, carving pale ribbons across the Lauderdale sky. Everything shimmered with excess—men in penguin suits, many of them rented, escorting women wrapped in gowns of every imaginable color as they drifted across the sparkling onyx carpet. The last pink glow of sunset clung to the Mediterranean clay roof of the historic Coral Hall, as if even the sky wanted a better look at her arrival.

His gaze shifted, narrowing.

The newly hired bodyguards moved easily among the wealthy crowd. Their slate-gray tuxedos made them indistinguishable from the elite guests. Bryn's idea of clever security. Blend them into the party so they could quietly hunt for the threat stalking XAna.

Her ex-fiancé.

Dallas Richards.

Tim's grip tightened on the steering wheel. The leather creaked beneath his hands.

They thought they understood the danger circling her. They thought a few hired men in borrowed tuxedos could protect her.

But none of them knew her.

Not the way he did.

Tim, too, had been specially requested to wear a tux.

His left hand rested on the steering wheel while the fingers of his right brushed an imaginary hair from the pristine cashmere sleeve. The simple motion stirred the memory of XAna's tender touch the day he had been fitted for the garment.

His nostrils flared as he recalled her nearness.

His cock hardened at the thought of that moment—
her delicate hands smoothing the front of the tux,
straightening the collar with careful fingers. A provoca-
tive gesture, whether she realized it or not.

An average man would have broken under such intimacy.

But he was not an average man.

Years of discipline had seen to that.

At a small meditation hall he had studied the art of
Japanese Zazen, beginning his training the moment he
learned she had moved to Broward County. He had been
only twenty-two then, but even at that age he understood she deserved a man capable of patience. A man capable of restraint.

So he had done the work.

He mastered the quieting of petty animal urges. He
sacrificed immature impulses. He trained his mind to
focus only on the endgame.

Becoming worthy of her.

Claiming her as his own.

Eight years had passed since then. Tim had been
there every step of the way, watching her transformation
—from the diet-obsessed young woman she once was to
the woman the world now admired. A globetrotting businesswoman. A devoted philanthropist.

Still innocent in many ways.

Yet spoken of everywhere as the most desirable
woman since Sophia Loren.

Her curves were softer now, more generous than
during her modeling days when she lived on salads and
discipline. Tim felt his heart thump with quiet pride.

The world might believe it wanted her.

But what the world desired...

Only he would soon have.

A rap on his window, a valet held up two fingers, indicating they were two cars from moving into position. He glanced in the mirror, watching XAna wait patiently in the back seat, he was feeling only peace about the next few hours, until looking ahead he saw three body men in position to do the job that was rightfully his to be done brought back the deep hurt he felt at being snubbed.

His honor was being challenged.

No amount of incense burning was going to bury the feelings these smug bastards triggered, damnit. XAna herself had sent him to Quantico two years ago for special training as an Executive driver. No longer was he a simple lackey behind the wheel but a skilled weapon of defense. He had taken strategic courses in collision avoidance and threat response. He was certified in all skills, just like these monkeys, and yet XAna still wouldn't allow him the honor of protecting her.

The pinch of anger eased. Tim drew a slow breath and reached for the discipline he had trained himself to use. Meditation. Control.

He summoned a practiced sati—one of his calming manifestation memories.

The day at Vera Wang's Florida studio.

XAna being fitted for the dress that would soon become her bridal gown. Their bridal gown.

The memory remained vivid. She had stepped from behind the golden curtain, her silhouette glowing through the fabric before she parted it. When she saw him waiting, she smiled softly and asked him to zip her up.

The request had been almost too intimate.

She had come to stand barely a foot in front of him, turning her back while facing the mirror. The gown hung open, revealing the smooth curve of her lower back through the unzipped seam.

Temptation had surged through him.

Every vein pulsed with the urge to do the opposite of helping her into the dress. To slip the gown from her shoulders instead and make her cry out beneath his love.

But determination won.

Barely.

With careful fingers he drew the zipper upward, closing the gown. When it was finished, she turned and spun before the mirror, the skirt catching the light.

Her face glowed with pure delight, like a young girl seeing her first prom dress.

This was why he served her.

Because beneath the glamour, beneath the fame and power the world worshipped, XAna still carried the heart of an angel.

A youthful heart.

After the fitting, she had taken him to Luis Pizzeria, their favorite restaurant, gifting him that day a Rolex, engraved 'My Knight'. The title she had given him the day he saved her from being mugged at the shopping mall. The words signified so much that he hadn't complained since. Well, not vocally to her.

He touched the watch on his left wrist—a beautiful, expensive gift from her.

The limo rolled forward toward the final security post, where another man would take over as her protector. The thought alone stirred his irritation.

No matter how much he loved the watch, she had still placed him in a tiny, useless box. And the new bodyguards knew it. They carried themselves like victors tonight, lording their positions over him.

The humiliation burned.

He recognized the childishness of it. He was pouting. Sitting in silence only made it worse, his thoughts circling the same bitter truth—this woman he worshiped believed she was in danger, yet still relegated him to nothing more than a hired driver.

A taxi.

The refusal to see him as the strong man he had become scraped against an old memory.

The schoolyard.

He could still see it clearly—those boys shoving him, laughing as he tried to keep his footing in the dirt. And then XAna stepping between them, fearless, chasing them off, lecturing them all as if she were born to command a room even back then.

She had cared.

She had seen him when no one else had.

But tonight... it didn't feel like she did.

Not as the man who had spent years becoming worthy of her—the only grace was she did not realize who he was—really was. Not yet. It wasn't time for his reveal.

But it still hurt. And he wanted the pain to go away.

Movement in the rearview mirror caught his attention.

XAna leaned forward in the back seat, checking her lipstick in her signature diamond compact. She looked nervous, though there was no reason for it. Her lips were already perfect, shimmering with silvery gloss over a bright pink stain. Her long golden hair was swept to one side, secured by the silver-lined pearl rose comb he had given her for her birthday.

She was a vision.

The gown she wore looked like something the goddess Aphrodite herself might choose. A fitted white bodice hugged her feminine curves so tightly they nearly spilled from the ruched silk, leaving no doubt about their fullness. A delicate gold chain secured the gown at one shoulder, while a braided golden cord rested low across her hips. The fabric flowed gracefully to the floor, a daring slit rising to mid-thigh and revealing the warm bronze glow of her summer skin.

When she had slipped into the back of the town car earlier, he had noticed the small detail he loved most.

The sandals.

Gold straps, barely a heel. A quiet rebellion against the towering stilettos the fashion world expected. After years as the third most famous supermodel in the world, XAna still hated high heels and only wore them when absolutely necessary.

Tonight, at the themed *"Women of Greatness"* MPowerU Charity Scholarship Ceremony and Silent Auction, she would outshine them all.

An ethereal goddess in white.

To him, costume or not, she was an original.

Even angry, he admired everything about her. The way she dressed. The way she worked harder than anyone else in a world where most supermodels simply married wealth or drifted comfortably through life on beauty alone. XAna had never been like them. She built empires. She gave money away. She carried herself with a quiet authority that made rooms shift when she entered.

She was one of a kind.

Even as her employee, he had never felt beneath her. Not really. With XAna there was always warmth—an ease that made him feel less like staff and more like a trusted friend. At times even family.

Which was why the sting of tonight cut so deeply.

He *was* family.

Seeing the pearl rose comb in her hair—the one he had given her months ago—softened the ache slightly. She had chosen it for tonight's special evening. That had to mean something.

Still, the comfort was thin.

His silence filled the front of the limo, heavy with the frustration he buried beneath the professional driver's mask he had worn since pulling the car from the Towers earlier that evening.

Her new bodyguards had made sure he understood his place.

A driver pretending to understand security.

Mitch had been the worst of them. Not openly mocking like the younger men, but colder in his professionalism. A quick glance, a tight smile, and that dismissive instruction:

Do what you're good at. We'll do what we're good at.

The arrogant prick.

Tim had swallowed the insult for XAna's sake, but it had cost him. He should have been beside her tonight, not behind a wheel. After everything she had allowed him to do—the training, the expensive classes, the certifications—how could she still refuse to see that he was capable of protecting her himself?

With only a few backup men if necessary.

Their turn for the drop-off approached.

Tim lowered the sound partition and glanced into the rearview mirror. XAna was staring through the tinted window at the sea of cameras and bodies crowding the carpet.

Watching the world waiting for her.

"I really should be with you tonight—by your side," Tim said, trying to keep the strain from his voice. "Let Mitch and the other two handle the perimeter. I can protect you personally now. I'd spot Dallas from a thousand yards away. I would never let him—or anyone—hurt you."

He hated the note of desperation creeping into his tone. It sounded like whining, but he needed her to understand his value.

"Those guys are just paid bullies," he pressed on. "They care about the dollar you give them. Remember the alley? I protected you then, and I didn't have half the training I have now. It should be me, not them. The stalker has never come near you when I've been at your side. He knows I'd kill for you."

The raw edge in his voice surprised even him. Six years he had devoted himself to her in every way he could. Tonight wasn't just her night—it should have been his moment too, the chance to prove the skills he had worked so hard to master. If she would only let him do his job, there would be no need for the next step in his plans.

But this new security team had made that impossible.

XAna trusted badges and bullets far too easily.

The balance between driver and protector churned inside him, stoking his temper. Still, he told himself that after tonight she would remember who had always been there for her. It irritated him that he even had to consider dealing with those pathetic men pretending to play heroes. He had hoped she would reconsider during the ride to the gala.

Sadly, she was disappointing him again.

"Timmy," she said gently, her voice warm but firm. "I know you would do your best. It doesn't go unnoticed how sweet it is that you'd want to put yourself in harm's way for me. But these men are trained for exactly this kind of protection."

She paused, choosing her words carefully.

"They're convinced Dallas might show up tonight. I'm not entirely sure myself—I can't imagine him being truly dangerous—but the threats have to be taken seriously. Arthur assures me these men are the best in the business. I only want this event to go smoothly. Its mission matters too much for unnecessary risks."

Her eyes softened in the mirror.

"I know how deeply you care for me. I depend on you more than you realize. Knowing you'll be here waiting to take me safely home if the worst happens gives me tremendous peace. You're more important than anyone tonight. You're my knight, ready to sweep me away from danger."

She smiled sweetly at him in the reflection, hoping to ease the sting.

"Besides," she added playfully, "I see you brought your best friend again. Gatsby tonight, is it?"

She nodded toward the passenger seat.

Tim glanced down at the book resting beside him. It had once been a gift from her grandmother—though XAna never knew that connection. Years earlier, as a teenager, he had worked for the elderly Mrs. Montgomery's landscaping company. He had taken the job because it allowed him glimpses of XAna during the summers.

The old woman had taken a liking to him, teaching him how to care for the famed O'Hara roses. Each week she handed him another classic novel, and they would discuss the story while he trimmed her favorite bushes.

XAna had never made the connection.

Nor had she noticed how the books had changed.

Now hollowed inside, carefully altered to house his pistol.

Tim allowed himself a small, private smile at the clever disguise. He liked carrying a piece of her grandmother with him. Another quiet sign, in his mind, that their lives were meant to be intertwined.

When he glanced back again, she was still speaking.

"Seems appropriate tonight," she said lightly, gesturing toward the glittering crowd outside. "With all the glitz waiting for us out there, I'm hoping your book proves far more interesting than the gala itself."

Her fingertips smoothed her hair near the pearl rose comb, a subtle salute to him in the mirror.

"Thank you for being such a dear friend."

She truly hoped the words would ease his disappointment. She understood why he was upset. What she wished he could see was how much she depended on him.

For eight years he had been far more than a driver.

He was her friend.

As he eased the sedan to the curb, one small detail lingered in his mind.

The way she had said his name.

Timmy.

The sound grated against him. He had asked her long ago not to call him that once he began working for her full time. The name belonged to another life, another version of him. Sometimes he wondered if she used it because she remembered him from their childhood, but if that were true she would have said something by now.

She never did.

Instead, she only used the name in quiet, intimate moments like this. Still, *Timmy* sounded weak. Needy. A boy's name.

That wasn't who he was to her anymore.

He was her friend.

Like family—her words, repeated to him many times over the years.

A dear friend, she had said after her father passed away.

That was the moment he had known things between them had changed. Her trust had deepened beyond employer and employee. Beyond even friendship.

At least that was how it felt to him.

Reaching forward through the opening in the tinted partition, she touched his shoulder and gave it a gentle squeeze.

"Now do me a favor," she said warmly. "Relax and enjoy your story. I'll handle my hostess duties, collect lots of donations for the women who need them, and afterward you can escort me home."

Her voice softened.

"Remember, I couldn't do any of this without you."

The sincerity in her tone settled his agitation. Tim nodded slowly, rubbing the spot on his shoulder where her hand had rested.

Then she turned away, her attention shifting beyond him to the crowd gathered outside.

Her eyes scanned the flashing lights and waiting guests, already focused on the work she had created for the evening.

Chapter 5

MPowerU Gala

Xana's eyes filled with happy tears as she gazed out the passenger window, overwhelmed by the sight before her. Her biggest dream yet was unfolding in front of her.

The entrance to the Coral Club shimmered beneath the night sky. A canopy of white chiffon flowed from the structure to the ground, cascading over a black onyx carpet flecked with gold that sparkled beneath the spotlights.

Not red carpet.

Onyx.

She had chosen it deliberately — a stone symbolizing abundance, vitality, strength, and protection from negative energy. Tonight was meant to say something.

This wasn't about lipstick or designer labels.

It was about power.

About women bold enough to chase their dreams and strong enough to catch them.

The event company *Dazzlers* had more than lived up to their name. Lights swept the sky in slow arcs, bright enough she suspected half of Dade County could see them. The air hummed with anticipation.

Press from across the country had arrived for the gala. Requests for interviews had flooded in — *People Magazine*, Page Six of *The New York Times*.

But her first interview would belong to *Fort Lauderdale Magazine*.

Some victories deserved to stay close to home.

The car rolled to a stop.

Instantly, the paparazzi surged forward, flashes exploding in rapid bursts. Cameras lifted. Voices shouted her name.

Before the door could open, Mitch was already there.

"Step back."

The command came out low and hard as he pulled the door wide. Behind him, Bruno and Duncan moved in like a wall of muscle. Bruno—Mitch's second-in-command—was built like a two-ton truck, and he used that size well, forcing the press back an arm's length at a time while lenses strained for the first shot.

Then she stepped out.

For a moment, the noise faded.

XAna turned slowly, taking it all in. The long rows of limousines and town cars. The crush of press. The relentless bursts of light reflecting off the black onyx carpet now beneath her sandals, its gold flecks glittering under the spotlights.

She knew she was probably smiling like a fool.

She didn't care.

She drew in a slow breath, wanting to hold the moment inside her lungs. For years she had dreamed of finding a way to give something meaningful back to the world.

And now, standing beneath the lights, with the crowd roaring around her, every shimmering detail told her the same thing.

Her dream had finally come true.

Yesterday, Bryn—brilliant publicist and loyal friend—had orchestrated private press tours of the new headquarters near the New River district.

Tonight was the result.

Hollywood's elite had come: actors, models, dancers, theater legends. Producers and magazine editors mingled beneath the lights, while the mayors of both Fort Lauderdale and Miami had placed themselves firmly on the *yes* list.

XAna could hardly believe it.

Her work—her dream—was rising above the storm that had nearly buried it. The headlines about her split with Dallas. The bitter fracture with Charla, once her closest friend and business partner.

Maybe the worst of it was finally behind her.

Maybe what remained was the future she had fought for—one filled with success, purpose, and opportunity for the women her charity served.

She glanced down the glittering stretch of onyx carpet. Fans lined the street, shouting her name, hoping for a glimpse of the arrivals.

Nothing was going to steal this night.

This night belonged to her ladies.

All the risks she'd taken.

All the warnings she'd ignored.

Somehow, she believed it would be worth it.

Arthur appeared quietly at her side. She slipped her hand into the crook of his arm, gave Mitch a small nod, and said softly,

"I'm ready to go in."

As they walked, Mitch's expression darkened with every step.

She understood professionalism, but the change in his mood had her scanning the crowd again. The sea of faces, cameras, and shouting voices suddenly felt less like celebration and more like something to watch.

Her gaze lifted to Mitch, searching for reassurance—some silent promise of safety.

None came.

Mitch wasn't the comforting kind of bodyguard. That role belonged—loosely—to the other three men on his team. They at least attempted sympathy.

Mitch simply did the job.

His eyes swept the crowd again, slower this time.

Most days, she found his quiet vigilance reassuring.

Tonight, though, a little comfort might have helped.

Especially when so much depended on this evening passing without a single misstep.

And the way Mitch's hand hovered a little closer to the inside of his jacket told her he wasn't taking any chances.

On most nights, the Coral Gables Country Club was quiet elegance—host to the occasional wedding or private gathering. A members-only sanctuary tucked away from the frenzy of Miami society.

But tonight was different.

As a favor to Arthur, one of the club's founding board members, the Coral had cleared its calendar entirely for the event. The staff had even granted the unusual request that her security team sweep the building for the past two days.

Tonight, the historic grounds looked breathtaking.

The club's signature coral-pink stucco glowed beneath the fading sun, flecks of diamond dust embedded in the walls catching the last light of evening and scattering it like sparks across the property. Sunset deepened the hues to rich shades of rose and amber.

Inside, more than five hundred crystal candelabras had been placed throughout the ballroom, their soft glow creating an intimate warmth that softened what was, in truth, a slightly overcrowded guest list.

Judging by the endless line of limousines and the wall of paparazzi waiting outside, nearly every RSVP had arrived.

She couldn't help but feel humbled by the support.

Miami International Airport must have been flooded with private jets.

Eighteen months of planning had led to this moment. And the evening was about far more than an elaborate soirée.

The Coral itself stood to receive glowing publicity after donating a generous portion of the venue fees to the MPowerU Scholarship.

This wasn't just her reputation—or her resources—behind the dream anymore.

Entire industries had stepped forward in support. Former magazine and marketing partners had donated their services. Social media coverage alone would span every major platform—videos, vlogs, and live feeds streaming across the world.

And the press...

Vogue.

Cosmopolitan.

Time.

People.

Each had already sent representatives days earlier to interview her in her private tower office for upcoming issues.

For one night, the Coral Gables Country Club had become the center of the world she had spent years building.

And every glittering light in the room existed for the same purpose—

The women of MPowerU.

She was deeply proud of the work being done.

The women's empowerment movement that had swept through Hollywood had brought both triumphs and controversy. Too often the headlines focused on the negatives—lawsuits that unraveled, accusations that proved false.

XAna wanted something different.

Something lasting.

MPowerU focused on ten women—carefully vetted, each one chosen after intense background checks and essays that revealed the same thing: determination. These were women who had struggled for years to build something meaningful and simply needed the opportunity to finally see their efforts bear fruit.

This night, with all its glamour and attention, was only the smallest part of it.

The real victory had already happened.

Each of those women had earned their place in the MPowerU scholarship program through grit, courage, and an unwavering belief in their own potential.

For them, the future was no longer an idea.

It was something they could almost taste.

As much as she hated the fear-driven layer of security surrounding the evening, she didn't regret it. Not tonight. The protection was essential.

This night belonged to the winners.

Amid the glitz and glamour—the celebrities, the mini makeovers, the shopping sprees they'd been gifted—these women were finally being celebrated. The last thing XAna wanted was for her nightmares to touch their dreams.

Arthur was ushered ahead of her up the stairs.

Behind him, XAna felt Mitch's steady hand at the small of her back guiding her forward while Bruno moved to her right, forming a wall of protection. The two towering men wore the Brioni tuxedos she had ordered and tailored specifically for the gala, the midnight-blue fabric catching the light as they moved.

They looked magnificent.

Brioni—the same legendary house that dressed Bond —had created them. Having worked with the designer before, XAna had called in a favor. He had been gracious enough to accept her invitation to the gala as her personal guest.

When she told him who the suits were for—and why —the trauma behind the added security, he hadn't hesitated.

"I would be honored."

He designed the tuxedos to move with the bodyguards' strength and speed, yet remain sleek and elegant enough for the evening.

Truthfully, if Mitch and Bruno weren't currently guarding her, they might have been the most striking men in the room.

Women would have been swooning.

She heard Mitch speaking quietly into the earpiece that doubled as his communication device.

A faint smile touched her lips as she remembered the first time she'd mistaken it for him talking to her. She had stood there trying to follow his instructions until he finally pointed to his ear, letting her know he was speaking to one of his men.

At the time, she had found it amusing.

Tonight, there was nothing humorous about him.

As he instructed Wayne—his number three—to move the crowd back from the stairs, Mitch's expression hardened, almost murderous.

XAna was grateful he took his job so seriously. Especially tonight.

Greeting guests and waving to the fans lining the staircase, they continued upward toward the Coral Club's Orchid Room, where hundreds of prominent guests waited for her arrival and the start of the evening's speeches and scholarship presentations.

At the final step, still gathering the chiffon train in her hands, XAna paused.

For a fleeting moment she felt like Aphrodite herself—the theme of tonight's gala: *Goddess of MPowerU.*

At the top of the staircase the scholarship recipients waited, each woman radiant with pride. Every one of them had chosen a mythical goddess to represent her strength.

Bryn had chosen for XAna.

Aphrodite—Greek goddess of beauty, sensuality, and desire.

Years ago she might have resisted the symbolism, still chasing some impossible ideal of perfection. Now she embraced it. A woman's curves, her individuality, her confidence—those were the very things worth celebrating.

It was the same belief that fueled everything she loved about her life: the beauty products she created, the brands she promoted, and most of all, the promise of this night.

Women championing women.

Aphrodite—mythical or not—felt right for the night, and for her.

Bryn was almost always right.

Taking one last look down the staircase, XAna watched the white chiffon train of her gown drift over the dark onyx carpet. So far, the evening had unfolded flawlessly.

The sky glowed with the last traces of sunset. The air smelled like a garden in full bloom. Fans and paparazzi along the street were still smiling, cameras flashing as she gave them a final wave before turning toward the great hall.

At the top of the stairs, Bryn and Janice flanked the scholarship winners. Bryn was already speaking with a reporter—no doubt arranging an after-event interview—while Janice checked the notes on her phone, making sure every detail of the entrance remained perfectly timed.

XAna smiled.

She could never have built any of this without them. Bryn and Janice were her backbone—and on some days, her brain.

Together they stepped toward the Orchid Room.

For a moment, despite the chaos of the past months —Dallas, Charla, and the shadow of the man stalking her —XAna felt like the luckiest woman alive.

Tonight, those nightmares would take a backseat.

Tonight, she intended to savor every glittering, hard-earned moment of her life.

She stepped through the doors.

And the room erupted.

A long sigh slipped from her as relief settled in.

The gala had been a success.

With the formalities complete, each scholarship recipient had received a standing ovation for her acceptance speech. Their first moments in the spotlight had been nothing short of triumphant. The room had been moved by their stories, and now press and guests crowded around them, eager to hear more about the futures they planned to build.

XAna couldn't have been prouder.

Across the room, Bryn and Janice kept the evening running like clockwork. Even XAna's quiet—if not entirely secret—plan to slip away early was unfolding just as she'd hoped as she threaded her gown through the ballroom doors.

Her dream ending for the night was simple: a private bubble bath and the chance to soak in the evening's success.

But first she would have to face the press waiting by the line of limousines outside.

Through the glass wall of doors, she spotted Mitch.

He looked perturbed—but when didn't he?

She made her way toward him, and as she reached his side, his arm slid firmly around her waist, guiding her toward the exit.

"Stay close," Mitch said. "We weave through them. Bruno's on the outside of the crowd. Five hundred twenty-two steps to the bottom. Two minutes."

"Let's go."

XAna touched his arm. "No. I can take a few questions. I promised Zeke—a blogger on X—he'd get a moment. It won't take long."

Mitch's jaw tightened, the line of his shoulders hardening. His cologne lingered sharp in the air, the quiet presence of a man used to command.

She met his gaze without flinching.

Direct confrontation had never come easily to her, but building the nonprofit she believed in had forced her to change. The threats, the stalking—whatever madness drove it—had taught her one thing.

She would not live like a victim.

Mitch studied her for a beat, then scanned the crowd. His hand lifted to the mic at his collar.

"Change of plans," he said into it. "She's taking three questions."

His eyes cut back to her.

"Then straight to the car. Flank."

"Thank you," she said with a quick smile. "I'll be fast."

Mitch grunted.

They moved as one. Mitch in front, Bruno and Wayne closing in beside them, the three men forming a tight triangle as they pushed into the crowd.

CHAPTER 6

DEAD MAN WALKING

Dallas watched XAna glide across the room, flushed with excitement in her silken white gown—*the great Goddess of Love and Sex.*

Ha. What a joke. The lie would be funny if it weren't so pathetic.

XAna was a cold fish in bed.

IIc took another hard drag on his cigarillo, the ember flaring in the dark as he watched her.

God, he'd tried with her. Tried to coax her into loosening up, trying new things. But XAna had never been willing. The few times she had—barely five in eighteen months—it was one round, then straight to the shower and back to work before bed.

Hell, it had felt like they were already married long before he'd even bought the engagement ring.

He'd tried to be faithful.

But five times in a year and a half? That was ridiculous for any man.

His needs had found other outlets—women, men, whoever appreciated the body he worked so damn hard to maintain. As the face of male fashion, admiration came easily.

And frankly, he deserved it.

Truth was, he was grateful he and Charla had gotten caught, not that he would ever share this with the overly precious XAna. They never would have made it, but damn, if she hadn't killed his chances to take her for half of what she was worth. The wedding, which had been put on hold for tonight's event, would have cinched it for him. What with no prenup, but no, her Timmy had made sure he was caught red-handed before making it down the aisle.

The plan had been simple: finish the gala, then slip off to the courthouse and say *I do*.

He'd even played the humble fiancé, begging her for no big spectacle. Just the two of them, he'd said. An intimate union.

A lie, of course.

She'd believed it—right up until the moment she and Timmy found him tangled up with Charla in her own bed.

Dallas took another slow drag, the ember glowing as he watched the lights of the gala.

Yeah, he would've married her. Then bought a beach house somewhere in Fiji, lived off her money with drinks flowing day and night, and when the novelty wore off... a quiet divorce. XAna hated scandal. She would have settled quickly just to keep her name clean.

Easy money.

Instead, here he was—Dallas Richards, once the prized face of RL Male Models—lurking in the shadows of an event he'd been promoting only eight weeks earlier alongside his long-legged ex.

Sleeping with her best friend had a way of making a man unpopular.

Still... tonight should've been his night.

After all the nights he'd endured the prudish princess sending him away because he'd had a little too much to drink—or taken a few too many pills.

He'd tolerated her small-town Midwestern innocence long enough. She might have carried herself like some untouchable saint, but the irony was almost funny.

XAna.

A name whispered around the world as the embodiment of sensual beauty.

And yet, with him, she had always played the innocent.

She was beautiful, and could be dangerously sexy for the camera, and though she had a body that was a bit too curvaceous for his taste, he had loved the shape of her ass. Many times, he begged her to let him touch and taste. Maybe someday was all he had ever gotten. If her refusal hadn't been a problem, her driver 'Timmy' would have been. Dallas could never figure out how he always seemed to have the perfect timing to interrupt their private moments.

More than once in the penthouse he'd had XAna alone, convinced he'd finally coaxed her into something a little less proper, when the door would swing open and in walked Timmy—always with some urgent work question.

Perfect timing.

It killed the mood every damn time.

Dallas had never figured out how the man managed it.

That frustration—and a dozen other reasons—was how Charla became an option. The petite brunette had never really been his type, but her jealousy of XAna burned hot, and his own irritation matched it perfectly.

The result had been reckless, angry sex—closets, spare bathrooms, even once in XAna's bed.

A little revenge for every night he'd been sent away feeling like some kind of deviant for having needs.

Until XAna caught them.

Even now he couldn't understand how she'd suspected anything. For a while it had been effortless. If a meeting with XAna went badly for Charla, a text would appear on his phone:

Fuck. Now.

Those angry little messages had become their signal.

The last time with XAna he'd pushed harder than usual, certain she'd give in eventually. When she told him to make an excuse, he'd tried to silence the protest and take what he wanted.

But once again—

Timmy.

Bursting in, calm as ever, telling him to get out.

XAna hadn't stopped him. The look on her face that night should have told him it was over, but not wanting drama in the media, the relationship continued until she happened upon Charla and him fucking like pigs on the edge of her bed. That was the end.He'd tried to make her see reason. Told her he loved her—he just needed more attention than she was willing to give. Charla had simply filled the gap.

But XAna wouldn't hear it.

Everyone called him fake. Said he'd used her.

Dallas snorted at the thought.

She was the fake one—smiling for cameras, flashing that sultry image the world adored, while behind closed doors she was cold as ice.

She was the fraud. Not him. Damn it.

The next day Timmy showed up at his temporary apartment with two boxes of his things and a restraining order.

How convenient.

Both he and Charla were dismissed with tidy letters from her attorney friend Arthur, each accompanied by a generous severance check—generous enough to clear without issue, provided they kept quiet.

Dallas had taken the money and kept his temper in check.

But as the job offers slowed... and her fame kept rising, especially with the buzz around the gala...

His resentment hardened.

After everything he'd put up with—her rules, her purity lectures, her endless restraint—

He deserved more.

His moment was coming.

Dallas watched from the shadows as XAna prepared to take a few questions before slipping away—just like she always did. Her quiet exits had become something of

a legend with the press. If they let her disappear gracefully, she usually rewarded them with a quote and a
photo worth selling.

It made him sick.

Who wouldn't want the cameras? The shouting, the
chaos, the attention?

Wasn't that the whole damn point of fame?

His shoulders shook with a quiet laugh of disgust.

Under his breath he murmured, "Well, angel
princess... tonight we'll give them a story."

The cigarillo ember flared as he took another drag.

"One they'll all pay for."

"Bad press is still press."

His smile thinned in the dark.

"Money, money, money."

Not one for following orders he disliked, Tim stood
behind a broad poplar tree, watching.

For several minutes now he had studied the disgusting ex lurking behind the first pillar at the Coral Gables
stair entrance. Dallas Richards shifted in the shadows,
eyes fixed on XAna as she descended. At one point the
foul man even groped himself.

Tim felt nothing.

No anger. No rush of fury.

Only calm.

He already knew what would become of the weakling
who had once dared to touch her. That ending would
come soon enough—and when it did, Tim would savor it.

Other men had drifted through XAna's life before.
None worthy of her, of course, but most had possessed at

least a trace of class. They had been easy enough to remove long before things went too far.

Dallas had been different.

She'd met him during modeling assignments in Europe—RL shoots, if Tim remembered correctly. At first she had called the man a friend. A mentor in the business. When she phoned home during those early trips, she'd sounded sincere when she said nothing was happening between them.

Tim believed her.

But he never trusted the jackal.

Dallas's face had been splashed across enough gossip magazines to prove what he was. A playboy. A parasite.

So Tim solved the problem the way he solved most problems.

He installed a tap on her phone.

A gift, really.

It allowed him to know her movements even before the press did. At first, he told himself it was simply to protect her.

But over time it became something more.

A tool.

A way to place himself between XAna and any man foolish enough to think he had the right to touch her pristine skin with unclean hands.

When she returned to the States, everything changed.

Pretty boy and XAna were suddenly engaged. Instagram and Tok announced it to the world before she even had the chance to tell him herself.

The rage that followed had been so intense the entire office felt it. People kept their distance. Even XAna.

At first that distance had hurt.

But solitude gave him something far more useful—time.

Time to research.

Time to plan.

Time to watch Dallas Richards unravel his own life.

Tim had only needed to wait. The man's weakness—his faithless appetites—would eventually destroy him. It was inevitable.

And it had.

But things were different now.

Four months ago, back in May and June, patience had still been possible. Now the game had changed.

His plans had to move faster.

Waiting no longer worked. She had misunderstood the notes of love, the care he had shown, the love he had tried to guide her toward. She refused to see what he had sacrificed for her.

Each note had been meant to help her understand her need for him to save her.

To remind her that he was the one meant to stand beside her.

Her protector.

Her knight.

Psychological triggers were all around him, everyone ignoring him. They told her to ignore his opinions on her safety. He wasn't a security specialist, they said.

He's just a driver.

The injustice of it gnawed at him.

Even the meditation exercises he'd once relied on to calm himself had stopped working. They no longer centered him. They only reminded him how long he had waited.

How patient he had been.

The truth was becoming unavoidable.

Soon, more blood would have to be shed.

But for Dallas Richards...not yet.

The waiting was almost over.

And when the time finally came, his princess—his pure love bride—would understand that everything he had done had been for her.

Forever.

The Dallas shit-show was about to begin.

The tall, lithe model drifted past him, wrapped in an aging tux and wearing that smug, cat-that-caught-the-canary grin. Tim still cloaked in shadows at just the right moment, brushing Dallas's side as if by accident.

The poisoned needle hidden in the ring on Tim's finger slipped in unnoticed.

Dallas stumbled, too busy catching his balance to realize what had happened. Tim steadied him with a firm hand, guiding him upright.

For a brief second their eyes met.

Tim leaned in slightly and murmured, "Careful... it's dangerous in dark places."

Then he released him and let the dead man continue on his way.

The fool simply shrugged his hands off of him, stumbling away rubbing his side. Dallas reeked of alcohol, making his work for him even easier. He hadn't recognized his voice, such worthlessness. He would never understand that the end for him was near until too late.

Dallas regained his composure. "Creep!" He felt his side. Looking backward, he was certain he had heard that voice somewhere before, but the shadow-stalker was nowhere to be seen. The bastard had nearly killed his grand entrance. Puffing his chest out, he made a straight line for the Queen of his Night. Time for him to rectify the damaged life she left him with and reclaim his rightful place as the star.

Five steps.

Four.

Three.

Dallas moved.

Two steps later his arm was around XAna's shoulders.

The bodyguards reacted too late. Mitch and Bruno had been scanning the crowd, not the man slipping through it. Everyone watched her. No one watched him.

The press gasped.

Now the cameras had them both.

Dallas leaned down and kissed her cheek.

"Go along with this and everything will be fine," he murmured against her ear. "You owe me."

Their eyes locked—his wild with panicked hysteria, hers wide with shock.

"There," he whispered. "That's a good girl. Now smile pretty for the press."

The reporters erupted.

"XAna! Are you and Dallas back together?"

"What does this mean?"

"Is this a reunion?"

Flashbulbs exploded in rapid bursts.

XAna tried to speak but the arm around her shoulders tightened painfully. She couldn't get a word out.

Mitch and Bruno moved in, attempting to pry Dallas away without drawing weapons or causing a scene. Dallas clung to her, his grip tightening.

"Call off your dogs, dear."

His voice was low, threatening.

XAna didn't hesitate. She drove her elbow hard into his ribs.

Dallas grunted, then yanked the sleeve of her dress as she twisted away. The fabric tore down the front with a sharp rip.

She screamed, clutching the torn bodice as she stumbled free.

The moment she slipped from his grip, Dallas bolted.

He shoved through reporters and cameramen, knocking equipment aside as he sprinted into the street.

"Duncan!" Mitch barked.

Duncan was already moving, launching into pursuit.

In the chaos, Timmy appeared beside XAna.

Mitch's eyes flicked to him, anger and disgust flashing between them.

"Orders not your thing?" Mitch muttered.

Then he pointed sharply toward the waiting car.

"Get her to the Tower Garage. Now. The men will handle the rest."

Mitch turned to XAna, his voice suddenly deadly calm.

"Duncan's after him. Bruno and I will assist Garrett, then return to the Tower."

He held her gaze.

"Go straight to your penthouse. Lock the door."

A beat.

"Let no one in."

His eyes cut briefly to Timmy, the warning unmistakable.

"No one."

XAna felt a cold ripple of fear run through her.

Timmy rushed her to the car and helped her inside.

Moments later he was behind the wheel, accelerating hard, blowing past stop signs and lights. Her Towers were only ten minutes away.

In the rearview mirror he watched her.

XAna sat huddled against the leather seat, staring at the torn fabric clutched in her hands. Shock had drained the color from her face. She shivered, still trying to cover herself with her arms.

The sight twisted something inside him.

He hated that she had endured this. Hated himself for not dealing with Dallas sooner. He had always known the man was capable of lies, of criminal behavior.

Still... the scene had been necessary.

Necessary for her to finally see what kind of man her ex-fiancé truly was.

And necessary to ensure Dallas remained the obvious suspect in the hunt for her stalker.

Tim rolled his eyes at the thought.

The men surrounding XAna were fools. Had none of them ever heard of a grand romantic gesture? His notes were poetry in action. Careful, thoughtful, elegant.

The work of devotion.

Not madness.

Every plan he made required precision. Elegance. The kind of care insanity could never produce.

They simply refused to see the love behind it.

Dallas Richards certainly never had.

He pulled through the Tower gate, which operated automatically from a button in his car; most had cards that gained access. XAna, as owner of the Towers, had a button that was especially for her parking garage private access area for her and her private guests.

The rest of Mitch's team was waiting for them, rushing the car. They jumped into action the moment he stopped. He was about to get out and help her to her penthouse, but Germaine, the largest of all the bodyguards, stopped him from getting all the way out.

"We have her from here. Park the car. Your shift is over."

His unkind words seemed to pull XAna from her stunned state. Palm raised, "Stop it! He's not a servant." She turned on Germaine, her eyes darkening in pent-up frustration. "He's my friend, and he just helped get me to safety." She turned to Timmy. "Timmy, thank you. You saved me again. Don't worry about me! I'm safe. Go rest. I'll call you when this is all under control."

"Ma'am, we really need to get you locked in the penthouse as instructed." Germaine's deep voice insisted, "We don't know where Dallas might be."

"Fine." She looked back at Timmy one last time, the hurt on his face registering as a look of betrayal. "I'm sorry."

Timmy watched as she turned to go into the Towers' private elevator.

Chapter 7

Burn It Down

The elevator opened onto the hallway outside her penthouse.

Germaine held up a hand, signaling her to stay back as he stepped out first, gun drawn, scanning the corridor.

It was all too much.

After a moment he nodded and guided her forward. Tomas, her doorman, opened the massive steel door. The heavy sound of it sliding shut behind her made the space feel less like home and more like a prison.

The darkness of the night was swallowing the happiness she had felt only hours earlier.

In the garage someone had mentioned shock. Maybe they had meant her.

When Tomas saw the torn dress, he immediately wrapped a blanket around her shoulders. Now he stood quietly beside her, worry etched across his face while Germaine moved through the penthouse with his gun raised, checking each room one by one.

Was this really happening?

Was Dallas truly this deranged?

The look in his eyes had been terrifying—his thin frame, the sharp smell of alcohol, eyes bloodshot from drugs or sleepless nights.

Yet she had seen him only a month earlier in Arthur's office, calmly signing the final documents. She had been more than generous considering the betrayal. Arthur had assured her it was the fastest and quietest way to make Dallas disappear from her life.

She had believed him.

She had been relieved to be finished with Dallas.

But tonight...

The wildness in his eyes had shaken her.

Germaine finished sweeping the rooms and declared the apartment secure. Returning to the living room, he informed her he was heading back down to the garage.

"Could you stay while I change?" she asked quietly.

He nodded.

When she returned a few minutes later, the torn dress hung over her arm. Staring at the rip, she handed it to Tomas.

"Tomas, could you send this to the cleaners? I'd like it cleaned before I have it repaired."

"Of course, ma'am." Tomas took the garment gently. "Rest now. Mr. Mitch and his team will make certain you're safe."

Germaine stepped closer, his tone all business.

"Mitch is on his way back with Bruno and Duncan. Dallas got away. City police have taken over the search. Mitch will come up once we regroup for instructions." He paused. "Do you need anything before I leave?"

She looked at him, her thoughts racing, grasping for something normal—something routine.

"My purse... I left it in the car." Her voice tightened. "My phone's in it. I need to check on everyone from the event. Bryn, Janice, the scholarship winners... they'll be frantic if I'm not answering."

She met his eyes.

"Please."

Tomas stepped forward. "I can go down with Mr. Germaine, drop the dress at the front desk for pickup, then bring her purse back up, if that's acceptable."

Germaine gave a short grunt. "Works for me. Let's go." He turned back to her. "Lock this door."

The men left, the heavy door shutting behind them.

XAna keyed in the code and listened as the alarm chimed, confirming the lock.

For the first time in minutes, she allowed herself to breathe.

Was it finally over?

Forty-five minutes crawled by. Then an hour.

Using the staff phone in the kitchen, she called each of the scholarship winners, taking comfort in hearing that every one of them was safely home. Arthur called as well, his concern genuine—exactly the kindness she had always expected from him.

Bryn and Janice checked in together on a Zoom call from the Coral Club. They assured her nothing else had happened, though most of the guests had left before the fireworks began.

XAna told them she didn't care about the show as long as everyone was safe.

They offered to come stay with her.

She thanked them but told them to go home and rest. She would be fine.

She hoped that was true.

When the calls were finished, she forced herself to keep moving. Sitting still made the silence of the penthouse unbearable, leaving too much room for her thoughts.

She turned on the television.

It was a mistake.

The news was already replaying the chaos. Footage showed Dallas running from police around a corner. Still images followed—her standing in the street, dress torn, mouth open in shock.

Only hours earlier the media had been praising the glamour of the gala.

Now every channel focused on the scandal.

Her ex.

She grabbed the remote and shut the television off.

All her effort to shield the evening from Dallas—and from the ugliness he brought with him—had failed. The entire event now looked like something out of a made-for-TV spectacle... or worse, a staged reality show.

The thought saddened her.

But more than that, it left her wondering if she could have stopped this from happening.

No matter how hard she tried, she couldn't make sense of his madness.

She clicked the television off in disgust.

That was when she heard it.

Voices—low, muffled—outside her door.

The security panel had already signaled that the elevator had reached her floor. She assumed it was Mitch or Tomas returning with her purse or an update.

What was taking so long?

She moved toward the door.

A sharp shout cut through the hall.

"No—wait!"

She froze.

It sounded like Mitch.

Two gunshots cracked through the corridor.

One.

Then another.

Two heavy thuds followed.

The steel door shuddered in its frame but held firm.

XAna couldn't breathe.

Her body locked in place, hands trembling as the silence that followed roared in her ears.

Had that really happened?

Maybe she'd imagined it.

No.

Those were gunshots.

She took a shaky step closer to the door.

An electronic ding sounded.

Then another.

Someone was trying to access the keypad outside.

Panic surged through her. She rushed to the panel and slammed the red key at the bottom.

The deadbolt override engaged instantly.

No code could open it now. Only a locksmith could break the seal.

Mitch's team had installed the secondary lock after the first letter—the one mentioning love in an elevator, proof the stalker knew she lived in the penthouse.

The alarm erupted.

A deafening siren tore through the apartment—loud enough to rival a hurricane warning.

The *Burn It Down* alarm.

It would bring every police unit within minutes.

She pressed her back against the wall, staring at the unmoving steel door.

Please...

Hold.

Just hold.

No voice answered from the hallway.

No footsteps.

No movement.

Only the shriek of the alarm.

XAna slid slowly down the wall, shaking.

She had no idea who was out there.

Who was hurt.

Or who might already be dead.

Help was coming.

She whispered it over and over, forcing the words past her trembling lips.

Help is coming.

Help is coming.

CHAPTER 8

CAPTAIN

Jared's old wind-up alarm rattled violently on the nightstand. It was alarm number one, handed down from his pops, its sharp ring carrying a rush of memories. He preferred it to anything that needed charging—and loved that one solid slap to the top shut it up.

But with Jared, one alarm was never enough.

His days at academy training had turned mornings into a drill. Next would be his smartwatch buzzing with notifications he'd ignored the day before. Then the big screen in the living room—twenty feet away—would kick on through his Alexa Dot, blasting headline news. Finally, the coffee maker would start, the scent of caffeine ordering him out of bed.

He reached past the empty whiskey glasses and condom wrappers, slapped the clock silent—just as alarm number two chirped to life in perfect comic timing.

Softer, but familiar enough to wake anyone nearby.

He shot a quick glance at the badge bunny beside him as she stirred.

Just in time.

His watch notifications read two missed calls, two unopened emails, and four texts with the slam effect - all from Garrett.

CALL ME BACK, ASSHOLE!!!

05:30 AM

Jared's head fell back, watching the ceiling fan blades spin above him. He ran his fingers through the top of his head, hair matted that was way overdue for a cut. He rubbed his eyes in irritation. The urgency of Garrett's messages put him on the defensive. Last night, he had caught the tail end of a ticker tape from CNN playing at Bab's Pub. Trouble at a celebrity gala involving a certain supermodel they all knew. Being here in Kansas City, he wasn't sure how much help he could be or aspired to be.

Looking to his right, Jared saw only a tangle of rich auburn hair and a shapely naked back. He idly toyed with the long strands draped across his shoulder, a smirk tugging at his lips. She'd warned him she was training for a marathon. She hadn't been lying. It had made for a hell of a workout—and very little sleep.

Stretching, he lowered the silk coverlet with a quiet whisper. No surprise there. Both of them were still naked. He usually slept in jockey shorts, but after hours of strip-search teasing, shower play, and too much whiskey, modesty had lost the battle. Cool air brushed his skin as he lifted the coverlet slightly, glancing at the plump curve of an ass peeking from beneath the sheet. Emerald sequins on her thong shimmered in the lamp's warm glow.

Sleeping beauty indeed.

Maybe she'd earn another night in his den of playdom. Usually, his loft was a one-stop destination—but...maybe.

He rubbed his eyes, head pounding. After a nine-day stakeout on a drug heist and the final takedown, he'd earned a little stress relief—some one-on-one playtime.

The brunette, Juliette, lay tangled in the sheets, her long hair spilling from her pillow onto his. She'd earned her rest after the drinks she'd served him at the bar—and the fun she'd served again here in his loft. She was a deep sleeper, which Jared secretly appreciated on mornings like this. He didn't do the morning-after *when can I see you again* routine. Usually there wasn't a next time. He never led a woman on. Once, long ago, he'd believed in a "next time." It hadn't ended well, and he wouldn't make anyone wait and wonder.

One eyebrow lifted as his lips curved in a smirk at the tempting view.

"Ah...maybe another time."

He pulled the covers gently over Juliette, slipped from the bed, grabbed his cell, and headed for the shower.

The text waiting for him complicated the rising steam. Flaxen-haired visions crept into his thoughts, pulling at something forbidden. He turned the dial hard. Cold turbo jets blasted the heat—and the thoughts—away.

Forty minutes later he was dressed and steady for the day: brown bomber jacket, white button-down, 5.11 cargo pants, and his favorite FastTac boots. Ready.

Slipping his chained badge that carried on it his mother's St. Michael pendant for protection around his neck was his finishing touch. His family wasn't Catholic, but he had made her a promise to wear it so he would have as much protection as he could get. Grabbing his Glock out of the hall safe, he stopped in the kitchen, filled his Yeti cup with black brew, and left the lovely Juliette a note on the bar. Any man can send a text, but a handwritten note always makes the ladies purr.

GM, help yourself to coffee.

Bagels are in the breadbox.

Had fun, lock up, please. TTYL, J.

Since being named the bachelor of the year in KC, his popularity demanded he refine his interactions with the ladies. Too many seeking marriage that wasn't on the table. Keep his intentions straightforward. Simple and sweet with no lies. His notes made him successful with the ladies. It was his bachelor signature. The ladies kept them as mementos, and it kept him out of the doghouse when he conveniently forgot to call after a playful night.

Relationships weren't his thing. There was a time in a distant memory, he had thought maybe, but NOPE that notion smashed on a midnight plane to Miami eight years ago. Since then, he had never attempted to travel the emotional road of entanglement again. And frankly, the ladies of KC and some from beyond were better off for it. This way he could wine, dine, and pleasure them into sweet dreams. They left happy and well satisfied, while he lived unscathed by the nonsense of wondering what might have been. God knows, his career was all he wanted to focus on in the daytime. One more glance at the doll beginning to awaken, he closed his loft door with a hushed click.

Climbing into his unmarked Tahoe, the morning air changing from chilly to brisk. The jacket was a smart decision, 45 degrees and only the middle of September. Winter was coming early.

His phone chimed. Reaching into his coat pocket, he pulled out his phone. Garrett again.

NOW Peckerwood!!!

Read 06:03 AM

God, he was intense for six a.m. Jared guessed he wanted input on a protection job that was starting to spiral. Knowing who the protectee was, Jared wanted no part of it. He needed to stay as far from that problem as possible.

He shot back a quick reply—*Driving*—and tossed the phone onto the passenger seat.

The drive to HQ at 6:30 a.m. was uneventful, another reason he preferred the morning shift. Pulling into his reserved captain's spot, he grinned. It never got old. A small perk he relished—especially when the rookies had to trek the quarter-mile underground path from the new Security Garage.

After last night's adventures, he definitely didn't need the extra cardio.

Entering his code at the officers' entrance, Jared by-passed the new metal detector.

"Morning, Officer Wendell. All quiet?"

He paused at the desk where the rookie was stationed.

"Yes, sir."

Efficient. Not overly friendly at this hour—but neither was he. His height and permanent scowl had been called intimidating more than once, so he respected her quiet stoicism. Some officers needed to be liked. Jared didn't. The reputation worked in his favor as a leader.

Voices drifted down the hall from the breakroom. For a Saturday morning, it was crowded. Most of the Special Crimes Unit had weekends off, but for the next two months schedules were different. Private tours were being given by Patrick Anderson—Jared's high school buddy turned IT genius, turned millionaire, turned mayor of Kansas City.

Patrick had been proudly showing off the new building—one he'd helped bring to life through the fundraiser galas he'd hosted over the past two years. And rightly so. The project was a win for every department in Kansas City. The added parking security meant safer arrivals for officers, and the new technology wing would expand their training in surveillance and cyber operations.

With Patrick's money, influence, and relentless drive behind the project, he easily could have named the wing after himself.

But that wasn't Pat.

Instead, he'd insisted it be called the **D. Marr Wing**, honoring Detective Marr, a young officer killed in the line of duty in 2020.

The facility now hosted training not just for officers, but dispatchers, Fire and Rescue, and even private security teams who leased the space. The equipment was state-of-the-art. With Patrick's IT background—and the fact that half the people he cared about worked somewhere in Kansas City's security divisions—he'd been determined to see it done right.

Mayor Pat could be a little pompous at times, but Jared loved him like an annoying brother.

Most of Jared's childhood memories had Pat in them—usually the two of them cruising for girls in Pat's Jeep. Later, when Jared bought his own, they'd rolled side-by-side down Noland Road during Cruise Week, convinced they were the cat's meow.

Older now... but yeah. Between Patrick's mayoral title and Jared's uniform, they were still doing alright with the ladies.

Pat liked to joke the uniform was the only reason Jared had taken first place in the Hottest KC Bachelor contest. But second place hadn't been bad for the Hottest Mayor.

The whole thing had been a fluff promotion anyway—Patrick's idea to stir buzz for the grand opening of the new HQ.

Standing in the breakroom's doorway, also a recent addition to the investigation wing, "Morning. Pretty loud for this early, and it doesn't sound like work. So, what's up? President coming to KC? Putin, again?" he wandered over and filled up his cup with black coffee and took a sip before he glanced up at the TV reports.

"Morning Captain. Just enjoying some Headline News eye candy—*XAna*, that model in Florida?" Hale raised his cup at the screen, "CNN's covered the fancy gala she hosted last night for her new charity, sounds like she went ahead with the event even after the stalker threats. Not smart. "

The giant TV screen filled with a collage of multiple photos of XAna's SI Swimsuit cover. The hottest red string bikini with gold fringe, Narco Sgt. Det. Hale's silenced in awe, while the rest of the room whistled in appreciation. Jared glanced up at the screen and his whole body stiffened—one part in lust, and the rest in aggravation. His first thoughts in the morning typically leaned toward this curvaceous memory, like this morning, and always required cold water to cool his jets.

Hale apparently thought he needed the play-by-play. "She's hot AF, but damn, seems like she might have a death wish. Details aren't in, but something went sideways. Two dead, one they think was a professional hired gun, Mitch Leano. Reporters are speculating about suspects, one of whom is her ex-fiancé, Dallas Richards."

"Yea okay, enough with a state that isn't our problem. How 'bout we find some real criminals in Kansas City today? Turn that down, load up on your caffeine, and head to your desk. Work to do." The news about Mitch was hard to conceive; his gut knotted up. Regretting not having responded sooner to Pat when a colleague had been killed. He hoped that the reporting by the news outlet was incorrect. The officers in the room had scattered at his command. He hated using his boss voice on a Saturday, but that was the job. Besides, he didn't want to think of her this morning. Or any morning.

Fifteen steps from the breakroom, Jared pushed open his office door.

Two irritated faces greeted him.

He smirked. "Morning. Let me guess—Garrett woke you up too?"

"What the hell, Jared?" the mayor snapped.

Being barked at first thing in the morning wasn't ideal, but when the mayor happened to be your high school buddy, it took some of the sting out.

"It's Saturday, Pat," Jared said, rubbing a hand over his face. "I'm barely awake. Can we take it down a notch?"

He glanced at Aiden, who sat back in the chair, calm as ever, watching the exchange with a faint smirk.

"Garrett's calling in five minutes," Patrick said. "To go over what he needs from us. You will take the call, and you will help him."

"Pat, seriously," Jared muttered. "I barely have any details. Let me drink my coffee in peace while we wait. Garrett can bring us up to speed."

Across the room, Aiden leaned back farther, the smirk turning into a full, shit-eating grin. He was clearly enjoying Jared's misery.

If he knew what was causing it, he might not be smiling.

Calling the mayor *Pat* on purpose wasn't the smartest move, but it was only 6:45 a.m. Jared had woken up with *her* on his mind, walked into work to see Ana splashed across the morning news, and now found Aiden and Patrick waiting in his office while Garrett's name flashed nonstop on his phone.

Lauderdale wasn't his jurisdiction.

He didn't want it becoming a Kansas City problem either.

He had enough on his plate—training a new rookie detective, Sam, for starters. Hell, he was already buried.

His fingers lit up his laptop, avoiding the mayor's glare of fascination. He wasn't fond of being confronted early in the morning, hell really any time. This wasn't his problem; he'd shout it if that helped people get the picture. Ana wasn't his problem. She was Garretts. The desk phone rang, and Jared hit the speaker button.

"Is she OK?" Getting right to the point.

"Yeah, dickhead, she's okay so far. She's just shook up, but Jared - *what the hell, man*? Why so long to get a callback?"

Jared hated the guilt trip, laden with snarky do your duty in Garrett's tone. "Yeah, well, you have us all listening now. Tell us what happened to Mitch?"

"Shit got messy at the Gala. Dallas, the ex, showed up, causing a media frenzy before he ripped her dress and fled. Duncan chased after him but lost him through all the fans gathered. Her driver got her back to the Tower safely. From there, her security team got her delivered to the penthouse, locked her in. The security team met in the underground parking for further updates and to plan extra shifts, upping the security. After the briefing, Mitch was escorting the doorman back, who was bringing her belongings from the limo. In the 10-second screen of a masked gunman trying to breach the penthouse, Ana heard a man yell out, 'No, wait...' right before hearing two gunshots. Both men are dead, shot in the head, no silencer. This killer didn't care if anyone heard the shots." Garrett sounded frustrated. Hard cases usually did that to you.

"Damn! Rough night." Jared said sincerely, but he was holding back. He hated to lose any members of security, people who put their lives on the line for others, but he was remaining distant.

Leaning over the phone on the desk with both hands, Pat said a little loudly, "Hey Garrett, it's Pat. What about the security cameras? Fingerprints?" His background in IT, his expertise could be helpful. Since Officer Marr's on-duty death, all members of KC law enforcement and the mayor's office have made finding those guilty of cop-killing a top-level priority.

"Nothing. But I was hoping I could forward the .avi files over to you so you can work your wonders? All the cameras in the East Wing went down. We don't think it's an accident."

"Please do; I'll look at them as soon as I get back to my office." Patrick's look, now one of relief knowing that he could help.

"Thanks, man, really." Garrett's grateful tone shifted back to grumpy. "Jared?"

"Yeah, I'm still here." Sipping his coffee to hide his anticipation of the *BIG* ask that was coming.

"With no new leads, no camera footage, no finger-prints, not even on the flowers or the note..."

Jared interrupted, "Flowers? The killer brought flowers to a break-in? What did the note say?"

"Same flower's, white roses, bloody from being thrown in the elevator on Mitch's body, the card simply said, '*She's mine*'. No prints before."

"Sounds premeditated?" Aiden interjected.

"They haven't called it yet; the FBI-Miami division is on its way to the crime scene. They have more experi-ence with stalkers turned murderers. I'm doing the best I can. I used to think it was Dallas, her ex, and he's still a suspect, but the camera's put the height of the killer last night at 6' tops. Dallas is 6'3 so it couldn't have been him."

"He could have had someone hired?" Jared asked, trying to help piece the puzzle together.

"We are going to be looking into Mr. Russell's finances, see if we can find any money leads. But guy's this is leading us to a place I don't want to go. Whoever it is, is skilled. The ability to blindside and kill Mitch, one of the best in the security world, and Tomas was just a kind old man doing his best to serve Ana. Best security, people around her who cared aren't safe, *Jared*, you know what I'm saying, right?"

Jared's stomach rolled at Garrett's implication. "Yep, this stalker knows her, and he knows the workings of the towers. Murder and a note sounds personal or for show, and if he wanted to take out someone she cared for, the stalker is amping up. Whatever he's planning, he's becoming aggressively impatient."

"Exactly, she needs to go into hiding. But I'm afraid that either the paparazzi will hunt her down in her usual places and give her away. The only thing we have on our side is the hope that this stalker doesn't know her true identity. *She needs our help, buddy.* I need you and your team to hide her in plain sight in KC as the old Analeise Montgomery."

Jared's heart tumbled—old or new Ana, either, he wished to avoid. To forget. He cleared his throat trying to sound logical. "Why here? Doesn't she have like five other houses?"

Suddenly, a loud thud was heard through the phone. Garrett had lost his patience. "I don't know what the hell your problem is; she's our friend. She needs us. The best I have, the only plan I've come up with, is to hide her in

Kansas City. She's already done most of the work for us by only being recognized in the world by her alias XAna. Her looks have changed considerably, which helps too. No interview has ever gotten her to say who or where she came from, and that's a plus in our corner right now. A small town in Missouri will be far enough removed because there she's only Ana. We have a plan to misdirect the press. I need your help."

The mention of her looks changing didn't help his problem. It made it worse. Deep inside, Jared's guilt was getting the better of him, but still he remained silent. Only Ana...that was an understatement.

"Patrick here, Garrett, just know you've got our full support. Jared will get on board, you have my word. I'm going to arrange my jet to fly into a smaller private airfield so I can pick her up. Can you help coordinate that from your end?"

"Mayor buddy, that sounds great. I'm so desperate I'd drive her myself, so thanks but we're gonna need a security team." Garrett was beyond caring if he sounded desperate.

"Jared will take over the logistics and staffing of extra security." Pat's look dared Jared to object. "Jared's in charge, but Aiden and Aj will be on standby as backup. I spoke with Trav. He said to call anytime. We all have her back and will take care of her when she gets here; you just find this bastard and put him away."

"Thanks. I'm off, gotta try to convince a woman who is pretty stubborn that she's got no choice. Her determination and hard work for her foundation have made her feistier than we remember. Today, she's sad and feeling tremendous guilt over Mitch and Tomas. After killing them, the murderer attempted to breach the penthouse again. Ana stopped his access with a fail-safe button Mitch had installed when he was hired. If not for him, the stalker might have gotten her too. But she's the same Ana we all love, still thinks everyone is worthy of being called her friend. With her fame and fortune, it puts her at high risk from all sorts of crazies. I'll have the camera footage sent soon, Pat. Maybe your team can find something. Oh, Jared, one last thing."

"Yeah, man, what's that?" Jared leaned away from the phone as if it were going to bite him.

"*Stop being a dick*! Pull your head out of your ass and help me protect her." The loud dial tone said tons. He was on Garrett's shit list.

"He's right; what is your problem?" Aiden said impatiently, curiously, his arms folded. "And no more I've got to drink my coffee jag" — what gives? Aiden's thoughts about Jared's moody behavior were almost funny. Almost.

Not answering that question. He sure the hell wasn't going into that with Aiden. *Fuck no*.

"Look," standing up from behind his desk, "it's way too damn early for psychoanalysis; nothing is wrong. I just have a lot on my plate right now. More pressure being Captain." God, he hated the lies coming out of his mouth. He wanted to gag. Being captain was an honor; he fucking loved his job. Pressure, such bullshit and Aiden knew it, they all thrived on pressure. Now, he was using the responsibilities of his title as an excuse like a pussy. *Fuck,* this was a mess, and she wasn't even in KC yet.

"Look, momentary lapse, I'm back." Holding his hands up, shaking his head, "You're right, she's our family, our friend—yeah, yeah OK. I'm in. I'll get a team assembled with overlapping shifts. I've got it handled, and by the time she arrives we'll be set to go." It was the best he could muster.

Pat smiled, finally feeling assured. Stopping at the door, he turned to look at both men. "Thanks, I'll get my side taken care of, too. Together, we will keep her safe. See ya." His iPhone rang as he left the room.

Aiden stood, hands shoved in his Wrangler jeans. Jared wasn't acting like himself. Normally, he was the first to volunteer when someone was in trouble, and this was their Ana. Something was very wrong with this picture, but he was pretty sure he would not get the answers today. He shook his head at Jared. "Not like you."

He was right. Aiden was almost always right, another one of the many things Jared envied. "Yeah, I know. It's nothing, just a hangover. I'll get it done." He sat back down at his desk, hoping he looked distracted with work as he began logging in.

Aiden shut the door, leaving Jared to brood over his now-cold coffee. This was a bad day, losing Mitch, an honored servant of the people, and now Ana was returning home to be protected by him. Maybe his day of reckoning for having touched the forbidden angel long ago was coming due.

And Mayor Patrick riding in on his white stallion so early on a Saturday, it had never been a secret. They all knew he had a big crush since school days, but Ana hadn't seen him that way. For her, in school there had only been Aiden, or so he had thought until that one day in his apartment eight years ago.

Jared shook his head violently; he couldn't go there again. Not in mind nor in body, he wouldn't make that mistake again.

She's single now - just dumped her fiancé for cheating, maybe this was Pat's moment to seize. He's a billionaire, the mayor of a great city, a brilliant IT man, and single himself. The picture seemed perfect.

Maybe Jared was letting his memories of her rattle him, maybe protecting the famous XAna or the returned Ana would be a simple protection detail assignment, maybe even boring, the Garrett would find her stalker and job done, she heads back to her world, fast.

Jared could only wonder, would it be fast enough not to leave a mark like she did long ago?

CHAPTER 9

THE PLAN

Garrett scanned the spacious living room until his gaze landed on the woman Jared had been so reluctant to help.

Ana stood at the window, staring out at the ocean as the night lights blinked off one by one with the rising sun. Her posture was rigid, her expression distant—almost numb.

When the locksmiths finally breached Mitch's fail-safe system and forced entry into her apartment, she had been waiting on the other side. The opening had revealed only a glimpse—two bodies already covered with sheets—but it had been enough.

She'd collapsed into Garrett's arms then.

Now she stood alone, silent, as if trying to process it all without anyone watching.

She kept her guest list in the building small—a detail Garrett respected.

He glanced around the penthouse. Tower I. Hard to believe the small-town girl from Missouri had built an empire big enough to raise twin skyscrapers along the Atlantic boardwalk. But he knew better than most how hard she'd worked. He'd known her since puberty and had always admired the goodness in her. To the world she was the glamorous billionaire XAna. To the people who'd known her longest, she was still the same salt-of-the-earth girl.

He moved slowly through the room, watching her from different angles. She stood tall at the window, spine straight, determined not to break. The sight pulled a memory from years ago—ninth grade.

Ana had been the new transfer student. During roll call the teacher had read her full name: *Analiese Montgomery*. Ana had stood calmly and corrected him.

"Please call me Ana, sir."

Garrett had thought she was brave even then. Mr. Haslebeck was old, bitter, and seemed to hate teenagers almost as much as he hated teaching. Being corrected by a girl with bows in her hair had made him snap, ordering her to sit down and calling her *Miss Montgomery* for the rest of the year.

That was then.

Every light switched on in the 5,000 square-foot apartment was glaring, reflecting off the polished floors as police milled about. She hadn't shifted; her gaze was locked on Shore Blvd through the panoramic windows. The air buzzed with the murmur of voices from detectives and FBI agents filling the expansive space. She was yearning for sanctuary, and he held the key, reachable if she conceded and went home.

Two months ago, he had told her he believed the notes were becoming more intimately angry. Insistent and angry. Initially, both of them agreed it was just someone who had gotten a crush and was hurt she wasn't responding on social media. It had sounded plausible. Last year's highest paid supermodel and named sexiest woman in the world, who could blame a crush or fascination? The words, though, had suggested more, like the person writing the words knew her personally, not from afar.

But with 24.5 million followers on IG and 10 million+ subscribers on YouTube, and TikTok being a number so large he chose not to commit it to memory, it was hard to respond to her friends, much less every fan. She had a publicist and a team of social media managers who looked after her pages and posts; she rarely looked at them; she was so busy. Still, it seemed to be a reason to believe he was just simply a misunderstood fan, but the murder of two men was no misunderstanding. It was a warning.

Two people were dead, both of whom had close access to XAna and her penthouse. Whatever was driving this person, it was now very personal. The bodyguard, Mitch Leano, was by far the best he had ever known. The minute he had met the man, his character and experience had commanded Garrett's respect. Losing officers of the law like Mitch and Marr were tragic losses.

He still couldn't wrap his mind around how it was possible that he had been caught off guard and shot. The older penthouse usher, Tomas, had been easier to understand, and yet again not. He was an old man who watched over the daily comings and goings of guests to the Penthouse; it was simply poor timing in Garrett's detective mind.

Garrett knew only one thing for sure: he wanted Ana gone. He wanted her away from everyone who knew her as XAna. The only hope was to send her back to KC as her former self. Garrett was thankful that Jared finally agreed to help. He imagined Aiden and Patrick pushed him too. Jared had been erratic and avoided his texts. A party might have kept him up late. But when Garrett reached him, Jared's words were clipped and distant. This was unlike the friend Garrett and Ana desperately needed.

Garrett knew he was stalling. Jared wasn't his problem now; it was settled, and his team in KC were going to take her on as a protectee. He could rest easy on that end. But now.

His bigger problem was still staring out into the darkness, sad, worried. It was time to discuss the plan and convince her to return home for a while, where her friends would wait to take care of her and keep her safe while he gathered more clues here. He only hoped that the stalker did not follow her to KC.

Packing had always been difficult for XAna, but today it felt impossible. She had no idea how long she would be gone.

Her heart still ached with the loss of two dear friends. She had begged Garrett to let her stay—for the funerals, to visit their families—but he had refused. Her presence would put everyone attending in danger.

The truth had landed like a punch to the gut, though she knew he was right. With no sign of Dallas, the FBI agents had agreed with Garrett's assessment. They didn't love his plan to hide her away, but without a better option they had reluctantly gone along with it.

Garrett's plan gave her only one day to come to terms with leaving her home and work before boarding Patrick's jet the next morning for her condo in Kansas City.

Bryn had hired two decoy models to pose as XAna, distracting the press from her real departure. One model would wear clothes Ana had worn in public—her sunglasses, her luggage—and even have Timmy drive her to the airport. The paparazzi would follow, snapping photos of the decoy boarding a private jet bound for Mexico City.

If another diversion became necessary, the second model would repeat the act—this time appearing to travel to her villa in Italy.

The plan sounded like something out of a Disney film if there had been anything humorous about it. But there wasn't.

Her home in Mexico City was the least tracked by U.S. media, making it the safest destination for the decoy. Few people knew its exact location in the mountains among the lakes. It was beautiful, and she had begged Garrett to reconsider letting her go there instead of risking a model's safety.

Garrett and Bryn had both refused.

This was not the time for heroics.

It was time to disappear.

They hoped.

She hated how many people had been pulled into the mess because of her. Even Kristin—the model standing in for her—was now part of the plan. At least the woman was being well compensated. When things returned to normal, XAna intended to make it right.

Still, she hated the chaos of it all. She thrived on order and routine, and now everything felt like it was spinning out of control.

Her frustration showed as she shoved clothes into her suitcase instead of folding them.

Across the room Janice quietly removed the wrinkled pile, smoothing each piece before folding it neatly back into the bag. Preparing for a secret escape from Lauderdale for God only knew how long.

Janice had been there the night before when Garrett explained the plan. In the blur of the conversation, XAna thought she had noticed a flicker of something between Janice and Garrett—some spark of mutual interest.

Then again, she might have imagined it.

Everything felt uncertain lately.

Her mind replayed the events again and again. This could go on for weeks... maybe months. No one could tell her how long it would take to find the stalker.

The thought made her restless.

She hated being forced into a life she hadn't chosen. She wanted her routine back. Her work. Her foundation. The women she had promised to help.

She worked hard not to hate anyone.

But whoever was doing this deserved every ounce of it.

Would she even be the same person when she returned? Would she still be XAna... or someone hardened by circumstances beyond her control?

When Garrett first told her the flight would be on Patrick's private jet, the panic had felt like first-day-of-school jitters. She had effectively lost control of every part of her life—even the plane she was escaping on wasn't her decision.

The lies to her staff made it worse. Most of them had no idea what was really happening.

The uncertainty brought back memories of her early days in Miami—when she barely knew anyone and never knew when the next job would come in. Those had been lean years, but she had survived them.

Still, she had never lived like this before—plotting and scheming just to stay alive.

She had argued fiercely that she needed to stay for the foundation. To the women she helped, disappearing would look like surrender.

Garrett cut her off before she could continue.

He told her she should be scared.

Someone trying to reach her had just killed Mitch—a highly trained former sniper and professional body-guard. That level of skill wasn't typical of a stalker.

Then Garrett revealed the detail he had kept out of the official report.

There had been a second bullet.

It had been fired straight through the note on Mitch's chest, scattering rose petals across the floor. Whoever did this had been furious about the new security.

The message had been simple.

SHE'S MINE.

The doorman Tomas had simply been collateral damage.

The stalker had escalated.

And he was growing impatient.

Garrett promised then he would do whatever it took to keep her alive—even if it meant making her hate him.

After that, her objections ended.

The thought that someone was murdering people close to her because of a twisted delusion made her sick. Some moments she wanted to crawl into the enormous closet behind her and never come out.

Hiding at one of her estates had lasted only minutes as an idea. Garrett quickly pointed out the obvious: the press had covered those homes for years.

Anyone could find them.

Their only advantage was the possibility that the stalker didn't know her real identity.

That uncertainty might buy Garrett's team time to hunt him down before anyone else got hurt.

By late afternoon the arguments were finished.

The plan was in motion.

Later that evening Garrett returned to explain everything to Timmy.

If convincing XAna to leave had been difficult, telling Janice and Timmy they had to stay behind was worse.

Janice accepted it first.

Timmy did not.

He finally agreed only after XAna promised him a day trip—just the two of them—when she returned. The look Garrett gave her when she made the offer was unreadable. Perhaps surprise.

No one really understood what Timmy meant to her.

But Timmy did.

And for the moment, he seemed satisfied.

Garrett laid out their roles. Janice would schedule deliveries and meetings throughout the week to keep the penthouse looking active. Timmy would continue driving her usual routes through the city, parking at the places XAna often visited.

The routine would help maintain the illusion—and buy Garrett time to hunt the killer.

Janice handled it with quiet strength. She had worked closely with Tomas for years managing the penthouse schedule. Now she would attend the funerals in XAna's place.

That alone made XAna grateful she was staying.

Timmy had taken the news harder.

At first he insisted he should come with her to Kansas City so he could protect her himself. His loyalty touched her, but his temper worried her.

If there had been more time, she might have taken him to dinner or let him drive them along the coast while he talked about whatever old book he was reading.

But there wasn't time.

Garrett promised him daily updates on the hunt for the stalker.

That seemed to settle him.

XAna believed Timmy's heart was in the right place. He took his job as her driver seriously—fiercely so.

And in his own way...

he believed he was protecting her.

CHAPTER 10

THE SEAMSTRESS

"Fuck!"

The word tore out of him in a hushed scream as he slammed the door behind him. The garment bag containing the white chiffon gown swung carefully from his hand as he crossed the room and laid it across the sewing table waiting in the dim motel light.

Being dismissed the night of Dallas's attack so abruptly by the agents had turned out to be convenient after all. Executive access to the Towers meant doors opened without question. It had taken only seconds to retrieve the dress unnoticed.

His nose wrinkled.

The smell in the room was suffocating—mildew, stale smoke, and something sour that clung to the thin carpet and yellowed walls. The cheap hourly motel offered little more than a sagging full-size bed and a flickering lamp, but weeks earlier he had dragged the sewing table inside, preparing for tonight's work.

He had planned for everything.

He had not expected the gown to need such repair, but he never left important things to chance.

Not when it came to XAna.

Not tonight.

Tim hung the garment bag from a hook in the wall and turned.

On the edge of the bed sat the greasy blonde junkie, blinking up at him with glassy gratitude. The threadbare dress she wore clung to her thin body, exposing far too much skin for either modesty or dignity. The cheap fabric hung loose over curves that still carried a faint echo of beauty.

For a brief moment the sight tempted him.

He disliked that weakness in himself—the crude hunger men carried in their blood. The need for flesh. For release.

Disgusting.

But useful.

Trina solved several problems at once. She knew how to sew well enough to repair the damage to the gown, and she was eager to submit to whatever he asked in exchange for the drugs he supplied.

A convenient arrangement.

She provided a controlled outlet for impulses he preferred to keep contained.

Because the desire he felt for XAna was something far more important.

Something sacred.

And that desire required patience.

The dark hours he spent in physical abuse of Trina's worn body, he could keep his composure. His darker more focused fetishes fed, freed the more innocent needs and desires for XAna, his treasure. All thanks to useless souls like Trina here, the cute druggie that he had picked up three months ago to pose as his love interest. He had found her serviceable to take some of the strain off his nerves as he waited impatiently for XAna to acknowledge their true destiny.

"Mend this correctly and I may have a reward for you," he said with sweetness that could cause a toothache.

"Yes, sir. Thank you, sir."

That was all the reply he ever got from the brain-cooked girl. He had trained her well. Trina had proven to be an eager student so long as his lessons came with soft words and a milligram or two of her favorite reward.

Tim gave his pet a casual pat on the head.

Druggies were easy to manipulate. Their need hollowed them out, leaving nothing but hunger. Once the craving took hold, self-control disappeared. They would do anything for relief.

It was almost sad, really.

Once upon a time Trina had possessed real talent. She had told him herself during the early days—boasting in that nervous chatter addicts used to fill silence. She had once believed she might become a professional seamstress.

Even worse, she had confessed her secret dream.

To be famous.

Like XAna.

The memory tightened his jaw.

Sharing that fantasy had cost her dearly. Two bruises. A week without drugs. Enough time to teach her the difference between ambition and delusion.

As if she could ever resemble his princess.

Trina blinked up at him now, her bloodshot eyes dull with exhaustion and chemical haze. Her skin had grown almost translucent from too many days hiding indoors. Blue veins pulsed faintly beneath the pale surface.

So fragile.

So far removed from the warm, sunlit beauty of his golden goddess.

The comparison alone irritated him. The very idea that anyone—*anyone*—might imagine themselves standing beside XAna was enough to make his stomach twist with anger.

But Trina still had her uses.

Once she finished repairing the gown he had taken from the Towers' dry-cleaning hold, restoring it to the pristine condition XAna deserved, he would reward her. One or two small snorts from the locked cabinet.

Just enough to quiet the shaking.

After that, she would serve another purpose.

Tim rolled his shoulders slowly, feeling the tension that had been building all evening.

Release would come soon enough.

For now, he watched the clueless girl work.

And waited.

Sitting in the darkened corner of the ten-by-twenty room, Tim listened to the sounds bleeding through the paper-thin wall beside him.

Moans. Rhythmic thuds. A woman's sharp cry that might have been pleasure or pain.

The place was a filthy no-tell motel—thirty-five dollars a night, cash only, no questions asked. The air smelled of mildew and sweat. In rooms like these, screams and groans were as common as the buzzing neon sign outside.

Tim closed his eyes.

One day, when he and XAna were finally together, things would be different. There would be no yelps of pain, no crude fumbling like the animals in the room next door. Only soft sounds of devotion. Gentle lovemaking.

Because he was the only man who truly understood what she needed.

He knew her better than anyone.

All those hours watching her private rituals—her grooming habits, her careful self-care, the way her fingers lingered over her skin—had taught him everything. Even the quiet moments when she applied lotion after a bath had become lessons to him.

He remembered the way the bottle caught the light in the recording. The small click of the pump. The lavender scent he imagined filling the room as she smoothed the lotion across her shoulders, her arms, the delicate curve of her neck.

Most people would call him a predator for watching the recordings again and again.

But they didn't understand.

It wasn't obsession.

It was devotion.

Every replay had been study. Each movement a lesson. The way her breathing softened when she relaxed, the way her fingers lingered over certain places as if her body itself revealed its preferences.

He had memorized everything.

One day he would be the only man who knew her completely. The only one capable of giving her the care she deserved.

To tend to her gently. Carefully.

Like a gardener who understood exactly how a rare flower needed to be nurtured so it would bloom.

XAna needed someone strong enough to guide her—someone who could anticipate her moods, protect her from the crude world around her, and care for her with steady hands.

Soon, he would be that man.

Tonight's news had been difficult to swallow.

Tim sat in the dim motel room, the weight of it pressing heavily on his thoughts. The media had already begun reporting it—XAna would be leaving. After the killings at her penthouse following the gala, she was planning to take an extended break away from the city.

The idea unsettled him.

He hadn't enjoyed killing the old man, Tomas. The little fellow had always been nervous, always watching too closely. Tomas had never been part of the plan. Wrong place. Wrong time.

Mitch, however—the bodyguard with more muscle than intelligence—that one had been satisfying.

Mitch represented everything Tim despised in men like him. He only saw the job in front of him, never the humanity around it. Protection, procedure, control. Men like Mitch believed their authority mattered more than the person they were hired to serve.

Tim had watched how he spoke to XAna.

As if she were a problem to manage rather than a woman to honor.

Her wishes dismissed. Her movements controlled. Every decision filtered through their so-called protection protocols.

A true guardian would have understood that serving XAna meant preserving the life she wished to live, not suffocating it beneath commands and restrictions.

Tim had seen the toll it took on her.

His special camera lenses had captured it many times—the quiet resignation in her eyes reflected in mirrors when she was forced to accept their rules. The small sadness when some simple request was denied in the name of security.

It had become unbearable to watch.

Mitch's role had always been one of service.

And on that day, he performed his final duty.

To die.

Of course, the man would receive the hero's funeral —flags, speeches, empty praise. The world loved celebrating men like Mitch.

But he didn't deserve it.

XAna had only one true protector.

Tim.

Now, because of both the necessary death and the unfortunate one, his plans were shifting. The situation required more time, more careful maneuvering around the investigations of the Miami detective who had already been meddling for months.

Detective Garrett.

The man had been slowing things down long enough, but now he had become a real problem. Sending her away—removing her from the world she belonged to —was an unforgivable interference.

It disgusted Tim how little any of them truly understood her.

None of them saw the woman he saw.

None of them knew what she truly needed.

The media's speculation was that she would go to one of her homes outside the US, that Mexico City or Milan was preparing for her arrival with fanfare. His cameras and audio mics in the penthouse had picked up every detail. His ears burned as he replayed them over and over. They were trying to hide her from him. Yes, he was stressed. Pissed and stressed over another delay. He wanted this over; he wanted his golden angel by his side, telling the world how grateful she was for everything he had done for her, that it had always been their fate to be together. He was fucking sick of waiting, and now a game of hide and seek?

There was nowhere she could hide. He knew everything about her. Years of study, longer than anyone imagined or had even guessed. He knew her every secret whim. The pathetic plans to hide her were an insult to his intelligence, an insult to his devotion, to his sacrifice. He loved her; she was his, and soon his rightful place at her side would come true.

It was only a clock strike away.

CHAPTER 11

AN OLD DISGUISE

As she approached the jet, her thoughts drifted briefly back to Timmy stopping by the apartment earlier that evening.

He had asked for a minute alone with her before she left. His words had been few, mostly a calmer repetition of his frustration about being left behind. Timmy believed she was being unfair, but she trusted Garrett knew what he was doing. Keeping Timmy in Lauderdale was part of the misdirection—one more way to throw the stalker off her scent.

Before leaving, she had given him a quick hug and reminded him of the promise she made—that when this nightmare was over they would take a day off together and do something fun.

The smile on his face when she kissed his cheek had looked genuine.

It was a small gesture meant to soothe his wounded pride. She hoped it had helped. Disappointing Timmy after everything he had done for her was the last thing she wanted.

XAna climbed the steps of Patrick's jet, still amazed that Garrett's escape plan had worked perfectly.

Not a single flashbulb popped at the private airfield.

With Bryn's help, the timing between her flight and Kristin's—the model paid to play her—had been flawless.

By the time XAna settled into the leather seat, her "double" would be in the private lounge preparing to board her FLL International flight for Mexico City.

The jet carrying XAna lifted quietly into the sky.

It was a Falcon 7X.

She knew little about jets, but this one was elegant from the outside in—much larger than she would have imagined capable of landing on the tiny hidden runway only miles from the Everglades. The small airport was used mainly by alligator removal specialists who flew in for weekends of hunting.

She had known Patrick's success in the IT industry had made him wealthy and famous. He had cornered the market on corporate social media software used by companies like Insta and Tokland. Still, she hadn't imagined someone with that level of notoriety would go to such lengths for her.

The extent of his care warmed her heart.

Patrick—well, she supposed now she should address him as *Mayor Patrick*—had kindly sent flowers along with a note explaining the details of her journey. His thoughtful explanation of how the plane had been scheduled just for her, and how he would personally meet her at another private airstrip an hour south of Kansas City, had left her touched.

She was bowled over by the gesture.

Especially when a new mayor must have countless political meetings filling his days. In barely two years in office, Kansas City was already seeing increased revenues and new funding for departments like the KCPD and KCFD. Patrick had even secured more than ten million dollars in private donations to upgrade the city's public nursing homes.

He was doing great things for the city.

And now he was going out of his way to help her.

While she felt incredibly blessed, she was also overwhelmed with guilt.

The flight from Lauderdale did little to calm her nerves. Thoughts of returning to Kansas City—of seeing old friends again and possibly putting them in danger—kept her anxiety simmering just beneath the surface.

But if she was honest, the biggest stressor was Jared.

Captain Jared.

Her hands began to perspire at the thought of him. Her heart kicked into a faster rhythm. She glanced down and saw her fingers trembling slightly. Pressing them into the soft suede of her skirt, she let the fabric soothe her nerves.

The three-hour flight gave her far too much time to think.

Thankfully, aside from the pilot and a single flight attendant, she was the only passenger aboard the small plane. She was grateful for the privacy. The constant head shakes and quiet, hysterical chuckles she kept letting slip might have made her look ridiculous.

All this over seeing a man she had slept with once.

One night.

Years ago.

And since he had never contacted her afterward, she had always assumed the moment meant nothing to him once he woke to find her gone from his apartment.

So why on earth was she so flustered?

The thought made her feel foolish, just as she had back then.

She gazed out the airplane window, letting her mind drift into the clouds below. That night with Jared remained partially blurred by everything that had happened soon afterward, when she first arrived in Miami to begin her modeling career.

Still, when she left Kansas City, he had been all she could think about.

She waited for a call. A text.

But that first week in Miami moved fast—fittings, photoshoots, learning how to navigate the whirlwind pace of the fashion world.

Then, nine days after arriving, everything changed.

She had received her first official modeling paycheck that morning. The amount stunned her. Feeling lucky and a little reckless with excitement, she decided to celebrate with a trip to the mall.

She bought small things for her apartment. Little luxuries she had never allowed herself before.

Her arms full of shopping bags, she rounded the corner toward the parking garage without paying attention to her surroundings.

That was when she was attacked.

The memory still made her stomach tighten.

Timmy had appeared from nowhere, scaring off the man before he could do worse. The attacker escaped with two bags and her phone, but Timmy had gotten her safely away.

Losing the phone forced her to get a new one, this time with a Broward County number.

By then Jared still hadn't called.

And with the new number, she doubted he ever would.

In the end, she convinced herself it had simply been one fleeting moment between them—something better left in the past.

Eight years had passed.

Yet even now she couldn't quite forget the way he kissed her. The hungry look in his blue eyes. The quiet intensity he carried with him.

All these years later she still felt a ridiculous flutter of nervous excitement knowing she was about to see him again.

She shook her head at herself.

How silly.

It was probably just the uncertainty of it all—wondering what he thought of that night. Wondering if he even remembered.

Especially now that he would be responsible for her security while she was in Kansas City.

For a short time, Captain Jared would quite literally be in charge of her safety.

Before her father, Jerome, passed away last year, he had made a habit of sending letters and newspaper clippings to keep her up to date on life back home.

Not gossip, he would joke.

Tea.

She had loved those letters.

Through them she learned Aiden—her ex-boyfriend —had finally married Tessa. They had moved out to the countryside. Aiden was also Jared's cousin.

AJ, Aiden's younger brother and former special operations soldier, was now traveling the world working in the oil industry, chasing adventure the way he always had.

Travis—Trav to everyone who knew him—had climbed the ranks of the KCFD and now served as Captain and forensic investigator. After losing his wife two years earlier, her father said Trav had buried himself in work.

That couldn't have been easy.

Reading those updates often left her with a quiet ache. She had missed so much of her friends' lives while building her own career.

And yet now they were the ones stepping forward to help protect her.

The thought weighed heavily on her heart.

But there had always been one part of her father's letters that made her smile.

His stories about Jared.

Jerome had clearly enjoyed writing those most. He had nicknamed him "The Hot Cop," teasing about his local reputation with women.

One evening her father had even called her personally, laughing as he described how Jared had landed on the cover of *Kansas City Magazine* as Bachelor of the Year.

She couldn't remember the last time her father had sounded so proud of someone.

Later that week the magazine arrived in the mail.

She could immediately see why they chose him.

Jared was beautiful.

The centerfold photograph showed him in uniform, his shirt slightly open at the collar. She had opened those pages more times than she cared to admit. The worn edges of the magazine were proof.

Leaning back against the neck pillow now, she closed her eyes, warmth creeping across her cheeks as she remembered the feel of his skin against hers.

She couldn't help it.

Part of her still longed for that moment again.

Jared could have easily been a model himself— rugged jaw, broad shoulders, the kind of height that made him tower over most men, let alone women.

The photoshoot had featured several members of the local Junior League fawning over him at a pub, the women laughing beside him as he leaned casually against the bar in a navy half-zip and tactical jeans.

He had always been good at telling stories.

His voice had a way of pulling people in, hypnotic almost. Back then, listening to him talk felt effortless and warm.

Those days were fun.

Bittersweet now.

Because this reunion would be nothing like the one she had once imagined.

For the foreseeable future, Jared and his team would be risking their lives to protect her—just as Mitch had done so bravely.

And that was never how she had dreamed of seeing him again.

At her father's funeral, Jared stayed in the back of the church.

He wore a black suit and dark tinted glasses that never once left his face. His lips hadn't cracked a smile the entire day. She knew because she had been watching him through the heavy veil that covered her own face.

Jared had handled many of the details for the processional. Over the years he and her father had grown close, bonded by their shared love of books and baseball. More than once she had called home only to find the two of them sitting together watching a game, sometimes with the rest of her friends gathered around.

She loved knowing her father had them. It eased the guilt she carried for being away so often.

During the receiving line at the funeral, Jared finally came forward.

He didn't say much. He simply took her hand, held it for a moment, and kissed her cheek.

"I'm sorry," he said quietly.

Then he stepped away.

She hadn't seen him again since that day.

The memory lingered as the plane finished taxiing.

Gathering her things, she paused in front of the mirrored wall near the aircraft door, studying the reflection staring back at her. She smoothed the collar of her silk white blouse. The satin camisole beneath showed just slightly at the curve of her cleavage. Her gold chain belt had shifted during the flight; she slid it back to the center of her waist.

Next came the Mary Jane's she had slipped off during the flight. She pulled them back on, pressing her heels firmly into the floor.

Her hair had been pinned loosely for the trip, the soft waves giving her an effortless, carefree look.

She did not feel carefree today.

Satisfied she looked presentable, she lifted her carry-on and moved toward the narrow staircase leading down from the plane.

The Kansas air was cool when she stepped outside.

At the bottom she paused, breathing it in slowly. The scent of grass and distant trees was so different from the salt-heavy air of Lauderdale.

For a moment she simply stood there.

Then she saw Patrick's limousine rolling slowly toward the plane.

She straightened slightly, reminding herself that this was temporary. Just a short chapter before she could return to her life again.

Still, the thought weighed heavily in her chest.

God, she hated being the reason her friends might be in danger.

Mayors didn't have the luxury of nerves, but Patrick's breath still caught as he watched from his slowly rolling car while Ana stepped down from the plane.

Years of harboring an oversized crush had done nothing to dull the effect she had on him. If anything, she seemed to grow more beautiful with time. The grace in her stride, the quiet confidence in the way she carried herself—years of living under public scrutiny had shaped her into someone who moved effortlessly beneath the gaze of cameras. Paparazzi, fans, reporters—wherever she went, she handled it all with polished professionalism.

From small-town heartthrob to the international fantasy of millions.

Patrick was still awestruck.

Despite the weight she carried—launching a cosmetic company, managing a philanthropic foundation, navigating a complicated love life, and now surviving a stalker who had murdered two people close to her—she walked toward him with remarkable composure. Outwardly she looked calm, though Patrick couldn't tell if that strength was genuine or simply the well-practiced armor of someone who had lived too long in the public eye.

Garrett had given him a quiet warning.

Ana was stronger than most people realized, the detective had said, but she also needed kindness. She was deeply resistant to the idea of putting anyone she loved in danger.

Patrick planned to keep that in mind.

When he had called earlier with the flight details, he had done his best to reassure her that returning to Kansas City—surrounded by friends who cared about her —was the safest plan. The sadness and frustration in her voice had cut him deeply. She carried the weight of those deaths as if they were somehow her fault.

He hated that for her.

The driver opened Patrick's door and he stepped out, walking toward her. When she reached him, he wrapped her in a warm hug.

Pulling back slightly, he smiled down at her as she tilted her head up to meet his eyes.

"Welcome home," he said. "I'm told that this week you're supposed to be just *Ana*. No X. Is that right?"

She stepped back, the corners of her mouth attempting a smile.

"I suppose it is."

The expression was sincere, but he could see the frustration beneath it. The mention of the extra letter was another reminder of a life that suddenly felt far away.

Years earlier her agent had suggested adding the X to her name as a shield—something that would keep the press from digging too deeply into her family's life back home. At the time the logic had seemed sound. It protected her father and his company while still allowing her to build her career.

She hadn't wanted to disappear entirely.

But she also hadn't wanted some of her more scandalous lingerie campaigns tied directly to the girl she had once been in Kansas City.

That had been her choice.

She had chosen to become the angel.

Not them.

"Come on," Patrick said. "Let's grab lunch at a small diner nearby. Then I'll show you the new headquarters of KC's finest. After that, Jared will introduce you to a few members of the security team. They may not all be there yet, but the one in charge certainly will be—and I suspect Aiden will show up as well. Ginger's waiting for us too. She's eager to see you."

He slipped an arm around her shoulders, offering what comfort he could. His chauffeur stood beside the open door of the Town Car.

"This is Manny," Patrick continued. "He'll be your personal driver whenever it's safe enough for you to move around town. Jared's team is already running perimeter checks. They're setting up security at your condo on the Plaza and at your father's place off Ward Parkway. I also had my IT team install additional cameras at your building."

Patrick nodded toward the man holding the door.

"Manny and I will do everything we can to make your stay here as uneventful as possible. Won't we, Manny?"

"Yes, ma'am," Manny replied with a polite nod. "We'll do our best."

"Nice to meet you, Manny. Thank you for your help."

She was always gracious, but Patrick noticed a hint of hesitation in her voice. He couldn't blame her. She wasn't here on vacation—she was hiding.

The last time she had returned to Kansas City had been for her father's funeral. Another heavy homecoming.

Patrick tried to imagine what it must feel like for her now, stepping back into a city that still carried memories of Jerome everywhere. He hoped tonight's gathering at Bab's Irish Pub might remind her how many people still cared for her—and that Kansas City was still home.

"Manny, let's get moving."

Patrick slid into the back seat beside Ana. Manny closed the door and settled behind the wheel, guiding the car into traffic toward headquarters.

Patrick glanced over at her.

She sat quietly, her hands folded in her lap, staring down at them as if studying the stillness there. The tension radiating from her was impossible to miss.

He placed his large hand gently over hers.

"We've got a bit of a drive," he said softly. "Why don't you tell me about your new project? I've only read bits and pieces, but it sounds like—despite everything—your gala made quite an impression on the world."

Patrick's curiosity brought a full smile to her lips, and Ana relaxed a little. Turning toward him, she began telling the stories behind the scholarship program—why she started it and the remarkable women she had met along the way.

Patrick listened to every word.

He understood what it took to build a charity people truly believed in. The hours. The persistence. The personal investment. He knew because he had built one of his own. In the early days he had funded it entirely out of his own pocket—an initiative to help underprivileged kids gain early access to the IT world. They provided laptops, workspace, and Saturday programs where the students could learn coding and programming skills.

He had loved the day Ana discovered the program. Without hesitation she had contributed to support it.

Not out of obligation.

Out of friendship.

He felt honored to spend this time with her. It wasn't some political courtesy. Yes, he was the Mayor of Kansas City—successful, respected in his own right—but he never forgot that she had once seen him at his worst. Back then he had been a cocky, money-driven bully of a teenager.

Now he hoped to be someone she could admire.

Patrick listened as attentively as any man could, though her beauty made concentration difficult. Her eyes brightened and her cheeks flushed pink as she spoke about each woman who had earned a scholarship.

This was the Ana he remembered.

Happy. Passionate. Always eager for the next adventure.

Even the faint movement of her hands as she spoke sent the soft scent of her perfume drifting toward him.

He could feel how deeply she cared for the people connected to her work. To Ana, colleagues quickly became family. Even her driver had been someone she helped guide toward career advancement.

Patrick had met Timmy once.

Something about him had always struck Patrick as oddly familiar—and vaguely irritated. The man had seemed annoyed by his presence for reasons Patrick couldn't quite place. At the funeral he had stayed glued to Ana's side, hovering protectively.

Patrick had tried to see it as loyalty.

Ana certainly did.

Still, something about the man left a faint unease in the back of his mind. If Ana trusted him this deeply, though, Patrick hoped he could learn to do the same.

Her heart made her easy to admire.

How Dallas had managed to lose her was something Patrick would never understand. Rumor had always followed Dallas on the fashion circuit—too much charm, too many women. Any man with sense should have counted himself lucky to have Ana beside him.

She was brilliant in business, generous with her employees, and sincere in her desire to make the world better. In her mind, beauty was simply part of the profession—not something she considered extraordinary.

Years ago, she had changed Patrick's life without even realizing it.

He had grown up under the influence of a father obsessed with money and status, a man who was rarely present. Patrick had absorbed the worst of that upbringing. He had been arrogant, dismissive of anyone without wealth, and cruel more often than he cared to remember.

Then came the last day of middle school.

Patrick had been showing off for some older boys, mocking a kid's worn clothes and thick glasses. The boy had been shrinking under the laughter.

Then Ana stepped between them.

Small, fearless, and furious.

She stood in front of the boy like a tiny Joan of Arc facing down the monsters of the schoolyard.

Patrick had been stunned.

She scolded them all—shaming them for their cruelty—but it wasn't anger that stayed with him. It was the sincerity in her voice as she defended the boy.

For the first time in his life, Patrick felt ashamed of himself.

Later he caught up to her and apologized.

Ana listened, then pointed calmly toward where the boy had disappeared.

"You should apologize to him," she said.

Patrick promised he would and immediately went back to find the kid—but he was gone.

He never saw him again.

But he never bullied another person either.

When it was Patrick's turn to speak, he filled the rest of the drive reminiscing about the summer after their senior year, when Aiden had reintroduced them all.

Every Friday the guys gathered at Evelyn Hills to show off whatever car they were rebuilding—engines, paint jobs, half-finished hot rods. It was the biggest entertainment their small town had to offer: twenty cars, a crowd of curious onlookers, and plenty of teenage bravado.

One night Aiden arrived late.

Word spread quickly that he was bringing someone for everyone to meet.

It surprised them all. Aiden and Tessa had broken up right after graduation when she moved away. They had dated since sophomore year and everyone assumed they would marry young. When she left, Aiden fell into a quiet funk. Hearing he was bringing a date to the weekly gathering was a shock.

Ana laughed softly as she recalled the moment from her side of the story.

Stepping out of Aiden's step-side pickup in heels had been intimidating enough. Walking into a circle of staring guys had nearly sent her running back to the truck. Her grandmother had bought her what the family jokingly called "the zipper dress"—a little too daring for an eighteen-year-old.

Patrick assured her the staring had only meant one thing.

None of them had expected someone like her.

Her long tan legs, her blonde hair, the way she carried herself—it had left them speechless.

"You looked like a movie star," Patrick said. "Or a model."

She giggled, blushing at the memory.

Seeing the stress ease from her face—even for a moment—felt like a small victory. Ana had always been dear to all of them.

Patrick studied her eyes as she rested her hand over his. His thoughts wandered to a possibility he hadn't allowed himself to consider before.

Could this visit become something more?

More than simply protecting her.

She squeezed his hand gently and smiled.

"Thank you, Pat," she said softly. "Truly."

Ginger approached the Town Car at a brisk pace, a tablet clutched in one hand.

"Good morning, sir," she said, glancing first at Patrick before turning to Ana. "Welcome home, Ana. I'm so sorry for what you're going through. The mayor has alerted all staff about the need for privacy and asked everyone to do whatever we can to help you not only stay safe—but feel safe as well."

Before Ana could respond, Patrick jumped in.

"Ging, we're planning to tour HQ. With the schedule, should we head straight to Jared's office and introduce her to the security team first, or start the tour now?"

Ginger shot Ana a quick wink.

Both women knew Patrick had a tendency to focus on schedules with military precision, sometimes forgetting the more human side of greeting people properly.

Lowering her glasses, Ginger glanced down at the tablet.

"Yes, Jared and Aiden are already waiting in his office with several of the officers assigned to security," she said. "You should go there first, then continue the tour afterward. And don't forget—you'll need to stop by the Fire Chief's office. They're finalizing plans for next week's pancake breakfast and the groundbreaking cere-mony for the new firehouse on Peak Street."

"Good plan," Patrick said. Then, with what sounded almost like hope in his voice, he added, "Are you coming along with us on the tour?"

Ana watched the exchange carefully.

Ginger paused her scrolling and looked up from the tablet she held like a digital lifeline to the mayor's sched-ule. There was something warm in her expression—ad-miration perhaps, maybe something more. Ana couldn't quite place it, but the connection between the two felt deeper than simple employer and assistant.

She wondered if either of them realized it yet.

"No," Ginger replied. "I'm needed back in the office. I only came out to say hello to Ana."

She stepped past Patrick and gently placed a hand on Ana's shoulder.

"We're all here for you," she said softly. "And hopefully tonight will show you just how firmly we're in your corner."

Ana blinked in surprise. "Tonight?"

Ginger glanced over her shoulder at Patrick with a knowing look, shaking her head slightly.

He hadn't told her.

Patrick wrinkled his nose at Ginger before stepping in to repair the oversight.

"I didn't mention it yet," he admitted. "I didn't want to overwhelm you with the flight, the tour, and the secu-rity briefing. But we're hoping you'll come to a small gathering tonight at Bab's—just a few friends. Let us show you how many people here would do anything to protect one of their own."

Ana hesitated.

Returning to Kansas City had already been overwhelming enough. Leaving her work behind, stepping away from her life in Lauderdale, hiding from the chaos that had followed her—it was a lot.

But Patrick and Ginger watched her with sincere warmth. She knew if she declined, they would respect her choice.

Her head dipped for a moment before she lifted it again with a small, genuine smile.

"I'd love to see the gang."

Chapter 12

Bumpy Re-Entry

Two days after Jared had been *toe-twisted* into this security assignment for XAna—aka Ana Montgomery—his stomach was still in knots. Too much waiting had given his mind time to wander back to memories still burning bright, reminding him exactly why he kept his distance from the very off-limits Ana.

Before sunrise he'd jolted awake from the same recurring dream—visions of their one night together, erotic enough that the hard-on dragged him out of sleep. A forbidden encounter that had somehow shaped so much... or perhaps so little... of his life.

They had never spoken of it again.

Her plane had landed two hours ago, yet there was still no sign of her—or Pat.

Jared texted Ginger, the mayor's assistant, for an ETA. She replied that they'd stopped for lunch and would head to HQ afterward to meet a few officers assigned to Ana's detail who were working today.

The mayor, she added, hoped Jared would walk Ana through the security protocols.

Jared's mood had darkened.

Jealousy wasn't an emotion he entertained often, and waiting around was even less his style. Together they made it almost impossible to find his give-a-damn.

Eight years and dozens of women since that night, yet knowing Ana was on her way made it feel like yesterday.

He stood at the office window, watching thick clouds crawl across the sky.

And just like that, his mind slipped back.

Back to the day she'd called.

"Hey Jared... are you home?"

The memory still hit like a jolt. Ana Montgomery—calling him.

Ten frantic minutes later he'd been racing around his tiny rookie apartment, shoving laundry into a closet and wiping down counters that were already clean. The place wasn't much—just a modest unit paid for on a first-year officer's salary—but suddenly every inch of it mattered.

Because she was coming here.

At 6'3", six months out of rigorous boot camp, he had been in the best shape of his life—and proud of it. He ran ten miles a day, played intramural baseball, and had enough sex to offset pizza and beer. Toned and tight in all the right places, his fitness showed in his dress blues, earned through the demands of his career with KPD—a job he loved.

He had been living every bachelor's dream: a small apartment a block from Country Plaza, steps from the best nightclubs and sports bars. His personal life—hell, back then he had no trouble managing a steady flow of blondes, brunettes, and a few redhead beauties begging to be frisked. Badge bunnies, they were called. Jared never saw the term as a bad thing. Some women simply found the idea of safety a turn-on. He was young and randy—he didn't complain.

But it was impossible to think of Ana Montgomery—the younger version of the woman arriving today—as a bunny.

When he first met Ana, she had been on the arm of his best friend, Aiden. Just another small-town night of boys cruising in their hot rods looking for their dream girl. Aiden's golden-god looks and smooth talk had brought the dream to reality with Ana. Jared hadn't been the only guy who went hard when they saw her step out of Aiden's step-side.

She wore a tight-fitting mini dress with zippers crossing her curves, the short skirt showing off long golden legs still shimmering from the summer sun. Her blonde hair fell in waves down her back to the curve of her ass. Every teenage guy there had fallen in lust the moment she stepped out of the truck. None of them could help it. The fantasy sucker-punched every raging hormone they had. Even then, to small-town boys, she looked like a supermodel.

Back then Jared had envied Aiden's almost arrogant ease with girls. As he got older, he realized it simply came naturally to him. Jared himself had always been more reserved. He had girlfriends in high school, but they were just that—girls who were friends. They double-dated with the group, laughed, hung out. No one he dated ever stole his breath the way Ana had.

Aiden's looks and baritone voice—deep even in early puberty—meant girls came running. But Ana was different.

She didn't run.

Quiet by nature, she often came across shy, almost innocent. Yet one look from those fiery eyes could lay a guy flat. When she laughed they turned cool slate blue, and when she thought deeply they darkened to sapphire. The deeper the blue became, the more mesmerizing they were.

Captivating.

The Ana of 2024 was lethal.

Recent media coverage showed her figure had changed in all the right ways. No longer living the rigid life of a competitive model needing a tiny waistline, she had bloomed into a full-figured, voluptuous woman. From photos and videos online, though she clearly stayed fit, she was unmistakably more womanly.

Images of her in workout gear showed perfect breasts that were now lush handfuls begging for a man's mouth, hips wider and more pronounced, made for large hands to grip. Her lower backside—he'd bet a year of his captain's salary—was now plump enough to tempt every man alive.

She was aging like the proverbial wine.

What made it worse was that she was the real deal—inside and out.

Ana was honest. Hardworking. Even as a teenager, though her family had money, she kept a job at the Henderson Center, a home for adults with special needs. She worked there because she cared about the residents—not because she needed a paycheck.

In Jared's mind, she defined angelic beauty.

There was something disarming in the way her eyes lifted to a man, making him feel like a hero—like a god. Yet that innocence was deceptive, because those same eyes held a sensual depth a man could willingly lose himself in, drowning in their liquid blue.

Loud footsteps in the hall outside his office shattered the memory. Jared turned, his hand dropping to his lap to hide the hard-on—no one there.

Damn it. Hard again, just like this morning in the shower. She still had that kind of power over him.

Fuck. How was he supposed to get through this?

The memory of her golden skin flashed through his mind. He squeezed his eyes shut, his body tightening with the ache of it.

Even back then he'd known he would never be that man. She was out of his league. Maybe it was the pedestal he'd put her on that first day, or the long nights he'd spent staring at the ceiling, hating himself for wanting his best friend's girl. Either way, she had never been meant for him.

Not that Ana would ever think of herself that way. She was too good to believe she was better than anyone else—her heart too big for that.

But to Jared, she deserved a real hero.

A month before her unexpected call, Aiden had shared interesting news—he'd run into Tessa, his ex.

Jared had heard the nervous excitement in his best friend's voice immediately. They'd met for coffee, Aiden said, and not long after he broke things off with Ana.

Jared wasn't surprised.

He had spent enough time around Aiden and Tessa back in school to know their connection was undeniable. When her family moved away and she ended things, Aiden had moped for weeks—skipping weekend ball games, barely wanting to hang out. He didn't date again until after graduation.

Then he met Ana.

She made him smile again.

Ana had that effect on people.

Still, Jared had always known it wasn't the same as what Aiden had with Tessa. Jealousy aside, he had been glad to see his old friend finally returning to himself.

For two years Aiden and Ana kept things casual. They only saw each other, but it stayed light. Comfortable. Easy.

For everyone.

Everyone except him...

...and maybe Pat, who had carried an enormous, deafening crush on her.

Broken up or not, Jared still hated how his loyalty had slipped that day. His body had kicked into overdrive, betraying every rule he'd set for himself. He'd repeated the word *untouchable* like a mantra, trying to corral his raging hormones.

It had been a joke then.

It was still a joke now.

Touching her had never been the plan.

He had tried to convince himself she was simply being her usual friendly, outgoing self. No big deal. After all, he had once told her that if she was ever in the neighborhood, she should stop by. She was just taking him up on it.

He should have said no.

Should have told her he was busy.

But the sweetness in her voice when she called—the surprise of hearing from her at all—had wiped his mind clean.

He wished now that he had refused.

For all his nerves of steel on the job, Ana had always been his Achilles' heel. She had been dynamite then, just as she was now. Dangerous in the same way too—capable of leaving him tongue-tied, stumbling over words... or worse, turning him into a cold, defensive bastard just to hide how badly she unsettled him.

Jared dragged a hand through his freshly cut hair.

Hell, he'd even cleaned himself up for her arrival.

The haircut reminded him of that day—how close he had come to putting on his uniform before she arrived. He was never insecure in uniform. He wore it with pride, not for show. Service meant something to him. His father had worn one. His uncles too. Even his sister had married a man in uniform.

It was a family tradition.

And he carried it proudly.

None of this would have been a problem if he hadn't taken that shot of Jack earlier. He'd needed a cold shower afterward, but there hadn't been time. Even now he preferred to blame the whiskey.

Not his damn libido.

Back then they had spent countless nights together—pizza boxes stacked on the table, old sitcom reruns playing while the three of them laughed until midnight. At first Jared had felt like the awkward third wheel, wondering if he was unintentionally cockblocking Aiden.

Looking back, maybe he had been.

But Ana always made him feel welcome. She rarely spoke first—whether from shyness or out of respect for Aiden, he was never sure—but every night he waited for the same moment.

Her greeting.

"Hello, Jared."

Something about the way she said his name warmed him every time. It didn't hurt that she had the kind of smile that could light a room, and eyes a man could easily get lost in.

When she looked at you, it felt like you owned the world.

Like you could be the hero in whatever story she was imagining.

Then came the knock on his door.

A soft tap.

His mind raced as he crossed the room, trying to figure out how the hell he was supposed to handle this moment. Part of him hoped seeing her today might finally kill the mystery—break the strange hold she had over him and his traitorous body.

His jeans were already too damn tight.

He muttered the reminder one more time before opening the door.

Untouchable.

But when the door swung open, the girl from every one of his dangerous fantasies stood there smiling at him.

And today that smile was meant for him.

Not Aiden.

Him.

She stood in the doorway wearing an emerald sleeveless dress, a thin belt circling her tiny waist. Simple heels. Skin glowing from hours in the sun.

Jared had been screwed then.

Just like he was now—standing here, waiting for Ana to arrive all over again.

A knock on Jared's office door snapped him out of his thoughts like a gunshot.

"Cap," Sam called through the doorway, "Mayor Patrick's car just pulled into the garage—his private entrance. Ginger says he's officially giving her a tour of HQ, but it's more than that, right?"

Jared slowly swiveled toward the voice.

Sam stood in the doorway, eager as ever. Twenty-four, newly minted detective, and far too curious for his own good.

Jared rolled his eyes and turned back to his computer without answering, choosing silence over the inevitable interrogation.

"Yep." Aiden's deep voice carried across the room. He dropped into the chair in front of Jared's desk, propped his boots on the trash can, and laced his hands behind his head with a grin.

Sam chuckled, tapping the doorframe. "Good to know. I'll be around when it's time for details."

"Don't start," Jared muttered.

If he stayed quiet long enough, maybe the conversation would die.

Five minutes. That was all he needed.

But everyone in this room knew him too well. His moods were rarely a mystery.

Frustration simmered under his skin. He could feel it rising, threatening to surface if he didn't get a grip. What he needed was a long drive and a clear head—time to work through a strategy before his temper gave him away.

He stood, crossing the room to lock a file in the cabinet. His keys clattered loudly.

Too loudly.

Everything felt too loud.

"Any updates from Garrett?" Jared asked abruptly, slamming the drawer.

Still pissy. Interesting.

"Nothing new on my end. You?" Aiden smirked.

"Forensics are still grinding through evidence while we prep a team for glam-doll babysitting," Jared said. "A quarter of my department's tied up on this thing. I still can't believe we're protecting someone who doesn't even want protection. If she understood the danger—or cared—she wouldn't have gone through with that gala. Un-fucking-believable."

The metal cabinet slammed again, echoing through the quiet office.

But the gasp from the hallway was louder.

Jared turned.

Mayor Patrick stood in the doorway.

And beside him—

Ana.

Ah, fuck.

The shock on her face twisted something in his chest. He felt like a grade-A asshole.

He hadn't been sure what to expect after a cross-country flight, but the image before him caught him off guard. Sensible heels. Pencil skirt. High-neck blouse tied with a bow. Her hair pulled into a neat librarian bun, glasses perched on her nose.

Serious.

Controlled.

And somehow still devastating.

He hated how much he liked the look.

Few versions of Ana existed that didn't electrify him.

Which made this assignment worse. Not only did he have to hide his attraction—he had to pretend they were nothing more than old friends.

Patrick stepped forward, ignoring the comment that should never have been overheard.

"Morning, Aiden. Jared." His tone carried quiet authority. "Is the team assembled for introductions?"

Jared caught the reprimand beneath the words.

Fair enough.

"Morning," Jared said. "Some are around. I heard you were giving a tour. If you're finished, I can call in the officers currently on duty and go over protocols."

He deliberately avoided looking at her as he returned to his desk. It was the only way he could stay focused.

But he felt it.

Her gaze.

Watching him.

He hated this entire situation—for her and for himself. His job was simple: keep her safe.

Safe from a homicidal psychopath.

And possibly from him.

Patrick was speaking, but Jared only caught the final instruction.

Call them in.

He hit the all-call button on the intercom.

"Sam. James. Step into my office."

They would take a minute, so he sat again and pretended to study the screen.

From the corner of his eye he watched Aiden step forward and pull Ana into a hug.

Jared looked away quickly.

Even now he wondered how Aiden had ever let her go.

Seeing her wrapped in Aiden's arms stirred an old, ugly question he'd buried years ago.

Did she still want him?

Jared hit the print key harder than necessary.

The sharp sound drew everyone's attention.

Aiden smirked.

"Seriously, man," he said, narrowing his eyes at Jared. "That time of the month?"

Patrick and Ana both glanced his way.

Jared ignored the bait.

He crossed the room again, pulling the printed pages from the tray before walking back toward them.

"For you," he said, handing the papers to Ana.

Their fingers brushed.

He pulled back instantly, like he'd touched a live wire.

"These are the officers assigned to your protective detail while you're in Kansas City. You know Detective James. Rodriguez is pulling overtime. Sam's our newest detective—green, but solid. He and James are on their way."

He gestured toward the second page.

"Emergency contacts and procedures. You probably won't need it. My team—with help from Aiden, AJ, and the mayor—will make sure you stay safe."

He never looked up.

Safer that way.

"Thank you," she said quietly. "The résumés weren't necessary. I trust you to choose the right people."

Her voice had softened with time.

Before she could finish, the doorway filled with two large bodies—James and Sam—both freezing when they spotted Ana.

Patrick stepped in smoothly to make introductions.

Jared watched the officers struggle to say anything more than *ma'am*, shaking his head.

Grown men struck speechless.

Patrick turned back to him. "Go ahead, Jared."

Jared moved behind his desk, using it like a shield.

"It's straightforward," he said. "Two additional officers rotate in later. While you're here, we ask that you stay in your downtown apartment unless absolutely necessary. If you leave, one or two officers accompany you depending on the situation."

He finally looked at her.

"No social events. No parties. For your safety—and for my team's—you follow the rules."

Her eyes locked with his.

Cold.

Blank.

He couldn't tell if it was anger or shock, but the warmth she had shown Patrick and Aiden was gone.

"Mayor Patrick's team acts as backup," Jared continued. "But the six names on that list are your primary contact. Understood?"

Her eyes flashed for a brief second.

Then she looked down.

"Understood."

Patrick stepped in quickly.

"Ana, you're among friends now. Right, Jared?"

Jared met the mayor's pointed look.

"Sure," he said flatly.

"Friends with a job to do."

Chapter 13

Unfortunate Pains

The sight of blood had never bothered Tim. Growing up with a father like his, you got used to it. Broken teeth. The snap of a belt. Bruises blooming under the skin. None of that had broken him. If anything, it had shaped him—made him stronger, more determined, no longer the weak boy who once stood helpless in the schoolyard.

What bothered him now was something different.

The loss of control.

Trina's screams the night before had been so loud the motel manager had nearly called the police. The walls in the place were paper thin, the kind where every cry, every movement carried down the hall.

That had been sloppy.

Stepping over her body, Tim paused.

Her blonde wig lay beside her on the floor, soaked dark with blood. The cheap strands were tangled around her shoulder, stuck to the spreading stain beneath her head.

For the first time in years, something about what had happened left a bitter taste in his mouth.

Not the killing.

That had been necessary.

What unsettled him was how far his anger had taken him before it happened.

The junkie he'd met months ago at the Elbow Room had been useful. A pathetic creature, eager to please if it meant another hit of whatever poison he offered her. She could sew well enough, and she never asked questions.

But the moment she dared slip on XAna's dress—the gown he had brought for her to repair—something inside him snapped.

Hours earlier she had been nothing more than a distraction, a crude outlet for the frustration building in his chest. But afterward, when the haze lifted, the sight of her sickened him.

Trina had crawled from the bathroom wearing the Aphrodite gown she had just finished mending.

The sight froze his blood.

The elegant white dress—meant for beauty, meant for grace—hung from her skeletal frame like a mockery.

He stepped toward her slowly.

"Take it off," he said quietly.

The calmness in his voice should have warned her.

But the foolish girl only smiled.

"Yes, sir. Anything for you."

She tried to move seductively as she removed the gown, as if pleasing him might earn her favor. What truly enraged him was the realization that she wore nothing beneath it.

The sacred had been touched by the impure.

The moment she hung the dress back on its golden hanger, Tim's control shattered.

The metal tip of the cane cracked against bone again and again. Her frail body folded under the blows while she begged him to stop.

Her voice broke with each plea.

But he had already gone too far.

The final strike silenced her.

Now the room was still.

It was over.

She had paid for her sins.

As Tim wiped away any trace of himself from the room, he glanced down at the body with something almost like pity. Trina had served her purpose.

Now it was time to move on.

Soon he would board a late flight to Kansas City.

His beloved was there now—surrounded by men who stared at her beauty but failed to understand her.

Failed to protect her.

Tim would change that.

He would finally deliver her to the life they were meant to share.

The truth—his truth, her truth, *their* truth—was beginning to reveal itself.

And the waiting was almost over.

After Ana and Patrick resumed their tour of headquarters, Aiden lingered in the doorway, leaning against the frame with the same shit-eating grin he always wore when he thought he'd stumbled onto a mystery.

"What?" Jared snapped, already irritated. He'd been unreasonably testy for three straight days.

Aiden dipped his chin, trying—and failing—to hide his amusement. "Nothing. Just... interesting, that's all."

Jared had no patience for the psychoanalysis.

"I've got shit to do," he said flatly. "I'm sure Tessa needs you for something."

He needed quiet. Time to process what had just happened so he could get his head straight and focus on the job.

Aiden chuckled and pushed off the doorframe.

"Okay. We'll see you tonight then, right? At Bab's? In a better mood?"

Tonight.

Hell.

Jared had completely forgotten about the welcome gathering Ginger and Pat had planned in Ana's honor.

"Yeah," he muttered. "I'll see you tonight. Might not stay long."

Aiden was already halfway down the hall when he called back over his shoulder.

"As long as you show up."

The office fell silent.

Jared leaned heavily back in his chair and rolled his neck, trying to work the tension out of it.

Damn it.

Even dressed like a prim librarian—buttoned up and serious—she had still turned him on.

What the hell was wrong with him?

He'd slept with plenty of women since that night. If someone didn't return his call afterward, he shrugged it off. No big deal.

But Ana?

He couldn't forget.

Or forgive.

And forgive her for what, exactly?

She had every right to treat it like a one-night stand. Just like anyone else.

So what was his problem?

He needed to convince his body that he didn't still want her the way he had all those years ago. Needed to get over the fact that she was miles out of his league now.

Besides, forgiveness wasn't even the issue.

Whatever had happened between them back then, Ana was still someone he cared about. A friend.

And she was in danger.

Hormones aside, he would protect her.

He could do that.

Be her friend. Be her shield.

All he needed was a night with the gang, some old-fashioned normalcy. Maybe then everything would reset, like 2018 had never happened.

It was a hell of a leap.

But he needed the break—from the sting of unanswered calls and texts, from the ghost of that night.

Yeah.

Maybe tonight wouldn't be so bad.

He could handle it.

Even if it wouldn't be easy.

Jared shut down his computer. He'd take the rest of the day. Clear his head. Then apologize to her tonight at Bab's.

He hadn't meant to hurt her earlier. The sharp tone, the attitude—he'd felt cornered, and that never brought out the best in him.

Patrick and Manny had her secure.

She was safe.

Grabbing his backpack, he switched off the lights and headed down the hallway.

He leaned into Rodriguez's office.

"Hey, Pam—heading out early. Gonna hit the gym and I'll see everyone at Bab's tonight."

"Sounds good, boss," Pam Rodriguez replied without looking up from the report she was writing. "See you later."

Jared liked his people. Every officer under him worked hard, stayed dedicated.

His step grew lighter as he turned the corner—

—and slammed directly into Ana.

The sudden impact stole the breath from both of them.

Jared's hands shot out instinctively, gripping her hips to keep them upright. When they steadied, only inches separated them.

Too close.

His hands were still on her.

Her scent—patchouli and rose—wrapped around him, warm and intoxicating. His body refused to step back.

His eyes drifted to her lips.

Soft. Pink. Slightly parted in surprise.

Ana lifted her head, her eyes glossy, searching his face. He couldn't tell what filled them—fear, confusion, maybe something else entirely.

Voices down the hallway snapped him out of it.

"Damn," Jared muttered, stepping back quickly. "Sorry. Wasn't looking."

Distance.

He needed distance.

Feeling her pressed against him had already been dangerous enough.

"It's okay," she said softly. "My fault. I was just standing here in the way."

She turned toward the memorial wall beside them.

Her fingers lifted, tracing the newest plaque.

Kevin Starr.

Jared's longtime partner.

A junkie had shot him in the line of duty last December. The whole city had mourned him. Jared had taken weeks of leave afterward just to process the loss.

God, he missed Kevin's laugh.

"I'm so sorry, Jared," Ana said quietly. "My dad used to send me the newspaper clippings about him. The stories people wrote... they were beautiful. He must have been an incredible officer. And friend."

Jared didn't answer.

He simply stared up at the wall lined with too many names.

Footsteps echoed down the hallway.

Patrick.

Ana stepped away, beginning to follow the sound. After a few steps she stopped and turned back.

"You're mistaken, Jared," she said.

Her voice was calm, but edged with hurt.

"I do want protection. I just hate that so many people might be put in danger because of me. That's all."

She held his gaze for a moment.

"Thank you. Truly."

The sting in her voice lingered even as Patrick rounded the corner, telling her it was time to head home.

Jared watched them walk away until they disappeared around the bend.

The hallway fell quiet again.

Kevin.

Ana.

The scent of her perfume still hung faintly in the air.

Her hurt expression.

His careless words.

He should have stopped her. Apologized.

But the moment had been too heavy, the right words nowhere to be found.

They had a lot to talk about.

Just not now.

All he could do was make it up to her the only way he knew how—by leading the team assigned to keep her alive.

If he couldn't stop wanting her…

He could at least give Garrett the time he needed to find the bastard hunting her.

That much, Jared could do.

Chapter 14

First Shift

"Don't let Jared's gruff bother you," Patrick said as he turned onto the street leading to her plaza condo.

"It's always worse in the morning. I'm sure he has a lot on his plate, and I know he's heavily concerned about making sure you're safe."

He placed his hand over hers in a warm, chivalrous gesture.

XAna admired Patrick's steady kindness. During the short drive they had talked about his plans for the district surrounding her apartment—more fountains, more bike lanes. Patrick loved cycling on the weekends and greeting voters along the way.

He wanted to improve the city she loved so much... and the world beyond Missouri.

She covered his hand. "I know, and I'm so sorry for being such a hassle. I hate this for all of you."

Patrick lifted a finger under her chin, gently tipping her face up to meet his eyes.

"Ana, you're home. It's our honor to help someone we care about so deeply."

The pause that followed felt odd. Ana couldn't quite read the intention behind his words, but the feeling she got wasn't simply friendship. There was something more masculine, more intimate in the way he looked at her.

He continued, "No more talk about being a hassle. You did nothing to deserve this monster's attention, and you have nothing to apologize for."

He made finger quotes. "The gardener—or whoever is responsible for this nightmare is seriously deranged."

Patrick gave her hand a gentle squeeze. "We're all sorry you're going through this. But I, for one, am glad you're here."

Ana smiled. Patrick was working so hard to make her feel at ease, but the mention of the moniker given to her stalker by the press sent a shiver down her spine. She was glad he turned away so he wouldn't see her smile traded for one of fear.

As the car came to a halt in the alley behind her condo, he made ready to walk her to the door. "Garrett and Jared will do whatever they can to get this person and lock them away for a very long time. As your friend, I too will make use of every instrument given to my position as mayor to make your stay more like a visit rather than a hideaway. Perhaps once this is over, you will let me show you the whole town and its changes, then let me take you to dinner?"

Ana hesitated because she still wasn't sure what to make of the request. She was sure he felt something for Ginger, based on his gaze. Patrick had always been someone she liked when they were young, but romance wasn't something she considered. She had known Pat the longest of all her friends, as they both moved into the same school district when the district was rezoned. She wasn't sure she wanted to risk another friendship the way she had with Jared. But she was single; perhaps he was right when all of this was over, who knew what she might want.

"I'd like that." Placing her hand in his as she gathered her purse. Manny was already waiting with her luggage outside the car, she stepped out. They had dropped her at the back entrance — another security measure.

Walking the ten steps to a large metal door, where a plainclothes officer stood, who politely nodded at the mayor. Then Pat turned her back toward him and said, "Manny and I will be by around 7ish to take you over to Bab's. Just a small welcome home party, private of course. I reserved the whole place tonight, so it will be only those we trust and those that love you." He winked, "Rest. I'll see you soon." Manny closed the town car door.

Ana thanked Manny as she watched him climb back in the car and drive away.

She turned back to face the young man standing, waiting for her. "Afternoon, Ms. Montgomery. Welcome home." He picked up her luggage and proceeded into the elevator, pushing the first floor, waiting for her to enter.

She stepped in, fished out of her purse the list Jared had given her. "It says you are the first shift, so that makes you…"

"Duncan, ma'am."

Seeing his full name and officer grade on the list, she relaxed. "Well, Duncan, it's nice to meet you. I'll be staying in until the Mayor's car comes back for me around seven, so light duty, I suppose, today." She smiled at the man who stood as if a military man. He was handsome, she noted. All the security field seemed to be handsome, men and women alike. All very athletic and strong with lean muscles.

"Understood, I'll be a call away then in the lobby." The elevator was normally a housekeeping and delivery entrance, but the sheet had instructions on it that told her it was to be used during her stay. A bell dinged, and door motion put them at the first floor where her door was, she stepped out, nodded politely at Duncan as he took her suitcases upstairs.

She was home for now; she supposed. It could be worse, couldn't it? She could be in a strange hiding place, not knowing anything or anyone. Acceptance was key in life. And for now, this was her life.

As she unpacked what little she had brought on the trip into her dresser and closet, she thought of Patrick's offer of what seemed like a date, having not thought anything about her romantic life in so long. It surprised her, especially after what she had witnessed between him and his assistant. She wouldn't be okay if that were the case, and besides, she needed to get clear of these mixed emotions she had for Jared.

Complicated to say the least. His ugly words had stung; it hurt that somehow after all these years he thought she was cruel and uncaring. Where and when had she ever been so unkind that Jared could make such a character assessment of her? There had to be more to his hatefulness than just the interruption to his work.

There was a moment when he handed her the list of details, their hands touched, briefly but oh the sparks. Her fingertips warmed as if held to a flame; they tingled. She thought he had felt it too when he reacted by yanking his hand away. The look of repulsion he gave her made her question whether she was the only one who felt the chemistry.

Knowing that he was going to be there tonight put her on edge. She found herself physically affected by just the notion of his presence. His youthful looks had matured into a more rugged masculinity. The button-down stretched to the limit by impressive muscles. His tactical pants fit his slim hips. Remembering her body against his in the hall brought a fever to her cheeks, she had stared wanting to memorize every detail from the golden tan of his face, his strong jaw that made her want to take her hand and stroke along the stubble, curl it around the back of his large neck and pull his lips to hers. In the precious seconds that passed, she was certain she had felt a bulge pressing against her stomach. And it hadn't been a weapon. He was more delicious now, aged to perfection, and she wanted a bite.

She wasn't the type to get nervous around men. But today, with Jared, her heart had raced like never before with any man. She supposed it could have been how angry he seemed that made her take small breaths when he was near, but something inside her said it was more. Desire or lust, two things that she hadn't really felt before.

She wasn't like other women, who saw every man as a banking opportunity or a love interest. For the last five years, traveling for work had been her focus. Dallas had been a model that was a constant in her work world, and it had seemed easy because they both understood the demands of being a top model. All the similarities of their worlds, somehow had blinded her to the things that stood out now in hindsight as drastic differences and red flags. She wasn't naturally trusting of relationships, her mom having left her dad to be with Cliff, her 'stepdad', and moved two states away, leaving her to be raised by her father alone. She rarely trusted love to last. Work lasted.

Her dad had taught her that. She had loved her life with her father, but she knew she had missed out on some things that a mother could teach. It made it tougher through the teenage years seeing her mom only a few weeks during the summer. They tried to bond, but with so little time it was tough. The divorce and, rather, the sudden "I'm moving" had been a shock. Only days before, the whole family had been on vacation at their cabin. After 15 years of marriage, she hadn't taken it very well. Her dad, stoically, had hidden the hurt, she thought more for her sake than his own. He had never dated and just kept being the successful dad he had always been, spending his free time with her or in his study reading books. While she had been lucky getting a successful dad, her love life had always taken a back seat.

Seeing Aiden this morning had been a sweet surprise; he had changed too since their younger years. He and baby brother Aj, both ex-military, both worked in the private security field when they weren't off having adventures of their own. She supposed she and Aiden were lucky to have ended their dating life as friends who would always care for one another. Not all could say the same. She was happy that he and Tessa had found each other again and were having a baby soon. Other women friends found it unusual to like the wife of an ex, but Tessa made it easy, and Ana admitted to herself that she enjoyed being unique. She believed it was the reason her life seemed to be filled with adventures.

Adventures that a relationship would only make difficult.

Chapter 15

Irish Pub Reunion

The flight to Kansas City from Orlando had been the latest nonstop Tim could find. After packing up the motel room, he had rented a car and driven from Lauderdale to MCO, so the 7:30 p.m. departure was the best option available.

The entire trip had given him too much time to think.

Being pushed aside for another security team in Kansas City had wounded him deeply. When XAna refused to let him drive her to the airport that morning, it struck directly at his pride. The dismissal gnawed at him, disturbing the careful serenity he had spent years cultivating.

She wasn't thinking clearly.

The stress she was under had to be clouding her judgment. It was almost as if she were suffering from a kind of temporary amnesia.

Tim blamed it on the shock of the previous night—seeing the two bodies lying in the hallway outside her penthouse.

When he arrived that morning, the police had initially stopped him at the barricades. Only after XAna insisted did they allow him through. The moment he called out her name, she ran straight to him.

Just as he knew she would.

He had made sure she saw the men.

Cold. Motionless. Their blood pooling across the floor.

Now, watching how she had treated him afterward, Tim briefly wondered if showing her the scene had been a mistake.

He shook his head.

No.

This was only a temporary lapse on her part.

She needed to see the blood. The consequences. She needed to understand how far he was willing to go to keep those unworthy of her away.

The idea that she believed he would simply step aside—after eight years of serving her, protecting her—was almost laughable.

As if he would take a vacation and allow someone else to do his job.

"Fuck no," Tim muttered, staring out the airplane window as the Kansas City skyline came into view below.

She was his responsibility.

His to watch over.

His to love.

He would not allow himself to be pushed into the background any longer.

He would show her how far he was willing to go.

To the ends of the earth, if necessary.

The engines roared as the plane began its descent toward the metro airport.

His moment had finally arrived.

Even if it had to happen here.

In Kansas City, Missouri.

Jared slid onto a barstool at Bab's, arriving before the rest of the crew after cutting out early. The gym had done its job—deadlifts, sweat, and a surge of endorphins had burned off most of the tension. Now all he wanted was good food, a cold beer, and a night of laughter with friends.

"Hey, J, you're early." Bab's voice rang out as she rounded the bar carrying a tray of freshly washed mugs. "You take off for something special, or does making Captain mean you get to be lazy now?"

Her sass was standard issue. Anyone who sat at her bar expected it. Bab's had once worn the same badge Jared did, but when the pub went on the market, she cashed in her savings and bought it. What she built afterward turned the place into a haven for cops, firefighters,

EMT crews—anyone who lived with the daily grind of emergency work.

She might have turned in her badge, but she still served the community.

Dartboards lined the back wall, and the annual Red vs. Blue tournament she started had become a major fundraiser for families of fallen officers. Every dollar went directly to funeral expenses, counseling for spouses, or help for the kids left behind.

Bab's had always been good police.

But here she was even better.

"Yeah, that's me," Jared said, raising his hands in surrender. "Lazy Daisy."

Bab's barked out a laugh. "Oh, I'm keeping that nickname."

"I'm gonna grab a table near the boards," Jared said. "If I could get a Bab's BBQ medium with steak fries, that'd be perfect."

Bab's nodded toward the waitress.

"I've got the beer if you've got the rest?"

The young blonde waitress, Val, nodded eagerly. She had that wide-eyed look people got around Jared. Bab's noticed immediately and smirked as Jared pretended not to.

"Yep," Val said quickly before heading off to the kitchen.

Bab's leaned toward him.

"Caught another fish, huh?"

Jared glanced toward the waitress disappearing behind the counter.

"She's sweet," he said, grabbing the beer Bab's slid toward him. "Just not my type."

He carried the drink toward the dartboard tables, shaking his head. Everyone always had an opinion about his love life—his mom, the guys at work, Bab's. They all thought he was missing out on some grand romance.

Maybe they were right.

Maybe they weren't.

The pub filled slowly as the evening crowd rolled in. Groups of firefighters and officers clustered in twos and threes, laughter mixing with the hum of music just loud enough to keep the energy up without drowning out conversation.

Jared loved this city.

For a place of half a million people, Kansas City still felt like a tight-knit town. Crime existed, sure, but the community was strong. Everyone seemed to know someone who knew someone.

It kept the city grounded.

Jared settled at a table facing the big screen TV as a Royals update flashed across the sports channel.

Val returned with his burger and fries.

"Thank you," Jared said.

"Anything else I can get you?" she asked, fluttering her lashes slightly as she leaned in.

She was more than pretty.

Tempting, even.

But another blonde years ago had already taken up space in his head he hadn't figured out how to clear.

He smiled politely.

"No, but thanks."

Val shrugged playfully.

"Maybe someday."

Then she sashayed off.

Jared watched the sway of her hips for half a second before looking back toward the bar, where Bab's was laughing at him from across the room.

He rolled his eyes.

Then he turned his attention to the real priority—the double deluxe burger dripping with bacon and spicy aioli, one of Bab's signature dishes.

The pub continued filling around him. Uniforms mixed with plainclothes officers. Booths lined the brick walls, decorated with Royals memorabilia and plaques honoring dart tournament champions. The KCPD owned most of those plaques, something Jared took quiet pride in.

Competition between the Red and Blue crews was fierce—but always friendly.

The interior still looked exactly the way Bab's had found it when she bought the place. Emerald leather barstools surrounded the three-sided mahogany bar, brass chandeliers casting warm low light over the room. The booths were upholstered in Irish tartan, giving the place a feeling somewhere between Midwest America and a Dublin pub.

But the real reason it felt like home was Bab's herself.

Jared had just finished the last of his fries when a slap landed on his shoulder.

"Buy me a beer, Hoss."

Jared turned at the familiar baritone.

AJ stood there grinning, with Aiden and his very pregnant wife Tessa just behind him.

"Nope," Jared said immediately. "Pretty sure you owe me one after losing us the dart tournament last week."

He shoved his chair back, punched AJ lightly in the arm, then moved around Aiden to hug Tessa.

"You're looking great," he told her. "Everything ready for the big day?"

"Everything's a go," she said with a soft smile.

Tessa was naturally quiet—she spent her days talking people through crisis situations as part of KCPD's intervention team. Socially, she saved her words. Right now she was on maternity leave, counting down the weeks until the baby arrived.

"I hope Aiden's treating you right," Jared said. "If not, I'll take him out back."

"You and what army?" Aiden shot back while helping Tessa sit, propping her feet on the pillow they'd brought along.

Aiden doted on her constantly.

Jared gave him hell for it anyway.

Aiden had officially retired from bachelorhood—the first of the group to do it. Jared, Trav, Garrett, and Pat were still famously single. AJ had a long-distance girlfriend none of them had met, but judging by the constant texts lighting up his phone, Jared figured he might be off the market soon.

One of those texts had cost them last week's dart tournament against Firehouse #7.

Still stung a little.

The Red vs. Blue rivalry kept things lively.

As they caught up, a shift rippled through the room.

Heads turned toward the entrance.

The mayor had arrived.

And with him—

Ana.

Bab's had posted a *Private Event* sign outside, letting the group slip in through the delivery entrance to keep the gathering quiet. Earlier that day a memo had gone out asking officers to keep the event discreet for Ana's safety.

Now the room buzzed with curiosity as people edged closer.

Jared stayed where he was.

Watching.

Ana had changed into something casual—yet somehow still looked like she belonged in a magazine. A navy cardigan over a white tee, jeans, dark glasses, and a baseball cap pulling her ponytail through the back.

Ralph Lauren ad, he thought.

He suddenly felt eyes on him.

Across the table Aiden watched with smug amusement.

Jared shook his head.

"Drama Queen just walked in," he muttered, pretending indifference as he drained his beer.

Maybe another drink would help him regain his chill.

"AJ," he said, standing. "Let's play darts."

He crossed to the dartboards and selected his color.

As he stepped up to the line, he glanced around the room—

—and found Ana looking straight at him.

In the crowded pub, somehow she had picked him out instantly.

Jared stiffened.

Their eyes held for a long second.

Then he turned back to the dartboard.

Damn.

But he wished.

CHAPTER 16
HARD TO GET

Ana licked her lips and sighed.

Her skin heated all over again.

Damn him.

The look he'd given her had been hot enough to bring the fever back—the second time in less than six hours.

The way he'd turned away afterward felt intentional. Not dismissive exactly, but he was damn good at making a woman feel like he was avoiding her.

The energy from the dart corner of the room had pulled Ana's attention immediately. It might have been the laughter drifting from that direction, but if she trusted the tingling awareness spreading through certain very sensitive parts of her body, she suspected something else.

More likely, she was being watched.

The focus came from a certain giant, blue-eyed, thick-built captain whose mood was unreadable.

He held her gaze longer than he should have. Longer than she should have allowed. Even from twenty feet away—with a crowd of bodies between them—her skin warmed beneath his attention. His presence carried an electric, unyielding pull.

Whatever message lived in his body language, she couldn't trust it. Yet it stirred secret places inside her she had no time to examine.

With a barely perceptible shake of her head, Ana forced the thoughts away before they wandered into wishes she had no business entertaining. Instead, she looked around the room.

The pub itself was dim, the mirrored windows shielding those inside from curious eyes outside. It was the kind of place meant for people who carried the weight of the city on their shoulders and needed somewhere to set it down for a few hours. Despite the dark wood and low light, the room buzzed with easy camaraderie. Laughter rolled through the air. Not a single frown in sight. Even the waitstaff moved through the crowd like they belonged to the gathering rather than simply serving beer and burgers.

On the flight here, she'd worried that the Jared she'd built in her mind might not exist at all. That when she arrived, he wouldn't even remember their night together. Worse, that he'd felt nothing for her—nothing like the longing that still made her dream of his touch during quiet, lonely nights in her bed.

Their interaction earlier that morning—and now—proved there was something between them.

What she couldn't figure out was why his energy radiated irritation directed at her personally. Not XAna, the victim of a stalker.

Ana.

The woman he'd once shared a single night with.

Her gaze drifted back to the dart corner. Jared's back was turned now, breaking the brief daydream.

Blinking, she turned and found Patrick staring at her, clearly waiting for an answer.

"I'm sorry," she said with a small smile. "What was it you asked?"

Patrick studied her with a puzzled expression. When they'd entered, three officers had come over to greet him, leaving her to wander the room with her eyes, learning the sounds and faces around her.

And, if she were honest with herself, hoping to catch another glimpse of the brooding captain.

Not that she would admit it.

The impulse came from a very specific part of her anatomy—an overly feminine, slightly desperate part she dearly wished would take a chill pill.

Mayor Patrick smiled down at her. "I was asking if you wanted to go to the bar for a drink?"

"Yes, I would love a glass of wine." Relieved to be distracted.

"Good. Come with me and I'll have Bab's start a tab."

Ana felt Pat's arm slide around her waist as he guided her toward the bar. The touch made her glance up at him in surprise—then, ridiculously, her eyes darted to the darkened corner.

Piercing blue eyes were already there waiting.

He was watching the exchange between Patrick and her. Gone was the humor and easy light she had seen earlier. Jared leaned against the wall near the bar, beer in one hand, darts in the other, waiting for AJ, who was loudly bragging to the room about his last throw.

Jared's gaze moved from Ana's face to Patrick's hand resting at her waist.

Possessive.

His lips tightened. No smile.

AJ's bragging faltered for half a second before he threw the dart.

The room buzzed with laughter and loud conversation, yet the fierceness in Jared's stare made everything else disappear. Ana's mouth went dry, her body going on high alert.

This wasn't nothing.

It was personal.

Dangerous... the hot, sexy kind.

A waitress stepped between them to grab Jared's empty bottle, thankfully breaking the spell.

Ana exhaled slowly.

She was definitely going to need more than one drink tonight.

Bab's watched the room the way she always did, making sure everyone was taken care of. Her elevated perch behind the bar gave her a perfect vantage point. From there she could read the room like a seasoned detective—old habits from the badge she used to wear.

It helped to see everything.

Who was laughing too loudly.

Who was sitting too quietly.

Who needed a listening ear, a firm word... or a free drink.

Tonight's crowd happened to be one of her favorites: local uniforms from every branch of service gathered to support the hometown beauty who'd returned despite a stalker and a storm of headlines.

Bab's hadn't met the woman yet, but she'd read the news. XAna—Ana—had refused to cancel her charity event despite the danger.

That kind of backbone earned respect in Bab's book.

Still, the stalker had already claimed two lives, dragging the whole situation into darker territory.

Bab's eyes drifted back across the room.

More specifically—to Jared.

And the blonde standing across the floor.

Her redheaded *Spidey senses* started tingling.

Because that look between them?

That wasn't curiosity.

That was history.

Something salty.

Jared—KC's proudly confirmed Bachelor of the Year, plaque hanging right on the wall of her Irish pub for all to admire—was currently staring down the small-town blonde who'd somehow become eye candy for men around the world.

Bab's polished a glass slowly, lips curving.

Well now.

This might be the best entertainment she'd had all week.

Watching those two light a fire across a crowded room without saying a word?

Oh yes.

This was going to be fun.

Bab's leaned on the bar, satisfied.

Yep.

She loved her bar.

Hearing her name called, Ana stopped lollygagging.

"Evening, Mayor," Bab's greeted him the same way she always did.

She liked Patrick—both the politician and the guy she called when the pub's computers decided to misbehave. The two beautiful people standing at the bar looked like a dynamic power couple, though something about the picture felt incomplete.

"Where's your other half?" Bab's grinned.

Everyone knew she meant Ginger. The mayor's executive assistant was rarely more than two steps behind him, notebook in hand.

Patrick laughed. "Very funny. Ginger had something come up tonight, but I'll be sure to tell her she was missed."

He brushed off the joke easily, used to Bab's teasing. She'd hinted more than once that he might want his eyes checked when it came to the only other redhead she knew.

Patrick always waved it away. Ginger was his executive assistant—his best one yet. She anticipated his needs before he even spoke them. Losing someone like that simply because he found her intelligent, attractive, and the wittiest woman he knew would be foolish.

His denial didn't stop the teasing.

Truth was, Ginger seemed just as determined to ignore the obvious connection everyone else saw. Bab's couldn't figure out why two people who worked so well together wouldn't just make the leap.

Ana watched the exchange with interest, quietly gratified. It wasn't only her imagination that had noticed something between the mayor and his assistant.

Bab's clearly saw it too.

"So then," Bab's said, leaning against the bar and giving Ana an appraising once-over. "What can I get you to drink?"

"Before that," Patrick said, "how are the systems running in the back? No problems, I hope."

Another thing Ana liked about him—he never acted like being mayor made him above anyone else.

"All good for now." Bab's nodded, then gestured toward Ana. "So this must be the infamous Ana. Welcome to Bab's Irish Pub. I'm Bab's. What can I get you to drink, since the mayor here hasn't been quick enough to offer?"

She snapped her bar towel playfully at him. Patrick had actually given her the *Red's in Charge* towel as a gift on opening day.

Ana smiled. "Nice to meet you. A glass of Chardonnay, if you have one. And thank you for the warm welcome."

"Coming right up." Bab's turned to grab the bottle.

Her electric red hair and equally vibrant lipstick made quite the statement. She clearly wasn't toning it down for anyone. Ana liked her instantly. She could easily see them becoming friends.

Patrick ordered a Heineken and told Bab's to stop with the theatrics. Ana only smiled. Their playful sparring felt natural—like family.

It was nice to feel that again.

She noticed a number of curious glances drifting her way. People were wondering who she was, what her story might be—but every expression she saw was friendly.

Bab's returned with their drinks just as several officers approached to greet the mayor. Patrick listened to each of them with genuine interest. It was easy to see why he was so well liked in Kansas City.

It was also easy to see how a handsome mayor like Patrick had landed on the list for *Bachelor of the Year* with Jared, too.

The two men made quite a pair—both single, both successful, and according to gossip and her father's stories, both enjoying very active social lives. Yet the magazine interview had quoted them both claiming they were forever bachelors, fully devoted to their careers and the city they served.

Ana took a sip of her wine.

Lucky her—she knew them both.

After a few more sips, she excused herself and slipped toward the hallway leading to the restrooms, hoping for a moment of quiet.

Halfway there, she glanced back toward the dart corner.

Three female officers hovered around the two very focused, very handsome men.

One of them caught her looking.

Jared.

Even across the crowded room, his blue eyes locked on hers.

Then he smiled.

Slow. Knowing.

The heat of it hit her square in the chest.

Ana spun on her heel and disappeared down the hallway.

CHAPTER 17

A PERFECT COUPLE

Jared silently berated himself.

He couldn't stop watching her.

The flash of the door opening had caught his attention, and his peripheral vision—always annoyingly precise—had found her instantly. She stood off to the side, observing the room the way someone did when they didn't quite belong. Home, but not home.

A fish out of water.

The moment Patrick's hand slid around Ana's waist, Jared saw red.

His grip tightened around the dart in his hand.

It was ridiculous. He didn't do possessive. Especially not over a woman.

Especially not this woman.

She was so far outside his world it wasn't even funny. Yet the sudden urge to walk over to Patrick—his mayor, technically his boss—remove the hand from her waist and deck him had nearly overwhelmed him.

Jared forced his attention back to the dartboard, pretending to listen to AJ's bragging while keeping Ana in the edge of his vision.

It had to be the alcohol.

Nothing else explained it.

Never in his life had what amounted to a one-night stand—hell, a mistake really—left him wanting... no, craving that level of desire again.

Every man in the room wanted her.

But he had already had her.

In his bed.

Her lush, naked body writhing beneath him.

And God help him, he wanted that again.

Patrick clearly wanted her too. Watching them together felt like a punch to the gut.

Reality.

He wasn't in her league. She wasn't the kind of woman who collected random one-night stands. She was a Maserati.

He was a Chevy.

She was fame.

He was just another cop doing his job.

They lived in different worlds, and there was no way he could compete with what someone like Patrick could offer.

He should shut this down now and spare himself the misery.

Only after Ana disappeared down the hallway did Jared realize he had been holding his breath.

He exhaled slowly—and noticed three gorgeous women flirting shamelessly with him and AJ.

He hated himself right now.

"Ladies, if you'll excuse me." Jared pushed off the wall. "AJ, I'm grabbing another drink. You want a round?"

AJ's booming laugh followed him toward the bar.

"If you're buying, I'll take two!"

The women giggled behind him.

"Bab's," Jared said when he reached the bar, "another Corona. Two Heinies for AJ."

His mood had darkened considerably.

Bab's didn't move right away. She leaned against the bar, studying him with that smug little grin she wore whenever she thought she'd figured something out.

In her bar, she missed nothing.

"What?" Jared muttered, already knowing he was the target of that look.

"All these years," Bab's said slowly, "I wondered about your taste in women. Brunettes, gingers..." She tilted her head toward the hallway Ana had disappeared down. "Now I get it."

Her grin widened as she slid the Corona in front of him.

Jared took a long pull from the bottle, letting the bitterness of the lime settle his temper before he said something he'd regret.

Bab's set the other two beers on the bar, amusement still dancing in her eyes.

She saw too much.

If she noticed his reaction, others might have too.

He needed to get a handle on himself.

"No idea what you're babbling about, Bab's," he said evenly. "Keep trying though. One day you might make detective."

He turned back toward the dart corner just as Bab's murmured quietly behind him,

"Maybe stop fighting it."

Jared grabbed the beers and headed back to AJ.

The words followed him.

Stop fighting it.

Damn it—he couldn't help it.

His mind was already running ahead of him, imagining storming down that hallway, finding her in the restroom corridor, and begging her to let him taste her again.

For days this time.

Not hours.

Stop fighting wanting her?

He never would.

But what if he didn't fight it?

Would it cost him everything else?

His friendships.

His career.

Everything.

Exiting the ladies' room, Ana hesitated in the dim hallway of Bab's crowded pub. The shadows gave her the perfect hiding place to spy on the man who, with a single look, could scorch her panties.

He stood now in the center of colleagues and friends as if he were a rock star. The men respected him. The women wanted him. The younger officers watched with open envy.

She leaned against the wall, watching him hold court as he told a dramatic story to the crowd.

He was so different from the quiet but enthusiastic rookie she had once met in his small apartment.

This man—laughing, commanding the room—was older, confident, completely in control. His massive frame radiated power, virile and unapologetically masculine.

He wasn't anything like the polished men from her modeling world. Those men were sleck and curated.

Jared was all hard edges.

He stood like a mountain—massive, immovable—with heat that seemed to rise from him like molten lava.

She had dreamed about that heat more than once.

The perfect blend of safety and dangerous passion.

Now, older and wiser, she could see how that intensity would translate elsewhere. Jared would be methodical with a woman, slow, deliberate… devastatingly erotic.

Her mind betrayed her.

She imagined those blue eyes locking onto hers, pulling her under like a tide.

You're mine.

Her body remembered him. His touch. His size.

Ana closed her eyes, letting the memory warm her.

Yes… the woman who got to lie in his arms these days was very lucky indeed.

When her eyes opened again, she found him staring straight at her.

"Fuck," she whispered.

He had spotted her in the shadows.

A mischievous glint flashed in his eyes before he deliberately looked away.

Damn him.

One look from the man he had become made her want to taste him all over again.

If only life offered do-overs.

Flustered, she stepped out of the hallway—and promptly collided with the mayor.

"Oh!" She laughed softly. "Hi there. Thank you so much for this lovely evening."

She gestured toward the lively room.

"I appreciate the warmth in here. After the foundation gala… and everything that happened to Mitch and Tomas… I've been feeling a little lost. But seeing everyone again has helped more than you know."

She paused, glancing around at the uniforms filling the room.

"I worried some people might agree with Jared—that holding the gala was arrogant or reckless. But these men and women... in any uniform... they make the world safer for all of us. Being here in their world tonight feels like the safest homecoming I could imagine."

She smiled up at him.

"And I know that's mostly because of you."

Patrick's arm came around her shoulder, his grip warm and sincere.

"Deep down," he said gently, "you're still our Kansas City Ana. That will never change."

He gestured toward the booths.

"Come sit with me. You can tell me more about your life—and about the foundation."

"I'd love that, Pat."

As they walked, Ana's gaze drifted back toward the dart corner.

Jared had slipped back into his element. Women and young officers leaned in eagerly as he launched into another animated story.

They adored him.

Jared had always been a natural storyteller. He could make a room roar with laughter—or fall silent with suspense.

And tonight he seemed to have no shortage of female attention.

Ana forced herself to refocus on Patrick.

"So," she asked lightly, sliding into the booth, "how on earth did you end up with Dallas Richards?"

Patrick laughed.

"Well, that's direct."

She laughed with him.

"You asked about my love life first."

"Well," she said, shrugging, "we were modeling for the same company. They paired us for a fragrance campaign—cologne and perfume from the same brand."

She took a sip of wine.

"It made sense at the time. Same schedules. Same crazy travel. Flying across the world at a moment's notice." She gave a small shrug. "And he's handsome."

Her expression sobered slightly.

"Though looking back now... I ignored a few red flags."

Patrick watched her quietly.

"I don't know how much Garrett has shared," she continued, "but he thinks Dallas might be my stalker."

She shook her head slowly.

"I can't wrap my mind around it. Yes, Dallas was angry about the breakup, but murder? My bodyguard and Tomas—the doorman—did nothing to deserve that."

Her voice softened.

"The notes at first were strange, but not terrifying. Now they feel different... personal. Like someone who believes I wronged them somehow."

She sighed.

"I know men sometimes mistake kindness for something more. Or take a thank-you the wrong way. But Dallas? Killing someone?"

She shook her head.

"I just can't see it."

Patrick saw the frustration in her eyes.

He placed his hand gently over hers and leaned closer.

"It will all be over soon," he murmured.

When they looked up, they found Aiden and Tessa standing beside the table, watching them with questioning expressions.

"Mind if we join you?" Aiden asked.

Patrick stood as Tessa slid into the booth. "Of course not." Ana could tell he meant it, though it was clear he'd hoped for a moment of semi-private conversation. His mayoral charm won out.

"Ana, how are you? You look great... considering." Tessa's concern was sincere. The strawberry-blonde woman glowed with pregnancy, and Ana had always liked her. She was good for Aiden.

Glancing at Patrick, Ana replied softly, "I'm okay. I'm in the hands of dear friends."

Tessa reached across the table with open palms. Ana placed her hands in hers.

"We're all hoping Garrett can speed things up and catch whoever is behind those notes," Tessa said gently. "It must be awful having your life turned upside down like this. Aiden and I are here if you need anything."

Ana squeezed her hands. "Thank you. It's been truly awful. I'm heartbroken about my doorman, Tomas. He was always such a gentleman—so kind to me from the moment I hired him for the towers.”

Her voice softened.

“I've sent flowers to his family and made sure they're comfortable with the funeral arrangements. And Mitch... I had only recently gotten to know him, but he was so dedicated to protecting me these past months.” She shook her head slowly. “I can't believe this is my life right now—or that so many people are in danger because of me.”

“Do you think it's Dallas?” Tessa asked quietly. “Like the news reports suggest?”

“Patrick and I were just talking about that,” Ana said. “Honestly, I don't know. I truly don't think Dallas is capable of murder. Yes, he's angry that our relationship— our partnership—didn't work out. But killing someone? I just don't see it.”

She took a sip of wine before continuing.

“When we got engaged, we signed a type of agreement - not a prenup but a contract to safeguard my brand and properties. Ridiculous at the time, but now I'm grateful. My attorney, Arthur—he's also a friend—insisted on it because of my business ventures and partnerships. He never trusted Dallas.”

She gave a small shrug.

“When I caught Dallas with my business partner, Charla, I lost them both. Looking back, I think part of me always knew I wouldn't go through with the marriage. Some of his business tactics made me question his ethics... but killer? No. I still don't believe it.”

She paused.

“I think someone might be setting him up.”

Ana exhaled softly and gave them a small smile.

"But I'm not a detective. I'm just glad to be home with all of you. Hopefully I can keep a low profile with these hats." She laughed lightly.

Aiden and Tessa smiled back at her. They made a beautiful pair. He was steady and quiet with a deeply kind heart, while she was bright and affectionate, clearly in love with both Aiden and the baby on the way.

"Are you staying at your father's place?" Aiden asked.

Ana shook her head. "No. I'm at the Plaza condo for now. I may stop by the house to check on the renovations, but it's not ready yet. It's being updated before we put it on the market."

"So you're thinking of selling it?" Aiden's concern was evident.

"Yes." She nodded slowly. "It's harder to come back there without Dad greeting me at the door or asking me to play chess. I miss him terribly. And honestly... the house deserves a big family. I don't see that happening in my near future."

"Well," Tessa said gently, "take your time. You never know what the future holds. Sometimes moments like this remind us where we truly belong."

Ana smiled. "That's true. Life has a funny way of surprising us."

"Pat," Aiden teased, "you're making sure she gets home safely tonight, right?"

Ana laughed and came to Patrick's defense. "Patrick has been wonderful. He sent his private jet to bring me home and arranged this entire evening. He's even offered to show me all the ways the city has changed."

Patrick beamed at the praise.

Aiden noticed.

It seemed the mayor's long-standing crush on Ana hadn't faded in the slightest.

Thankfully, both women in his life—Tessa and Ana—were secure enough not to be bothered by past relationships. Ana and he had always been more friends than lovers. She had entered his life during a time when he felt lost, when Tessa had moved away and he believed he might never see her again.

Life, however, had a way of circling back.

He loved Ana and admired her deeply for everything she had accomplished. But Tessa was his forever. After everything Ana had endured, he hoped she would find that kind of love too.

Aiden's gaze drifted around the room as Patrick and Tessa began discussing Ginger and why she wasn't there tonight.

Across the pub, he spotted Jared watching their table.

More specifically... watching Ana.

Aiden lifted a hand, signaling him to come join them.

Jared shook his head and turned away, refocusing on AJ and the group of officers gathered near the dartboard.

Something was definitely off.

Aiden knew Jared cared about Ana. Yet ever since Garrett's call from Florida asking for help, Jared had been acting as though Ana was the last person he wanted to see.

And now, from across the room, the man couldn't take his eyes off her.

Aiden glanced back toward the booth.

Ana was listening politely as Patrick and Tessa talked—but her gaze had drifted past them, toward the dart corner.

Toward Jared.

There was a flicker of hurt in her eyes.

Interesting.

Had he missed something between those two... a long time ago?

Chapter 18

Caught Watching

Aiden caught him staring at Ana again.

Damn.

If he wasn't careful, his friends would notice just how affected he was by the bombshell blonde. Sure, he could blame it on being a red-blooded male, but staring like this—lost in thought—was bound to start a conversation he didn't want to have.

Especially with Aiden.

His phone buzzed in his hand.

Jared swiped the screen. "Gables here."

Garrett's voice came through immediately. "Hey, is Ana still with you guys at the pub?"

"Yes. What's up? Something new?" Jared's lips tightened. The news couldn't be good if Garrett was interrupting her welcome-home party.

"One of the decoys was attacked going through DFW International. She's in the hospital—shaken, a few bruises—but airport security couldn't catch Dallas. He slipped away again."

"Dallas?"

Jared turned sharply, eyes finding Ana's table across the room.

He gave Aiden a look.

Aiden understood instantly.

Jared motioned toward Patrick and nodded toward Ana. Time to end the night.

Patrick glanced around the room and saw Jared approaching, phone sliding into his pocket, his expression grim.

"Looks like it's time to call it a night, folks," Jared said quietly when he reached them. "Mayor, if you could see Ana back to her condo and wait there, I'll join you shortly after I brief the team and adjust the schedule."

"Of course," Patrick said smoothly. Turning to Ana, he offered his arm. "Let's get you home."

Patrick took her hand and tucked it into his arm.

Aiden watched Jared as Ana and Patrick passed them on their way to the door. Jared's eyes never left her.

Yeah.

That was more than a protective instinct.

"I'm going to hit the ladies' room before we go," Tessa said. "Back in a minute."

The two men watched with matching smiles as she waddled toward the hallway.

Once she disappeared, Aiden turned back to Jared.

"So what's up? Was that Garrett?"

"Yeah. Dallas struck again. One of the XAna decoys in DFW. She's okay, but Dallas got away." Jared lowered his voice. "Airport security footage shows him looking... wrong. Drugged, maybe sick. He was holding his side."

Aiden frowned. "Anything else?"

"Yeah." Jared glanced around, waiting for two officers to pass before continuing. "New information suggests it might not be Dallas after all."

"Does Garrett have a name?" Aiden asked quickly. "What's the news?"

He knew he was rushing Jared, but he didn't want Tessa overhearing anything alarming. Stress wasn't good for her—or the baby.

"Another murder in Miami," Jared said quietly.

"Miami? What's the connection?"

Aiden glanced toward the bar where Tessa had paused to chat with Bab's. Good—another minute.

"A woman was found dead next to a sewing machine," Jared said. "Looks like an overdose. Prostitute. But Ana's white ballgown from the gala was in the apartment."

Aiden blinked. "What?"

"Hanging in the closet," Jared continued. "Freshly repaired. The tear Dallas made when he grabbed her during that press interview."

"How would she get the dress?" Aiden asked. "Did she repair it? Steal it? What's the connection?"

Jared shrugged. "Garrett found a rose petal there too. Beyond that... more questions than answers."

Aiden exhaled slowly. "That rose petal makes it significant, wouldn't you say?"

He elbowed Jared—a silent signal to shut it down.

Tessa was heading back.

"What did I miss, Captain?" she asked cheerfully, sliding her arm around Jared's waist and sticking her tongue out at her husband.

Jared looked down at the pint-sized woman with the basketball belly and smiled.

"Nothing," he said lightly. "Just telling Aiden what a lucky man he is."

He gave her a quick hug.

"Alright, enough manhandling the precious cargo," Aiden said, pulling Tessa toward him. "Give me my bride and go find your own."

He kissed her soundly, then swatted her bottom playfully.

"That's for making me jealous."

Tessa laughed, burying her face in his shoulder.

Aiden looked over at Jared. "Keep me in the loop. I'm a text or call away."

"Thanks, man. I need to brief the security detail, but I'll catch you up tomorrow."

Jared watched them leave the pub arm in arm.

He was genuinely happy for them.

Aiden had his forever.

Maybe he and Ana still had unfinished business of their own. Maybe once this was over—once they caught the psycho behind it all—they could finally say the things left unsaid.

But one detail still gnawed at him.

The dead prostitute's phone had shown a flight reservation from Orlando to Kansas City. The plane had already departed earlier that evening and would land in about an hour.

The building where the girl died had no security cameras, leaving them with no proof of who had booked the flight.

Garrett suspected it might have been the girl herself.

Jared doubted it.

Maybe a boyfriend. Maybe a john.

Still, the coincidence felt far too convenient.

How had she gotten Ana's dress?

Why repair it... only to overdose beside the sewing machine?

None of it made sense.

They were miles from identifying the bastard behind all this.

Jared rubbed the back of his neck, already planning the next steps—briefing the team, adjusting shifts, tightening security.

He hated that Patrick was probably just now getting Ana home.

He needed to update them both.

If this new lead meant the threat had shifted, Ana could be in even more danger.

Maybe she would recognize the dead girl—from a modeling event, a charity gala, somewhere.

God, he hoped she didn't know the victim.

CHAPTER 19

EYES BEYOND

"Tim?" the Uber driver asked through the window before stepping out.

Timmy leaned down. "Yes. Broadway Street."

"Yes, sir." The driver closed the door as Tim slid into the back seat, then walked around the car and settled behind the wheel.

Timmy had chosen the luxury sedan upgrade to blend in with the other cars downtown. Normally he avoided such extravagances, preferring to save his money for future spending on his veritable treasure—XAna.

In Lauderdale, he had the personal use of the town car. In Kansas City, he had access to her father's antique Mercedes. But officially he wasn't on duty yet.

He had ignored her request that he take time away while she went into hiding.

In hiding from him.

As if he would ever hurt her.

The thought made him see dead bodies scattered like necessary sacrifices—proof of his devotion for making her believe he wanted anything other than her light to shine brighter.

Death had been required.

Trina—the drug-laced floozy—had fulfilled the highest purpose of her life when she repaired the gown XAna would one day wear when she married him.

Dallas, though not dead yet, served as the perfect distraction for the lackeys in the Miami and Kansas City police departments.

Mitch and the doorman?

Sweet revenge. One for mockery, the other for being in the wrong place at the wrong time.

Each death had been necessary.

The doorman had been unfortunate, but unavoidable. He might have told her who killed Mitch.

It hadn't been part of Timmy's plan.

But it had been *God's* plan—perfected in real time.

Taking the life of someone truly innocent was proof enough.

XAna was meant for him.

The Uber driver—Juan, according to the dashboard app—was rambling about things to do in Kansas City, trying his best to sell the city to his passenger.

What a tedious job.

Driving strangers around, pretending an ordinary place was exciting.

"No," Timmy said quietly, staring out the window. "I'm not here for work. I'm here to defend my queen."

"Oh man," the driver chuckled. "You here for chess? Tournament in town or something?"

Timmy turned his head slowly.

The Latin driver had more intelligence than most.

Still wrong.

But clever.

"Yes," Timmy replied calmly. "That's correct. I'm in a life-or-death game of chess."

He leaned forward slightly.

"And I have no intention of ending up dead."

The driver glanced at him in the rear-view mirror, searching for humor in the comment.

All he found was a cold stare.

Juan said nothing after that.

He drove the rest of the way through the night traffic in silence.

Timmy liked how easily most people were frightened.

A look.

A hint of danger.

The mere mention of death.

They all shriveled.

Not his XAna.

Two days ago, after they found the murdered body-guard and the doorman outside her penthouse door, she had been magnificent.

No fear.

Only sorrow.

His innocent bride-to-be.

The scene had been harsh, yes—but Tim believed she was already awakening to their connection.

Somewhere deep in her heart she was beginning to wonder who was behind the beautiful roses... the love notes... the devotion.

Her frustration with the police presence and Detective Garrett's hiding plan wasn't fear.

It was impatience.

She was tired of waiting.

Waiting for the day he revealed himself.

The moment their lives would finally intertwine.

Forever.

Inseparable.

Timmy smiled faintly.

He couldn't wait either.

For the moment when all his sacrifices would prove the depth of his love.

The kind of love earned only through suffering.

Love given.

Love returned.

Jared had been as thorough as possible with both Ana and Patrick so they could fully understand the danger.

The news linking another death to Ana's stalker had shaken her deeply. This time it was someone she didn't know—someone she believed had no connection to her or her company.

The photo of the dead woman had shocked her.

But the detail that unsettled her most was the dress.

Her gala gown.

How had it ended up there?

"When was the last time you had the gown in your possession?" Jared hated bringing up the gala night, but they needed every detail if they were going to keep her safe—and find whoever was hunting her.

"The night of the gala," Ana said quietly. "Tomas took it for me after I asked him to send it to my cleaner to be mended. It was the last thing I ever asked him to do."

Her voice softened.

"He couldn't have had anything to do with this. He cared about me."

Jared saw the flash of pain in her eyes as she remembered that final moment. The loyalty she felt toward someone who had simply worked for her said a lot about who she was. With her wealth and fame, that kind of kindness spoke volumes.

"No," Jared said gently. "We don't believe he was involved. At most, he was an unknowing link in the chain. We just need to figure out who could have taken the dress from the Towers. Garrett is working on it."

"I know you all are," Ana said. "And I'm grateful. I just wish this nightmare would end." She hesitated. "But there's more you're not telling me, isn't there? Please... maybe I can help."

Her voice carried a quiet sincerity.

Patrick stepped in beside her. "Yes. Don't spare her, Jared. She deserves all the information. Being forced to hide is hard enough—let her feel like she has some control."

Jared found it interesting that Patrick had jumped in before he'd even finished speaking. He bit back the sharp remark that threatened to escape.

"I know she can handle it," he said calmly.

His eyes met Ana's. The hope—and surprise—in her expression stole his breath for a moment.

"We believe the person who brought the dress in for repair may be the same person who helped that woman overdose," he said carefully. "And we have reason to believe they're on their way to Kansas City."

Ana's mouth opened, but no sound came out.

Her eyes widened with fear—and sorrow.

Jared's instinct was immediate. He wanted to step closer, pull her into his arms, reassure her.

But he hesitated a second too long.

Patrick didn't.

He turned Ana gently toward him. "We're going to make sure you're safe. You have our word. Jared and his team, Garrett in Miami—we'll do everything in our power to stop this. Trust us. We won't let anyone harm you."

"I believe you," Ana said softly.

Then she turned her face back toward Jared.

"But who is going to keep *you* safe?"

Sucker-punched—that's how Jared would describe the feeling.

Had he heard her right?

Who is going to keep you safe?

He couldn't make sense of what he had just witnessed. Patrick had meant to reassure Ana that she was safe, but her attention had shifted to him. Were her fears centered on him—or on him and his team?

Surely she couldn't really be worried about him after the way he had treated her in his office.

But then again… that was Ana.

Always worrying about everyone else.

Damn. I'm a jackass.

He had let his pent-up frustration get the better of him. A restless night of dreams and an entire day reliving memories while waiting for her arrival hadn't helped. For two days his body had been wound tight, desire and distraction twisting his thoughts into knots.

That rant in his office had been nothing more than a poor attempt to hide his feelings for her. Fear—plain and simple. Fear he still wasn't ready to name.

But none of that mattered right now.

If he didn't get his head straight, he could put Ana—and his entire team—in danger.

He forced himself to let her comment slide.

"You let me worry about everyone's safety," he said calmly. "Let the Mayor and his private security focus on helping you enjoy your stay. Ana, we *will* find this bastard."

Jared tried to ignore Patrick's hand resting at her waist.

He failed.

He smiled at them both, though the irritation in his eyes betrayed him.

Damn it. The complications of emotion and physical desire were a beast.

"Let us walk you out, Jared," Patrick said, moving around them toward the door.

Jared glanced down at Ana. She was staring off, lost in thought.

When she noticed him watching her, she gave a small smile and started to step forward.

Jared turned, blocking her path before she could move toward the entry.

They stood only inches apart.

Close enough that he caught the faint scent of her perfume. Close enough that his body wanted to memorize it.

He gently lifted her chin.

"Hey," he murmured, his voice low and steady. "We've got you."

The moment his hand touched her face, he felt her tremble.

Ana looked up at him, trying to appear brave.

A breath escaped her parted lips before she spoke.

"I know you do," she said softly. "Thank you. Truly."

When Jared and Ana reached the entry to her condo, Patrick stepped ahead and held the door open with one arm. He extended his hand.

"Thanks, man, for everything you're doing. The city was right to trust you to keep them safe. We're lucky to have you—and I'm grateful to call you a friend, even if you are a stubborn ass."

Jared shook the mayor's hand. Once again, he was struck by how easily Patrick could switch from politician to friend—offering sincere thanks while slipping in a playful jab.

Usually it didn't bother him.

Tonight, with Ana standing beside them, it did.

"Thank you, Mayor," Jared said. "Sorry I interrupted your evening with such somber news. Hopefully you can pick up right where you left off."

Patrick blinked. "What are you talking about?"

Jared's tone had carried a hint of jealousy. A brief *what the hell* look flashed across Patrick's face. He glanced at Ana. She looked at Jared. The strange undertone confused them both.

"When I arrived," Jared said, shifting his stance in an attempt to appear casual, "it looked like you two were deep in conversation. Bottle of wine, fireplace... felt like I walked in at the wrong time."

Inside, he was anything but casual. The jealousy crawling under his skin irritated him as much as it surprised him. For days this entire situation had been messing with his head, and he was starting not to care who noticed.

Ana's cheeks flushed at the insinuation. She looked ready to snap back at him, but Patrick beat her to it.

"I was simply helping Ana relax before Garrett's updates," Patrick said smoothly. Then he added with a grin, "Though honestly, who wouldn't be tempted by this beauty?"

Patrick slid an arm around Ana's shoulder and gave her a playful squeeze.

Jared immediately recognized the bait.

He watched Ana's face carefully, noting how her eyes searched his, trying to understand where his comment had come from.

Patrick caught her look of dismay and laughed it off.

"I'm not the type of man to let opportunity pass me by," he teased. "Nope, not me. I'm enjoying every moment."

Jared knew the tone well. Patrick was being Patrick—light, charming, harmless.

But this wasn't the night for games. A murderer was headed to Kansas City, and someone could get seriously hurt.

He needed to get out of there before his temper—or something worse—got the better of him.

Jared stepped down the stairs and turned back once, looking up at them beneath the glow of the porch light.

Ana's lips were no longer smiling. They pressed into a thin line of disappointment.

In a low, silky voice he said, "I get it, Mayor. Smart man."

There it was again.

That edge in Jared's voice—full of implications Ana couldn't quite understand.

Her mouth opened to respond, but before she could speak, his attention shifted.

His head turned slightly.

Something prickled at the back of his neck.

Jared scanned the quiet, tree-lined street.

Ana noticed the change immediately. When his hand moved instinctively toward the gun at his hip, alarm crept into her voice.

"What is it? Did you hear something?"

Jared's eyes moved slowly across the parked cars.

Seven vehicles.

The same seven that had been there when he arrived.

Nothing out of place.

Still...

Something felt wrong.

The street was too quiet for a weeknight.

He forced himself to relax.

"Nope," he said lightly. "Probably just a cat or something."

He glanced back toward the house.

"I'm going to check in with the team. We've got unmarked cars both in front of and behind the building. Ana—you're safe."

Then he looked at Patrick.

"I'll reach out tomorrow. Thanks again for the kind words. You should take Ana back inside and enjoy the rest of your night."

The moment the words left his mouth, Jared cursed himself.

Had he really just implied Patrick should take Ana inside and sleep with her?

Patrick's eyebrows pulled together.

That was enough.

Time to go.

Jared turned and stalked down the block.

What he should have been focusing on was the fact that someone might already be watching them.

Watching Ana's condo.

Watching *her*.

Someone close enough to strike.

His instincts—his cop's intuition—told him it was true, even if his eyes couldn't yet prove it.

That's fine.

Whoever you are...

Touch her—

and you'll learn what pain really feels like.

Tim's lips curled as he reveled in his brilliance.

From his vantage point, Jared would never see him.

He stood in the shadows of the parking garage across the street, looking down toward the condo entrance as the Captain walked away. A redbud tree cast an extra veil of cover, giving him a perfect view of everyone coming and going from XAna's building.

The men protecting her were a joke.

His stomach twisted with disgust as he watched Patrick slide a smug arm around Ana and guide her back inside. Of all the men to touch what belonged to him, this one tore at his soul.

In his mind, the mayor already lay dead.

He pictured dark blood spreading across the pavement, pooling around Patrick's lifeless body.

The image soothed him.

Tim's plans for the mayor were already elaborate, but every extra minute Patrick spent alone with his queen only meant Tim would draw the torture out longer.

He pulled out his phone and opened the security app.

One tap brought up the camera feed labeled *Living Room – Condo.*

The screen lit up with the image of them sitting together on the couch in front of the fire.

Tim watched Patrick place his arm around Ana, comforting her.

Rage surged through him.

He shut the phone off.

This anger needed somewhere private to breathe—somewhere soundproof.

His apartment.

Once there, he would listen to the audio feed and learn exactly what those fools had told her. It couldn't be news of his arrival; he had timed everything perfectly to coincide with her welcome-home party.

Not even XAna expected him yet.

So it had to be the news about Dallas… and the decoy.

Leaving the airport earlier, Tim had glimpsed a news update about a reported sighting of Dallas attacking someone he must have mistaken for XAna.

Timmy's body warmed with satisfaction.

The cameraman had caught a glimpse of Dallas on video—pale, hunched, sickly, like death was already stalking him.

Tim's stomach shook with quiet laughter.

I happened to him.

That needle he had slipped into Dallas's side the night of the gala had begun its quiet work. Poison working slowly through the kidneys and liver.

Dallas's body was already failing.

The stress of chasing XAna would only speed things along.

Tim gave him another week.

Maybe less.

Then all of Dallas's problems would finally end.

It was more mercy than the man deserved for the way he had treated Tim's XAna.

Begging her for a ménage à trois when she had been nearly innocent.

Then cheating on her with her own business partner.

He was lucky Tim hadn't already carved him into pieces and fed him to the alligators back in Florida.

Soon Dallas would be nothing more than a memory.

One more piece of the past erased.

Leaving the future clear—

for Tim and his XAna.

Chapter 20

Reset

After leaving Ana and Patrick at the condo steps, Jared walked the secured perimeter, checking in with the night watch and asking if they had seen anything suspicious.

His senses were on high alert.

The two officers had nothing to report. They had already run the plates of every vehicle lining the street—each belonged to a condo resident. From their perspective, it would be a quiet night.

Jared hoped they were right.

Still, he told them to watch for the slightest movement that didn't fit the neighborhood before leaving them to their post. When dealing with someone like Ana's stalker, danger came from unpredictability. There was still no clear connection between the killer and Ana, though it was obvious the man had a twisted romantic fixation on her. The love notes had turned into demands for attention, warnings that their time together was coming.

From experience, Jared trusted his instincts. When his gut tightened or his skin crawled, it meant something was wrong. And when the person at risk was someone he cared deeply about, those instincts mattered ten times more.

He drove slowly around the block.

It was a perfect fall evening, calm and cool, but something still felt off.

His senses were screaming warning, yet he couldn't explain why.

Ana's return to Kansas City had his mind spinning, that was certain. But maybe it wasn't just the unease of the case. Maybe he was misreading everything—the charged moment in the hallway at headquarters, the heat between them at the pub.

Still...

It felt like things had been left unsaid.

His body definitely thought so.

The thought of tasting the soft skin at the nape of her neck crept into his mind. Of tangling his hand in her long hair as he pulled her close and claimed her mouth with a force that promised no regrets.

God.

The desire for her burned like a torch.

Other women had always been easy. Fun. Like Juliette the other night. He liked women who understood the rules—no strings, no expectations. He gave them everything physically, and he liked to believe they left satisfied, even happy, with the arrangement.

But Ana had never been like that.

She had always been a slow-burning fire inside him.

One he knew could burn everything down if he let it.

For two days now his body had been wound tight. The reminders started during the briefing with the team. As the officers reviewed the files on Ana's fame, catcalls and whistles had echoed through the conference room.

He had hated that.

If he didn't have a history with her—if she wasn't Aiden's ex—he knew he would have added her to the long list of possibilities without hesitation.

Instead he had shut the room down, ending the commentary about the photos of XAna dressed like an angel in the massive case files and redirecting the team back to what mattered.

Her protection.

Later, though, temptation had gotten the better of him.

He had gone through the files alone, memorizing the lingerie campaigns the brand had chosen for her, the lace framing her breasts, the delicate strings of swimsuits she had worn on beaches across the world.

Every image had tightened the tension coiled inside him.

He wanted her.

And if he didn't find release soon, focusing on the case was going to become impossible.

He needed to shut down this train of thought.

Ana was untouchable.

He could easily call one of the women in his phone, but the idea left a bitter taste in his mouth. Using another woman just to erase thoughts of Ana felt wrong.

This much internal debate was driving him crazy.

Never in his life had the thought of a woman kept him from finding company for the night.

Yet Ana sat in his mind like a barricade, cock-blocking every other option.

This shit was insane.

Before his Chevy completed the third pass around the block, his phone buzzed with two notifications.

One was a text from Patrick thanking him again for his quick response and attention to detail in helping Ana feel reassured.

The second was a voicemail from an unknown number.

He played it.

Ana's voice filled the truck, soft as a whisper.

"Jared, I got your number from Officer Sam. I just wanted to say thank you. I know you're doing everything you can to catch this person. I'm grateful. Truly."

The line stayed open for a moment, as if she wanted to say more.

Then he heard her quiet voice again.

"Goodnight, Jared. Be safe... please."

Headlights swept across his truck as another car passed.

It was the mayor's town car.

Jared hated the surge of relief that loosened something in his chest when he realized Patrick hadn't stayed the night.

He shouldn't care.

But he did.

The problem was, he cared far too much.

Instead of turning toward his loft, Jared steered north onto the expressway. Driving fast on the empty highway usually helped clear his head.

An hour later, when he finally reached his place, his mind was still tangled with thoughts he didn't want.

Ana's face.

Her quiet plea for his safety.

The way she looked at him when he tried to comfort her at the condo.

Patrick's hand on her waist.

Her body.

Aiden.

Every thought led somewhere he didn't want to go.

Earlier that night, when Patrick pulled her close, Jared had nearly punched his friend. Which was unfair—Patrick had mostly been comforting her after the awful news about the attack on the decoy and the murdered woman in Miami.

Patrick was a good man.

Friendly touches Jared could handle.

But that last one—his hand tightening at her waist, his words baiting Jared—that had pushed him dangerously close to losing control.

Patrick had made his intentions clear.

He wanted Ana.

And Jared?

Jared wanted to pull her against him, feel her body against his chest, and forget every reason he had to stay away.

But the moment he acted on that impulse, everything would unravel. Years of restraint since their one night together would disappear.

And that could not happen.

Besides, Patrick made more sense for her than Jared ever could.

Patrick was friends with Aiden—but not family. He didn't share the brotherly bond Jared did. Every lustful thought Jared had about Ana felt like a betrayal.

Patrick was free to pursue her.

Jared wasn't.

His irritation simmered.

Normally he was calm, sharp, controlled. Now he felt edgy, snapping at everyone—including her.

The truth was simple.

The woman who had haunted his dreams for years was now under his protection.

She wasn't a stranger.

She had been his friend.

They had shared one reckless night when he was a young rookie still dazzled by the world.

Now he was a seasoned officer with authority in Kansas City.

And she...

She wasn't the girl he had once known.

She was a glamorous supermodel and successful entrepreneur. Sexy, confident, playful, yet still as kind as ever.

Still completely off-limits.

And his body didn't care.

She had become a fantasy for millions.

But she had been his fantasy first.

Every magazine cover, every campaign photo over the years had only made the memory stronger.

The problem was she wasn't anonymous.

She was Aiden's ex.

And once—very briefly—she had been his.

At the pub every movement she made had sent heat through him. All he had wanted was to close the distance between them, remind her of those reckless hours they once shared, and see if that fire could still burn.

He needed release.

Memories of the previous night—tossed sheets, restless sleep, dreams of Ana riding him, her hair swaying wildly—followed him as he stormed through his loft.

If he didn't have time for a woman tonight, he at least needed rest.

But before that could happen, he needed to calm down.

Opening the frosted glass door of his oversized stone-tiled shower, he turned the knob fully to hot. Steam quickly filled the bathroom.

He pushed his jeans down his muscular thighs, his body still tense.

Normally he would carefully hang each piece of clothing, but tonight he simply stripped off his shirt and tossed it aside.

For a moment he paused in front of the mirror, already fogging with steam.

He studied the reflection staring back.

Older now. A few scars earned on the job. Not the young man he once was.

But women still noticed him.

His mind drifted back to the moment at the pub when he caught Ana watching him from the hallway behind the bar.

He was almost certain there had been desire in her eyes.

His fingers brushed the rough stubble along his jaw, the fine hair across his chest.

He wasn't vain, but he kept himself in shape.

That look she had given him...

No.

He wasn't imagining it.

His body responded instantly.

She liked what she saw.

He stepped into the steam, letting the water drench his gigantic frame while his mind filled with erotic images of Ana. Grabbing the shower gel, he lathered his body; the showerhead set to power pulse, hot water poured over his face, soothing him. Eyes closed, his hands gripped his cock as he imagined Ana standing under the water, the spray trickling down her skin, those cobalt eyes darkening as she watched him, her teeth gently biting her lip as she took him in her hand, cheeks flushed warm red from desire and the steam. Her eyes playful, watching him lose control as she stroked him slowly at first then speeding up, her breath matching her pulls on him. He could see her kneeling before him in the sudsy water, her head angled upward and the soft words, "May I?" slipped past her lips just as she took him in her mouth. Wet, soft, her tongue flicking the tip, teasing him, her body rocking, matching the rhythm of his cock as it moved in and out of her mouth. The release came so forcefully his other hand had to grip the showerhead above until the waves of pleasure subsided. Tension released, but not his desire for the one thing he could not have and could not forget.

Ana woke with the memories of the night before replaying in vivid detail.

Since arriving in town, she couldn't predict Jared's moods. When she first saw him, he had seemed cold, almost angry about being assigned to her protection. At the pub, when he caught her watching him from behind the bar, his expression had shifted—playful, teasing, but still intense. Then at her condo, after delivering the grim details about the latest tragedy tied to her stalker, he had turned thoughtful and kind.

He had her on an emotional roller coaster.

And then, on her front steps, everything shifted again. The moment Patrick's arm slid around her waist, Jared's mood darkened instantly. His joking comment about making every minute count had carried a sharp edge, the tone suggesting she and Patrick wanted time alone together.

The mixed signals left her breathless—and strangely aroused.

She didn't understand him.

Most women might fantasize about standing between two powerful, handsome men. Patrick was tall, lean, and commanding in his political confidence. Jared, on the other hand, was something entirely different—broad-shouldered and powerful, a man built like strength itself, with eyes capable of melting resolve.

She wasn't immune.

Listening to them circle each other in what felt suspiciously like a quiet contest over her had left her unsettled. Maybe it was the danger she was living under, the isolation of hiding away, but she couldn't deny how the protective attention stirred something inside her.

Patrick's concern felt steady and reassuring.

Jared's presence felt like danger.

The moment his eyes dropped to her lips the night before, she had forgotten how to breathe. The raw desire in his gaze had sent a shiver through her body, just like when his fingers lifted her chin and forced her to meet his eyes in the doorway.

It was no wonder she had fallen asleep replaying every moment.

Every look.

Every word.

Every touch.

Even this morning after a long night's sleep, her body ached to feel the passion his mood suggested. Her hand slid under the strap of her nightgown, finding her breast, squeezing, wishing it was Jared's broad hands and not hers.

Her neck arched, her eyes closed, imagining his lips on her neck, she let her hands roam under the satin gown, pulling it up. The chemistry was electric between them, even more than in the past. Before when they were younger she had thought him handsome, last night, those eyes brewed with dark, sexual intensity, an energy giving off hot flashes of electricity and she wanted to feel the shock of it.

Her fingers sought to ease the aching in her, finding her wetness, stroking, oh how she wanted him. Her body didn't care about the chaos her world was in, the dangers that were lurking; her body's needs were on the edge of a cliff begging for release. She wanted Jared Gables. She wanted a do-over.

Chapter 21

Funeral Planning

Tim awoke with renewed purpose.

His sleep had been restless, his mind replaying the image of Patrick touching his XAna in ways far too familiar. He should have been waking beside her, brushing a kiss across her lips before devouring her slowly for hours. Instead, another morning passed with him forced to wait.

Watching the recordings of XAna failing to stop Patrick's vulgar touch had left him in a foul mood. The contempt stirred a flood of ideas about how to hurt the stick-figure of a man who had once humiliated him as a teenager. XAna's inability to see the truth right in front of her was further proof of how persuasive a politician could be.

It was unfortunate that Kansas City would soon need a new mayor.

The thought filled him with delight.

Closing his eyes, Tim pictured the morning headlines—citizens sipping coffee as they read about the tragic demise of their beloved icon, bachelor number two. The public, like XAna, would be forced to accept the truth: their city's prince had been a sleaze, secretly making deals with drug lords.

His plan was poetic justice.

Tim disliked improvising, but this brief game of hide-and-seek required flexibility. The final pieces were not yet in place. His contact from Miami was arriving today—the last piece of the puzzle.

But first, he needed to be near his angel.

She would need him soon.

When he returned to his apartment the night before, he reviewed the security feed from the cameras he had planted around XAna's Plaza condo. The unwelcome visitor had stayed well past midnight, pretending concern while pawing at her like she belonged to him.

The way the mayor looked at her—eyes heavy with lust—made Tim's jaw tighten. Patrick's careful words of comfort were nothing but lies. Deception was a politician's trade.

Watching his childhood bully's hands on his angel had nearly broken his composure. His teeth ground together until he tasted blood. The metallic salt on his tongue sharpened his resolve.

Soon, the long-awaited revenge against the great mayor would begin.

Though Tim couldn't help thinking it was a shame Patrick's humiliation would occur in secret. Tim's own had been public—on a school campus, in front of everyone.

The mayor deserved the same.

Mockery.

Fear.

Public shame.

But making him a martyr would ruin everything. XAna had to see Patrick for what he truly was—a greedy bully who delighted in humiliating others.

Watching the recordings last night confirmed it. XAna remained blind to the truth, mistaking Patrick's pursuit for kindness.

She wasn't to blame.

She was innocent.

She couldn't yet see the predator beneath the polished smile.

But she would.

Soon she would understand what Patrick had created years ago with his cruel words—taunting him about smelling like skunk cabbage, calling him weasel-sized, humiliating him in front of the girl he admired.

Those insults had followed Tim every day since.

They had shaped him.

Hardened him.

Turned him into something far more dangerous than the frightened boy Patrick once mocked.

One day soon, XAna would see him clearly.

She would understand that Patrick had forged his own executioner.

Poor little rich boy.

Soon he would scream like the damned.

For now, though, his beauty needed him.

Tim retrieved another of his book safes before heading out for his morning walk. The design was ingenious—his favorite invention.

At a glance, it looked exactly like a classic novel. The cover was professionally bound, the edges mimicked real pages, and the size was identical to a hardcover book.

Hidden inside, however, were tools of necessity: a Walther P22 handgun, vials of sleeping serum, and others far more lethal.

Even XAna believed it was merely a book.

He loved that about her.

Her innocence.

Her ability to see goodness in others.

It was the same kindness she had shown years ago when she stepped between him and Patrick's cruel friends. She had seen a boy in pain and offered compassion without hesitation.

That moment had saved him.

What hurt most was how long it had taken her to recognize the man he had become.

He knew she loved him.

She had proven it in countless small ways over the years.

Once the obstacles were gone and she saw the results of his work, she would understand everything.

She would run into his arms.

Grateful.

Just as she had that first day.

One final choice—and she would choose him again, proving their destiny as man and woman.

But first, his mayoral reveal had to unfold perfectly.

Crystal meth clean.

Tim smiled to himself, pleased with the wordplay.

All those nights studying hacking would finally pay off.

There was still much to prepare before Patrick's suffering could begin.

But first, he needed to be near XAna.

It was time she learned the truth about the people she called friends.

Once she saw the light—

she would choose him.

CHAPTER 22

UNSETTLED RIVALRY

Patrick's booming voice echoed down the hallway before he even appeared in Jared's doorway.

The mayor greeted officers as he passed the connecting offices, loud enough for half the station to hear.

"Jared, are you listening?" Garrett asked through the phone.

Jared dragged his attention back to the call. Patrick's arrival was distracting him more than he liked to admit. Last night's awkwardness—and Pat's constant goading—were still getting under his skin.

"Yeah. Go on."

He set the phone on his desk and tapped speaker just as Patrick stepped into the office, Aj close behind him.

"Pat's here," Jared said. "Aj too."

"Good," Garrett replied. "That'll save time. I don't have long. The FBI office here in Miami is breathing down my neck to take over since this is such a high-profile case. Here's what we have so far."

The line crackled slightly.

"We're closing in on Dallas. Last eyewitness says he looks sick—eyes bloodshot, big bags under them. Clothes suggest he might still be wearing what he had on two days ago at the airport. Not typical behavior for a vain supermodel. Sounds like the stress of the chase—his for her, ours for him—is catching up to him. Shouldn't be long before we have him in custody."

A pause.

"How's our Ana?"

Jared grimaced slightly at the word *our*.

Patrick stepped forward. "Our Ana is doing well. The pub gathering helped. It made her feel more at home... safer."

"Good," Garrett said, relief and exhaustion mixing in his voice. "Because I wish I could say we're closer to solving this, but the scent's gone cold. Other than the Dallas connection, the last twenty-four hours have given us nothing. Both the FBI and my team are starting to think Dallas might be a distraction to the real killer. Too many threads lead away from him."

Jared leaned forward.

"Doesn't mean we're not still hunting him for the gala attack," Garrett continued. "But he's a lower priority now. The frustrating part is every time we think we've got something solid, it disappears. Parts of this feel deeply personal and angry... and then suddenly it goes cold, almost random. Experience tells me it's not over."

Another pause.

"Jared, have your guys noticed any movement since she arrived?"

"No," Jared replied. "Pretty uneventful. Maybe too quiet. She's only been here two days. Overnight detail reported nothing unusual. My guess? Either the killer doesn't really know her personally—which makes her being here smart—or he's on the move and we need to stay sharp. Pat's team is reinforcing our detail. Aj and Aiden are ready to step in at a moment's notice."

"Hey, Garrett," Aj cut in. "Aj here. You know we've got your back—and Ana's. Whoever this psycho is, he'll have to go through all of us first. We miss you, man. Come back and visit sometime."

Garrett chuckled faintly. "After we catch this lunatic, I might do that. Maybe even bring a friend. And Mayor—I appreciate the resources Kansas City's providing."

Patrick cleared his throat. "Happy to help, Garrett. But I do have to pull some of my security detail. I've got an unplanned meeting in St. Louis on Thursday. I'll try to keep it short, but it can't be helped."

Jared studied him.

Something flickered across the mayor's face—nervous, guarded.

It didn't fit.

After last night's display with Ana, it made no sense that Patrick would suddenly step away now.

Patrick continued talking about how Jared had everything handled and that his team would return within two or three days.

Jared glanced toward Aj leaning against the wall.

They exchanged a look.

Aj caught the strange frequency too.

Shuffling sounded on Garrett's end.

"I've got to run," Garrett said. "Agents from Miami just walked in. I'll keep in touch. If anything suggests the stalker's heading toward Kansas City, I'll let you know. I'm going back to the beginning—I feel like I missed something. Jared... take care of Ana."

The line went dead.

Two sets of raised eyebrows turned toward Jared.

"Nope," Jared said immediately. "I've got nothing."

He turned back to his desk, shutting down the unasked question hanging in the room.

Patrick checked his phone and slipped it back into his pocket.

"Well, I should get going. Lots to do. Jared, keep me updated. I'll have my phone on me at all times, though I may need to call back later. Cell service in the conference center is terrible."

Jared watched him carefully.

"So what's going on? I thought you were sticking to Ana like glue after last night. Something wrong?"

He thought his tone sounded only mildly accusatory.

Aj's raised brow said otherwise.

Patrick barely slowed his stride as he headed for the door.

"No, everything's fine. Just a complicated meeting. I'll have more information for the city when I get back. Aj, good seeing you. Jared."

He turned the corner without looking up from his phone.

Aj leaned back in his chair.

"Well... that was odd. Pat rarely flips on the formal *Mayor voice* with us."

Jared shrugged, turning back to his computer.

"So... anything you want to tell me about Garrett's little instruction? Why *you* in particular?" Aj asked, propping his boots on the desk.

Jared swiped them off. "Feet off my desk. And no—as I said, I've got nothing."

He kept his back to Aj, hoping his face wasn't giving him away.

"I think Garrett's just tired. Long hours make a man ramble."

Aj smirked. "Interesting. I never thought of you as clueless when it comes to women."

Still staring at the screen, Jared shrugged. "Maybe some pretty girl walked into Garrett's office and scrambled his brain. I'm sure it was nothing."

Aj chuckled.

"And now you're irritated and trying to run me off. Even more interesting."

He stood.

"Alright, keep your secrets. I'll figure it out eventually. I'm heading to Aiden's—grabbing dive gear from his garage. Let me know if you need another shift."

"Will do."

Aj disappeared down the hallway.

Jared leaned back in his chair, hands folded behind his head, staring at the ceiling.

Garrett's words replayed in his mind.

Take care of Ana.

Where the hell had that come from?

He had never—*not once*—hinted to anyone about what had happened between him and Ana.

Ever.

So why say it now? In front of Patrick and Aj?

Had Ana said something to Garrett?

Mentioned their one night together?

The thought made his brain spin.

Did she regret it?

Or worse—

did she remember it the same way he did?

Chapter 23

Sweet Reuniting

The Uber slowed in front of XAna's favorite Kansas City café.

He leaned forward. "Give me just a minute."

Four days apart was too long, and he wanted their reunion to start perfectly—with her favorite danish and a chai latte topped with whipped cream.

He could already picture how it would unfold.

First the smile.

Then the lecture.

Then the moment she would admit how much she had missed him.

The time had come for him to take his rightful place, and this ridiculous game of hide-and-seek had played out perfectly.

Being separated from his bride-to-be had been torture. He knew she must be missing the daily routines they shared. If it hadn't meant more waiting, Tim might have been grateful the idiots planned for him to stay behind. It would only make their reunion more tender.

He slid into the back of the Uber waiting at the curb, finally on his way to awaken his beauty from the nightmare of being without him.

His heart pounded at the thought of seeing her bright blue eyes light up with happiness at his surprise arrival.

Their last tender time together had been during the days after her father died. He had helped plan the funeral, staying late into the evenings when she begged him to linger after dinner. She would lean against him as they relaxed in front of the fire while rain tapped softly against the windows.

He had thought of taking things further then—but he waited, savoring the tenderness growing between them.

He had chosen to let her grief and need for comfort slowly melt them together into something inseparable.

Since their return to Lauderdale six months ago, XAna's business has been keeping her too busy to even have dinner out. He even complained about coffee dates, as she called them, seemed too much to ask for. That was when he began taunting her by sending the roses with crass notes of obsession, but he needed her to see him.

He needed her attention; he wanted her to focus on him. To see he was the perfect partner. He had only intended to drive her back into his arms and fully recognize that she needed him, but after Janice spoke with Garrett, the two of them, convinced she was in real danger, had pleaded with her to seek a professional team. Tim happily admitted he had taken the task very seriously; he wanted only the best for his queen, even her fears should only be of the scariest variety. Thinking the more fear the more she would lean on him again.

For the first few weeks, his plan to frighten her had worked. A team of so-called professionals was hired, and initially she came to him for a second opinion, which he loved. But then the private schedule meetings without including him began. Still not blaming her, but it pissed him off. She began trusting them more than she did him. Spending less and less time with him. So, more notes followed, hoping she would seek him out. She didn't. Mitch had made sure of that, and in doing so he had sealed his fate.

It was in the loving that he planned all his deeds for her. Even the finishing touches on his plans for the great Mayor were, in a way, out of love. His heart needed her to see the truly, radically evil human he was, to put once and for all a divide so great between them she never missed him once he was dead.

Using a sickeningly sweet tone, he repeated aloud Patrick's last words to her the night before: "Ana, beautiful girl, we are all here for you. You can trust Patrick." The ickiness stuck in his gut made Tim shiver.

Those same words had made him want to kill in that moment. The man was shameless. He was still the gamer he had always been around decent humans. Creating fake worlds like he did in virtual reality games, lies and deceptions made to give the feeling of kindness and warmth. Tim's anger amped again, and he needed to refocus. His hatred of the mayor was sometimes overpowering. The lust for revenge was intoxicating, and the mix of devious plans using his own IT company against him was the last detail that would make all Timmy's suffering worth it.

"What do you mean, Rodriquez? Who's where?" The call coming at 7:30am on his day off was unexpected. Jared was tired; it had been two days since he had last seen Ana. Nights of sleeplessness, waking from fitful dreams of scenarios that he wanted to play out in real time but still knew he shouldn't.

Officer Rodriquez stood in the open door of Ana's condo on Plaza Street staring down at the man in a white button up, black blazer and faux leather loafers then at his driver's license spoke into her phone, "Some man by the name of Tim Scott? I don't have him on the accepted list of visitors. Do I let him in? Who is he?"

Jared enjoyed Rodriquez, he smiled picturing Mr. Scott, Ana's driver who was not supposed to be in Kansas City and was definitely not on the list, being stared down at by the abnormally tall Latina who stood even an inch taller than him when in heels.

"Yes, I know him, but he's not on the list and not supposed to be in town. Have you asked him..." Jared stopped talking, hearing a female voice in the distance.

"Timmy? What are you doing here?" The voice had a name; Ana had come downstairs. Clearly, she was surprised by the arrival.

"Ummm boss, Ana's hugging the man now? Should I stop this reunion? Seems she knows him well?"

Hugging, fuck what kind of driver is arriving unannounced?

"No, I'll stop by early this afternoon and sort it out, get him on a temporary list and run the normal checks; no one stays without doing our due diligence." He hung up after Rodriquez affirmed his orders.

"Timmy, I thought you understood I wanted you to take some time off? What are you doing here?" Ana tried to control the concern in her voice.

"I was worried about you; I want to help, to be here for you during this time. You shouldn't be alone." Tim knew she wasn't alone but couldn't let on. She couldn't know the detailed care he took to protect her just yet, but soon.

"Timmy, I know you do and I'm so lucky to have you always in my corner, but I wanted you far away to keep you safe. I couldn't lose you like I have lost Mitch and Tomas. That would break my heart, don't you see?"

Tim's heart swelled. He turned with pride in his eyes to look at the officer standing still in the doorway. The eyes that narrowed as she looked between him and Ana showed surprise at Ana's declaration and didn't quite believe it. Timmy believed it, and soon everyone would hear her shout it from every facet of her mega world. This was his XAna and now that she had made it known, her secret heart's desire, to another person. Once again, defending his honor. His heart was full. All the past tiny dents to his pride forgiven. Her proclamation now and to come made every insult he had endured in the past months' worth it.

"Officer Rodriquez, I'm sorry for any confusion, but please put Timmy on whatever access list you have for the time that he is here. He is a cherished member of my world, and he is always welcome. We will go to the gym now to work out." The officer watched them walk off, perplexed by the dismissive tone. Her boss might be right. Maybe it was time to investigate this, Timmy.

"Is that I hope a Chai Latte and caramel apple Danish from Betsy's Internet Café?" she winked at him in a friendly manner, reaching for the proffered goodies, nodding at him to follow her down the hall.

"Let's go play." He loved the way she always viewed activities as playtime. A child at heart. His steps fell in line with hers down the halls to the private gym connected by an inner courtyard accessible only by code. He was with his everything again, and all felt right in the world, for now. So much more was to come; he was giddy with excitement but contained it to simple camaraderie.

Today, he would live on the beauty of being reunited with her again and savor the sweetness of how they knew each other so well, that all soon would know it was true

love, not mere friendship. He truly felt nothing could
spoil this day for him.

CHAPTER 24

MEETING MR. SCOTT

Jared had managed some much-needed gym time, a hot shower, more coffee, and a call from Rodriquez about their uninvited driver.

They had found nothing in the preliminary background check on Mr. Scott's license. Completely clean—which could be good... or very bad. No tickets. No warrants. His professional history was straightforward. He had started as a cab driver in Fort Lauderdale and Miami, later working privately for XAna through Lyft. When she landed her Angel contract, she hired him as her full-time executive driver after he completed the FBI Executive Driver course at Quantico.

That part surprised Jared.

According to Officer Rodriquez, Mr. Scott was on the puny side—tall, thin, almost weightless—with unsettling ice-blue eyes. Not exactly the type she pictured attending Quantico. But Pam believed every security professional should look big and sturdy.

Jared skimmed the report again. Nothing unusual. Plenty of drivers took the Quantico executive driving course to strengthen their résumés. Maybe it was Scott's underlying possessive tone that had triggered Rodriquez's instincts. Or maybe it was the lack of connections. No real family left except a cousin in California. Very little personal history.

Jared preferred backgrounds that were full—family ties, work history, even messy credit reports. When a file came up nearly blank, alarms rang in his head.

Something felt off.

But feelings could be wrong.

If he was honest, part of the disturbance might simply be jealousy. From what he could tell, Mr. Scott was the person Ana spent the most time with—and clearly he was more than just her driver.

Driving toward Ana's condo, Jared reminded himself to keep his ego in check and maintain distance. No surprises. No distractions.

No glances at her backside.

No flirting.

Just focus on the job.

When he arrived, Sam was outside relieving Rodriquez from her shift.

"Anything new?" Jared asked as he stepped out of the Tahoe.

"No, sir. Mr. Scott and Ana went to the workout room about an hour ago and haven't come back yet." She checked her phone as it buzzed with a text. "They must be pretty close. Ms. Montgomery scolded him a little for coming to KC."

She slid the phone back into her pocket.

"Eight years he's worked for her," she added. "That kind of loyalty suggests we can trust him... if she does."

"Maybe," Jared said. "But until this killer is behind bars, we assume nothing. Go home, Sam. I've got it from here."

"Happily," she said. "These light duties bore me. Night, Captain."

Jared watched Rodriquez's athletic stride disappear toward the parking garage. She was a damn good officer.

And he agreed with her—waiting and watching wasn't his strength either.

"Sam," Jared said to the other officer, handing him a sheet. "Latest update from Miami. I'm going inside. I want to meet Mr. Scott and get a feel for our newest guest."

"Sounds good," Sam said. "I'll walk the block while you're in there. Check the security gate in back and talk to the garage attendant about any unfamiliar vehicles."

"Perfect."

Jared climbed the stairs, his steps heavier than usual.

No drama today.

That was the goal.

He let himself into the condo's glamorous foyer and paused.

From the outside, the building looked like a standard Georgetown-style brick flat—nothing special. Inside, however, Ana's signature elegance was everywhere. An eight-foot gold-leaf mirror dominated the entryway. A crystal chandelier hung above the marble floor. A curved staircase swept upward toward the bedrooms.

All this splendor... in what she considered her *spare* home in Kansas City.

He wondered what the other properties looked like.

He'd seen glimpses in magazines, though the camera usually focused on the model in the room rather than the room itself. Still, he imagined more white furniture, gold accents, and sleek surfaces.

His place was the opposite—brick walls, wood floors, worn leather furniture.

The contrast made his chest ache.

Another reminder that he and Ana lived in completely different worlds.

He was Kansas City—rough around the edges, practical.

Ana was something else entirely. Ethereal. A fantasy.

It was Thursday afternoon. He was working.

And she was working out with her private driver.

Maybe they really were too different.

Laughter drifted down the hallway beyond the staircase.

Jared stopped.

It was Ana.

And if he guessed right, Mr. Scott was with her.

The sound carried genuine happiness as Ana playfully pleaded with him to return to Lauderdale.

Then they rounded the corner.

Jared's eyes immediately found Ana.

All of her.

She glowed from the workout, a towel draped over her arm. Her hair was pulled into a loose ponytail, damp strands clinging to her flushed cheeks. The bright coral leotard beneath her leggings clung perfectly to every curve.

His body reacted instantly.

Thankfully, his tactical slacks were loose enough today that he didn't need to adjust himself like a teenager.

Ana gasped when she saw him.

The sound cooled his reaction quickly.

Jared shifted his focus between her and the man beside her.

"Mr. Scott, I presume?" Jared said coolly. "What brings you to Kansas City?"

Ana immediately stepped in.

"Jared, this is Timmy. He came to help."

She glanced apologetically at Tim.

"I did ask him to stay in Fort Lauderdale," she admitted. "But he's here now, and he's welcome. I hope the security team will make him feel welcome as well."

Her eyes softened.

"He's very important to me. While he works as my driver, he's also a dear friend. He was there for me after I lost my father—more than anyone else."

Her tone was gentle but firm.

Not a request.

Jared understood.

Still, he wasn't lowering his guard.

Holding Ana's gaze, he addressed Tim.

"Welcome to Kansas City, Mr. Scott. How long will you be staying? We'll want to make sure you're safe as well."

Then his eyes locked onto the man standing beside her. Timmy returned the stare without flinching.

"For as long as Ana needs me," he said calmly. "I'm here to keep her safe from anyone with bad intentions."

"I want to go out!" Ana declared. "Patrick said I'm not a prisoner, so why can't I go out? If the great Captain won't take me, I'll convince Officer Sam. I think he's on duty today."

She was taunting him, but she was also tired of being scared. She wanted her life back—even if it was just for a few hours.

"Timmy's right," she continued. "Garrett practically conned me into coming to KC because he promised I wouldn't feel trapped. He said no one here knows Ana—the real Ana—not the exaggerated alter ego my agent created. This is Ana land, not XAna land... so why not?"

Even to herself she sounded childish.

Timmy nodded in agreement.

Jared slid him a sharp side-eye.

"For the biggest reason," Jared said coolly, "it's my Saturday off. Second, it's unnecessary. According to the duties assigned to your protection detail, unnecessary activities are strongly discouraged because they require... additional considerations."

"Considerations like what?" Ana's lip curved into a full pout.

Damn it if he didn't find that sexy too.

"Considerations like calling ahead to warn store managers that armed officers will be walking through their businesses. Like the risk of taking someone who looks like you into public where any Tom, Dick, or Mary might decide to ask for your number—or worse."

Her eyes lit with curiosity.

"Someone who looks like me?" she teased. "How exactly do I look, Captain?"

Was she flirting... or just being difficult?

"You know damn well what I meant," he snapped. "This isn't a game, Ana. Your safety isn't the only factor here. The officers protecting you, the citizens in those stores, the owners, the shoppers—it all has to be considered. In case you've forgotten, a twenty-year veteran was killed trying to protect you."

The light in her eyes dimmed.

His words were harsh, but she didn't think he meant to hurt her. Still, they made her feel selfish.

And she was tired of that accusation.

"No, damn you, I haven't forgotten," she shot back. "My heart breaks for his family—and for my doorman's. But I'm in Kansas City, not Miami. There's been no sign of my stalker or Dallas here. I'm not under lock and key, Captain. I just wanted to feel the air, the sunlight... some freedom."

She took a breath, forcing herself to calm down, and shook her head slightly toward Tim.

Jared watched the driver closely. Tim had looked ready to speak—maybe even defend her—but when Ana gave that small shake of her head, he stayed silent.

Still, anger simmered in the man's eyes.

Jared turned back to Ana.

He had never heard her curse before.

Now she looked... defeated.

"But I see your point," she said quietly. "You're right. I don't want to put anyone else in danger. I wasn't thinking about the bigger picture."

She swallowed.

"I'm sorry, Jared."

She refused to look at him as she turned toward the stairs.

"Okay—wait."

He hadn't meant to sound that harsh.

And she had a point. So far there had been no sign of anyone suspicious... except the driver she insisted on calling a friend.

"How many stores would it take for you to feel less like a prisoner?" he asked.

Her eyes lit up instantly, childlike excitement replacing the sadness.

"And before you get carried away," he added quickly, "by *how many* I mean which *one* store."

She rushed forward and kissed his cheek before he could react, blushing slightly as she did. Then she spun toward Timmy, giggling as she hugged him too.

Both men stood frozen as she dashed toward the stairs, tight leggings hugging every curve.

The imprint of her body still lingered against Jared's chest, his cheek tingling from the kiss.

From upstairs her voice echoed excitedly.

"Thank you! I promise we'll make it quick. I have wigs, glasses, hats—I can change at every store we visit! And we could take my dad's car. No one would recognize XAna in that because I'm always driven by Timmy. He's almost as famous as I am!"

Is he now?

Jared studied Mr. Scott carefully for a reaction.

Surprisingly, he saw nothing.

Just those icy, unreadable eyes staring back at him.

"So, Tim," Jared said calmly, "you're welcome to tag along—if you follow my orders."

He waited.

Tim's voice was cool. "No. I haven't unpacked yet and need to run a few errands. I'll see Ana later."

"Okay."

The man walked out without another word.

Strange.

Jared wondered if Tim had feelings for her. They certainly seemed close. Hell, Ana could drive any man mad with desire. Maybe the driver was jealous. It would explain why he'd shown up after she'd clearly told him to stay in Lauderdale.

The mention of Sam irritated him.

So the rookie had a fan now?

He told the officers he was taking Ana on a quick outing because it was his duty as captain.

But was it really duty... or was he keeping her to himself?

Jared glanced up the staircase.

Ana was still talking excitedly from her room.

"You'll see! I have ways to disguise myself—my features and everything!"

Her laughter floated down again—light, bright.

His Ana again.

Jared rolled his eyes and muttered toward the door.

"I doubt that."

Nothing could hide those curves.

Women and shopping.

He was doomed.

She wouldn't stop until she got out, and he'd make damn sure it was quick.

Before the door shut behind him, he heard another burst of laughter upstairs.

She might be happy.

But he sure as hell wasn't.

Jared headed toward the officers on duty to inform them of the outing.

This was a mistake.

A big one.

CHAPTER 25

SHOPPING DANGEROUSLY

Officers Sam and Rodriquez followed three cars back in the tail unit as Jared drove Ana's antique silvery-blue Mercedes-Benz Pagoda 230SL through the Plaza district.

He and all of Ana's friends had coveted the car back in college. Jerome Montgomery had restored it himself, slipping a souped-up V-8 under the hood and installing a muffler system that disguised the engine's real speed. The car looked like a pristine vintage classic—but it could move.

Jerome had given it to Ana as a Christmas gift when the restoration was complete. Since his passing, it had remained at her condo.

Jared tightened his grip on the wheel.

Jerome had been a good man. A great father to Ana. The kind of guy who treated her friends like they were his own kids. During football season you could find half their crew piled into his den watching games on the massive screen in his man cave.

Jared missed him.

Ana did too.

It was another reason Jared had forced himself to push past his anxiety about protecting her. He owed Jerome that much.

From the driver's seat he glanced over at Ana.

She was dressed head-to-toe in loose workout gear—thank God. When she'd come into the garage earlier she'd proudly announced she was disguised as a "Kansas City housewife running errands."

The Yankees cap sat low over her face. Her long hair had been pulled into a ponytail and braided. The over-sized sunglasses helped.

Still... the fitted tank underneath her sweats showed more cleavage than he was comfortable with.

Even disguised, she was unmistakably Ana.

Yet at the same time... she was almost a stranger now.

Funny how her leaving years ago to chase her dream had left a hole in their friend group. Now she was back home when she needed them most.

Jared tried to let go of the past.

They had known each other for years, but not in the deep, confessional way people imagined. They had grown up in the same orbit—friends, family almost—but they had never shared secrets or dreams. He hadn't even known she was leaving for modeling until she was already gone.

Most of them still felt that bond.

For Jared, though... it was more complicated.

Out of the corner of his eye he saw her smiling at something outside the window.

She looked lighter today. Younger somehow.

Not like the woman who had arrived dressed in black beside the mayor—tired, guarded, angry at being forced into hiding.

If a quick trip to the grocery store helped her breathe again, then it was worth it.

It wasn't helping him.

Being alone in a car with Ana had the opposite effect. Every time he looked at her he wanted her. That fact alone made focusing on the job harder.

Her lips.

Her eyes.

Her hands folded in her lap.

She consumed his thoughts.

Jared forced himself to stay alert, circling the Plaza blocks twice before parking. Anyone trying to track them would have lost the trail.

He had no proof the stalker was even in Kansas City, but he wasn't taking chances.

Ana hadn't questioned the extra turns. She simply trusted him.

This was the first time they'd truly been alone since she arrived.

It wasn't how he'd imagined it.

For years he'd wondered what it might feel like—just the two of them again. In his fantasies they were definitely naked.

Instead, they were driving to buy groceries while watching for a stalker.

Silence filled the car.

Neither of them mentioned the past.

And Jared sure as hell wasn't going to.

Focus.

He cleared his throat.

"Okay," he said, switching into command mode. "Here's the plan. I park two streets over from Baker's. The tail parks one block down. We stick with your disguise—with one change."

Ana turned toward him.

"We go in as a couple."

Her eyebrows shot up.

"For this trip," he continued, "I'm your Mister. You hold my arm when we walk. We act normal. Talk about groceries, complain about prices, whatever couples do. Relaxed but fast."

"So you and me," she said slowly, pulling off her sunglasses, "are a couple today?"

That smirk appeared again.

"Stop," he warned. "I'm serious. Do you want to go shopping or not?"

"Fine, Mr. Mister." She stuck her tongue out at him. "Hold your arm. Talk about fruits and vegetables. Blend in. Relaxed but fast. Did I miss anything?"

He should've been grateful she listened.

"One last thing," he said. "Today you're Joss. I'm still me. Talk to as few people as possible. Someone could get hurt if we draw attention."

He paused.

"And I'm paying. So try to keep it under a million."

Her giggles filled the car.

God, he loved that sound.

The florist shop was their first stop.

Ana immediately told the owner Jared never bought her flowers.

The woman shot him a glare. "Well we'll fix that today."

Ana laughed so hard her shoulders shook while he paid for a ridiculous bouquet.

The grocery store was worse.

She spent twenty minutes inspecting fruit like a sommelier while bending over every produce bin in the building.

Jared tried to focus on security.

Instead, his eyes kept drifting to the way her sweats hugged her backside.

Men noticed.

More than one adjusted himself.

Including Jared.

Finally they grabbed groceries and stopped for coffee.

Her order surprised him.

Mocha latte.

Whipped cream.

"What?" she asked when she caught him smiling.

He shrugged.

"Just surprised. Most women skip the whip."

"Oh really?" she said sweetly. "Do your women not enjoy whipped cream play?"

Jared nearly choked.

She poked his arm. "First tip, Captain—women adore being compared to other women you sleep with."

He froze.

"And second," she continued, licking whipped cream off the lid, "I'm not a model anymore. I run a cosmetics company for *real women.* Real women eat what they want."

She took another sip.

"So yes. I like whipped cream. And caramel. Some-times chocolate too."

Then she smiled wickedly.

"Black coffee seems a bit... boring."

Her sudden edge stopped him cold.

She stormed around the corner toward the street.

Jared followed in two long strides, ready to argue—

—and almost ran straight into her.

She had frozen.

The groceries slipped from her arms.

All the color drained from her face.

Jared looked past her.

White rose petals scattered beside the Pagoda.

At first he thought it was paint.

Then he saw the red.

Blood.

Rage detonated in his chest.

Fuck.

He had let himself get distracted.

"Eleven-ninety-nine. Corner of Tenth and Walnut," he barked into his radio. "All units respond."

Sam and Rodriquez's unmarked car screeched into view from the parking garage.

"Sam," Jared snapped, already grabbing Ana's shoulders. "Take her to the Mansion. Now. I'll stay for backup."

Ana hadn't moved.

She stared at the petals like stone.

Her day out—gone.

"Ana," Jared said sharply. "Look at me."

Nothing.

His voice hardened.

"No more condo. Sam's taking you to your father's house. It's safer."

Still nothing.

Fear twisted into fury.

"Ana, go with them. Now!"

She flinched.

Good.

Anger replaced the shock in her eyes.

Better angry than frozen.

Sam guided her toward the car.

Jared turned back to the roses.

Blood soaked into the pavement.

His jaw tightened.

Someone had come into his city.

And Jared intended to make them regret it.

Chapter 26

She's Mine

Two little words, covered in blood.

she's mine

"OUT shopping? What the hell? You needed a play-date? I want this bastard caught." Patrick's voice blasted through the speakerphone. Loud and clear. The mayor didn't just sound angry—he was furious. They all were. "That was too close of a call. Are we certain it isn't a copycat?"

Aiden and Aj stood with their arms folded, leaning against either side of the doorway to Jared's office. Both men shook their heads but didn't offer any defense.

Jared rubbed the back of his neck, closing his eyes and forcing himself to stay calm.

"I suppose it could be," he said slowly, "but my gut says it's him. The stalker's here. Which means he knows more about her than we thought."

"Then find the fucker and put him in county jail," Patrick snapped. "He can't be invisible with all the cameras around the Plaza. I'm out of pocket a few more days, but I'll check in. She's depending on you to keep her safe. Be ready with a full report when I do."

The line went silent.

Jared stared at the phone.

"Garrett, you still there?"

"Yeah," Garrett replied after a beat. "I need to break off and update Agent Sanders at the FBI field office, but I'll check back in."

The call ended.

"Well... okay then," Jared muttered, dropping the phone onto the desk. "I guess Mayor Patrick has spoken. As if we aren't already working on it."

His fist slammed against the desk with a heavy thud.

"Fuck. That piece of shit was close. I knew taking her shopping was a bad idea. Fuck."

He looked toward Aiden.

"What do you make of the note?"

Aiden pushed himself off the doorframe, sliding his hands into the pockets of his jeans.

"That note wasn't for Ana... or XAna," he said evenly. "It was for you. Whoever this prick is, he clearly doesn't want you anywhere near her."

Jared's lips tightened.

"I agree. What do you think, Aj?"

Aj shrugged, still leaning against the door.

"It was definitely meant for you," he said. "But the question is why. Does he target anyone close to her... or just you? Either way, this guy feels like a loose pedal on a bike with bald tires."

He shook his head.

"Makes him unpredictable. Which makes him lethal."

Jared exhaled slowly.

"Well, I'm glad we're all on the same page in this nightmare." He dragged a hand through his hair. "One of you go check on her at the mansion. I've got work to finish here, and I want to talk to Garrett about Mr. Scott. Something about that guy is rubbing me wrong."

He hesitated.

"I don't care that she likes him... I just can't figure out why."

"Really?" Aiden folded his arms again, a smirk creeping onto his face. "Interesting stuff, J. By the way—how was she when she got dropped her off at her dad's place? First time she's been back there since the funeral. Had to be rough, especially after a day like today."

Jared closed his eyes.

Damn.

In the chaos, he hadn't even thought about what returning to that house would mean to her.

He was screwed.

Aiden and Aj both noticed his silence.

In perfect unison they said, "What? Spill."

Jared shook his head.

"I didn't take her," he admitted. "Sam and Rodriquez did. I haven't seen or talked to her since."

He braced himself.

Aj stepped forward first.

"What the hell, Jared? Are you really this much of a prick?" Aj snapped. "She's terrified, and the one person she trusted to take her shopping lets someone else drive her to safety and doesn't even check on her? I don't get it. Something's been off with you lately. Everyone's been saying it."

He shook his head.

"I defended your stupid ass. Now I'm starting to wonder if they were right."

Jared didn't answer.

Aj wasn't wrong.

And the worst part was, if his friends started digging, they might figure out the truth—that he and Ana had unfinished business.

Aiden stepped forward, raising a hand toward his younger brother.

"Alright, Aj. That's enough."

Then he turned his attention back to Jared.

"But I'll tell you what we're not going to do," Aiden said calmly. "We're not going to check on Ana."

Jared blinked.

"You are."

Aiden pointed toward the door.

"You finish whatever work you've got here, then you get your ass over to her dad's place. She's alone there except for the shift officer. She needs to know she can trust you."

He paused.

"And you owe her one hell of an apology."

Aiden shook his head slowly.

"Good luck convincing her you're still her protector after today. But if the planets align… maybe—just maybe —she'll forgive you for being this damn thoughtless."

Jared leaned back in his chair.

He could only hope.

After Aiden and Aj left him in peace. Garrett called back. He explained that with this recent development; the FBI was now focusing on KC, and they wanted to schedule a meeting with him for the following week.

He told Garrett he was glad they were moving fast. Garrett agreed.

They spoke about Mr. Scott. Garrett didn't have a clear opinion of him either, though he said he found him usually agreeable. He said Tim was pretty bent out of shape when he was asked to stay behind.

Garrett said he had seen it as someone who cared for the long-term employer and wanted to do his job. The only thing he thought was a little strange was that he put so much emphasis on being her protector rather than driver.

Jared wasn't sure about anything anymore. He wasn't able to shake the frustration he felt with himself at dropping her in the hands of an unknown shift officer. Trey was a good man, but they hadn't formally introduced him because he was just filling in until Sam finished his reports. Sam was back on duty now and would be there when he arrived to make his apologies.

Lying around feeling frightened about what had happened that afternoon wouldn't change the truth. Once again she had tried to assert her independence—and it had blown up in her face.

Somehow he had found her.

Here.

In Kansas City.

Her hometown.

She grabbed her silk pillow and screamed the word *HOW?* into it.

To make matters worse, she had forced Jared to take her shopping. She had used his sense of duty against him. All for what?

She couldn't even decide who she was more angry with.

Herself—for being ridiculous, as if shopping were a necessity. Shopping wasn't a need for her. She had more than enough, and she knew it. Most days she was grateful for the life she'd built.

But having her freedom stripped away was eating at her.

At twenty-one she had left her father's home to find her own way in the world. She had traveled to foreign countries alone without fear.

Now she couldn't even walk into a grocery store without danger.

Maybe her anger was really aimed at Jared. He had been such an ass on the street. Comparing her—or any woman—to another had irritated her enough that she had stormed ahead without him, breaking the one rule he had given her: stay at his side.

He had a remarkable way of making her feel shallow and small because of the world she lived in.

What she hated even more was how badly she wanted him to desire her.

But how could he when she kept proving his point?

From an outsider's perspective, she had looked exactly like the spoiled woman he imagined. Her choices today had put everyone in danger.

Her chest tightened.

The thought of Jared getting hurt because of her made her stomach twist. No matter what had passed between them, she cared deeply for him. She wouldn't be able to live with herself if the stalker harmed any of her friends.

She had to keep herself centered during this strange imprisonment. Otherwise she would go stir-crazy inside a house that already made her miss her father terribly.

Especially now that this *fucking* criminal kept finding her no matter how hard she tried to hide.

A small smile crept onto her lips.

Her father would have scolded her for that language. He always said a potty mouth was never pretty on a lady.

She had argued with him about that more than once. Cuss words were everywhere—books, movies, music— and sometimes they were the perfect expression.

Language was expression, she'd told him.

But he would always smile and say, *"I'm not wrong, sweetheart. It's simply not ladylike, and your grandmother would want you to choose better words."*

Well, right now felt like the perfect moment to express herself however she pleased.

Still... maybe there were better ways to release her frustration.

She threw the blankets aside and jumped up, quickly making the bed.

She would cook.

Wasting the groceries she had bought wouldn't help anything, but at least she wouldn't feel like a wasteful human being.

She slipped into the new swimsuit she hadn't yet worn and pulled a bright red floral skirt over it. Still irritated, but improving, she decided she would cook spicy pasta with the ingredients she had bought with equal parts money and fear.

She'd heat the hot tub later.

Letting her hair fall free from the braid, she studied herself in the mirror. As she pulled the long strands forward over her shoulders, a memory surfaced.

Even while driving earlier, she had felt Jared watching her.

In the tight space of the car, alone for the first time in eight years, her body had hummed with electricity. She had controlled her breathing the way she did in Pilates—slow, measured inhales and exhales.

Neither of them had mentioned the past.

But she couldn't shake the feeling that he had wanted to.

They had slipped easily into that familiar rhythm—him bossy, her rebellious, teasing each other with words.

While she shopped, she had caught him watching her more than once. Every time she leaned over a bin of tomatoes or grapefruit searching for the ripest one, he would quickly turn his head when she looked back at him.

As if he didn't want to be caught staring.

The truth?

She had liked it.

She *wanted* him to look.

But on the walk back to the car his words had ruined the moment. They made her feel judged again, as if nothing she did could ever earn his approval.

He had even questioned her coffee order—and then compared her to other women.

The image of him in bed with someone else had drained all the joy from her brief taste of freedom.

And then she had done the one thing she absolutely shouldn't have.

She had walked away from him.

The rule had been simple: stay at his side.

But no.

She had acted like a jealous woman and stormed ahead as if there wasn't a killer stalking her.

Seeing the roses had frozen her in place.

She still wasn't certain, but the red on those white petals hadn't looked like paint. Some spots were too dark, others too liquid.

Blood.

It had splattered across the passenger door of her father's car.

Every thought of freedom vanished, replaced by dread and a crushing sense of being hunted.

She felt judged from every direction.

By Jared.

By the stalker.

By the entire situation closing in on her.

To her, those roses looked like an act of hatred—not love.

She stormed into the kitchen.

If she was going to reclaim her mood, she needed music.

Something loud.

Something sensual.

Something that would move her body enough to quiet the chaos in her mind.

She cranked the music and began pulling pots from cabinets and utensils from drawers, slamming each one shut as if the noise might silence her thoughts.

But two questions refused to leave.

She closed her eyes and let the music take over, swaying to the rhythm.

Yet with every movement, her mind drifted back to them.

Why doesn't Jared see her?

And why does her stalker hate her?

Why?

Chapter 27

Truce

The scent of Italian cooking filled the air as Jared moved quietly through the house.

For a home under protection from a stalker who had already killed trying to reach her, the place looked nothing like he expected. Lively salsa music pulsed through the rooms at a volume better suited for a party than a threat. Ana hadn't even noticed him enter—something that spoke volumes about how seriously she was taking the danger.

Anger flared.

He had been heavily pushed into taking this assignment, and a protectee who didn't respect the effort his team was making to keep her alive rubbed him the wrong way. For a moment he considered turning around and walking out.

Let her find someone else.

His steps grew heavier, deliberate stomps echoing down the hallway as if daring her to hear his irritation.

But deep down he knew he wouldn't leave.

This was Ana.

Whatever had happened—or hadn't happened—between them in the past, his conscience wouldn't allow him to walk away after what had happened earlier that afternoon. He would make sure she was safe tonight. Then he'd go home, watch a game... maybe call Tory again.

He could use the distraction.

Turning the corner, he froze.

Then instinctively stepped back into the shadows.

Every reasonable thought vanished.

Every reckless instinct woke up.

Ana moved through the kitchen like sunlight brought to life—barefoot, tan curves swaying, long blonde hair flowing down her back as she twisted and spun with the rhythm of the music.

She turned his direction.

Jared stepped farther back, suddenly feeling like the stalker himself as he watched her. Any man alive would have done the same.

She was dancing like she believed she was completely alone.

The Ana who had arrived at headquarters days ago had been stiff and businesslike—hair pulled into a tight bun, sensible suit, dark glasses, designer bag clutched like armor. That woman had seemed determined to hide every ounce of her femininity.

This woman was the opposite.

Hair loose.

Skin glowing.

A red floral island skirt that dipped shorter in front and swayed behind her hips. Beneath it, a soft off-the-shoulder white bodysuit clung to every curve.

She wasn't the Ana he remembered from years ago either.

That girl had been thoughtful... a little shy about her beauty.

This woman was something else entirely.

A minx.

All business in public—but here, alone, she was pure sensuality. A femme fatale with no audience but the music itself.

He had forgotten the danger.

Forgotten his job.

Her movements were hypnotic. Each sway of her hips left him thirsty. Each turn showed him another glimpse of sun-kissed skin. When she lifted her arms and gathered her hair above her head, his eyes traced the curve of her back and the tempting shape of her hips beneath the skirt.

The bodysuit hugged her breasts.

The skirt floated around her thighs.

Her eyes were closed as she twirled again, lost in the rhythm.

Jared's body reacted instantly.

The music—something with a warm island beat—wrapped around her like it belonged to her. Everything

about the moment felt like Miami sunlight brought indoors: the music, the scent of garlic and tomatoes simmering, the glow of her skin even in early November.

She had aged beautifully.

Voluptuous where it mattered.

Perfect for his large hands.

The music sped up.

So did her movements.

A woman being hunted should have been more aware.

Damn her for making him furious with worry while
mesmerizing him at the same time.

He leaned against the doorway, fighting to remember why he was there. His brain screamed protector. His
body begged him to stay exactly where he was.

Just one more second.

Her fingertips drifted along her collarbone, grazing
the edge of her bodysuit. His pulse kicked hard as she
bent at the waist, tossing her hair forward before rising
again, golden strands cascading over her breasts.

It looked dangerously like seduction.

But she clearly believed she was alone.

Her hands wandered over her hips, tracing the lines
of her body in rhythm with the music. Fingers slipped up
to adjust the fabric across her chest, gathering the soft
curves together before releasing them again.

Jared forgot how to breathe.

He had never seen her like this.

Her hair spilled past her waist, brushing the small
curve of her backside as she swayed. The music carried
her movements, every step smooth and intoxicating.

He was hard as steel.

She bent again, this time gripping the hem of the skirt as she straightened, letting the fabric flare around her legs as she spun.

One more inch and he might have crossed the kitchen just to stop himself from watching.

Then she tossed her hair from her eyes.

And saw him.

She froze.

A burst of laughter escaped her as she covered her face with a curtain of hair before rushing to turn down the music.

"I didn't see you there."

"Good show," Jared said dryly, clapping once.

"Ha... thanks."

She turned back to the stove, lowering the music until it hummed softly in the background.

"I thought Officer McDade and Samuel were watching me tonight."

Samuel?

Jared's jaw tightened. She was already on a first-name basis with the newest detective? Samuel might find himself reassigned to washing squad cars.

"They are," Jared replied. "I stopped by to make sure the perimeter was secure. You should be able to sleep tonight. McDade and Samuel will stay on duty until seven. Then Jonathon and I take over."

"I see."

She stirred the pasta quietly without looking at him.

Was she avoiding him?

Had the roses shaken her more than she was letting on?

Whatever the reason, if she didn't want to see him, he'd make himself scarce.

"Okay," he said after a moment. "If you need anything, everyone's on speed dial. Your panic device will alert them instantly, but nothing's going to happen tonight, so—"

"Would you like to join me?"

The question stopped him.

His first thought: *I'd rather eat you.*

His body was already running on pure adrenaline.

"Ana," he said carefully, "you haven't even looked at me. And you expect me to believe you want me to stay for dinner?"

She turned then and stepped closer.

Those eyes nearly stole his breath.

"I'm sorry," she said softly. "I wasn't sure you wanted to talk to me. I keep remembering what you said at headquarters—that you thought I didn't want protection. You were wrong."

She bit her lip nervously.

"That's not it. I just hate that so many people are risking themselves because of me. People I care about. I hate all of this."

She hesitated.

"And I guess... I'm embarrassed about how we left things that day."

Embarrassed.

In all his years Jared had never heard a woman describe a night in his bed that way.

"Well," he muttered, "on that note I'll see myself out."

"No—wait. Jared, please."

Her voice softened.

"I made too much food. You might as well sit and eat with me. I can't finish it all."

She paused.

"I'd like to hear about your life."

Then, almost shyly—

"Let's call a truce... whatever this awkwardness is."

He told himself it was the smell of garlic and basil that made him stay.

Or the dance.

Definitely not the eyes.

"It does smell good," he admitted. "And the entertainment was top shelf."

She giggled.

God, he loved that sound.

"So we have a deal?" she asked, wrinkling her nose.

Jared was already lost.

"Deal."

Chapter 28

You're Next

DAMMIT! The big-ass oak tree and clinging vines were blocking most of the view into the kitchen. He looked over at the man lying unconscious and snickered. *"All muscle, no brain, should have looked behind you."*

Honestly, the man lying in the leaves should thank him; the rookie wouldn't have any memory of this.

He would have killed him simply from his name crossing the supple lips of his angel, but Sam, the younger officer, wasn't a threat. Mostly, he was just in the way for the moment.

On spec, he didn't mind violence, but he hated waste. Murder or mayhem should be artful in action, part of a story and have purpose. Each of the people he had chosen was part of his love story for his angel. Necessary deaths, not merely casual killings for fun's sake, though there were some that gave him a warm sense of satisfaction.

Each death had a special reason. He likened it to his favorite form of art, books. Every classic novel included a protagonist, a hero, a heroine, and an obstacle that they had to eliminate to achieve their happy ending.

And XAna and his story was still being written, but Sammy boy wasn't a character, so today he got to live with a mighty headache for interrupting his work.

Muffled conversation in the distance distracted his thoughts about what came next for the man lying prone in the leaves. He hated the country. Looking back towards the rear of Ana's inherited mansion, he saw her carrying out a tray of food and Captain Jared following with wine and beer.

Tim's jaw clenched, his teeth aching with a silent scream of impending disaster.

"Touch her, you filthy bastard, and you're the next one dead."

No man from XAna's past made his blood boil more; only he knew that his precious angel had once been intimate with the *pig*. Only Tim knew how many times the mighty captain had attempted to contact her after their night.

In his opinion, the man wasn't fit to wear a badge; he was a coward. He gave up after only five phone calls and ten text messages. He hadn't even tried to contact her when her dad died last spring. Being overly arrogant, he had been the one leading the processional, which Timmy supposed was a little something, but XAna, his XAna deserved more than a petty gesture.

She deserved the world, the universe, and he was just the man to give it to her on a crystal platter covered in white O'Hara roses. Only the best for his queen of innocence. But the Captain, too muscular, though seriously he had seen bigger, and too stupid, had dropped the ball and lost her. Then he moved on to every redhead and brunette in the metro area.

He was worse than a coward; he was brawny trash. He deserved to die, and he would — but in good time. This setup was the best yet. He chuckled to himself about his brilliant conspiracy. Taking out his oldest revenge and landing it with a Pulitzer Prize, the Captain himself finishing the job, perfection.

It was utter genius, and after completing it, he would protect and cherish Ana. The closing chapter would be her full surrender to him, the hero, and to his vision of their perfect life.

Hearing Ana giggle from 50 yards back in the woods behind the house was almost too much. The sound taunted him; her laughter should be saved for him. His reserve of wrath this strong was usually for moments of killing, but tonight as he watched the lights dim, the sun setting, and the low hum of intimate conversation beginning between two friends reconnecting.

"Damn, damn, damn", Tim, feeling the blood rage in his veins with a need for reckoning, he kicked a large fallen limb out of his way. The crack of the dead wood sounded too loudly; he watched Jared's eyes search the forest for the source of the noise.

He could feel the eyes trying to penetrate the dense woods, but like a sign from the heavens, a deer crossed over into the backyard to graze. His own evil skills of planning couldn't have timed that better, but now the captain seemed more relaxed with his gaze now centered on Ana.

Fists tightened, his face turning scarlet to hold back a scream, he let out a whisper.

"Fuck it all to hell!"

CHAPTER 29
THE RULES

"Cheers to...?" Ana paused, lifting her glass. "To finally catching this evil person so all my friends are safe—and so we can both return to our normal lives."

Jared raised his beer and clinked glasses but stayed silent. She seemed eager to return to the life she'd built far away from friends and family. Another reminder that he didn't really know her at all.

He took a forkful of the carbonara she'd made. "Spicy. This is superb."

"Well, you caught me doing the two things that help me de-stress—cooking and dancing." She dabbed her mouth with her napkin and took a sip of her frozen drink. "When you had me dropped off so abruptly..."

He started to speak, but she lifted a hand to stop him.

"No, please don't apologize again. I understand. It was awful, but I get it—you needed to report about the roses and get me somewhere safe."

She hesitated, looking up at him with uncertain eyes.

That look was familiar.

This was the Ana he remembered.

"You see, I haven't been back here since the funeral," she continued softly. "Leaving was hard. I felt guilty for not coming home more often, even though Dad always said he understood. That didn't stop me from feeling like I'd let him down."

She glanced down at her glass.

"When I got back to Florida, I did what I always do—I worked. I had foundation projects waiting, so I asked the contractor overseeing the kitchen remodel here to handle the rest of the updates and get the house ready for selling. I just... haven't had the time to come back."

She paused, watching his face as if expecting judgment.

He had none.

She had built her own life, and Jerome had always been proud of her.

"Jerr talked about you constantly," Jared said. "Whenever we were over for games or chess, he bragged about your accomplishments—especially the work you do for women. He wasn't angry. He missed you, sure. A lot. But we all did."

Her eyes brightened instantly.

She was beautiful when she smiled.

Hell, she was always beautiful to him.

She blushed slightly—probably the wine.

"With my schedule so packed, I leaned on my staff for updates. My team is incredibly loyal and competent. I trust them completely. Timmy, for instance—he'd give his life for me."

Jared noted the certainty in her voice.

"They sent detailed progress reports on the house," she continued. "So I let them manage things while I focused on planning the gala. But when I flew back here, I made the choice not to stay at the house. I felt guilty about selling it. Timmy and I talked about it right after the funeral... maybe it was too soon."

"Gotcha." Jared finished his beer. "So you're selling the house? Makes sense—you've got three other homes."

She tilted her head.

"Actually four, if you count the condo on the Plaza. Remember?" she said with a small smile. "Timmy made a good point—this house deserves a family. Kids running through it. A life I can't give it right now."

Timmy certainly seemed to have influence.

More than just professional?

"I imagine letting go is tough," Jared said. "All those memories with your dad."

"Memories with a lot of people," she said quietly. "But yes... harder knowing Dad isn't sitting in his library reading some mystery novel or waiting to beat me at chess."

Her voice softened.

"I miss him terribly."

She finished the wine in her glass and gazed out toward the darkening woods.

Watching her, Jared realized how little time he had given her earlier—to pack, to prepare, to process being forced back into this house. His fear for her safety had overridden everything else.

He shifted the conversation.

"So how did the idea for EmpowrU start?"

She nodded slightly, recognizing his attempt to lighten the mood.

"Before I answer that," she said, rising from her chair, "let me grab you another beer. You can refill my drink while I clear the dishes."

He watched her walk away, unable to ignore the natural sway of her hips. Ana had always come alive when she talked about something she believed in.

He loved watching her eyes light up.

When she returned, she carried his third beer and two slices of cherry cheesecake topped with a dollop of cream.

"Do you really want to hear this?" she asked, searching his face.

He took the beer and the plate.

"Truce, remember? Tell me the story."

She smiled faintly.

"Well... it wasn't much of a leap from the goals I had for the cosmetics company. After making more money than I ever imagined—and meeting so many incredible people as a model—I started wondering what came next. I was far too young to retire, so cosmetics felt like the logical step."

She shrugged.

"But it wasn't enough. It was just the catalyst."

"As I traveled promoting the products, I kept meeting these amazing women. Hard-working, ambitious women who wanted the best the world could offer—but couldn't afford it."

Her voice grew stronger as she spoke.

"They were trying to go to school, raising children, supporting parents... all on salaries that barely kept them afloat. Listening to them day after day, hearing their dreams and exhaustion, it broke my heart."

She looked down at her hands.

"One day I realized I could do more than just make their skin glow."

"So I talked to Arthur—my attorney and an old friend —and he suggested creating a philanthropic foundation. Women could submit their stories, their goals, even business plans. The first thirty applications we received... each one was more powerful than the last."

She met Jared's gaze.

"I know holding the gala seemed reckless. But those women deserved recognition. Even if I underestimated how dangerous my situation had become, I still believe in what we're building."

Jared nodded slowly.

"It sounds worthwhile. I'm sure those thirty women —and their families—will appreciate the scholarships."

He paused.

"Was the old friend you mentioned Charla? The partner mentioned in the news reports?"

"Yes," Ana replied. "We modeled together in Europe for three years. She became my best friend. Starting the company together felt natural."

She sighed softly.

"But she could tell I wanted something more meaningful than just profits. She was the one who encouraged me to speak with Arthur."

She gave a small, bittersweet smile.

"It's funny. Charla also introduced me to Dallas. I never imagined she wanted him for herself... but I guess I saw what I wanted to see."

She glanced toward the woods again, as if wondering whether he thought her naïve.

When she looked back, his expression held only understanding.

"I'm sure ending both relationships was hard," he said. "But you survived the legal battle and the breakup. Now you've got your company and the scholarship program. Once we figure out who's behind this... you'll be able to focus on those again."

He hesitated.

"Has it ever crossed your mind that it could be one of them?"

"Charla is all bark and no bite," Ana said quietly. "Dallas... I used to think he was too weak to be violent. But the way he looked at the gala—angry, desperate—I don't know anymore."

She took another sip of wine.

Jared reached across the table, brushing his fingers lightly over her hand.

She startled, looking down at the contact.

Wow. She was wound tight.

"With luck," he said gently, "this will be over soon. But maybe we should hold off on public galas until we catch this bastard. Deal?"

"Deal."

Her smile returned, bright and warm.

Then she tipped back the last of her margarita like it was a shot of whiskey.

"So... I've always wondered something," she said, hiccupping and giggling. "Do you remember that sleepover when Aiden, Pat, you, Garrett, and Travis showed up and we played spin the bottle?"

Jared nearly laughed.

"Of course I remember. Why?"

"When the bottle landed on me during your spin, you kissed my cheek instead of my lips. All the other boys—including Aiden—kissed whoever they landed on. Even Patrick kissed me."

She tilted her head, studying him.

"How come?"

"I was being loyal to Aiden," he said.

Partially true.

The real truth was he wouldn't have stopped at one kiss.

"But Aiden still took his turns with the other girls," she pointed out. "And Patrick definitely didn't hold back."

Jared shrugged.

"Well... I'm not them."

She smiled softly.

"No, Jared. You never were."

Her eyes sparkled.

"I always admired that about you. You made everyone laugh—especially the girls. You were just as handsome as the others, but you never strutted."

She paused, grinning.

"Well... not until recently. *The Diamond of Kansas City.* Dad and I laughed so hard reading that article. It sounded like something straight out of Bridgerton."

Jared groaned.

"That photo shoot was a nightmare. Every woman in that article—and half the city—got the wrong idea. HQ didn't stop teasing me for weeks."

She giggled again.

"Oh poor Jared. Too many women, so little time."

"Alright, that's enough from you," he said, finishing his beer and pushing back his chair.

He was about to offer to help with the dishes when she cut him off.

CHAPTER 30

PLAYING WITH FIRE

"So, Captain, before you showed up, it was my intention to soak in the hot tub to unwind. Your officers are still guarding the house, right? So, you could take the evening off and join me? It would be safe, would it not?"

Safe for who? Her from a stalker, yes. From him? Not so much.

The last hour had him struggling to maintain control. He alternated between listening to her stories and fantasizing about her mouth while watching her wet her lips or lick cream from her fork. A hot tub and her? No, *not a good idea.* They had called a truce, but part of him would always be on the ready from honeyed memories of the past. They definitely did not need to tempt fate again. But damn, he was sorely tempted.

He told her he needed to go check in with the men, but clearly she was feeling the liquid courage because while she had asked, she hadn't bothered to wait for the answer. She started unknotting the sarong as she walked to the tub and turned on the jets. The knot undone, the skirt floated to the ground; he forgot to breathe. The top turned out to be a one-piece bathing suit, thong, *oh damn kill me now.*

"Ana, I'm still here." Thinking that the wine must have made her forget.

"Oh, trust me, I know you are." Her tone deeper now, more sultry.

Did she realize she was playing with him, or was it the wine? Was she flirting with him? He tried to force himself to turn the other way, but he couldn't. Every move was still mesmerizing him. She took the pins out of her hair, giving it a wild shake so that it all hung loose and fell to graze her glorious backside. Offering him a full view of her peachy perfection orbs. His dick hard as the barrel of his gun. He needed to get himself in check.

Her words cut through the air, a hint of daring that echoed and intensified everything he felt. Catching him staring, she asked, "Jared, surely a bachelor like you has seen a bathing suit before?"

She giggled, the alcohol had her teasing him, "Come on, the water is deliciously warm, I have a suit inside that was my dad's, might be loose but should be close to your size or you could go sans bathing trunks if you wish?"

"Ana, don't play with fire," Jared barely choked those words out when she bent over to add a solvent; scenting the water with aromatic bubbles.

The thong completely disappeared further into his dreamland as she did a deep bend over the water. With every rational thought vanishing, his hand moved naturally to his arousal, the intensity growing beyond reason's reach. Between the beers, her two glasses of wine, the night air, the thought of fucking her again and nibbling on those perfectly rounded peaches she was offering his bewildered eyes, he was in danger.

"I'm not playing with fire, Captain. It's water, remember? Come on, join me. You're not scared of little ole me, are you?"

At last, she stepped a foot into the water and climbed over the edge. Jared thought this would save his sanity, but then she eased in, the water rising and enveloping the creamy white suit. But instead it was his undoing; the water wetting the suit made it sheer enough to give him a tasty view of her areolas.

God, he wanted to suck on those nipples. He knew from personal experience that when she was relaxed; they were the size of sand dollars, but when she got excited they twisted into tight thimbles. His brain had only one track now, he wanted to know was, was it the cooling night air or arousal? He wanted to take a taste test, suck on them until she was begging for everything he desired. So much for his well-honed restraint; it was toast if he didn't leave soon.

His sensible mind reasoned out why he should stay and watch the show. Giving him excuses like her inebriation state and a hot tub; she could hurt herself. He couldn't leave her alone now. She was drunk. Someone should make sure she doesn't drown.

"No, I think I'll stay over here in the safe zone and watch." His voice was getting gruffer with arousal.

"OH, so you like to watch?" A bubble of laughter escaping followed by a tiny hiccup.

The bubbles in the water were mixing well with the third glass she was now consuming. She was feeling brave, but her heart raced at lightning speed at the idea of letting him watch her play. It seemed such a sensual suggestion; her body hot from the water and the feel of his eyes that had darkened while he watched.

"Is that how you play now that you are older, Captain? You watch your special ladies?"

Oh, damn, no sooner had the words left her mouth than she regretted them. She wasn't sure what she was prepared for tonight, but she knew she didn't want him thinking of any other woman.

Jared smirked. So when she gets tipsy, *the kitty comes out to play.* Again, another side to her he did not know, but this daring slightly lit from alcohol Ana, he might very much like to join. He would play with her *kitty,* make her purr in all the right ways. He rose from his chair and moved to lean against the brick of the home.

"My turn, are you sure you really want to hear my stories, Ana or do you want something else?" Fuck it, if she was gonna play, he'd play too or at least until she sobered up and changed back into the Ana all business like.

She blushed deeply; she had played with fire, and being the alpha he is, Jared's words were a challenge meant to shock and intimidate her into stopping game but she had a surprise for Mr. Manly, all sex and no commitment, she wasn't the frightened.

She was no longer the young woman he might remember from the past. In this very moment, with the help of bubbly and bubbles dancing, she was anything but afraid.

The past few weeks had taught her life was precious; not a minute could she spare in fear of going for what she wanted, and here was the man she had fantasized about for years. In the flesh, sitting calmly yet telling her with his eyes that he wanted to pounce like a feral panther. Each look screamed that he wanted to lick her up like a bowl of yummy cream. But he was holding back. She wanted a 'do over' damn him. A do-over that was long overdue.

"What if I wanted something, Jared?" her voice shaky but her words direct.

Jared strolled closer to the jacuzzi, grabbed a towel, "Come here."

Her mind raced, maybe the alcohol or maybe because she had pushed him too far. Maybe he was going to reject her this time; maybe he had regretted long ago.

The look in his eyes looked very stern as she rose from the water and came to the edge of the hot tub. He held out his hand and helped her til she was standing inches from him. He wrapped the towel around her arms, rubbing them dry. "So what is it you think you want?" His voice was like melted butter.

God, he was so beautiful in a rugged, intimidating way. Shoulders wide, arms roped with muscle, his giant neck meant for her mouth to kiss and suck on. Having him so near, she was losing her nerve.

"A do-over." Breathy she found the words. The drinks, the nearness of his powerful body, his scent, his masculinity — always so overwhelming, but in a good way. The words seemed like a child's words, and she felt silly but couldn't walk back from this now. She had dared.

"A do-over, huh? You sure that's what you want? With me?" He was playing with her now.

Being out of the water, the night air becoming chilly, she bit her lip and nodded.

He took hold of the towel, bringing her within breathing distance. "Look at me." A hand crept underneath her wet locks, pulling her closer to him.

"Tell me why you want a do-over." She couldn't tell his tone was heavier, sounding almost bored with the idea. Had she read him wrong, she just couldn't tell.

Perhaps he needed convincing. She thought she felt the heat of tension at dinner, but maybe it was wishful thinking. When she had caught him staring, he had played it cool, but she was certain she had seen him adjust when he thought she couldn't see him. Why was he playing it off as if he weren't interested?

"Tell me, Ana, convince me. Why do you want a do-over with me?" She looked up into his eyes. There were glints of laughter within them.

He was taunting her. Hell yeah, he was. He was playing it nonchalant, his ego hell, his body needed to be sure this was not a dream. That this was Ana asking him for a redo, a night in bed with him.

Seven years had gone by, and dozens of beautiful women had come willingly, knowingly, to his bed. Every brunette and redhead, all to forget one night with the blonde angel before him. Damn straight he wanted her answer; no, he needed her answer. Had she been thinking about it as much as he had for the past four days?

He had been taking matters into his own hands since she had arrived. Fantasizing about her lips, her scent, her hands, her ass. Tight bun and all, glasses making her look like a schoolteacher, he was the errant student, and he wanted punishment. But that was just fantasy. Tonight, tonight the very alive, very real bombshell was standing less than a foot away from him, asking him for a remake of years past. He damn well needed to know why!

She pulled back to let the light shine on her face. She wished she were as confident as the wine had made her seem. But now, his coolness made her worry he wouldn't like her answer. That he might reject her reasoning. But answer she would. All in or all out.

"Because I think we could do the memory better." Simple and to the point.

Jared searched her eyes to see if she was telling the truth. As a police officer for five years, an FBI-trained interrogator, and lead detective for three, he was skilled at detecting lies. Her answer was not coy; it was plainspoken. Her voice had wavered, but not out of deception but rather of desire; her brow creased, and the biting of the lip told him she was worried he might not believe her. But he did. Maybe he was mistaken — infinitesimal chance of that — but for the woman of his dreams, he would risk it.

She shifted, trying to appear more confident after her confession. Her mouth opened to speak, but he leaned closer to her and whispered.

"If you want a do-over, my rules." He pulled away from her ear, his grin that of a proverbial Cheshire cat knowing he was going to lick the milk saucer clean.

She was going to respond, but the look in his eyes took her by surprise. A curiosity shone in them as he searched her many features. When his hand came up to touch her face, his fingers made as if to hush her, but then his thumb stroked her bottom lip. She couldn't think. His eyes stared at her lips; her tongue darted instinctively at the touch wetting the tip of his finger. His eyes flamed with an intensity so delicious it made her tremble.

"Rule 1, First, Say Yes," his fingers pressed against her lips once more, "not yet, listen first then make your decision. Saying yes is crucial because once you do, there will be no going back. Say Yes and the Second Rule I will demand."

While his blue-gray eyes still sparked with playfulness and daring, his words were confusing. Did he want her to say yes, or was he trying to intimidate her into saying no? Was he being so cold in his rule requirement because he hoped she would be the deal breaker? So he didn't have to let her down because he didn't want her?

The alcohol and heat from the waters were clouding her thoughts, sending her into doubtful overthinking.

"Second rule: *if* you say YES tonight, you will give me your full surrender; you will be all mine. Mine to touch, to tease, to pleasure with my fingers, my lips, my tongue, my cock until you beg me to give you what you want with no promises, no regrets. Yes, from these succulent lips is the entry price to play.”

Ana looked down at the large hand holding the towel.

She knew what she wanted.

His two rules were a lot.

At first, she had felt them cold, but then she remembered his warmth, his kindness, the desire that flashed in his eyes, and all doubt left her mind.

She looked up, ready to answer, but he shifted away from her. “Go inside Ana, I will shut down the tub and douse the torches. You will catch a cold. Go shower off. I won’t leave until you are out of the shower.”

Chapter 31

Challenge Accepted

Jared knew he could be a cold bastard.

She had wanted to speak, but he shut her down. The way she had yanked the towel from his hands and stomped inside told him she thought so too.

Still, he had seen it—the flash of confusion in her eyes. The hesitation when she looked away after he laid out the rules.

It had been the right thing to do.

Tonight's game had gotten out of hand. He still wasn't over the last time.

They needed space. Time to think clearly. It was safer for both of them.

That sharp little tongue of hers had nearly been his undoing, but her hesitation had warned him to slow down. All the wine, the flirting—hell, after all this time he still wanted her.

Still caught in her spell.

He drained the last of his beer.

His gut tightened, his body throbbing with the effort of holding himself back.

What if he had just given her enough time to reconsider?

What if she changed her mind in the shower?

Fuck, thinking of her in the shower, *naked*, water pouring over her, down to the sweet valley between her thighs, what had he been thinking, playing it so cool? Acting like he could take it or leave it. He was certifiable. If she said yes, he couldn't leave it. No man would.

For Ana, his body would win out. Logic didn't have a chance when she was asking him to take her to bed and make a fresh memory.

Trying to restrain himself was becoming physically painful; his erection for the past hour wanted him to give in. He had to be insane, but his instinct was to self-protect.

Babs had been right the other night.

Ana was the reason for all the brunettes. All the redheads.

He snuffed out the tiki lights one by one until the patio fell into darkness, lit only by a distant streetlamp.

A rustle sounded from the trees.

Jared paused, looking east into the woods.

Probably Sam making his rounds.

Or just the deer coming back.

The thought lingered a moment longer than it should have.

Then he shook it off, gathering the remaining dishes and heading for the back door.

If Ana changed her mind, it would be for the best. He could go back to the life he knew.

The life he loved.

But as he reached for the handle, a quieter thought followed him inside.

Could he really?

Ana heard the back door close and shut off the water. The cooling sprays had been a quick remedy for the alcohol-induced boldness, but they weren't enough to chill the heat Jared stirred deep within her lady parts. The frigid water nipped at her special places, making her wish the icy bite was from his mouth. Her hand lifted to pull at her nipple, her head leaning back against the shower wall. Never had she felt this wanton.

Stepping out of the shower, Ana finished drying off, his dismissal still gnawing at her.

She needed answers.

A thousand questions chased each other through her mind. Had it been her hesitation? Her nerves? Was he truly a *take-it-or-leave-it* kind of man—or only that way with her?

At first his eyes had burned with eagerness. He had seemed almost thrilled by the idea.

Then, just as she was ready to say yes, he shut it down. Pushed her away.

Maybe the shy girl he remembered had disappointed him. With his reputation as a twenty-first-century Casanova, he was probably used to women far more confident than she had been that night.

Maybe her offer of a do-over hadn't tempted him at all.

The thought stung.

And yet...

The quiet intensity of his rules still echoed in her ears. The way he had made her meet his gaze when he explained them—especially that second rule—had left her nearly breathless.

Wanting more.

Far more than she should.

She wanted to know the man he had become.

Then his attitude changed.

The heat vanished, replaced by something cold. His tone turned sharp, almost parental—mocking her, ordering her inside like a child.

She stiffened.

At nearly twenty-nine, she was no child.

She was a woman. A woman who wanted this man.

So what if rule number two only promised one night? One night was exactly what she wanted.

One long, hot, unforgettable night in Jared's arms.

Rules be damned.

Closing her eyes, she lifted the towel he had handed her and pressed it to her face, breathing in the faint trace of his aftershave. The scent wrapped around her, warm and intoxicating, making her pulse quicken again.

Standing that close to him had nearly undone her.

For one wild second she had wanted to grab him and kiss him senseless.

Her eyes flew open.

This time they narrowed with a new focus.

Determination.

Tonight she would have him.

She would be his—and he would be hers.

No more kitten, Captain Jared.

Tonight you get the lioness.

Decision made, she reached into her dresser and pulled out a deep fiery red satin robe, sliding the silky fabric over her skin. There were no details beyond the softness of the material, no lace, no edging, simple.

Her confidence and determination growing; *I dare him to say no to me in this.* The perfect choice for seduction on both of their terms. He and his rules were in trouble if he thought she were going to shy away from an opportunity to feel him deep inside her one more time.

After all she had endured these past months—and the years spent dreaming of him—she had earned the right to give in. Tonight, she would be the woman of her own fantasies, the woman she knew she could be with the right man. With this man. Jared. Tonight she would be bold, playful, and undeniably sexy. And yes—his rules be damned—she would be a woman with desires and demands of her own.

Walking down the long hallway, she thought back to their one and only time. She had known very little about the world of intimacy, having only been with one man before, Aiden, Jared's cousin, and certainly hadn't been prepared for a night of sex. They had only been friends; she thought.

The first time was a quick and passionately clumsy act, but the sweetness of his gentleness with her made the memory stick. The way he had looked at her with awe at every kiss or touch had left a lasting impression.

She wanted to taste the man he had become since she left town; she wanted even more to show him the woman she was now.

The woman she was in this moment knew exactly what she wanted with no hesitation. A woman who wanted another night in his arms, a long, satisfying, memory-making night of playful temptation til their skin glowed with tantalizing sweat. She wanted a taste of everything, try new things in the arms of a man she couldn't forget.

His hot and cold manner had her thinking that even if he remembered their night, maybe it wasn't as she re-membered it. She had found his every move skilled and charmingly determined to give her pleasure rather than take his own.

Her daydreams always circled back to one thing—showing him just how well she could please a man. Most of that confidence came from the pages of erotic novels rather than experience. The three men before Jared had been little more than lessons. Aiden had been sweet but better suited as a friend; their spark had never truly lit. Dallas, her ex-fiancé, and one other had been disap-pointing enough to barely qualify as lovers.

None of them came close to Jared. In truth, she doubted anyone ever could. Not for her.

She gave herself one last look in the full-length mirror. Hair clipped up in a silver claw, she tugged a few loose ringlets free. Chin lifted, she studied her reflection, proud of her nerve. Tonight she would show this man of steel she could give as good as she got. After all, he was the one who had thrown down the gauntlet—take it or leave it.

Tonight, she was going to make it very hard for him to leave it.

Jared heard the light footsteps in the hall long before she appeared. He fought his first instinct—to pull her into his arms and smother her in kisses before she even had the chance to speak. Instead, he forced himself to stay still.

His ears tried to ignore the whisper of fabric brushing her skin with each slow sway of her hips. His eyes tried—and failed—not to linger on the wet ringlets clinging to her glowing skin. The red satin caught the dim wall sconces as she moved, flickering like a warning.

While she'd been in the shower, he'd spent the time reconsidering her offer. The smartest move—for both of them—was simple: tell her the house was secure, the perimeter locked down, cameras running perfectly, then leave as quickly as possible.

In his day job, red meant warning.

It meant stop.

But his body had already chosen go.

One of his heads was telling him to do the right thing, but the other only wanted to watch the deep dark red satin robe she wore with its tempting lush view of the deep valley between her pillowy breasts fall to the floor.

One long, wet ringlet was laying in the sweet spot between her breast; he wanted to trace its path with his fingers and then his tongue. Lick a trail to heaven. He was harder than steel for this woman. She came to a stop in front of him, the shadows of the room making it hard to read her expression, yet while she wasn't saying any-thing, the nightgown was a telling choice. It screamed, *take me off and fuck me.*

More than ever his engines revved, but her earlier hesitation had him in neutral. His sexual appetite was limitless for this woman. He was great in bed. That wasn't ego; it was experience talking. The women who had shared his evenings with he dedicated his skills to perfecting. To leave every woman who gifted him with their intimacy left satisfied. He never lied to any woman. He gave as good as he got and then some. A woman's sat-isfaction was a man's ecstasy, if he was doing it right.

Ana was not just any other woman. She's the one and only woman that had left him wanting more. *Scarred* was how his pals had mocked him with all the bachelor jokes; they mocked his perpetual singlehood. But who could blame him, she was the whole package.

His will power was hanging by a thread. His fingers ached to grab her around the waist and crush her to him, kiss her until she gave in. It was a yes or a no this time - he wouldn't accept anything less.

The first time had been built on assumptions. He'd fumbled it, never believing the girl he'd dreamed about would actually walk through his apartment door. Back then he'd been young, inexperienced, and obsessed with his career. Sex had been little more than a distraction. Ana had been the one temptation he hadn't had the strength to resist.

Even now, with her standing beside him in the fire's glow—the look in her eyes, the gown, her scent—he couldn't deny he wanted a do-over too.

Which was exactly why he needed her answer to be yes or no.

Years ago, the morning after, he found her gone. A week later, while hanging out with the gang at the pub, they told him she had left the next day on a plane to Florida, moved away. *Left the actual fucking state.*

At first, it made sense. She was ambitious, and a modeling career was a tremendous opportunity for a Midwest beauty, but after a while the unanswered texts, the unanswered phone calls had left him raw with insecurities. Leaving him asking questions that were still unanswered. Had he hurt her? Had she been disappointed in his bed? Had she been ashamed it happened, or had she still been in love with Aiden and he had overstepped? He had told himself that the calls were simply out of concern and not male ego, but the truth was hell yeah he had wanted to know if she regretted it.

Tonight, if she answered yes, he would make damn sure there were no regrets left behind, not for him and certainly not for her.

Ana took a step backward. This was it, her moment to make all her fantasies come true. Strong, beautiful Jared, desire in his eyes — she saw it now. He wanted her, but he was giving her a chance to say no. She knew that if she did, he would do the honorable thing and walk away.

It's just who he is, who he has always been. Kind and caring. Her eyes scanned the good guy before her, strong arms to hold a woman close, his towering height; both sexy and intimidating, jaw line chiseled like a roman statue, an intensity that could scorch a ladies panties off, yes, he was good man but he was also *deliciously hot*.

A yes to him meant giving her one more night if she were brave enough to accept his terms. Yes, never had a three-letter word seemed so important.

A yes was serious business. *Dangerous even.*

The time before there had been no words, just two bodies colliding in fast acrobatic movements, clothes falling, tongues lashing, hands grasping in a moment of heated desperation, and then it was over. They had lain there in silence, and then she had realized he had fallen asleep.

She left never saying goodbye to him, as she had the other friends in KC. Timing had killed that opportunity. She had hated herself for weeks, regretting leaving, saying nothing. Truth was, she was a little embarrassed, unsure if he had thought she had come to his apartment for sex or worse, that maybe he regretted it because she had been really inexperienced in bed.

Beautiful alpha males like Jared were rarely without beautiful female companionship, especially rookie cops fresh from the academy. Aiden and Aj had teased him about his many badge bunnies on their days off in front of her at parties. Often she felt the ugly twinge of jealousy; she hadn't even then known how she felt about him. His phone always in hand, lighting up with an offer of fun.

When she arrived in Miami, her little world of Kansas City had gotten swept away with the hustle of starting her modeling career in a new city. There had been no time to wonder all the what-ifs or maybes.

What scared her was that tonight, if she said yes, the same was possible. Never knowing what could be because they weren't offering anything beyond a one-night do-over. No dreams of tomorrow, no wishes to be fulfilled beyond the long hours of breathless anticipation of losing herself mind, body and maybe her heart in each other's arms. It was a passionate offering but also merely a physical answer to chemistry that was undeniable for them both.

Tonight was her chance. A rare moment to make up for all the nights she had secretly lain in bed stroking herself to the memory of his long athletic body pressed hard against hers, and all she had to do was take a deep breath and say the magic word. And damn if she was gonna let a night in his arms pass her by.

But first, his requirement of rules and her 'yes' implied he wasn't certain she truly wanted this moment to happen. Tonight, she would erase any doubt in his mind that she was a woman who wanted him; desired him with every fiber of her being.

The chaos of her world could wait on the other side of her locked doors; tonight she would shelter in his arms and forget everything else.

She could feel the heated tension in his body as she walked over to the fireplace, picked up the remote, pressed buttons that closed the curtains to the back patio and ignited the fire behind him.

Soft jazz music played, all the little details of her many fantasies of a moment with Jared were coming to life, and a part of her was coming to life as well. A part of her that deep down she believed only Jared could help her reach. She walked around him again. He let out a breath of — was it frustration or impatience; she didn't know, but she enjoyed making him wait. She smiled to herself.

"Ana, I will need you to say the word," his voice was tight.

Leaning over, the red satin of the gown drawing tight against her backside, she placed the remote on the coffee table, turned back towards him, and walked within two feet of him. Looking up into his eyes with more confidence than she had ever felt before with a man, she bit her lip before the simple word slipped out, "*Yes.*"

CHAPTER 32

SAY YES

Yes.

One tiny word.

The tables were turned. Blue eyes sparkled; happy but uncertain as she waited for him to find his words.

She was offering him the night of his dreams; any other female, a yes would have been nothing to him.

But Ana wasn't any other woman.

She wasn't a one-night stand.

She was a forever.

Jared stepped back, letting his eyes take in every inch of her. For the first time since that night long ago, he was truly seeing her.

It felt as if he had been asleep for days.

The Ana he remembered had been a kitten—wide-eyed and innocent. She had welcomed his kisses with shy eagerness, naturally affectionate as she embraced him and his awkward attempts to please her.

That softness was still there, glowing beneath her skin.

But the woman before him now carried something more.

Confidence. Fire. A quiet sensuality that hadn't existed back then.

Not because of experience—he would bet his badge no man had ever loved her the way she deserved—but because she had grown into herself.

The kitten was still there.

She had simply become a lioness.

She was still drop-dead gorgeous, but something about her tonight had shifted.

Maybe it was the satin clinging to curves fuller than he remembered. Maybe the sensual patience in the way she waited for him to make the first move. Maybe it was the daring glint in her eyes.

Something was different.

Then he saw it.

If he had blinked, he might have missed it.

She wet her lips.

Her pulse fluttered at her throat. Her breath slowed, careful and deliberate.

She was aroused.

She wanted him.

Not the wine. Not the moment.

Him.

Jared.

The realization shot through him, all the way to his toes, electrifying every nerve in his body.

She wasn't just offering a night.

She was choosing him.

Now the question was whether he would give in.

He had laid out the rules. One night. No promises.

But looking into her eyes, seeing the desire there—and knowing it was meant for him—could he really keep it to that?

The brave lioness before him deserved more than a few hours of passion. She deserved a lifetime with a man who could make her body sing.

Bathed in the orange glow of the fire, her body waiting for his touch, Jared realized something dangerous.

He wanted more than one night.

Hell, he wanted far more.

But he also knew he didn't deserve a woman like her.

She was crystal, and he was a mug.

She was city lights, and he was rambling back roads.

She served a world, and he served a city.

They were miles apart.

And the truth of that hurt more than he expected.

He should stop this now.

But he knew he wouldn't.

Even if he tried, he couldn't say no.

Ana shifted slightly, fidgeting. He had stalled too long. He had made her say the words, and now he was the one hesitating—second-guessing the moment, her answer, even his own selfishness for wanting a night of passion while danger still hunted her.

She should tell him to leave.

Instead, her hand drifted to the tie of her robe, holding it loosely closed.

For the third time that night, his breath caught at the playful confidence flashing through her.

Jared reached for her.

Her chest rose and fell with the quick rhythm of her heart, her lips parting softly at his touch. His fingers brushed her cheek, warm and smooth beneath his hand.

She looked up at him, eyes fixed only on his.

And in that moment Jared knew something dangerous.

If he wasn't already falling for this crazy, wonderful woman—

he soon would be.

"You want me?" he wet his lips. The sight took all words away. She could only nod.

"Show me" he studied her closely for any hesitation. "Take your hair down for me. Slowly."

Ana let go of the robe ties. Using her hands, she pulled the claw out and let the hair fall around her.

His fingers played with the ringlet that had caught his attention earlier, slowly twirling it. Her eyes widened as his hand slid to the strap on her shoulder, letting it slip free.

That was all the restraint he had left.

His arm wrapped around her, pulling her close. His other hand slid to the back of her neck, tangling in her hair as he drew her face to his.

His lips brushed hers first—soft, testing.

He wanted to savor her.

He sucked gently on her full bottom lip, but the taste of her only made him want more. His mouth crushed against hers as their tongues tangled, heat surging between them. He stroked her tongue with his, then pulled back just enough to nip her lip.

The connection was instant. Electric.

Years apart, and within seconds of touching her they were already burning.

Breathing rough, he broke the kiss and rested his forehead against hers.

"Come sit with me," he rasped.

Sit? Had he changed his mind, she wondered as he led them to the leather couch in front of the fire. He sat first. As she sat next to him, he maneuvered her around in front of him, his hands going back to the tie on the robe. A gentle pull and the robe parted slightly. She was wearing a lacy bra and panty set in shades of delicate pink, which showed off her Florida tan; her skin was flushed. His fingers traced the lines of the bra, his longest finger dipping beneath the fabric to tease her nipple; soon that taut nub would be in his mouth but not yet, if one night was all they had he was going to make it linger. He watched her eyes as his hand continued its path downward towards her navel. The slow tease had her eyes glowing, and her pulse had quickened. He loved it, loved the way simple petting made her light as bright as the fire in the room.

His finger lightly danced across the top of her panties. Her breath caught in hope he wouldn't stop there, but he did. He grabbed her hand and pulled her until she was straddling him, he used his arms to press her against his bulge. A soft moan escaped her lips as she tried to steady herself by placing her hands on his shoulders.

His fingers slid under her panty, grazing her clit, teasing his fingers stopped she watched as he brought his fingers up to his face, licking them it was pure raw desire she saw in his eyes when he said, "I've dreamed of this taste for so long. We skipped over the best parts last time, the fantasy does not compare."

"What if reality me isn't as great as the fantasy of the angel in the magazines?" Hating how nervous that statement made her sound, but the truth was Jared was the one man she wanted to be real with, to be fully the woman she was with the man she desired. What if he was like all the others and only wanted the magazine cover?

"Magazines?" The thought of how many other men must pursue her out of a physical-only rutting dog fantasy to stroke their egos rather than actually care about her and her satisfaction. Obviously, it had crossed her mind a lot if she were asking him now at a time like this.

"No, beautiful Ana", softening his touch to reassure her, "angel you is gorgeous to be sure, but the fantasy for me is of the woman you are today, knowing what I know intimately of the young woman long ago....that's the fantasy I've been spinning. The chance to know the woman you have become and all the ways you've learned to pleasure and be pleasured and to explore even more ways to make you cum. Seeing the many sides of this woman I've long desired flourish and offer herself to me, her body for me to discover each curve and crevice with my hands, my mouth, my cock until she's begging for more?

No, I want more than the angel on a magazine, I want you and your fully ripe body as I see you now, your tits that have blossomed in to full handfuls and your ass that makes my tongue jealous of that thong you are wearing now.

His words did more than relax her; they released her inhibitions; they made her instinctively grind on him.

His hands moved to the back of her hips, a grin lit his face up as he felt her silky skin. The glorious peaches he had witnessed at the hot tub were in his two hands, and squeeze he did. Relishing how luscious in size it was and so firm, "I love your ass. It fits perfectly in my hands." His large hands pressed her harder against his crotch. "Feel what you do to me."

Ana, could feel every inch of him beneath her, the small panties barely sheathing her within and she was already wet. "Yes, I feel all of you."

"Not yet you don't but soon my lioness, soon," he pulled her mouth to his taking her as fully with his tongue as he would with his cock, he dragged his lips to her ear, "take your hair down for me, slowly."

The words were so simple, but from him they seemed dangerous, erotic somehow. She wanted to please him, to pleasure him with words and movements. Like he was her, the man whose lap she sat fully on was not the inexperienced man she knew long ago, this man was lethal in the powers of seduction. She was no match for his experience, but in desire they were a matched pair.

She pushed herself back from him, letting him look his fill as she let the robe slip off her shoulders to lie around their legs, then she reached up and pulled a pin and the clip loosened, her blond locks tumbled down over her breast, the tips reaching the cleft of her ass. So full, so gorgeous, this woman before him was a goddess in his eyes. His goddess for the night.

His hands reached up and gathered her hair in his fist, letting the soft tendrils fall where they would come to lay on her luscious breast, he leaned forward to kiss the tops of their fullness, a sharp intake of breath escaped her, he grinned and took a nibble of the sweet flesh, the breath she had been holding released with a pang of a sigh, she reached up and pulled his head more fully to her, his lips began to devour her delicious globes, his hands reaching around behind her to release the clasp, then she shrugged and her breast were on full display, he sat back to take her all in, big beautiful mounds of glory his eyes took in, his hands again teasing them as he tweaked her nipples and watched her close her eyes, taking his advantage while she fully took in the moment, he lifted one glorious orb to his lips, taking in the nipple and sucking hard. Her eyes flashed open at the shock. "Oh, Jared," she whispered, "Yes, more please."

"Is that how you became so skilled?"

"Skilled at what exactly, Ana?"

He was teasing her mind and but he couldn't help himself, he loved the way her body flushed the most gorgeous heated pink when she was baited. He leaned down and took her nipple in his mouth.

"You know damn you." Giving him a lighthearted shove, she couldn't concentrate when his tongue was doing amazing things to her body.

"Oh, this, Ana?" Taking her whole nipple in his mouth, his tongue swirled deliciously. His arrogance was unreal, but if she were honest, it was also a big part of what she loved about him.

"Yesss," she hissed as his teeth grazed her nipple. "Yes!" Pulling his face from her breast so she could think.

His facial expression became serious. His hand tipped her face up so he could see her reaction, "Your body."

"Excuse me what, my body what?"

He shifted his weight, adjusting his length against her tender opening. "Your body tells me what it wants. Like now, you're wet for me, your skin is flaming, its magic the way every little move I make, your body sparks the most sweet rupture of fireworks, and knowing it's my touch that is causing it is a very big turn on." His hips pushed at her entry, making her back arch, giving him more access to lean down and lick the tender flesh of her throat.

His scruffy face made its way to her magical spot just below her ear lobe underneath her hair, his lips pressing deep wet kisses, his rough tongue licking her to a wildness on the secret spot no one knew but him, she was losing herself, but damn he knew just how to make her purr. She needed more, wanted more of him deep within her, her hand reached between them, spreading her legs wider to center him, she wiggled her hips, trying to get his tip inside but he stopped her, grabbing her hair gently but enough she was forced to meet his gaze.

"What do you want, Ana?"

She knew what he wanted to hear, but this was dangerous. The passion between them was already undeniably the hottest thing she had ever experienced, but now it was becoming intensely emotional. Of course not on his part, but giving him what he wanted to hear, she wasn't sure how she was going to come out of this one night in his bed without being scorched. She was falling for him not just from one night in bed or rather two, this was a man she had known since they were teens. He had been a dear friend for so long before anything physical had ever happened, he had always made her laugh with his sharp witty sarcasm or comic impressions, he was a good man who loved his community who served his family and friends as if it were his duty, and his lovemaking was on a scale out of the realm. Yes, she could love Jared for all of these things...she knew now that he wanted her but tonight it was as if he needed her and only her.

Needed her soul to be his just for this night, this moment, and the look in his eyes, the feel of his hard body grinding against her wetness as he waited for her answer, she couldn't deny it, so why try. Just for tonight, she told herself, she could give them both what they need.

She tilted his chin up at her, "You, Jared, I want you and everything you are. Say yes to me."

Beyond a deep low groan, Jared's only answer was to slide his shaft fully deep inside her, lips crushing hers, and what she thought was a soft yes slipping past his lips.

When they finally lay exhausted but fully satisfied, it was peaceful. The quiet sounds of their breathing slowing down to a restful state, he rolled on his side. Her body was still backed up to his, and she was nearing sleep. He needed to use this time to dress but he lingered a minute watching her so still, so beautiful. He picked up a long lock of her hair, brought it closer to his face and took in her scent, he wanted to bottle it just for him. The fantastical thought stung him back to reality. The night was over, morning would soon be here and a change of shifts would be here soon. He needed to gather his clothes and leave her bedroom before he was found and the spell broke like a cold bucket of water.

Quietly, he eased his feet to the floor, pulling on his jeans, his tshirt that was on the floor, the sight of her white lace panties next to it made him ache for more, but the clock on their magic ran out at sunrise. Walking around to her side of the bed, the clang of his belt woke her, "Shhh, sleep beautiful."

He turned but she grabbed his hand pulling, her eyes drowsy but her lips with a gentle loving smile, she said "So I guess we are now how you say *finished business*";

Placing his fingers to her lips, kissing her forehead, he whispered, "Hush now, get some sleep."

Her hand slipped out of his and she laid her head down still smiling, still hauntingly beautiful. He stared a moment more committing the vision to memory.

As he got to the door, his heart knew for him, they would never be finished business, the door closed with a quiet click like an exclamation point.

CHAPTER 33
WAKE UP CALL

"**F**uck!" A low but crisp whistle pierced the silence of Ana's living room. Jared didn't even turn towards the sound. He knew it too well..

"WOWser, what happen Cap, you fall in lurve?" Kate snickered, knowing her boss's affliction with the real word, love.

"Shut up," Jared grimaced. Kate knew him *too* well. "Were you smart enough to bring a cup of coffee to go with that sass?"

A chuckle slipped out. "No, sir, but there's a fancy Keurig in the kitchen." She picked up the pace and followed the crank out front.

"Good to see you working for a change. Didn't think you were going to make the rotation?" Jared liked Kate, his first ever female former partner, and he shared the same level of snarky comebacks. It's what had made them fast friends and good workmates. Kate was more on the independent side; she chose not to socialize with the officers, much preferring to keep it all business. She would make a good captain one day. Still walking towards the kitchen, knowing she was close on his heels. It wasn't ever easy to get her to drop a bone when she smelled a good story.

"Wanna talk about it?" Two feet behind, Kate matched his stomping pace. She knew he was gonna be an unfocused nightmare today if he didn't get whatever was causing the massive frown off his chest. She pressed forward. "This is the one, right? The only girl who had a chance? The reason you choose only brunettes and redheads?"

Kate understood she was pushing his boundaries, but something was stirring below the surface, and she wanted to help. It was time he stopped denying that his bachelor status was really a way of self-preservation. Macho bullshit covering his insecurities.

Jared abruptly halted, saying, "Stop." He turned on the tall officer, his eyes squinting. His mood, like that of a cornered animal, gave away how serious the problem was to Kate.

Double wow! This must be the real deal. Taking a step back, she raised her arms in mock surrender. She shook her head; the topic dropped.

"Any updates from Miami? Anything from Garrett?" Jared needed a change of topic, but the questions were only a brief pause. He would have to sort out later what he was feeling. Right now, he needed the team to do their job. He also needed the coffee to do its job; provide a steaming caffeinated jolt out of the fantasy land that his mind and body wanted to remain in.

"Nothing you don't have in a thousand texts from Garrett, but CNN has updated reporting that Dallas is missing. Ana's ex-business partner isn't missing a beat; she's all over the news trying to remove any connection to him and her; declaring she hasn't heard from him. Not sure I believe her; she's slimy. I guess fame will get you followed and friended by all kinds of trouble."

Jared agreed but didn't want to linger on how many frenemies might be plotting against Ana.

"Check the parameters, silence and no news is not a good sign. This bastard didn't kill and then simply slink away. He sent us a message just yesterday; he's here, and he wants us to know it. I'm sick of playing his game. Send a text to the team to meet here in 45 minutes. We need to change tactics; this is taking too long. We need to go on the offensive."

"Where's Sam? Did you send him out? I came inside thinking I might find him in the foyer, but he wasn't there. I checked the rest of the house, the last stop being Ana's bedroom."

The mention of her bedroom broke through Jared's focus, flashes of Ana's soft skin against his, her taste. Fuck, he needed to shift gears back to the missing murderer.

Kate waited as she watched mixed emotions flash across Jared's face. His mouth grim, she hid her worry as a good detective does.

"No, I didn't send him anywhere. Send out the order for everyone to assemble before you make the perimeter check. Perhaps Sam's back in the woods. It's a large acreage to cover. Radio if you need backup or don't find Sam."

Lieutenant **Morris** nodded before shutting the front door.

The room atmosphere was lighter, no one shining an inquisitive light on his unchecked emotions and erratic behavior. Walking down the hall to the enormous kitchen, Jared's shoulders relaxed, but his mind needed something stronger. Breakfast for the team would be a great distraction.

Sauntering over to the coffeepot, he spun the coffee pod holder around, his fingers landing on an orange-capped pod. It read Cinnamon Hazelnut. Less than a minute, the aroma filled the air, reminding him of Ana's lips, sweet with hints of spice. Damn, he was a goner. While he waited for the miracle in a pot to finish brewing, he determinedly turned himself towards the fridge, pulling eggs, bacon, and tomatoes out. This was a healthy distraction for his stomach growling and his mind. He knew his heart would remind him again as soon as she came out of the bedroom. As he grabbed his cup, thoughts of waking Ana up with a cup of java, knowing she was still naked, brought a secret smile to his lips. He was definitely ready to say *maybe* one day. Refocus Captain. *Geesh*.

The front door opened, Sam and Kate walked into the kitchen together, Sam holding the back of his head.

"What the hell happened to you?" Jared questioned, but his and Kate's looks were matched in concern. He stepped closer to look at the wound. Sam held in his hand a large rock with a small amount of blood on it. "What's with the rock?"

"I was gonna ask if you knew. One minute I was doing a fence check; the next, nothing. I woke up in a pile of leaves with my head against a rock. I had heard movement in the woods but didn't get very far on the search, and I remember nothing after. Ana out on the patio, and loud music was the last thing I remember seeing or hearing."

Jared's mind flashed the memory of hearing the deer coming out of the woods, but that wouldn't explain the big knot on the side of his head. Disgust with himself bubbled up inside him. He had been distracted again, and he was preoccupied. Damn, he wanted to punch something hard, but he needed to remain in command of the situation. "You get cleaned up, keep trying to remember any detail, it's possible you tripped, Kate and I will finish up breakfast for the team while we wait for the others to arrive.

The rookie detective left to wash the dried blood and dirt off his head, while Kate and he spoke quietly. He made her repeat everything again — the details of how she found Sam, the distance from the house, any signs around the area.

"Boss, you don't really think it was an accident, do you?"

Kate was intelligent, and she had a good intuition about his leadership style. She knew he was offering up options, but inside, no, he knew it wasn't an accident.

Both of them now laying out the food on the island buffet style, he said, "No, I don't, but until we have proof, we will roll with it's a possibility. For all concerned, especially Ana, we need to keep the panic to a minimum. But as of today, we are doubling down our efforts."

Kate just nodded as Sam walked back into the room. He'd let the young officer feed himself and then off to the hospital to get checked out. He seemed disoriented but okay. They would refrain from telling the rookie anything more until the doctor cleared him. The team would be here soon, and he would give them his new plan of attack.

Now, more than ever, Jared was ready to take this piece of shit out. Enough is enough.

"Do we all understand the new focus of our security details? No more waiting, he's here, in KC and we need to find him and put this case to bed." Jared wanted clarification from the team before Ana came out of her bedroom. He was pleased with the team's agreement that a more offense tactic was smart.

Sam chimed in between bites of his sixth biscuit with honey, "Sir, you said he? Is it certain now that we are definitely on the lookout for a male perpetrator?"

"Yes, Garrett and I agree, along with the FBI, believe with a 95% degree of certainty that the perp is a male. He believes he loves Ana/Xana; he believes she's already destined to be with him. Mitch was six foot four, but the angle of the shots at point-blank range suggests he is between six foot and six foot two. Combined with the possessive tone of the notes and the dead prostitute, we are convinced that this is a man *"in love"* with her. But Sam, no one is to know that we have ruled out the possibility that it could be a female. We want this creep to think we are still clueless; it will give us the advantage when we close in on his identity."

"Gotcha, 10-4, boss." Sam, being a newbie, still enjoyed using code speak. Assisting on cases like this would increase his maturity as an officer. Jared liked his eagerness, as the more senior officers could be cranky with babysitting assignments.

"Okay, everyone has their orders. I think I heard Ana's door open upstairs, so she should be down any minute. Let's keep it light and business as usual. Finish up and everyone return to their shifts. Watch for text updates."

Kate had shifted closer and turned away from the rest of those gathered, leaning towards him. *"Business as usual, huh?* Interesting. Good luck with that." She looked over her shoulder at him, winking in rebellion.

"Shut up, go do your job." Once again, his friend determined to psychoanalyze him and his love life.

The sun was peaking through Ana's bedroom curtains, heavenly scents of cinnamon coffee wafted with hints of bacon and waffles were the only thing giving Ana motivation to stop replaying last night in her head for the umpteenth time and ready herself to face the world that was noisily humming downstairs. Sitting before her vanity in her satin robe, she brushed the *'about last night'* tangles out of her hair; thoughts of Jared's hands in her long locks warmed her cheeks. The memory of how brazen Jared had made her feel and act, not really made her but more drawn out of her were sending tingly chills through her body. She should be shocked at the desire simmering between her legs again only hours after the man who had made her feel every inch the woman she had craved so long to be. She was a little sore from all the various positions they had played with last night. With no other man had she ever been inspired to be a little dangerous in intimacy. All other encounters had her being pursued, waiting for the man to take action, but Jared, he brought out this mouthwatering hunger in her like the scents of syrup and freshly squeezed orange juice were doing. Yup, he was that yummy in every way.

While her body hummed, her heart and mind were definitely on the confused spectrum. On the one hand, she had asked him for a do over and he had granted her wish. On the other, do-over sounded finite, as if there would not be a repeat performance, definitely not what she was prepared to accept.

She wasn't sure she could stay detached; his touch and his words had ignited more than passion, his tenderness had shown her that maybe there was a chance for something more. A connection like theirs shouldn't be wasted, but what if he didn't feel more for her than lust? She was walking a tightrope of confusion. Was he just doing his duty protecting her, or had what she felt long ago been more? Her heart was in limbo, her mind spun as she donned a pair of casual wide leg sweats, a white tank, put her hair up in a messy bun with just a few tendrils falling around her face, it was her *I'm happy and I don't care* look.

A rare view but today her looks were the last thing she was concerned about, what was more pressing as she listened to doors opening and closing and many footsteps downstairs, were concerns of the *walk of shame* awkwardness with Jared or possibly the rest of the officer's.

Staring at the mirror one last time, her cheeks rosy, her lips swollen from the tiny nips he had made over and again. Her hand came to her mouth, a smile, a glint in her eyes. Was he thinking about it too? Would they be able to tell by looking at her that she had been well-loved last night? If not love, she supposed maybe it was well-lusted?

With a confidence she hadn't felt in a very long time, she took long strides to the bedroom door, taking a deep breath and a shrug of her shoulders, *no time like now to find out.*

Sunlight beamed through the kitchen window, bringing warmth to the room. Ana looked around, seeing all but one face turned towards her with a smile of greeting.

A round of good mornings happened as she made her way to the coffee corner. She popped in her favorite pod, scooped two spoonfuls of sugar and a pour of creamer into the cup setting it on the drip tray. She reached for an orange before turning back to the officers in the room. Jared was still turned away from her, tapping away on his phone. Remember, he said one night.

"How did you sleep?" Kate smiled down at her. So, someone had figured it out. Maybe that's why he wasn't greeting her as the others had. She glanced at the instinctive officer in blue. Being a model, one would think Ana would be six feet tall, but she had lucked out; her height hadn't mattered as much as her measurements and hair. Kate, with a height of well over six feet, would have made a fabulous runway model. Dark burgundy hair that shined almost cherry red when the light hit it, high cheekbones, and the officer wasn't as buxom as Ana is now, she would have made it big. Hyper-focusing on the other woman's attributes gave her time to think of how to answer the cheeky question.

"Well, I slept very well, thank you for asking." Taking a sip of her coffee, she gave a quick glance toward the captain, who was keeping his eyes focused on a message on his phone. She directed her gaze back to the entire room. "Why is everyone here? I love a good brunch gathering but wasn't expecting one. Has something happened?"

The doorbell interrupted everyone's train of thought. Jared turned at the sound, his eyes drawn tightly together. Again, not expecting company, he sent Officer Rodriquez left to answer the door.

There stood Mr. Scott, another goodie bag in hand. What is the deal with this driver? So happy in the morning, does he not realize Ana is in danger?

Chapter 34

Misunderstood

"Good morning" Timmy stopped in the kitchen doorway, feigning surprise at seeing the large gathering. Surprise wasn't how he would describe how he was feeling right now, but the look on his face was practiced art.

His stomach still clenched from having watched far more of last night's camera feed than was comfortable. He had known before he arrived that the six officers had assembled to meet about Sam and a new plan. Ugh, they thought themselves so clever.

"Oh, should I come back later?" He looked over at Ana, who gave Jared a quick glance before answering. Another disappointment. How many black marks must he endure on his rose?

"Of course not; you are most welcome. Come. Fix yourself some coffee. What have you brought me?" See, his heart felt a temporary relief; she was still his XAna, always a gracious host. He made his way through the throng of uniformed and plainclothes officers. Carrying the box of fresh croissants, he could feel Jared's eyes on him.

The sight of the big twit made his teeth grind. His mind reeled with images of XAna offering herself to him. The bastard had taken advantage of her alcohol intake. He had no moral code. Knowing that after Jared played the starring role in the precious mayor's death scene was the only soothing to his soul. He nodded hello to the captain, who simply nodded.

Tim was savoring Ana's adoration of his gift of pastries with glee at the detectives' irritation. Not quite full satiation, but it was a start.

In disgust, Jared cleared his throat, turned full, leaned his back against the sink and announced, "Okay, I'll update Ana; let's move forward with our plan, Garrett's onboard. Sam, get that bump checked out before your next shift." The look on Ana's face said she wanted to ask, but then she thought better of interrupting. "Everyone check in before noon with details."

Collectively, you got it, went through the room. Footsteps, see ya's, and dishes clanking as the men and women dropped them in the sink. Ana was very impressed that there was no argument, no back talk from Jared. His team respected him and followed orders without hesitation. She watched him in admiration, finding the lingering looks between him and Timmy curious. *He couldn't be jealous, could he?*

She noticed Timmy seemed very intense this morning. It was clear he didn't like Jared, which she hoped would change once they got to know each other better. She wasn't used to the people in her life having this much angst, and she certainly didn't need more worries.

Once the officers had left, Jared crossed the kitchen. "Perhaps you would like to discuss this in private?"

Ana looked at him confused, "Why, I already explained to you, Timmy knows almost every detail of my life?" Holding up the plate of scones, "See he even knows my favorite scones, I can't see why he would need to leave the room?"

Tim hated the name Timmy. He controlled his angry bitch retort only because she had told the hulking idiot that he knew her every detail. Watching his newest target be forced to accept that she was determined to keep him here with her helped to put a momentary bandage on the repetitive injury to his lessor nickname she called him when flustered.

The reason she was flustered, though, only reminded him she had betrayed him last night.

He had waited outside until three in the morning, waiting for the captain to leave the house, but that never happened. He had watched as Jared seduced her in the living room, watching him paw at her, no finesse, no romancing before they disappeared into the only room in the house he didn't have cameras installed yet. She had let the slime's oversized hands touch her. He didn't want to blame her.

He blamed the invasion of the overgrown, blue-eyed dandelion daring to trespass in his garden.

Gas had been added to the flame of his fire-edged hatred, now burning uncontrollably for the captain. Staying awake plotting on how to make his death dishonorable was the only way he could stand to face the two of them.

They each seemed to have trouble looking one another in the eye, and the rare times he witnessed it, his XAna had turned a shade of royal red. His ears burned from the contempt he felt for this man, who was polluting what was his. Payment for such an offense was going to be at a very high and excruciating price. He would beg for the torture to stop, and so would XAna.

He didn't hold her responsible; Jared's visit was unexpected, and she was surprised. The bottle of wine in the trash cleared her of wrongdoing. She had been too inebriated to show good judgement. He was disappointed that she had let herself get so sloppy, but there it was in the trashcan plain to see. A gentleman would never have pursued a lady in distress. But he would teach him manners happily.

"Alright," Jared disliked the thin angry man standing too near Ana and the gleam in his eyes told him that Mr. Scott damn well knew it was getting to him, "First, we are investigating what or who might have put the large knot on the back of Sam's head. Last night while doing a perimeter check, it's possible that he tripped, but with a killer still at large, there is a possibility that it wasn't an accident, so we are erring on the side of caution." He paused, seeing a flash of concern in Ana's eyes, waiting to see if she wanted to inquire more about Sam.

Her countenance showing her resolve to hold her questions, he glanced at Tim. He found his gaze fixed on

Ana. Tightened lips and veins in his neck bulging from gritting his teeth spoke of unreleased rage, which piqued Jared's interest. He continued, "Second, Garrett and I agree that the appearance of the bloody roses yesterday in the alley is a significant sign that our killer knows about you more than we hoped. The only good thing is he's showing himself to be pathetically predictable. This will give us the upper hand. We can't say for sure if he knows of your father's mansion, only your condo on the Plaza; however, we are not taking any chances. We are going to go on the offensive. I won't go into too much detail only to say, we are going to have a few surprises of our own should he decide to show up here. We hope to find out more of what occurred in the woods last night with Sam, so I have ordered a forensic team that will be here within the hour to scour the woods for any signs that it wasn't an accident."

Jared stopped talking. He stepped closer to Ana, his movements making her eyes swing up to meet his, and her lips opened as she took a breath from the nearness of his body, he too, felt the intensity of being so close but he wanted her full attention, "Ana, I owe you an apology for last night. I regret that my distraction allowed for a breakdown in your protection. It won't happen again."

"But...", she stopped before she could form the words that would give more away than she wanted yet, especially in front of Timmy, "I see," she looked away from him, "I understand, thank you, I know you didn't mean for it to happen. I hope Sam is alright. I'm sorry too."

Jared hadn't expected her to apologize or to say she understood; it left him wondering if she really understood. It was his job to protect her, and he had allowed himself to get caught up in the fantasy of being with her one more time, of making her fully his, that he had let his team down. It was unacceptable, not making love to her, never had he felt such unbridled passion nor had he ever wanted to stay and find a woman awake in his arms or be the first to see her beautiful eyes open, or brush her lips with his to awaken desire again. Somehow, now he doubted his own words. Had he said them wrong?

He wanted to explain the meaning behind his apology, but a glance to the side reminded him that now wasn't the time. Tim stood beside her, smiling strangely at him with a queer grin.

He really did not get this guy.

Was he after Ana as more than an employer, or was the irritation he had shown earlier more about the woman she was and he wanted her for himself? Other than showing up unannounced, Jared had no reason to dislike the man, but somehow he did. There was still something about the way he appeared when he was least wanted that irked Jared.

"Okay, well I need to ask you to please stay around the house today. The scene investigators won't need interior access to the home but will wander the property outside and in the property's wooded acreage; they shouldn't bother you. Can I count on you not to venture out today?" he paused, giving Mr. Scott a look of determination, willing him to get that interference would come at a cost, "not with anyone?"

Ana looked over at Timmy, his eyes slivers of distrust. "Yes, I will be here working on some emails for the scholarship ladies. No going out today, I promise." His apology had turned her conversation style into the brisk, terse words like when she first arrived at Headquarters. Yup, she definitely had not understood, but he couldn't focus on that now; he would need to find a moment to clear the air later.

"Okay, well I need to file all this information at the station, so I'm going to leave now. I probably won't be back today, but text if you think of or need anything. Just no more shopping trips until we have caught this disgusting psycho." Before turning to go, Jared stopped and put his hand on Ana's shoulder. "We are going to find this creep; it's only a matter of time."

Chapter 35

No, For Now

Ana and Timmy stood in the kitchen watching the broad, masculine frame of Jared disappear down the hall. When the door shut behind him, Ana turned back slowly, confusion clouding her expression. Disappointment flickered in her eyes.

Tim was relieved to see the oaf gone. The sooner he had Ana alone, the better.

"So, angel," he said smoothly, stepping closer. "Lunch always relaxes you. Where should we go? The Fogo or would you prefer some of Kansas City's famous BBQ?"

He couldn't have cared less about the warnings Jared had just thrown around. The arrogant fool had even dared to touch her in front of him.

Tim could protect her.

He had chosen *Fogo de Chão* deliberately. The Brazil-
ian steakhouse existed in Kansas City, but it was also one
of their favorite places in Lauderdale. A quiet reminder
of the life she truly belonged to—the penthouse, the
ocean, the world far away from this small Midwest city.

For a moment, it worked.

Recognition sparked in Ana's eyes. A soft glint of
memory passed across her face as thoughts of the penthouse she loved drifted through her mind.

Tim watched it happen, pleased.

His smile widened with hope—something that unsettled Ana, especially after Jared's fierce warning that
danger was closing in.

Though she hated feeling trapped, she wouldn't en-
danger herself and her friend further, but she didn't
want to disappoint Timmy either; she had a bad feeling
about the madman, and Sam's being injured made her
sad. She needed to take the day to process her night with
Jared and his words.

She didn't want to go out and, honestly; she needed
some time alone.

"Timmy," she paused when she saw him flinch at his
name, "Sorry, Tim, we need to follow Jared's directions. I
can't afford to put anyone else in this maniac's eyeline.
What if he hurt you? How could I live with myself if anything happened to you or anyone else for that matter?
I'm just going to stay in and do some work, read a little,
and rest. I wish you would reconsider going somewhere
where it's safer. Truly."

She cares. There's that confirmation again, making
his heart sing, his blood pulsing through his veins like a

symphony at its crescendo point. That bastard from last night had no chance with his angel. He was her primary concern; she had just said so. It was a positive high watching her tender care of him; it only reinforced how much all the killing, the maiming he had done was mirrored in her actions. Her watching out for him, her defending him to Jared, her determination to let all her so-called friends know how important he was and nothing could come between them. These moments were what he had lived for until now, and the coming days would only bring them that much closer.

He put both of his hands on her shoulders, "No, don't you see, now you need me with you more than ever, with danger around every corner, I am the only one who can truly," he paused on her special word, truly was a word she used when her heart was sincere, a detail he adored about her, "know exactly what you most need at this time? I can't leave now, but I can run out and pick you up something for later? What do you say to dinner in, soup and salad from Fogo?"

Ana's expressions running the gamut from disappointment to endearing concern, he loved this beautiful woman and hated all the nonsense confusing her, but in the end Tim knew she would make all the right choices.

"I suppose dinner in would be a wise idea. Thank you for the suggestion. Soup from Fogo sounds delicious. I'll have a fire burning, and we can eat at the table in front of the windows while we watch it rain. Let's say 5ish? I want to get a lot of my correspondence completed and check in with Bryn and Janice, plus I need to get to bed early. I'm done in with all that's been going on."

Ana watched curiously for the long minute it took Timmy to respond. He looked perturbed, but she had gone along with his idea, so she couldn't figure out why he looked disappointed. She was certain she had seen a flash of disgust when his lips curled downward. She wondered if he could have guessed that Jared had spent the night? Had it upset him?

"Well, I could just order it in and stay with you all day. We can read and work in front of the fire if you wish. I don't have to leave your side for a minute. I can be her for as long as you want." Trying his best to hide his aggravation at being dismissed. Didn't she know how much she needed him? Did she really prefer that buffoon of a detective to him?

"Timmy, sorry, Tim, I know you mean well, I just need to concentrate. I have so very many things on my mind, and you would be a distraction in the best way. Please let me do my work this afternoon, and then I will focus all of my attention on you and our lovely dinner."

Timmy looked back at her. She was appeasing him; he knew besides he could use the time to take out some of this pent-up anger from last night's events on his new guest. Yes, this would give him plenty of time to get his own emotions vented out so that he could fulfill her every need tonight. The clock was counting down faster, and he was glad. His patience was at its end.

"For you anything, I will do some special work of my own and return with our meals and we can sit together like we did when your father passed away. It was raining then too. I'll bring us a bottle of Electra that you love.

How does that sound?" He smiled down at her, tipped her chin up to look at him; she seemed surprised at the touch.

It was an odd moment between them. Had Timmy developed a crush on her, she hoped he hadn't misinterpreted her care for him. She did care, but not in a man-woman way. She pressed his hand against her face for a blink of a second, then took it down and held it.

"Timmy, you are so very dear to me, I would love to share a bottle of Quady with you and talk of our long years of friendship. I can't wait. Thank you for being so understanding. I'm going to go change and then get to work. You can let yourself out. See you later." She squeezed his hand, let it go and walked down the hall.

Tim was once again irritated at the name Timmy. She clearly didn't know how deeply it upset him or why he hated it so, or she wouldn't use it. He knew she didn't mean it to sound degrading, but more maternal out of kindness, but he didn't want her maternal love; he wanted her all-consuming, lust-driven desire for him. Not a mommy love. He was her protector, not her his.

His hand still warm and tingly from her touch, he could still feel her face beneath his fingertips, so soft. An angry flicker of thought reminded him that Jared had touched his angel last night in more intimate ways. His fist hardened, he needed to punch something and fast. The liquid heat pouring through his veins was putting his plan at risk if he didn't get ahold of himself soon.

And he had just the way to relieve that itch. Dear, dear Patrick was awaiting his next visit. Now he had the time and the full desire to make something take away his pain. A brief trip to the woods was just what the doctor ordered to cure what ailed him this very day.

Tim opened the front door, stopping to turn and look at the stairs Ana had taken to her bedroom, a jolt in his manhood at the possibilities yet to come. *Soon, my angel,* as he closed the door behind him, *soon you will be mine and only mine.*

Chapter 36

Educating The Mayor

Patrick's lungs burned, his throat raw, but he forced out one last shout, hoping someone—any-one—might hear him.

Hours of struggling against the ropes had drained what little strength he had left. Anger simmered beneath the exhaustion. He still didn't know who had taken him or what they wanted. If it was ransom, they were wasting their time—he wouldn't give them a damn thing.

It had been hours since the man had come back.

Blindfolded, Patrick couldn't see the structure around him, but the air carried the heavy scent of raw wood. A cabin, maybe. Somewhere remote. No traffic. No voices. No sign of life outside the walls.

No food. No water.

It hurt to shout, but he did it anyway.

"You know people are looking for me!" he yelled hoarsely. "You won't get away with this!"

He froze.

Footsteps.

Slow. Just outside the room.

Patrick lowered his voice, instinctively listening as the door creaked open.

The silence from whoever stepped inside made his skin prickle. The shoes moved closer to the chair where he was bound. His clothes clung to him, soaked with sweat and blood from the first beating.

Patrick's mind raced.

Was the bastard moving slowly on purpose—stretching the moment, feeding on his fear?

"Hello? Who are you? What do you want?" Pat hated how scared he sounded, but no water in 12 hours would make anyone desperate. He was pretty sure he was drugged with something because his arm was hurting from some kind of wound.

"So.Many.Questions. Mayor." The voice was very close now. His mind in overdrive, the man, whoever he was, stood so near that he could smell his breath. "Let us see, as a gracious host, I should begin by answering your questions in order. First, you obviously forgot that you had an undisclosed meeting on your calendar. If memory serves, you didn't even tell the lovely Ginger how to reach you, shame she's been a full panic trying to reach you." Tim snickered. Condescended to the bastard that egged the bullies on that day in the schoolyard. He was relishing the evil. His intention to take his anger out on the poor little rich man was going to be more fun than he had originally thought.

Pat could almost taste the hatred in this man's words. He was enjoying Patrick's pain, reveling in it like it was some kind of game, but why did he hate him? Was it a business deal gone sour? Had he dated a woman who was married and not known?

The mention of Ginger made him seethe with hurt and anger at her. He had thought the meeting was on the up and up. A rare opportunity too sweet to pass up for the citizens of Kansas City, when he had been told that the deal must be handled in secret, he thought it strange but his ego pushed him to say yes. He aspired to be the best mayor KC had ever known. It was vain, but also it was because he wanted to make his grandfather, his only living relative, proud of him. He should have done more research, and he damn well should have told Ginger how to reach him. This son of a bitch must be using his cell phone to read his messages. Fuck, he wanted out of here.

"I believe you sent her a text yesterday saying you would check in with her within a week. So, the answer to your question of whether someone is looking for you is… hmmm, probably not." Evil laughter filled the small room. The dense air had to mean that it was very compact. No A/C.

Pat's shoulders slumped in defeat. Lack of even a sip of something was affecting his clarity of memory. In four years, he had never gone a week without talking to the woman who wasn't just the best damn executive assistant in the state but who had become an especially important part of his world. The redheaded vixen who could draw a man's attention and make them dance to her tune had long ago become his best friend. Knowing now that he might never get to tell her what she meant to him made his gut fill with regret.

"Did you drug me?" The words came out more like a whimper.

"Why no? You were already high when I found you, Mayor. You really shouldn't use recreational drugs when you are serving as mayor of a fine city like Kansas City. Tsk tsk tsk. Shameful, really."

So, he was right. The jackass had drugged him. The last thing Patrick remembered was getting into the back of a limo with....his head popped up.

"Timmy?" Thwack, the backhand had been unexpected. Patrick's head fell to the side, his cheek stinging, his lip bleeding, he tasted his own blood.

Whispered words near his ear surprised him, and he cringed away. "Never call me that again." His kidnapper pulled the blindfold off roughly, pulling hair as it went.

"My name is Tim," he said, his back turned as he walked towards the only light in the room. Seeming to check windows.

Patrick's eyes tried to acclimate to the darkness of the room. Only a kerosene lamp lit in the far corner of the tiny cabin. Now he knew he was at Jared's hunting cabin. How had Timmy found out about the cabin?

Pat looked down at his body, he smelled of dirt and sweat, the clothes he was wearing were that of a homeless man, second-hand clothes, shoes with holes in them no socks, he could see the needle marks in his left arm, red from infection. Blood stains down the front of the shirt.

Watching the mayor inspect his clothing, he couldn't help but tease in a high pitch tone. "Ah, what's the matter, Mr. Moneybags? You don't like your secondhand clothing?"

Tim began walking slowly in steps around him. Another thwack. Pat's head went forward violently. "I didn't either, you piece of dog waste. That's correct, isn't it? You called me dog waste when the other boys were kicking me in the nuts?"

Pat didn't move fast enough, too tired to pull his legs together to help limit the impact of Tim's boot to his crotch. He couldn't breathe. The pain made his eyes bulge.

"Why are you doing this? Is this because I bullied you or helped people bully you? Listen, that day when Ana...," Pat's words went silent as another unexpected blow was landed and his eye instantly swelled.

"Never speak her name again; you aren't worthy to say her precious name. And she is not Ana any longer, she's my XAna. This should silence you soon enough." Tim administered the last of the remaining vials he had used on Trina. She had come in handy even after she was gone.

Patrick's eye blurry and his arm tingling from the drug, he watched as the violent man paced slowly around him. He was insane. He clearly thought Ana was only XAna now, and somehow, he believed she was his.

"Okay, okay, I won't say her name, but the day when she protected you from us, I changed. I came back to apologize to you, but you were gone. I swear, man, I'm sorry."

The poor little mayor was terrified and begging him. Sweet, painful begging like he had done each time one of the other boys had followed Pat's orders. Tim was living high on every pathetic syllable that was coming out of this piece of filth's mouth. As if he would believe him. The boy grown into a man was well known for his slick business ways. He was just an older version of the teen that had tortured him so long ago. Nope, he wouldn't be buying what he was selling; it was too late. His fate was sealed many years ago.

Attempting to seduce his sweet angel was the nail in his proverbial but soon to be very real coffin.

"Your attempts at making me believe your pitiful lies have failed. I have to go again, back to my Ana's side." He watched Patrick's eyes light up in fear. The sad man pulled at his tie trying to free himself to attack him. Tim was almost humored with freeing the man from his bindings to see him in action. It would be fun to physically challenge the IT man who sits behind a desk all day. Show him he's not the little boy on the playground any longer. Almost tempted, but not quite.

"You leave Ana alone. She has done nothing to you. I did it. Hurt me, but leave her alone." Patrick's plea fell to a whisper as the drug and his weakness from nothing to eat overcame him.

"I would never hurt my angel; she and I are having dinner by the fire tonight." A tear ran down the mayor's cheek. "Don't worry, it won't be long now. Though I initially had a long drawn-out plan of torture for you, now I simply want XAna all to myself. Once I have the honorable Detective Gables in full pursuit of your criminal ways, both of you will meet your end together."

Tim came behind him, checking the zip ties at his wrists and ankles one last time.

"Scream all you like, it's five-plus miles to the nearest highway, and as gallant Jared owns 25 acres surrounding this place, there's not a soul in sight. But just so you don't wear yourself out too much, here's another taste of your favorite treat. That should keep you very chill for the next day or so."

Tim strode to the large wooden door, his footsteps heavy. "Tata for now, Mayor Patrick." His snickering could be heard for a full minute until a car started and drove off into the night.

Chapter 37

So Disappointing

Pulling up the long drive, Jared already knew what he would find. Rodriquez had sent a text with a pic of Mr. Scott's black town car in the drive. The lack of background information about the determined driver was making him second-guess his usually dead-on instincts. There was something missing. He was too invested in Ana as XAna. Like he wanted to erase her past existence.

A lot of exec drivers savored time away from their employers. Not Mr. Scott, he seemed to see himself as some sort of guardian or more, and sure Ana was kind and generous, Jared had yet to see any kind of intimate exchange from Ana to Tim beyond basic courteous concern for him. The way she referred to him as Timmy was almost maternal. She had said they talked about selling the house like they were a team or a couple, but he only got kind, professional vibes from Ana for her driver. There was a puzzle piece missing. But what?

He parked alongside the sleek sedan. Just as he was opening the door, his cell rang. "Gables." He closed the door again as the rain patted his windshield.

"Jared, it's Ginger. Sorry to bother you, but have you heard from Pat?"

Though she was trying to sound professional, Jared heard heavy concern in her tone. "Not since Tuesday, when is the last you spoke to him?"

"Monday evening, he said he was leaving on a business trip. He said it was too good of an opportunity to pass up, but he wouldn't tell me who it was with or what it was about, said he was required to keep it hush. He said he would reach out to me the earliest opportunity, but then I got a text saying he'll call me in a week. Jared, I've got a bad feeling about this. In my last four years with him, he has never once not needed an update on his schedule at least every other day. Now it's been three days and only one text telling me it will be longer."

"Ginger, how long had the meeting been on the books?" Jared agreed; most days Patrick wouldn't know what to do without his Lois Lane. Normally reserved and collected, Ginger was not sounding calm.

"That's the thing — it wasn't on the books; it came up out of nowhere. All he said was that it was an opportunity for him to make genuine change for Kansas City students and that he couldn't pass it up."

"So no time, place, or anything?" Jared was now pissed at himself. He should have been more assertive with Pat when he was acting squirrely at their meeting and on their last phone call.

"No, Jared, nothing. I wish I did, but he said he couldn't discuss it even with me. It was part of the agreement he made. I've tried calling; it goes to voicemail. Texts just stay unread."

"Okay, I'm going to call the office and have them triangulate his cell, see which towers pinged. Maybe we can get an approximation of where he is and then have officers be on the lookout. I don't like this, but Ginger, believe me, we will find him. I'll reach out tomorrow morning to update you on what I'm able to find out."

"Thank you Jared, he's much more than a boss to me. Please find him." With that, the line went dead.

Jared hated how upset she was. He had always wondered if there was more between the mayor and his assistant, but in public they were always professional, so it was hard to tell. She was a beautiful woman to be sure and her expert level of care was beyond compare; he had thought to himself once to maybe make a play for her but once Pat saw his eyes laser in; he threatened to chop off all of his protruding parts. He had found it endearing that Patrick cared so much, but maybe it was more for him too, and duty was keeping them apart.

Jared closed up his Tahoe and made his way up the mansion's long walkway. Officer Sam was standing his post at the front door.

"Evening, Captain. Yep, he's inside. They just had dinner and now are reading by firelight." Sam smirked when his boss's tongue clicked in irritation and gave the junior officer the side-eye.

"Awesome. I'm going in. It shouldn't be long. I'll update you when I come out. Keep your eyes peeled, near and far. I have a sick feeling that our killer is far closer than we think. Something's off. How's the head?"

"Yes, sir. I'll be here when you come out. I'm good, doctor cleared me."

Jared patted the young officer on the shoulder. "You're doing great." He turned and walked inside.

The entry empty, he shut the door behind him softly, not wanting to alert them of his presence yet. Sometimes, eavesdropping was just what his job required. Catching people unaware so that he can see them at their most real. Hear them in this case. He soft-padded towards the entry of the living room, hearing little bits of chatter from the center of the large living area that looked more like a hotel lobby than a family gathering room. Even upon entering, he would still be a good thirty feet away from them. He leaned his head around the wall. They were seated close together on a settee in front of the fireplace, talking about the rain coming down outside.

Jealousy burned in his stomach, seeing them. This emotion was tied not just to last night but also to his role as her protector. He found it odd for a driver to sit so near their employer, intimate one might say, but Jared squashed the word out of his mind. He watched as the driver looked down at his phone and quietly put his arm on the back of the couch up behind Ana.

He watched for any reaction from Ana — nothing. She either didn't mind her driver being so familiar, or she wasn't paying attention, or worse, she needed comforting. The thought made his head spin. Possessiveness like he had never known before, not even with Patrick, had he felt such a need to stride over and throw the obnoxious prick's arm off from behind her. He cleared his throat; it ached from the tension in his neck muscles tightening.

Ana turned at the sound. "Jared, we didn't hear you come in." Her body spun further into Tim, his hand reaching up to hold her shoulder, until Ana looked back at him with a quizzical gaze, she stood. "Come in, get warm by the fire. Timmy and I just had dinner, but I could warm something up?"

Jared had initially come over wanting to discuss last night. After this morning's conversation, he was still pretty sure that she had misunderstood him. He wanted to clear things up between them, but now he also needs to talk to her about Patrick.

"Coffee would be great if you have it." Give him a little alone time with Mr. Scott.

Ana smiled. "I don't have one perking, but it won't take but a few minutes and I can have a steaming cup for you. I'll be right back. Perhaps you could catch Timmy up on the case? Maybe he can help your team out while he's here? Be back in a moment." She flashed those baby blues at them both.

The two men stared after her until she was gone.

Jared took a seat on the chair across from the long couch. Tim stared at him, waiting cooly, his demeanor that of a Cheshire cat, so proud of himself for having an intimate evening with a beautiful supermodel. Jared hated to disappoint the man, but he was about to put a damper on any hope he might have of romance.

Jared shifted in his seat. "So how long are you planning to stay, Mr. Scott?"

"Oh, I'll always be at XAna's beck and call. As long as she is here, I will be close by." Tim gave the smug bully a smarmy grin. He thought his eagle glare and oversized masculinity would make him cry uncle, but little did the detective realize that he was the one who should be frightened.

Jared wasn't deterred. "I see." He took in the man in full — his clothes neat, but there was what looked like a dried bloodstain on his shirt. "Did you cut yourself?" Using his hand, he gestured to Tim's shirt.

Tim looked down. Damn that stupid, worthless mayor had gotten blood on his shirt. With quick thinking, he said, "I cut myself shaving earlier to prepare for our evening at home." Again, the arrogant grin appeared.

It was making Jared want to scratch it off his face. It was time to take this guy down a notch.

"Hmm, looks like maybe it's been a couple days since you shaved?" He smiled at the man, hoping the next words might hit their mark. "I'm certain Ana would be happy to let you have time off to do your laundry?"

Taking a deep breath and holding it, he wasn't about to let this bastard get the better of his temper. "XAna," reverting to his beloved's new name, "is always so loving, so generous. Don't you worry, she takes good care of me." His eyes became slivers as he pierced the gaze of the almighty detective.

"Tell me, is it detective or do you really prefer Captain, as in Captain America? Kinda juvenile, don't you think?" Tim aimed his words carefully, punch for punch.

Jared's head shook in pity-laugh. Obviously his words had hit their mark, the act of controlling his breathing and then an attempt at mocking his title. Yes, he hit home. The weasel wanted Ana for himself.

"Your coffee is served, Captain." Ana came strolling in just in time; Jared couldn't take much more of this game of words. Something was telling him he needed to know more about Mr. Scott.

"We're fine. Look I wanted to know if you have heard from Pat?" Jared hated that one aspect of him wanted her to say no, but the part that cared for his friend needed her to say yes.

"Not since Monday. Why?" Her facial features scrunched in distress. "Is he missing?"

"We don't think missing just yet, simply not checking in. Ginger said he had an unexpected meeting with weird requirements of secrecy come up, and she hasn't heard from him in two days. I'm asking everyone he knows." Jared tried his best to sound confident.

"Please share with me anything you find out. Please, Jared, Patrick can't be hurt because of me. I couldn't live with myself." Ana had placed her hand on his shoulder for a moment.

Tim watched the panic in XAna's delicate features. He needed to stop this sickening caring for Mayor Patrick. He moved to stand next to her, taking her hand in his. "XAna, with all the secrecy perhaps your mayor Patrick is doing something seedy. Maybe he needs all the cloak and dagger because he's doing underhanded trans-actions; you know politicians are never squeaky clean. They are all smooth in the ways of the crooked hand-shake. XAna don't worry; if anything, your mayor may just be off having a fling with a married woman. You never really know about a politician. They are all sleezy users."

Ana shook his hand out of hers. "Timmy, my name here in Kansas City is Ana, please use it. It's the only way I can make sure I keep all of my friends safe. And you don't even know Patrick; you met him for five minutes. He's a good and kind mayor. He really cares about the citizens of this city, and he cares deeply about me. I will never believe that he could be involved in anything sinister, and Patrick would never be with a married woman. His father was a serial philander, he had five stepmothers. It hurt Pat tons what he watched his mom go through it. Besides, he's in love with Ginger." Pausing, reading the shocked expression on Tim's face. "I'm sorry, but please never say those things again in my presence."

Jared almost felt bad for the poor man. Again, only almost. He was proud Ana cared so much for Patrick. Obviously, he wasn't the only one seeing the fire between the Ginger and Pat. It also gave him hope that the feelings between him and Ana had a chance.

Tim kept his calm and turned to leave. At the door he looked back and said good night, Ana. No XAna, just Ana, closed the door behind him. His rose was dying. Seething.

Chapter 38

Dismissed

Everything had been going perfectly. Dinner, wine by the fire—every hope he had finally coming true. Until the ox showed up.

Timmy had known the moment the man stepped into the hall, grateful once again for the timely alert from his surveillance cameras. The warning had given him just enough time to drape his arm along the back of the couch at the perfect moment. He had loved the way it made the detective hesitate before fully entering the room.

But now, hearing XAna's words, he sat stunned.

His heart felt blown wide open.

How could she?

In front of that... that nothing. A vapid piece of flesh.

He had no excuse for her. No way to understand how she could cut him so deeply. Rage simmered beneath the surface, the tips of his ears burning as his hands gripped the steering wheel so tightly the town car drifted erratically down the road.

His anger pressed the pedal to the floor.

Then his thoughts scattered, searching desperately for some explanation for why she would hurt him like this. The road blurred ahead of him and he slowed to a crawl, realizing he had already taken several turns on the back roads without remembering them.

If he wasn't careful, he would wreck everything.

He forced himself to breathe, trying to steady his racing heart. His hot breath mixed with the cold night air, fogging the windshield just as his thoughts clouded his mind.

How had he misjudged his angel so badly?

A sick feeling crept through him.

Used.

Dirty.

And worst of all... every dream he had built around her was fading before his eyes.

He loved XAna, why wasn't she calling him back to the house? She wasn't acting like herself. This was her confused by the past reminders of her old self, *Ana,* and being used by Jared; her mind was clouded by the sleezy moments in bed with him. When she left Lauderdale, she had been wholesome, but now she had been made unclean by the detective, who was a disgusting lothario.

He would never cherish her body the way he would; he didn't know how to be a gentle lover, taking his time

to coax her as she deserved. The detective's wasteful encounters with too many women would have made his
lovemaking twisted nasty tricks. She would never get
used to that kind of touch.

It had scattered her beautiful mind, made her forget
who she really was and how special she was to him. Tim
closed his eyes. He couldn't stop the ringing in his ears,
the images in his head. Horns blaring caused him to open
them again, jerking the car back across the yellow lines.

The air in the car sucking the life out of him, never
had he felt such fury in his soul. Seven years, he had used
his talents only to make her happy. Now she was risking
losing him for this man, who would throw her away when
the next woman came his way. A devious smile formed
on his lips. He would have to teach her an important lesson: the difference between a man willing to kill for her
and a man willing to use her.

The car sped down the dirt road to the cabin. Oh
dear, Pat, your moment might come faster than originally planned. No more Trina to take his frustration out
on, the precious mayor his XAna was so desperate to find
would have to do.

Still staring at the closed door, "I'm sorry about that,
Timmy didn't really mean it. You really haven't gotten to

see him at his best. He saved me, you know." Ana sat back down on the settee, looking into the fire. Jared moved to his chair, watching her as she told her story.

"About two weeks after I arrived in Miami. I didn't know anyone but my agent and a few models. That day I had just gotten my biggest check ever from a modeling gig. I had walked to the shopping mall to buy new sheets for my apartment—a little splurge." She paused, sliding him a sly smile.

"When I came out of the department store, I had packages in both hands and, honestly, I was feeling so much pride at my independence I wasn't paying attention to those around me. Stupid, but I was younger." The shame she felt was apparent in her bowed head, "I rounded a corner towards the parking garage, a mugger was waiting, I never saw him, never heard a footstep until his arm was around my neck, my packages, my purse all falling to the ground, I screamed but not from the attacker. Out of nowhere, Timmy appeared. He was able to get the man off me. He saved a few of my things, but not my purse or my phone, unfortunately. I never saw either item again. But without Timmy, I might not be here. The attacker had a knife; Timmy found it on the ground a few feet away from us. I was terrified. Trembling, he took me to my apartment, no charge. Then, he went and got soup for me."

"He was so gentle and so reassuring. I initially wanted to tuck my tail and run home, but Timmy told me he would always make me feel safe, and ever since he has always been there for all the awful things that happen in life. The mugger, Dallas, Charla, he is always watching out for me with anyone I date. Truly, he's been like a very dear brother to me. I don't know if you know it but it was Timmy who called the ambulance for my dad when he found him on the floor of the kitchen. I trust him, so I really mean it, you haven't seen him at his best." Her eyes pleaded with Jared to understand.

"I didn't know how important a role he played in your life, perhaps I have not seen him in the best light? You say he found Jerome in the kitchen? Were they having a meal?"

"No, I guess Dad had gotten up in the middle of the night. Timmy said he heard a noise and went to check it out, and that's when he found him, lying there barely breathing. It was so awful, I wouldn't have made it without Timmy." Sadness touched her features.

Jared found all this heroism interesting. Sure, it seemed these were the acts of someone sincere, but it also seemed like it was too convenient that he was always in the right place at the right time. Jared didn't like it; something was wrong with this picture. The man who just left the house wasn't upset at being reprimanded as an employee, more like a lover rejected. Someone who is always there at the right time, just to save the day? He didn't like it when things were too neatly explained.

A look into Jerome's death might be necessary. He stood and moved to the small couch, sitting beside her. He put his arm around her, pulling her close.

"Look, I'm sure Tim will be okay once he gets over the hurt. I guess from his reaction that he's not used to your acting like an employer?"

"I suppose not. In Lauderdale, when I'm not working, it's just him and me. So we spend a lot of time together; lunches, going to the gym once in a while, or out on the Water Taxi." She leaned on his arm, enjoying the feel of him. It was comforting.

"So, is there more to this relationship? You've called him 'brother, best friend, now you use phrases like *our own life*, is it more? Perhaps that's why he left so mad?" Jared let his eyes scan the room, not wanting his facial expressions to give away he was secretly hoping the answer was a fat NO.

Ridiculous, he envied the time Tim got to spend with her. He was never jealous.

"No," she wrinkled her nose at him, "not once has Timmy made a move. The most he's ever done was sit here on the couch and hold me as I cried about my father. In fact, that was his plan tonight: to have dinner and watch the rain, while I told him stories of Dad by the fire. Like we did in the spring after his funeral. He was really such a support through it all."

Jared hated to tell her, but his gut was telling him that plan sounded a little like a man hoping to relive a close moment they had shared. And there was only one reason a man would do that, and Jared didn't fucking like it at all. He knew men like this, ones that couldn't get a woman without appealing to past moments, preying on their heartbreaks in life to get a feel. Shit, this guy was good.

"How many years has he been with you full time?" He pressed on with questions, trying to sound like he was just asking out of curiosity. He didn't want to alarm Ana yet; he could still be wrong about the driver.

"Since about three months after I moved to Florida from Missouri, actually, we had that in common. It was like he was a friend from back home. Anyway, he was a taxi driver originally, that day he saved me from the mugger, he was waiting on a person who had called for a cab in front of the mall, I was so lucky it felt like fate had put him in my path. So, from that moment on, I would only call his cab number for a ride to appointments. Then he started working for Uber, and I became his only client during the daytime, and then when I was hired to be an Angel, I bought a town car and made him my executive driver. I truly don't know what I'd do without him; he knows all the ins and outs of my security systems, all the cameras here and in all my houses. He volunteered to oversee the installs were done correctly. He's been so protective of me, I feel so terrible. I was awful to him just now. I need to call him." She stood up, searching for her cell.

Jared didn't want her calling him. Mr. Scott needed a cool-down minute. Ana's stories of him didn't sit well, that he had access to her security, why would a professional driver need access to her cameras? For the first time, Jared wondered if it was possible that Timmy was our stalker. Would his devotion go that far? He needed time and more information.

He walked over to where Ana was rummaging around through some mail on a side table; she didn't hear him for the television beeping with a breaking news report.

"Breaking news: The Mayor of Kansas City, Patrick Anderson," at the mention of Pat, Ana and Jared both stopped still looking at each other than back at the screen, "the youngest mayor the city has ever had has been reported missing. Unconfirmed allegations are trending on social media that the mayor was last seen getting in a limo leased by drug lord El Kadif, an international businessman in town on a land purchase..." Jared turned the TV off..

"Look I wanted us to talk about last night, but I have to go, I need to get back to the office, Aiden and AJ will be waiting for an update and if they've heard this news, they will be chomping at the bit. Something isn't right, and if we don't narrow down the suspects or follow up on the signs, something far worse could happen."

"I know, please go. We can talk about it later...or not. We said one do-over, that's all. I'm not holding you to anything more. Truly." Ana put her hand on his arm. "Just please find Pat."

Nodding, he made his way to the entry, one hand on the door handle, when he suddenly turned and took three large strides to stand in front of her, inches separating them, grabbed her by the waist, pulling her hard against him. His lips crushed hers in urgency, desperation and frustration from her determination to let him off the hook, willing her to hear him when he spoke these next words.

"We have unfinished business; we will talk later." He lifted her chin, her eyes glowing and soft. Damn, he wanted this pair of eyes looking at him for the rest of his life. The realization slammed him like a loud clap of thunder and lightning. He kissed her gently. "I'll be back for more." He let his finger tap her nose and gave her a wink.

CHAPTER 39
COOLING OFF

The second swing of the frying pan was the moment Tim finally felt calm again.

Patrick's scream had split the room. Blood ran down his chin, dripping onto the floor. His broken wrist still hung twisted against the chair, the rope biting into swollen skin.

Tim stood there for a moment, breathing slowly.

Better.

The mayor's pain had been beautiful at first. The screams, the begging, the blood running down his face. Tim had almost lost himself in it.

But losing control wouldn't make him worthy of XAna.

He wiped the blood from his hands and splashed water on his face.

Not frantic anymore.

Disappointed, yes.

But calm.

He couldn't let XAna see the ugly parts. She needed to know he had done her a favor—not how much he had enjoyed doing it.

The cabin still needed to be ready.

The final act of a very long play.

One he had written.

Edited.

Starred in.

And now the finale was coming.

Tim moved around the room gathering the pans he had used, humming quietly as Patrick whimpered behind him.

The drugs were wearing off.

Good.

Pain made people honest.

"You were never good enough for her, Patrick."

His voice was soft as he carried the pans to the sink.

"Never."

Patrick stayed very still in the chair. Breathing hurt. His ribs throbbed where Tim had struck him with the metal ladle. Every inhale tasted like blood.

Tim returned slowly.

"Don't you see?" he said gently.

Patrick tried to speak, but the swelling in his mouth turned the word into a wet grunt.

Tim tilted his head.

"You didn't hear me."

He stepped closer.

Patrick could smell his breath now.

"I said... don't you see?"

Patrick nodded quickly. The movement sent pain shooting through his skull.

Good enough.

Tim smiled.

"Can you believe she prefers that derelict detective to me?"

Patrick's eyebrow twitched despite himself.

Tim noticed.

"Oh, you didn't know."

He chuckled softly.

"Yes. She and the great Captain have been intimate."

He leaned against the counter.

"Twice, actually. Once years ago before she moved to Florida... and again last night."

Patrick said nothing.

There was nothing safe to say.

"Disgusting, really," Tim continued. "Her angelic skin being groped by that oversized french fry."

Tim shrugged.

"Shocking, right?"

Patrick stared at the floor.

Tim didn't need answers. He was already having both sides of the conversation.

Patrick watched him move around the cabin, wiping counters, scrubbing the floor, humming to himself.

Why was he cleaning?

His wrists burned where the rope cut into them. Two of his fingers had gone numb. His vision swam every time he tried to focus.

Tim filled a bucket with bleach.

Patrick's stomach turned.

"You know," Tim said casually, dipping the mop, "I've spent years making sure the wrong men didn't touch her."

The mop slid slowly across the floor.

"Some came and went."

Tim smiled faintly.

"Some... disappeared."

Patrick felt cold despite the blood running down his neck.

"I drove them to their dates," Tim continued. "Picked them up. Dropped them off."

The mop scraped softly across the boards.

"I watched."

He glanced up.

"And when necessary..."

A small shrug.

"...corrected things."

Patrick swallowed painfully.

"The ones like Dallas?" Tim continued. "He had it coming."

Another slow pass of the mop.

"Her father too."

Patrick's head jerked up.

Tim stopped mopping.

"Oh."

He smiled.

"You didn't know that either."

He walked slowly toward Patrick.

"Really, anyone who stands between me and my angel deserves what happens to them."

Tim leaned down close enough for Patrick to smell the sour sweat on his skin.

"You see that now, don't you?"

Patrick nodded weakly.

Tim reached out and gently brushed Patrick's hair back.

Patrick flinched.

Tim's hand tightened suddenly, yanking his head back.

"You see," Tim whispered, "none of this would have happened if you hadn't been exactly who you were."

Patrick's scalp burned under Tim's grip.

"If teenage you hadn't been such a rich, entitled little prince... my angel would never have needed to rescue me."

Tim released him.

Patrick sagged forward.

"So really, Patrick... I should thank you."

Tim smiled again.

"And for that kindness..."

He gestured casually.

"I'll let Jared do the honor of killing you when he arrives."

Patrick's heart slammed against his ribs.

"Then I'll kill Jared."

Tim's eyes brightened.

"And my XAna and I will finally return to our life together."

He checked the room.

Clean enough.

"Time is almost up."

He pulled a phone from his pocket.

"No fairy godmother tonight."

His smile widened.

"Just her future partner and lover coming to save the day."

Tim held up the phone.

"I thought you might enjoy this part."

Patrick barely managed to whisper.

"...yes."

"Oh good."

Tim's fingers moved quickly across the screen.

"Now that the cabin is ready for my dearest XAna..."

He winked.

"...I'll send her a message."

Patrick's stomach dropped.

"Using a backdoor through Jared's phone."

Tim looked up at him, amused.

"You arrogant prick."

His thumb hovered over the screen.

"You're not the only one who knows how to hack software."

Tim smiled.

"Sending it now."

> Ana, I'm asking Tim to come drive you to my cabin in the woods, no one knows how to get there or about me, we can talk about last night and plan our next steps.

Sending... 04:23 PM

Pat watched Timmy, his face changed from goading to insecurity, doubt. Sending the text was playing with his emotions.

Tim almost hoped that she would turn the request down flat. Tell that beefcake that she had nothing more to discuss with him but if she did that would mean his plan would not finish. That his time with his angel for all the world to see would be delayed. His patience was at a breaking point but his heart wanted her to return his love.

Ding. The sound of a reply felt ominous.

Jared, I will be ready when Timmy arrives. You are right we need to talk. A

Read 04:25 PM

Timmy threw the phone across the room. Pat watched as the man started pacing again, hands pulling at his hair, grunting with loud stomps on the wood flooring, screaming, "Timmy...TIMMMY...how many fucking times have I said I don't like the name TIMMMMMY. FUCK...."

The room went deathly silent, Tim stopped pacing, calmly he walked to the phone on the floor, broken screen but still working, slid it into his pocket.

"So," he let out a breath while staring down at the figure leaning away from him in fear, "the final countdown has begun. Not much longer mayor Pat for you or the mighty Captain."

He stepped to the cabin door opening it, it was beginning to grow dark as the sun set, he looked over his shoulder with a laugh, "Don't go anywhere."

Chapter 40

Explain The Driver

Finding Aiden and Aj in his office ready to hurt something was to be expected. Jared wanted to strangle whoever was fucking with his friends.

"You heard?" Jared said as he strode over to his desk, taking off his wet jacket. "Sorry it took a bit with all the rain coming down."

"Yea, Garrett is calling, he texted he has news we aren't going to like. Where were you?" Aiden sat in his fave chair, leg crossed. This was the side of Aiden that could be scary. Jared liked him better when he propped his feet up and hands behind his head, Aiden calm, cool, and collected.

"Ana's, just checking in." Jared avoiding his best friends chin up gaze, he knew Aiden could read him better than anyone and he wasn't ready for the conversation to come. "Interesting moment with Mr. Scott while I was there. I'm hoping Garrett's call isn't what I think it is."

The cell on the table lit the room, dark had fallen outside, Jared hit speaker, "Garrett, you've got Aiden and Aj too. Give us a new lead we need to catch this prick."

"Hey guys, sorry it's not good, the Mr. Scott isn't who he would seem."

Aiden leaned up, elbows on his thighs, having not met him yet, he could only guess but the look on Jared's face was speaking loud that this was bad. "Okay, who is the Mr. Scott."

Garrett continued, "look it's all just coming in, don't have everything, but it seems he's someone that went to Chapel Hill Middle School with Pat and Ana. He then went onto highschool at Olathe High while Pat and Ana moved to Park Valley High on the North side, Timmy Jones, which is his real name, his parents divorced, he left Olathe and went on to Technology Development Center, where he graduated with honors in computer programming. During the summers he worked as a landscaper for a Mrs. Montgomery, Ana's grandmother until she passed away. The next note is that he appears to have moved to Miami about 3 months before Ana did. Got a job driving cabs. Relationships are sketchy but guys, the FBI believes this is our man, a partial finger print was found at the prostitutes apartment, we can't say 100% now but they are getting close."

"Great work Garrett, but we have a bit of a problem that heightens our need to find Patrick."

Jared stopped talking when Aiden lifted out of his chair, Aj coming to sit on the desk edge.

"I just left Ana and she had a fight with Tim over Patrick, he was stunned by her words, he left pissed, I think he felt betrayed by the fact that she defended Patrick after he was claiming that he was possibly in leagues with criminals."

"Nifty timing considering the latest news reports that alleged the very thing." Aiden's face hardened.

"Sounds like we might have found our man, now we need to find Patrick. Aj and I will head over to Ana's and stay with her, can you ping Mr. Jones' phone, he won't be expecting it since he thinks, we are bumbling this investigation?"

"Just did, Jared man, you are gonna hate this." Garrett went silent then he was heard speaking to another officer in Miami. "Are you sure? Damn."

"For fuck sake, what?" Jared was losing his chill quickly, nervous for Ana.

"Man, his phone is pinging at your cabin. Did you give him directions to your hunting cabin?"

"Hell No! Okay, Garrett, let's wrap this up, places to be." Jared's sharp tone was speaking volumes, this was more about Ana than he was letting on.

"Go get him, bring this nightmare to an end." Garrett's line went dead.

"Okay, you guys go take care of Ana, I'm gonna call in reinforcements. Take care of her for me." He heard the words come out of his mouth before thought, he refused to look at Aiden, who had sat back down hands folded behind his head. Fuck.

"So, were you gonna tell me, eventually?" Aiden was smirking. Bastard was going to play with him.

"Yup," Jared shrugged still gathering another clip for his glock from his locked drawer. "Eventually."

"Nice, so it's true, you have feelings for Ana?"

Aj jumped off the desk, "Whoa what? You have feelings for Ana? Hold on you have feelings? Wow, this is awesome, more Kansas City women for me." His laugh was a raucous one.

"Shut up," Jared turned to Aiden, "I don't understand, you knew? How?"

Aiden smarmy grin got wider, "Whelp, you have my pregnant bride and her pregnancy sixth sense to thank,.." Aiden rolled his eyes and shrugged his shoulders, "Guess she was right, she said she saw you and Ana in a heated stare down at Bab's and she got a dangerously delicious feeling that was either hate or deep love. My hormonal wife has a flare for the dramatic, but seems she is correct, or do you hate Ana?"

Jared put his glock away in his holster, "I don't hate her, but we have been denying it for 8 years, so I don't know what to call it. Yet. I'm going to talk to her after this bastard is in jail or dead."

"Well, I only have one rule, don't fuck this up so bad we all can't be friends, my wife will kill you, she likes Ana, she is impressed by her realness and her bravery. And I won't protect you from her. I'm on Tessa's side, and Ana's. But I think she will be good for you, if you can work out logistics. She's headed back to Lauderdale after he's caught, you know?"

"Yea, I know that too. Now if we can save the slumber party talk for later, I have to go catch a madman." He passed Aiden, tapping his fist against his shoulder, "Thanks man. I love her. Taken me too long to figure it out, damn sure would've taken me longer to figure out how to tell you."

"I get it. But from now on just spill. Deal?" Aiden extended his hand.

Jared accepted with a tug, given the bro hug. He was glad Aiden had found Tessa. Now he could process his feelings for Ana without lingering guilt.

"Go. We will take care of her for you."

Ana slipped into the back of the town car. Timmy was very quiet and focused on the highway. She was glad he had come to pick her up and take her to Jared's cabin. Hoping the drive would give them a chance to talk, but so far he had left the glass separator up.

She leaned forward to scratched the glass, motioning for him to let it down. He glanced in the mirror, his eyes still showing hurt. She hated that she had been so harsh with her words.

"Tim, I wanted to say I'm sorry, I treated you terribly, you didn't deserve it. It's just that Patrick is a dear person to me. I would never let anyone speak about you that way, it's just how I am with my friends, don't you see?"

Friends, now they were friends? He pressed harder on the gas, he didn't want to hear anymore, soon she would see the truth, she would understand how deeply she was hurting him. Choosing Jared and now all this love for Patrick. "I understand, it's fine."

Lies like the ones she was telling herself.

"Are we okay? You seem still mad?" Ana wanted to pierce through this dark mood, she had never felt him so cold.

"Soon everything will be cleared up. You will see me in a new light." His eyes slid from the road to reflect at her in the rearview, this wasn't her Timmy anymore.

There was something in his demeanor, his words didn't sound like her Timmy, the one who had rescued her so many times.

She was frightened. "Timmy, you know how much I care for you don't you?"

Cared? Who hurts someone they care for? He couldn't look at her anymore, she was lost but that all would change soon, focusing back on the road, he turned the wheel onto the dirt path to Jared's cabin, "Yes, my angel, I know. All will be well soon."

Ana sat back in the darkened corner, her hands clammy and clenched, she suddenly felt a sudden urge to reach out to Jared but her phone was in the trunk with her luggage. Timmy had never called her anything but XAna, now he called her angel? His angel? Something was wrong, but she didn't know how to change his mood. Lights ahead suggested they were near Jared's cabin, no other vehicles were around, which worried her more.

Chapter 41

She's Gone

Jared was pushing the Tahoe as fast as it would legally take him. He had called in the reinforcements which had taken up a few minutes, causing it to take longer to get out of the city.

Jared's cell rang, Aiden's number coming up. "Gables."

"She's not here." Aiden sounded both pissed and worried.

"What do you mean? Is she out with Rodriquez?" Jared's heart skipped a beat.

"We found Rodriquez behind the bushes, knocked out or drugged. The way she's wobbling, Aj and I think drugs. This man is more weaponized than we think and way more determined."

"And now he has Ana and a good chance he has Patrick. Fuck!" Jared's fist slammed on the steering wheel, blood rushing to his brain.

"Where are you now?' Aiden asked, in the background he heard Aj asking how far out?

"I'm seven miles from turning off onto my road, once I hit the dirt, the camera's will notify him I'm arriving. Unfortunately, there will be no element of surprise."

"J, you need to punch it. I've got a bad feeling, this guys clever, he's been under our noses the whole time. Years he's spent with her, learning her every habit and we don't have any clue yet why he's got Patrick, if he does. So suck it up and run those tires bald. Aj and I are 40 minutes out, we would have been closer but we stayed until the EMT showed up for Rodriquez, they said she was going to be ok but needed to find out what he had used to drug her."

"Thanks for the update, but Aiden, he has Patrick, I'm sure of it." Jared's gut was knotted like a lead balloon, he had Pat and Ana now, Jared wouldn't live with himself if anything happened to either of them. "And I'm holding steady at 85mph. No sense in wrecking on these curves in my mood. When I get there, I'll go to the side of the house and cut the Wi-Fi wire – that will shut down the camera's, and he won't know you are coming. Back at you about the get here now. I need all the backup I can get."

"When you get there play it smart, stall for time so that we can lend you support. Don't play the hero but don't get your ass beat like a pussy either. If he suspects, and I bet he does, that you have feelings for Ana and she you, your life is in danger. He killed Mitch, and he was only a protector, a lover he may very well slice and dice."

"He can fucking try, but I won't go down quite so easily, now that I'm finding out she's the one I want to take a chance on."

"I get it so get to her and remember play it smart. We want all three of you back in good health."

"Yup. Thanks guys." Jared's line went silent.

Aiden pocketed his phone, Aj looking over from the driver seat, "You really cool with him and Ana?"

"Any time Jared has bit down hard on anything, he gave it all his heart. Nope, as long he doesn't get his ass killed or Ana or Patrick, I'll be happy as a hog in a mud puddle."

Aj grinned, "Well I'm surprised but honestly maybe they are made for each other. We all have had a crush on her but Jared daring your wrath, must be more than a crush."

Aiden shrugged, "Floor it man, we need to be there already."

Aj rolled his eyes at his big brother, "Just remember you said that."

Timmy rounded the car, opened her door then preceded to get her overnight bag from the trunk. The slam of the door surprised her, she was being thrown off balance.

"Timmy what's going on? Are you still angry? I'm truly sorry, I never meant to hurt you." Her voice filled with anguish.

"Come in, my angel, all will be right with the world very soon." Though his words were kind they were said in a cold way, they didn't sound sincere. "Follow me, there's a nice fire already built, you can warm yourself by it."

It was like he wasn't hearing her, or ignoring her pleas. She stood frozen, it was getting chilly out. Timmy turned back, "Have you changed your mind? Your Captain will be so disappointed."

His words, 'your captain', was he mad at her? Rustling could be heard in the dark woods, only a flicker of light could be seen coming from the fireplace through the window was causing her heart to race frantically, so much that she had forgotten she was meeting Jared here.

"No, I haven't." She willed herself to put one foot in front of the other, thinking maybe when they got inside, she and Timmy could sit by the fire and have a long talk.

Another hope dashed, she had another disappointing choice. Oh XAna, perhaps the only way for you to see me clearly is through a great deal of pain. He hated the idea of physically causing her pain but in this moment, she was stabbing him in the back. A small amount of pain for the good of their future might do the trick.

Timmy stepped in as if he owned the cabin, like he was familiar with the layout. But how could that be if Jared had just shared the location of the cabin today? Ana's hands were clammy, nothing was what it was yesterday. Ever since she spent the night with Jared, she hadn't been able to get her bearings. Now Timmy was acting jealous. She wished Jared was here now.

She stepped into the dimly lit room, while Timmy held the door open, it was hard to see in the small entry and the smells weren't what you imagine a cabin might be; it smelled clean but not like spring clean but more of an antibacterial clean. Heavy on the bleaching scent, so strong it was almost nauseating. Timmy set the luggage down, "please make yourself comfortable, it won't be long now."

"Why are you being so formal? Timmy, let's sit and talk for a minute...," she stopped.

She heard something.

She turned towards the flicker of flame from the dying fire. There was someone sitting in front of the fireplace, her eyes acclimating to the room.

Who is that?

"Timmy, who else is here?" Strangely, she felt like she knew who it was, slowly she made a hesitating step towards the chair.

"You're right, it's too dark in here, let me light the kerosene so that you might see what I have done for you. A special guest has been waiting your arrival."

She watched him walk to the farthest part of the room, the room glowing brighter with the flick of a match.

She turned, her mouth fell open.

Ugly pride crept into Tim's voice. "There. See your beloved mayor."

CHAPTER 42

THE TRUTH

"**P**atrick!" she cried, rushing to the chair. "Timmy, why is he tied up? Who did this to him?"

Her hands hovered over the swollen bruises around Patrick's eyes.

She whimpered.

A hand seized her arm and yanked her away.

Tim dragged her to the center of the room where a dining chair faced Patrick. He shoved her down into it. Pain shot through her arm from his grip.

When he released her, she looked up at him, tears filling her eyes.

"Why, Timmy?"

The backhand came so fast it stole her breath.

"What have I asked you repeatedly?" he said, his voice eerily soft. "Do not ever call me Timmy."

He patted her head.

Ana sat frozen, her hand rising to her cheek. It was the first time anyone had ever struck her. Her head throbbed. She tasted blood where she had bitten her lip.

Her fingertips brushed the torn skin.

"Tim... I'm sorry," she whispered, panic breaking through. "Please help me understand. Why are you like this?"

There was no holding back the tears now. The man in front of her was a stranger. The helpful, gentle Timmy she had known was gone.

Had she missed this all along?

Tim lifted his hand again.

She flinched.

Instead of striking her, he gripped her chin and pulled her face closer.

"I'm sorry, my angel," he murmured. "When this is over, I'll buy you two dozen O'Hara roses to make it up to you. But you must never call me that again. Timmy died long ago—thanks to you."

His smile widened.

"Don't you see? I'm proving my loyalty to you... just like you did for me all those years ago."

Ana stared into his eyes.

They looked kind.

But they were empty.

"I don't understand," she said, shaking her head. "Timmy died? What are you talking about? Do you mean when I hired you? That wasn't loyalty—I did that because I cared about you."

The words tumbled out in desperate confusion.

Behind him, something shifted.

Ana glanced past Tim and saw Patrick stirring in the chair.

"Patrick—"

She tried to stand, but Tim's hands slammed onto her shoulders, forcing her back down.

"Ow!" she cried.

"He's Timmy Anderson, Ana. From middle school. He's going to kill me for bullying him. Isn't that right?"

Patrick had nothing left to lose. He stared the maniac down.

"Oh, you tell the story so poorly." Tim smiled. "How sad the tales of your death will be—so many questions left unan-

swered. Especially with your office being investigated by the DEA for connections to a Colombian drug lord."

He clicked his tongue.

"Tsk, tsk, Mayor. It seems your days of being an evil tyrant aren't quite behind you."

Tim stepped behind XAna, stroking her hair and rubbing her shoulders.

The touch made her skin crawl.

Ana leaned her head away so she could see him.

Tim Anderson.

A flash of memory surfaced—a thin teenage boy lying on the ground, surrounded by bullies. Patrick had been one of them. Ana had stepped in that day, pulling them away.

After that, she had only seen Tim once or twice in the school halls.

The man standing behind her now was different—short hair, expensive clothes, confident. When they met again in Miami, she hadn't recognized him.

But looking at him now, she saw it.

The same wounded expression she had glimpsed whenever he thought she had disappointed him.

"You changed your name?" she asked slowly. "Why didn't you tell me who you were?"

"I wanted a fresh start." His voice softened. "I didn't want you to see the boy anymore you helped save that day with your kindness, I wanted you to see the man."

For a moment his eyes warmed.

Then the anger returned.

"I've been showing you my love every day since I moved here. I came ahead of you when I learned about your position at Agent Inc.—to prepare, to be there when you needed help."

Ana frowned, confusion tightening her voice.

"How could you know I was moving? I never saw you again after we went to different high schools."

"I worked for your grandmother one summer," he said. "Landscape crew. Until she passed away and the house was sold."

His smile returned.

"I loved that job. It gave me access to make sure you were always safe. She's the one who told me how much you loved O'Hara roses. Mrs. Montgomery was a wonderful woman."

Ana searched her memory.

She had spent most summers at her grandmother's house—swimming, reading at the library, talking for hours about boys and dreams.

She vaguely remembered a young man with long hair working somewhere on the property. But the estate had been large, and the workers stayed far from the house.

"That was you?" she asked. "Why didn't you say anything?"

"You were always busy," he said softly. "Friends visiting. Washing your car in the backyard... yellow shorts, white T-shirt."

His eyes slowly moved down her body.

"So beautiful. Even when you were wet."

Ana looked down quickly, her stomach twisting.

The truth slammed into her.

Timmy was her stalker.

Her pulse quickened as cold dread spread through her chest. She forced her expression to stay calm. One wrong look could set him off.

She had to keep him focused.

Keep him talking.

Maybe even turn his anger away from Patrick.

Looking back up, she wiped away a tear.

"Don't you realize," she said gently, "we could have spent time together during those summers?"

If this twisted obsession was his version of love, maybe she could redirect it.

He had said he loved her kindness.

She had to use that now.

"No, you were still hanging out with Patrick, and you had a new boyfriend, Aiden. Your grandmother would tell me when I came to tend the roses. She talked about you all the time." His voice softened. "It was the only time I ever took my earbuds out. She showed me kindness... like you."

Ana reached for his hand, stopping his gruesome massage, she began rubbing it with exaggerated care.

She flinched as the thought struck her—those same hands had held the gun that killed Mitch and Tomas. Now Patrick was bleeding in front of her. How many others had Tim hurt in her name?

She glanced at Patrick. He looked furious.

And fragile.

"I wish you had told me," she said, forcing warmth into her voice. "After all, I saved you that day. The least you could have done was say hello." She hesitated. "Can you tell me something I don't understand? Why the notes with blood on them?"

He didn't hear the disgust in her tone.

"The notes were how I brought you back to me," Tim said proudly. "Too many people were distracting you. I needed you to remember who saved you." He frowned. "They weren't supposed to happen more than once, but your job... that gala... it ruined my plans. I had to remind you who your hero was."

Ana studied his face.

He believed every word.

The bullied boy she had once defended had grown into something far worse. Whatever damage had shaped him, he was killing people she cared about.

She had to stop him.

"Why don't we just leave Patrick here," she said softly, offering a weak smile. "We could go somewhere private and talk."

"Once we finish my plan, we'll fly back to Lauderdale," Tim said dreamily. "We'll never be apart." His smile hardened. "But first, the mayor has an appointment."

Ana's control cracked.

"Tim, please don't kill him," she blurted. "I'll do anything. He's my friend. Please."

The words left her mouth and she cursed herself. Stay focused.

"You'll go to jail, Tim," she said quickly. "I don't want that for you."

"XAna, my angel... he must die." Tim forced her head down so she had to look at Patrick. "He touched what's mine. No one stands between us."

Patrick groaned weakly in the chair.

"But you're right about one thing," Tim continued calmly. "I won't be the one to kill him."

Ana blinked.

"What?"

"The Captain will have that honor."

"What are you talking about? Jared and Patrick are friends."

"Sweet, innocent XAna." Tim smiled. "Your friend here is a wanted criminal. And Captain Gables is going to shoot him for hurting you."

Tim's fingers brushed her swollen lip before he brought them to his mouth.

Ana recoiled.

"Patrick isn't a criminal," she said. "What are you talking about?"

"Oh, but the information I provided to the news suggests otherwise. Channel 29/40 seems convinced he's working with a Colombian drug lord."

The grin stretching across Tim's face made her stomach drop.

"Ana," Patrick rasped. "Tim leaked the story. He set this whole thing up. He thinks he's protecting you."

Each breath cost Patrick visible pain.

"Don't worry about me," he forced out. "Just get away from him. He'll hurt you too."

An electronic chime suddenly pierced the room.

Lights flashed on the security panel.

Someone had arrived.

Outside, tires skidded in the dirt.

An engine shut off.

Tim slowly lifted his head.

And smiled.

CHAPTER 43

OUR TIME HAS ARRIVED

Tim released Patrick's hair so violently the chair slammed upright with a crack against the hard-wood floor.

Ana flinched.

Tim walked calmly back toward the kitchen. From the counter he picked up a pair of black plastic gloves and slipped them on. Then he opened a drawer and pulled out a book.

Ana blinked in confusion.

Was he going to read to them?

Tim noticed her watching and carried the book over.

"Do you recognize this?"

He turned it so she could read the title.

The Great Gatsby.

His favorite.

She nodded slowly. "It's one of my grandmother's books."

He patted her head.

"That's right. But there's a detail you've always missed, sweet innocent XAna."

He opened the cover.

Inside sat a handgun.

"It's also a gun safe. Cleverly disguised."

Ana's eyes widened.

Tim smiled, delighted.

"Do you know why this is my favorite story, Angel?"

She shook her head, staring at her hands.

"Because every character in it is misunderstood." His voice softened. "Gatsby was a nobody who spent his life becoming somebody... just to win the love of Daisy. His angel in pearls."

He leaned closer.

"You see, I'm the Great Gatsby."

His eyes shone.

"And you are my Daisy."

He paused, smiling faintly.

"But I detest daisies."

"Yes, I know, my love. So I chose the O'Hara rose."

Tim turned toward Patrick.

"Oh, dear Pat... say your prayers. Let's not have any dramatic attempts at bravery that might accidentally hurt XAna."

With the back of his gloved hand he brushed Ana's hair behind her ear. Then he bent and kissed her cheek.

"Soon," he whispered, "all my work will have brought us together."

Outside, Jared killed the engine on the Tahoe.

Tim would understand the meaning of the flashing alert lights. Jared had seconds.

Moving quickly to the rear of the cabin, he found the Wi-Fi cable feeding the deer camera.

His Leatherman snapped open.

One cut.

The red warning lights went dark.

Jared circled to the front and looked through the cabin's single window.

Inside, Tim stood behind Ana, who sat frozen in a chair facing the fireplace.

A gun hung loosely at his side.

Patrick's feet were visible across the room, tied to another chair.

Jared shifted his grip on his weapon.

Then Tim's voice rang out.

"Hello, Captain."

Tim turned toward the window.

"Why don't you come join us?"

He smiled.

"We've been waiting for you."

Jared caught the sick humor in Tim's tone as he stepped onto the wooden porch. The boards creaked under his weight.

"I'm unarmed," Jared called. "We can do this peacefully."

The doorknob turned.

Tim opened the door with his arm wrapped around Ana.

"No funny business," he said calmly. "No tricks. We wouldn't want XAna hurt."

Even now he used her professional name.

Jared stepped inside, raising his hands. He slowly turned in a circle.

"See? No weapon. You can put yours away and we can just talk."

As he finished the turn, he quietly pushed the door closed behind him so any movement from Aiden or AJ outside wouldn't be heard.

"Of course I believe you," Tim said with a smirk. "Ever trustworthy, aren't you, Captain?"

His grip tightened on Ana's shoulders.

"You were trusted to protect my XAna... and instead you violated her." His voice sharpened. "Using your charm on an innocent woman. Men like you take what they want for a single night and walk away."

He leaned closer to her.

"I saved you from him, Angel. I heard his rules. One night. That's all men like him can manage."

His smile returned.

"But don't worry. I'll repay him for that soon enough."

The gun lifted slightly.

"First we dispense justice for Mayor Patrick."

Jared kept his focus on the gun as he stepped farther inside. Only then did he glance toward the chair.

Patrick's head hung forward, barely conscious. His face was swollen, blood drying across his shirt.

Rage burned through Jared.

Tim would feel every blow for that.

Jared looked back.

Tim stood behind Ana, the gun now resting against her shoulder as he idly twisted a strand of her hair.

"I've waited long enough," Tim said. "You're going to kill the mayor now. Be quick. XAna and I have a life to begin."

Jared tilted his head.

"Why would I kill Pat?" he asked calmly. "You've already beaten him half to death... and destroyed his career with those false allegations."

Tim's face lit with pride.

"Ah. The Captain is smarter than he looks."

His hand stroked Ana's hair again.

"Maybe," Jared said. "But I'm curious. Why does the mayor have to die?"

Tim smiled.

"It's simple."

He brushed Ana's hair like she was a pet.

"He touched what belongs to me."

Ana's eyes squeezed shut in disgust.

Jared nodded slowly.

"And what exactly is yours?"

He glanced deliberately at Ana's face.

"She doesn't look like she agrees."

Patrick stirred weakly in the chair.

"Jared..." he rasped. "He confessed... he killed Ana's father... and Dallas too."

Patrick's head dropped again, slumping unconscious.

Jared's stomach tightened.

Ana's face drained of color.

Tears slipped silently down her cheeks.

Jared forced himself to stay calm.

"How?" he asked Tim. "We ran toxicology. No poison. No medication error. The coroner ruled it a heart attack."

He leaned slightly forward.

"So how did you do it?"

Tim chuckled.

"You poor fool."

He spread his hands.

"Money."

"That's all it takes to rewrite a toxicology report. A coroner with gambling debts... a few quiet threats to his children..."

He grinned.

"And suddenly poison disappears."

He laughed.

Ana exploded from the chair.

"You killed my father?" she screamed. "How? Why?"

Her voice cracked with fury.

"My dad was kind to you! Just like my grandmother!"

Tim barely reacted.

"You bastard," she shouted. "We treated you like family. You stayed with us for holidays. We bought you gifts."

Her hands clenched into fists.

"I never treated you like a driver. I treated you like a friend."

Her voice broke.

"How could you take my father from me?"

Jared watched her tremble—face flushed, body rigid with rage.

And Tim...

Tim was smiling.

Timmy's gun was now fully trained on Ana.

Jared didn't move.

One wrong step and she was dead.

Ana's words were hitting Tim harder than any weapon. Jared wanted her to stop pushing him—but watching her stare down a killer, shame and fury burning in her eyes, filled him with pride.

The girl he had crushed on years ago was still there.

Only stronger.

Bab had been right.

Ana was a badass—at work, with her friends, with the stubborn courage that made her stand here now, risking everything for the truth. For Patrick. For her father.

And suddenly it hit him.

Hard.

He loved her.

Her mind. Her fire. Her heart.

And if she still needed a driver when this was over, it would be someone he hired. Or he'd drive her himself.

But first he had to deal with Mr. Scott.

Tim's expression shifted.

The smug smile was gone. His lips pressed tight, the reality settling in—his dream was collapsing.

That made him even more dangerous.

He paced in short circles now, his free hand dragging through his hair, the gun wavering in the air.

Then he let out a broken wail.

"XAna... you weren't supposed to find out. That wasn't part of the plan."

Jared caught Ana's eye.

He subtly circled his finger near his hip.

Keep him talking.

Ana gave the smallest nod.

Good.

She understood.

"Tim," she said softly, "please stop pacing and tell me why. Did my dad do something to hurt you?"

Tim froze.

His face turned toward her while the hand holding the gun now pointed at Jared.

Ana gasped.

"I overheard you and your father talking," Tim said bitterly. "He told you it wasn't appropriate to spend so much time with your driver. He wanted you to put me in my place."

His voice rose.

"My place is beside you."

He shook his head.

"He wanted you to stop loving me. I couldn't let him do that."

Ana's hand covered her mouth.

Her world shattered.

Her father had died for doing what any father would —protecting his daughter.

And she had told him Tim was important.

That he had saved her.

It was her fault.

"Tim," she whispered, tears streaming down her face. "You killed my father. How could I ever love you now?"

Her voice hardened.

"You murdered my dad. My doorman. My bodyguard. You hurt Patrick."

She shook her head.

"No one could love someone who's done that."

For the first time, she wasn't stalling.

She needed the truth.

Tim backed slowly toward the window, glancing outside.

Seeing nothing.

His eyes were bloodshot.

"You forgot Dallas," he said hoarsely. "If you're listing my sins... add Dallas."

Ana blinked.

"Dallas? I thought he was just sick. Missing."

She glanced at Jared.

He gave a grim shake of his head.

"Oh, Timmy," she said, her voice cracking. "How could you kill all these people I cared about?"

Her expression hardened.

"I hate you."

The words struck like a slap.

"I wish I had never saved you."

She turned her back on him.

Tim's face twisted.

Sadness—

Then rage.

The name echoed in his ears.

Timmy.

His arm lifted.

The gun rose.

Jared moved.

He launched forward, slamming into Tim with all his strength.

"GET DOWN, ANA!"

Two shots exploded.

Glass shattered.

Jared drove his shoulder into Tim's gut just as the window behind them burst inward.

Aiden and AJ had arrived.

But Tim still fired once more.

The bullet tore into Jared's left shoulder.

The two men crashed to the floor, wrestling in the broken glass.

Then another shot cracked from outside. Tim jerked. The bullet punched through his chest.

Jared drove a final backfist into Tim's nose. Tim's head slammed against the hardwood floor.

His eyes rolled back.

Blood spread across the boards beneath him. His lips moved weakly. *"I loved her."*

The last breath left him.

Jared pushed himself up, clutching his shoulder.

Tim lay motionless.

Blood pooling beneath his chest.

Ana shrieked and rushed forward, dropping to her knees beside Jared.

The door burst open.

Aiden and AJ stormed in with weapons drawn as sirens wailed in the distance.

Aiden pulled Jared carefully off Tim's body, the dead man's arm still tangled around him.

AJ hurried to Patrick, slicing the zip ties from his wrists before grabbing water from the kitchen.

The sirens grew louder.

AJ helped Patrick sip slowly while they watched Jared struggle to his feet, clutching his shoulder.

Ana stayed at his side, steadying him as Aiden examined the wound.

"Looks like the bullet grazed you," Aiden said. "Took some skin, but most of that blood is his."

He nodded toward Tim's body on the floor.

"Can't say I'm sorry to hear that," Jared said through a grim smile.

He looked down at Ana.

Her eyes were red with tears, her shoulders stiff with shock. The truth about her father had shattered her.

Behind them, an officer entered.

"Hey, Cap," Officer Sam said. "Looks like you got him."

"We all did," Jared replied, nodding toward the others. "You'll want to confirm his confession. He admitted the coroner falsified the report. Said he killed Jerome and Dallas."

Sam nodded. "EMTs are outside."

"Good," Jared said. "I'll leave this to you."

He squeezed Ana's hand.

"Aiden, AJ... appreciate it. I was about five seconds from tearing him apart myself."

Aiden smirked.

Jared's arm throbbed, the pain finally settling in.

"I need to be seen too," he said lightly, glancing at Ana. "You're going to take care of me, right?"

She shook her head.

"You need a doctor," she said quietly, gesturing toward the ambulance lights outside. "Both you and Patrick do."

Her eyes filled again.

"Please. For me."

Patrick was being lifted onto a stretcher. Ana moved beside him.

He barely opened his eyes.

"I'm so sorry, Pat," she whispered. "Get better... and remember there's a beautiful woman waiting for you who's been sick with worry."

His good eye opened wider.

"Ginger."

Ana smiled faintly and kissed his cheek.

"Don't mess that up."

Patrick managed a weak grin.

"I'll try."

Jared stepped beside the stretcher.

Patrick glanced at him.

"What she said."

Jared nodded.

The EMTs carried Patrick outside.

"Go," Ana said softly. "Get checked out. I'll come see you before I leave."

Jared hesitated.

"I don't need an ambulance," he muttered. "Aiden can drive me."

Aiden stepped in immediately. "Get in the damn ambulance," he said. "Don't make me drag you."

Jared sighed.

"Fine."

He turned to Ana and lifted her chin gently.

"But we're talking," Jared said in a stern quiet voice. "Count on it."

She tried to smile, but it barely formed.

"Okay, Jared. We'll talk."

He walked away toward the ambulance, frustration tightening his shoulders. Ana watched him go.

Patrick hurt because of her.

Jared hurt because of her.

And her father...

Her chest tightened.

The memories of the past hours pressed in on her until she felt like she couldn't breathe.

Kansas City suddenly felt suffocating.

She wrapped her arms around herself as the ambulance lights flashed across the trees.

She needed space.

Needed distance from everything that had happened here.

For the first time in nearly a year, she was free.

But the freedom hurt.

An officer pulled a sheet over Tim's body inside the cabin.

Ana turned away.

Aiden approached quietly while AJ talked excitedly beside him, adrenaline still rushing. Ana barely heard him.

She climbed into the Chevy S10.

Her mind was made up.

Right now she didn't want uncertainty.
She wanted something solid.
Something she knew.
Home.
She needed to go home.

Chapter 44

2 Long Weeks

Two long weeks had passed since Ana had flown back to her world in Lauderdale. According to Aiden, she had left the very next morning after calling the hospital to check on both Pat and Jared.

At first, Jared had been furious.

He had woken up to a message lying beside the call button on the hospital bed. The doctor had insisted he stay overnight because of a possible concussion. Jared hadn't liked it, but he figured it would give him time to think about what he wanted to say to Ana the next day before she left.

No such luck.

When he stopped by Pat's room before leaving the hospital, Aiden was already there. It was Aiden who told him Ana was gone.

Just like all those years ago.

No conversation.

No clearing things up.

Just gone with the wind.

For the first few days he kept telling himself she would call.

Ana had always been good about circling back, even when things between them were awkward. She never liked leaving things unresolved. So he waited. Every time his phone buzzed, a small, stupid part of him expected to see her name light up the screen.

It never did.

The silence gnawed at him more than the bruises or the stitches in his side.

The same damn pattern.

Years ago they had shared one unforgettable night—heat, laughter, the kind of connection that made a man think maybe the universe had finally thrown him a bone. And then she had disappeared from his life just as quietly as she had slipped into his bed. No explanation. No follow-up call. Nothing but unanswered questions.

He had spent years convincing himself that night hadn't meant anything to her.

Now here they were again.

Another moment.

Another disappearing act.

He had been pissed for days. He tried burning the anger off the way he used to when he was younger—

through distraction, through women, through anything that dulled the edge. But the interest just wasn't there.

His body was healing.

His heart felt like it had been cracked open.

Aiden noticed. So did Aj.

They dragged him to Bab's for a beer and a burger.

Jared sat there twelve days later, chewing his food without tasting it, staring at the table like it had personally offended him.

"So," Aiden asked around a mouthful of fries, "whatcha gonna do?"

"Nothing."

Jared shrugged, draining his beer before setting the empty mug on the table and lifting it toward Bab's for another round.

"It's over. She's where she wants to be and I'm where I'm needed. End of story. Just a momentary lapse in judgment. Got caught up in the drama and thought it meant something. Clearly it didn't."

"Hmmmph." Aiden leaned back with a crooked smirk. "So you're gonna chicken-shit this out, huh?"

"Hey, she left," Jared snapped. "She chose not to talk. Again. Not me. You heard me tell her we were going to talk. You heard her say, 'Okay, we'll talk.'"

Bab's set the fresh beer in front of him just as he grabbed it and took a long pull, slamming the mug back down hard enough to splash foam onto the table.

"See?" he muttered. "Ridiculous. Let's drop it."

Aiden's fist hit the table with a crack.

"Okay, yup," he said flatly. "Love is chaotic. Yup, it's a pain in the ass sometimes. And yup, women can be the damndest creatures on earth to figure out. But that damn sure doesn't mean we let them win before we've said our peace."

Jared stared stubbornly at his beer.

Aiden leaned forward.

"And if I recall correctly, I told you I'd kick your ass if you made this difficult for the rest of us to remain friends. Did I not?"

Jared pretended not to hear him.

Aiden nodded slowly. "That's what I thought."

He pointed toward the bar.

"So here's what's gonna happen. You're going to man up, take the ticket Bab's is holding, and catch the flight that will take you to her. Bring her back or don't. That part's up to you."

Bab's stood there with her arms crossed, one hand holding what might—if he had the guts to try—be the luckiest ticket of his life.

Jared looked over at Aj.

Aj finally chimed in between bites of his burger.

"Hell, man," he said, wiping his mouth. "I'll drive you to the airport just to shut up all this love nonsense."

Aiden and Bab's burst out laughing, each smacking Aj on the shoulder.

Bab's slid the ticket across the table.

"Get gone," she said.

Then she glanced at the clock.

"And I mean now. Your flight leaves in one hour."

Ana was signing the last of the legal documents to formally change her name on company records to Ana "XAna" Montgomery.

Leaving Kansas City after so much emotional turmoil had forced her to confront something she hadn't expected—her heart hated that she had ever let her birth name slip quietly into the background. Her family, her father, and her grandmother were part of her history there. She had only ever intended to shield their privacy from the paparazzi, not sever her connection to their memory.

Since returning to Lauderdale, she had kept herself busy with company details—reviewing contracts, answering questions from each scholarship recipient, and helping organize the next round of foundation meetings.

She and Chloe had grown closer as well, spending more time together now that Janice was finally taking Garrett up on his long-standing offer of a date. So far there had been one coffee outing and one candlelit dinner at Shooter's on the Waterfront. Janice had returned to the office glowing with happiness, even managing to schedule more time away from work—something Ana had begged her to do for years.

Ana was thrilled for her.

Janice deserved to be loved.

Loved.

The word lingered longer than she liked.

She still hadn't heard from Jared.

Every evening she found herself standing in the bedroom of her oceanfront home, watching the moon climb slowly over the Atlantic, wondering if the silence meant what she feared it did. She didn't blame him if he was angry. After everything that had happened, she had rushed home leaving nothing but a note beside his hospital bed.

Work kept her mind busy.

But not her heart.

So she poured her heart into the work instead.

Like today.

Taking back her name.

She only wished she could hear Jared say it one more time.

Smiling at the foolish thought, she shook her head.

Setting the pen down, she handed the documents back to Arthur. He studied them for a moment before looking up with a warm smile.

"Good girl. Your father would love that you're doing this."

"Thank you, Arthur. For everything."

She walked around the desk and wrapped her arms around him in a tight hug. In Lauderdale, he was the closest thing she had to family. Pulling back, she wiped a stray tear from her cheek and made a silent promise to herself to spend more time with him—not just when she needed legal advice.

Arthur slipped the paperwork neatly into a file.

"So," he said casually, giving her a knowing wink, "anything new to report from Kansas City? Anyone special?"

Her expression softened instantly as Jared's face flashed through her mind.

"For a moment I thought maybe," she admitted quietly. "But I suppose there never really was a chance. Oh well... at least the nightmare is over. That's what matters."

Arthur studied her for a beat longer than usual.

"I suppose so," he said gently. "But keep your eyes open. You never know what might appear when you least expect it."

He brightened suddenly.

"Say, would you like to have dinner with me tonight at our special restaurant? Your treat."

The dimples in his cheeks were so deep they showed clearly through his white beard.

Ana laughed.

"I'd love that. I'll run home and change. Shall we say 6:45 so we can watch the water taxis drop off the beautiful people?"

She loved Shooter's—the golden sunsets over the Intracoastal, the boats gliding along the waterway, the soft buzz of laughter drifting from the dockside tables. Lauderdale had always felt alive there.

"Sounds perfect," Arthur replied. "Max will drop me off. If I'm a few minutes late, grab our usual table."

He wagged a playful finger at her.

"Now off you go. Get gorgeous. We're celebrating your return in style tonight, so wear something beautiful. I promise you—it will be a night to remember."

She narrowed her eyes playfully.

"Really? Well then, I suppose I'll wear something special just for you. You sneaky devil. I know you have something up your sleeve."

Arthur placed a hand over his chest in mock innocence.

"Me? No ma'am. Just an old man lucky enough to take out his favorite girl. Now go."

Ana stepped out of the office with her heart lighter than it had been in weeks. Her smile widened as she walked toward the elevator, the warm Florida sun spilling through the windows.

Life in Lauderdale had its rhythm again.

But a small piece of her heart still lingered in Kansas City.

Oh, how she wished...

Chapter 45

Unfinished Business

Jared had taken an Uber to the restaurant—Shooter's, as Janice had instructed. It was an odd name for a romantic dinner spot, but the more he thought about it, the more he liked it. Janice had told him it sat right on the waterfront, where boats drifted by slowly and the evening air smelled faintly of salt and citrus from the ocean breeze. After dinner, she had suggested they take the Fort Lauderdale Water Taxi for a moonlit ride along the Intracoastal.

According to Janice, it was one of Ana's favorite things to do.

Jared had taken an immediate shine to the woman, even though they hadn't officially met yet. Anyone willing to orchestrate something like this for two stubborn people clearly had a good heart—and a wicked sense of romantic strategy. She and Arthur, Ana's longtime attorney, had clearly worked together to set the whole thing up.

Janice had also filled him in on something that caught his attention immediately.

Ana had reclaimed her full name.

Ana Montgomery.

"XAna" would remain, but only as her middle name now—no longer the persona she hid behind in the public eye. Janice had explained it casually, as if it were just another administrative detail, but Jared couldn't help wondering if it meant something deeper. Maybe Ana was reclaiming more than paperwork. Maybe she was reclaiming pieces of herself she had once set aside.

Maybe that meant there was room for him too.

Still, he refused to let himself hope too much.

The Uber driver continued weaving through the city, taking what felt like a scenic tour of Fort Lauderdale. Jared didn't mind. It was his first time here, and the place did not disappoint.

Palm trees lined the streets in elegant rows, their leaves rustling softly in the warm night air. The city felt alive—art galleries glowing behind glass storefronts, upscale restaurants buzzing with laughter, luxury boutiques still lit up along Las Olas Boulevard like a runway of polished glamour. Beyond that stretched the waterfront itself, where sleek yachts floated beside dockside hotels and beachfront towers.

The entire place had a polished, sun-soaked beauty to it.

Not exactly his style.

But he could see why a certain gorgeous blonde called it home.

Ana fit here. Perfectly.

The glamour, the lights reflecting off the water, the easy confidence of the people strolling along the boulevard—it all matched her energy in a way that made sense.

And yet...

She had fit in Kansas City too.

That thought lingered.

The Uber slowed as they approached the waterfront district, and Jared felt something twist in his stomach. He wasn't usually a man who got nervous about meeting a woman. Hell, most of the time he was the one calming the other person down.

But Ana wasn't just any woman.

She was the woman.

The realization still felt strange in his chest. He had spent years refusing to put that word to the feeling, pretending what he felt for her was something simpler—something temporary, something easier to dismiss.

But somewhere between the bloodied roses, the long nights guarding her safety, and the way she had danced barefoot in that kitchen... the truth had settled into his bones.

He loved her.

The word still felt foreign.

Heavy.

Real.

And tonight wasn't some casual dinner where he could flirt his way through a conversation and see where things went. This wasn't a Netflix-and-chill situation with the quiet expectation of ending up tangled in someone's sheets.

This was a grand gesture.

A leap.

And he had no idea how it would land.

He was walking straight into the unknown.

Ana had left Kansas City without a word.

Again.

The woman had a habit of disappearing from his life that he was getting real tired of.

Leaving wasn't the problem.

But leaving without talking—after everything they had been through—that still burned.

He had told her they would talk.

She had looked him in the eye and agreed.

Then she had gone home.

Aiden had spent nearly an hour talking him down from that anger. According to him, Ana hadn't run away from Jared—she had run away from everything else.

The blood.

The chaos.

The terror of the last few weeks.

Aiden had explained it in the blunt, practical way only he could.

"Ana works," he had said. "That's how she copes. She doesn't sit around worrying—she fixes things. Being back in Lauderdale gave her control again."

Once Jared let that explanation sink into his thick skull, it made sense.

Still...

He wished she had given him a chance.

That was all he wanted.

Not a guarantee.

Not a ring.

Not some fairy-tale promise of forever.

Just a chance.

A chance to see if the years of silent longing between them could turn into something real.

Mayor Patrick had weighed in on the situation too. The man had been on speakerphone from his hospital bed, still recovering but sounding very much like himself. Ginger was furious with him for not sharing the secret meeting. Once he was out of the hospital bed, he would make things right with her.

Patrick was practically climbing the hospital walls trying to get discharged so he could track her down.

Before she left, Ginger had spoken briefly with Jared. She had asked about his injuries, her voice tight with worry, and told him to pass along a message to Patrick—that she needed to speak with him when the time was right.

Patrick had no idea what that meant.

Luckily, the political fallout from the case had ended up working in the mayor's favor. Once Jared's team cleared him of wrongdoing, the investigation had unraveled the rest of Tim's operation. The local drug dealers who had helped Tim execute parts of his plan were now behind bars, along with the Miami contact tied to the prostitute Tim had murdered.

Justice had finally caught up with the pieces he left behind.

But even from his hospital bed—with Ginger remaining silent and his own recovery still underway—Patrick had made one thing very clear.

If Jared didn't follow through with Ana, he would personally see to it that Jared regretted it.

Patrick's exact words had been something along the lines of:

"If you don't get on that damn plane, I will fire you myself."

Apparently, the mayor wanted Ana visiting Kansas City more often.

So technically, Jared had no choice.

Fear or not.

Doubt or not.

He had come all this way to see it through—for her and for himself.

Either they had a chance.

Or they didn't.

Tonight he was finally going to find out.

Ana sat on the pier beneath a wide umbrella, watching the sun dip low behind the tall iron buildings that framed the skyline. Boats cruised slowly along the waterway, some easing up to the dock to drop off passengers heading toward the restaurants lining the shore. She loved the water taxi service. It was one of the things that made Fort Lauderdale feel magical—like a small piece of Venice tucked into the Florida coast.

She closed her eyes and let the evening settle around her.

The gentle lap of water against the pilings.

The hum of music drifting from nearby patios.

The easy laughter of couples enjoying the warm night air.

Her skin still held the warmth of the sun.

After leaving Arthur's office she had gone home to change, slipping into her favorite off-the-shoulder dress —a brilliant shade of orange that complemented the golden glow her skin still carried from several quiet days resting on the beach. It had been a much-needed break, time to breathe, time to think... and time she had spent thinking about a certain stubborn Captain.

She could picture him easily.

Probably sitting at Bab's, a beer in hand, maybe throwing darts with Aj while pretending he wasn't thinking about her at all. Since returning home, the thought had crossed her mind more than once—what it might be like if Jared ever came to visit her here.

Would he like Lauderdale?

Would the easy rhythm of the water, the salt air, and the slow sunset evenings feel foreign to him... or would he settle into it the way he seemed to settle into everything?

For so many years she had never allowed herself to dream about happily ever after. Oh, she had liked the idea of it well enough, but the reality of her life had always kept it at arm's length.

What she wondered about wasn't forever.

Just a chance.

A chance to see where the heat and electricity they had shared—twice now—might actually lead. A chance to see whether, without criminals chasing them or the press circling overhead, they could spend an ordinary day together.

Just one normal day.

She knew she had been wrong to leave Kansas City the way she did.

Jared had wanted to talk.

She had promised him they would.

But a part of her had been afraid of that conversation. Afraid that whatever he might say could shatter the fragile hope she had been clinging to. After everything that had happened in those seven frantic days, she couldn't bear the thought that his kisses might never happen again.

So she ran.

Back to the world she understood.

Back to the life she knew she could control—her company, her charity, the friends who surrounded her, and the penthouse overlooking the ocean that had always felt like her sanctuary.

Cowardly, perhaps.

But she had been exhausted... and heart-weary.

Thinking of friends reminded her that Arthur was late.

That alone was unusual.

She opened her eyes and reached for her phone just as it buzzed in her hand.

A text message appeared on the screen

07:00 PM

It was from an unknown number, but the J suggested it was Jared, but how could he know what she looked like? She turned in her chair scanning the pier left and right, then back down at her phone, then back out into the restaurant, there at the bar he stood, black suit jacket, white dress shirt and jeans leaning so cocky up against the mahogany. Damn, he was beautiful...and so here. She giggled, her shoulders trembling, her hair shaking in disbelief watching him walk toward her.

"What? How?" Her phone went off again, this time it was a text from Arthur.

07:01 PM

Her eyes glistened, tears of joy blurring the words as she looked up. Jared stood beside the table. "We need to talk," he'd said.

He was here. In the flesh, in her Lauderdale, the man she loved asking her to talk.

His grin was all she needed; she launched herself, colliding with him, lips meeting in a fervent kiss. His arms tightened around her waist, lifting her. He set her down, only after minutes of passionate embrace, in her favorite restaurant, the murmur of voices and clinking silverware fading as the room erupted in applause. This was the happiest she had ever been. They had a chance.

She took his hands, staring up into his beautiful blue eyes, "Okay Captain, let's talk."

Thank you so much for reading Ana and Jared's story, if it moved you, a short review on Amazon helps other readers find them too.

SHATTER AGENDA

MAYOR PATRICK & GINGER'S STORY

Mayor Patrick Young would fire his assistant if she weren't missing.

After weeks of making pro and con list, he finally gave into his desire and confessed his attraction for Ginger McGraw, the auburn beauty, who by day acted as his Executive Assistant; his right hand. Days later in the midst of planning their *first official date* for the coming weekend; she had vanished. Something was terribly wrong.

In the last two years working with him; never had she gone off track. She was beautiful, hard-working, and smart; smarter than him, always keeping him on task with project planners and meeting schedules. He was baffled. The last thing she said was that she needed to tell him about her past. When he found the simple resignation letter on his desk with a forwarding PO Box address for her last check in somewhere Nebraska, he had driven to her townhome. All her belongings were still there, her car in the garage, but no Ginger. NO explanation, no excuse, *just gone.*

His Ginger; had she left him or was it something more?

Two years ago, Ginger Brown was put in the witness protection program. Her new identity as Ginger McGraw was given to her by the US Marshals after she named her ex-husband as the leader in a fentanyl ring out of LA. The agency found her a new life in Midwest America, a new name, new IDs, and a new career working for a handsome, recently elected mayor of Kansas City. Being from a faster-paced Hollywood lifestyle, she found the political life suited her. The mayor and she shared similar outlooks. They both preferred planning to spontaneity; schedules are life. Both were homebodies *and* workaholics, and there was undeniable chemistry. Passion for work she understood, but Ginger never expected passion *for a man* to burn this brightly. For two years in Mayor Patrick's employment, she had grown fond of his single-minded ways, his flirty comebacks when he went off schedule, and she found him irresistible.

In a shared stolen moment, neither of them could deny how they felt any longer. Not ready for public scrutiny, they agreed to keep their relationship private. But secrets have a way of coming out when you least expect them. Timing was not on their side, arriving home late, she found a sheet torn from her calendar on her doorstep with a knife stabbed through the date of what would have been her first official date with Patrick. Her worse nightmare was coming true. Her ex-husband had found her, but now he was threatening her new life with the man she loved.

She couldn't risk causing chaos to the mayor or his office. She wouldn't. So she fled in the night. Taking only the money she had in the bank, to a place she knew no one would find her.

Walls closing in, their chances crushed by someone who wants vengeance.

Ginger, now on the run with no clues to follow; will the Mayor risk his career and unravel the secret past of the woman he desires, or will he accept her leaving as fate?

Secret Agenda's can be fatal.

COMING 2026

Acknowledgments

From the bottom of my heart, I want to thank my daughter for being the inspiration behind every important decision I have ever made since her miraculous birth. For the betterment of her world, I chose to move bravely forward in publishing this story of Jared, Ana, and Timmy. You walked through every page with inspiring creativity and forethought. I admire all that you are; kindness, generosity, creative, caring, and beyond grace-filled. Your heart is everything to me. Thank you for being the reason I strive to be a better human everyday.

To my friends, not named but who have inspired characters in this story, thank you for being unique and worthy of a thousand stories. I am so grateful.

To my author friends, who again, not named, took the time to answer my questions, give advice, and for seriously simply being great humans and writers. Sincerely grateful.

To my non-traditional beta readers, beyond grateful for the feedback. Hope to see you for the next book.

To the Readers; Last but certainly NOT least. Thank you for choosing to read my first story published. I am so very thankful.

***A Note from the Author – March 2026**

Thank you for reading *Full Surrender*. This edition includes minor updates and refinements made in 2026 to improve the reading experience.

If you enjoyed Ana and Jared's story, I would be incredibly grateful if you left a short review on Amazon. Reviews help other readers discover the series.